# Lisa Alther

# BEDROCK

 Alfred A. Knopf   New York   1990

THIS IS A BORZOI BOOK
PUBLISHED BY ALFRED A. KNOPF, INC.

Grateful acknowledgment is made to Ice Nine Publishing Company, Inc.
for permission to reprint an excerpt from "If I Had the World to Give," words by
Robert Hunter. Copyright © 1979 by Ice Nine Publishing Company, Inc.

Library of Congress Cataloging-in-Publication Data
Alther, Lisa.
Bedrock / Lisa Alther.—1st ed.
p.   cm.
ISBN: 0-394-57755-8
I. Title.
PS3551.L78B4   1990
813'.54—dc20          89-43360
CIP

Manufactured in the United States of America
First Edition

*For Carey Kaplan*

Many thanks to the following friends for all the good suggestions and stolen jokes: Richard Alther, Sara Alther, Blanche Boyd, Andy Canale, Jody Crosby, Brenda Feigen, Françoise Gilot, John Izzi, Steve Izzo, Carey Kaplan, Rollie McKenna, Janice Perry, Kate Pond, John Reed, Mary Twitchell, and Vicky Wilson. With special thanks to Jody Crosby for the years of unflagging patience and encouragement while this book was *in vitro*.

# 1  Roches Ridge

An ivory BMW with two pairs of skis on the roof descended a long hill, granite cliffs spiked with fir trees rising up on either side of the road. The driver, Turner Shawn, had a pleasant, ruddy face and a sparse crop of graying blond hair. His wife, Clea, dressed in stretch pants and a turtleneck, sat beside him studying Roches Ridge, Vermont, which lay below them in the winter sun, on a granite outcropping that plunged down to the marshes of Mink Creek, where the creek flows into Lake Champlain.

Clea Shawn was a sophisticated woman. Men had insisted they loved her in several languages. By this time she'd been in love so often that her heart felt like a sponge mop. On a regular basis passion had seized her up, swirled her around, and squeezed her dry. These were not flings, they were obsessions, the kind that dominate days and dictate dreams, that compel salmon to leap up waterfalls and men to ride down them in barrels. She had come to regard the symptoms—the flushed face and clammy palms, the pounding pulse and restless nights, the wish to buy new sheets and work out at her health club—with dread.

Yet Clea was a woman who adored love. Hormones had always been her recreational drug of choice. An aficionado of that moment when fervor swamps common sense, she lacked a gift for restraint.

Snow was piled hip-high along streets that outlined a central green with its Victorian bandstand, bronze Civil War soldier, and War of 1812 cannon. White frame colonials encircled the green. In the distance in one direction was Camel's Hump, capped toothlike with snow; and in the other, the Adirondacks. Although she'd traveled the world, Clea had rarely seen a spot so lovely.

"Turner, this place is gorgeous." She felt alarm as her palms turned clammy. Turner nodded and smiled. After their bout of lovemaking that morning, on the orange shag carpet in the condo overlooking the Alpine Glen ski trails, he'd have agreed if she'd maintained the earth was flat. "The old man can still put it to you," he'd murmured as he lay beside Clea, who lacked the heart to admit she'd faked her orgasm, another disturbing symptom of fresh passion in the offing. Her obsession with Turner had subsided after all these years into sororal affection—warm and comfortable, but lacking the note of complication and compulsion she required. A safety strap from a ski pole in the roof rack began slapping against the roof.

While Turner inspected the ski rack, Clea zipped her parka, took her Nikon from the back seat, and began snapping shots of peeling colonial cornices and returns. Starr's IGA, St. Sebastian's Catholic Church, the Community Congregational Church, a grade school with a soccer field behind it, Al's Getty station, the Center for Sanity, a volunteer firehouse, a doctor's office, Coffin's Funeral Home, Casa Loretta, the Karma Café, Earl's Barbershop, Orlon's Bait and Tackle, with a fly-specked sign in the window: YES, WE DO HAVE NIGHT CRAWLERS!

Everything a person really needed, Clea concluded as she stood before the redbrick post office, the only structure in sight dating after 1880. She felt suddenly ashamed of the junk that cluttered her life, the urgent trips to Bloomingdale's or the Atrium to find the right place mats or neck scarf, her tangled web of illicit relationships. It was clear that Roches Ridgers lived simple, honest lives, requiring only the essentials.

Casa Loretta was paneled in barn board. Turner and Clea sat at the Formica table, regarding a pink plastic rose in a ceramic bud vase and eating Ridgeburgers brought by a woman with a remarkable bleached blond hairdo piled eighteen inches high, with spit curls at the ears. A badge over her left breast read: HI, I'M LORETTA. ASK ME ABOUT OUR SOUTH OF THE BORDER SPECIALS. John Denver sang "Rocky Mountain High" from the neon Wurlitzer in the back corner.

"Turner, I like this town," Clea heard herself confess. She'd fallen in love with cities before—New York, Paris, Bombay, Kyoto, Sydney— but never with a village: She had always been opposed to settlements of fewer than one million, unless they were situated in foreign countries, which made them picturesque rather than merely boring. In fact, she'd spent her first twenty-one years trying to *escape* small towns, and the small minds that sometimes infest them. Her particular crossroads to bear was Poplar Bluffs, Ohio, eighty miles upriver from Cincinnati, on a limestone cliff overlooking the Ohio River. Population 3,813, mostly senior citizens who passed their days behind morning glory vines on front porches, discussing brands of denture adhesives and abhorring the behavior of all ambulatory townspeople. Clea had fled to Cornell, then to New York City.

Turner was unimpressed, being accustomed to Clea's mentally setting up housekeeping in each spot they visited. And they'd visited plenty, with his international marketing career, vacations with their children, and Clea's photo assignments for travel magazines.

"I really mean it, Turner." Abruptly Clea found herself longing to get back to the basics, not recalling that the basics might include tedium, loneliness, disease, violence, and death.

"Good French fries."

"Turner, all you need is an airport. I've got enough contacts now so I can live anywhere. And the children love to ski." An empty nest belonged in the forest, not on East Forty-ninth Street. Theo was in his last year at Hotchkiss and Kate in her first at Smith. Clea had always led an active life apart from them. But last September she'd been appalled to discover a giant cavity in her heart, which parenthood had evidently been filling. The day the children left for school, Turner left for Rome. Clea spent the afternoon crying in bed. Those infants who'd sucked so hungrily at her breasts, who'd clutched her fingers when confronted with strangers, were now going on blind dates and opening checking accounts and picking majors without her assistance.

"Clea, you're like an express train." Turner laughed. "I can either climb aboard or stand aside."

"And all these years you've climbed aboard, my love. In sickness and in health."

"Infidelity and out of fidelity," he added with his sweet smile. "Ever since I first saw you at that DU freshman tea at Cornell. Drunk on whiskey sours. Black hair falling across one eye. Singing 'Roll Your Leg Over.' Off-key."

"We could keep the brownstone. A pied-à-terre. What's all this money for anyhow?" On top of her free-lance fees she had income from her parents' estate. And Turner earned the salary of a successful corporate executive.

"You're forgetting that you love New York, Clea. You'll get over this mugging business. Just give it time."

*Clea was kneeling among Big Mac cartons in an alley off West Eighty-eighth Street. A man in a torn maroon parka held a gun to her temple. With his free hand he tore the gold hoops from her earlobes.*

*"Please don't shoot," she whispered. "I've got two children."*

*"Lady," he said, cocking the pistol, bloodshot eyes burning through the holes in his leather ski mask, "I wouldn't care if you ran the orphanage."*

"What about Elke?" asked Turner, faintly alarmed.

Clea shook her head. Elke. Elke and she talked on the phone most days and lunched every week. "She could come up here. I'd visit her. Letters. The phone. God, Turner, I can't plan my life around Elke." The time when she *had* planned around Elke had passed. They first met in Elke's studio while Clea photographed her for *American Artist.* Afterward, Clea's every waking moment, and much of her sleep as well, was tinctured with a yearning for Elke. But after Saint John, when it became clear they weren't going to run off with each other, the urgency slackened a bit, if not the affection and respect.

A diminutive man in cowboy boots and a string tie with a turquoise thunderbird clasp was paying his bill to Loretta. Possessed of the brown wizened face and fetal carriage of a mummy, he paused to sign a petition demanding reinstatement of Vermont's death penalty.

Loretta looked up from the cash register to smile at Clea, hair piled atop her head like an osprey's nest. Clea said, "This town is absolutely beautiful."

"Couldn't say. Been here all my life."

The man in the string tie said from the corner of his mouth, "Not yet, let's hope, Loretta."

And Clea's poor roving heart stood still.

Back in New York, Clea struggled to put Roches Ridge out of her mind with her usual round of household maintenance, photo assignments, health club workouts, and dinner parties. But one stormy afternoon she sat at the mahogany claw-foot desk in the fourth-floor office of her Turtle Bay town house, sorting through photos from the Alpine Glen ski weekend for a *Vermont Life* feature. The stunted urban maple in the courtyard tossed and lashed, splattering the windowpanes with rain. One photo showed sunlight glinting off icicles on the gingerbread cornice of a large white Victorian house on the Roches Ridge green. Clea remembered taking the picture, but she didn't recall a frail young white-blond woman in a high-necked Edwardian gown, who played a golden harp in the front window. It looked almost like a double exposure. Clea loved this kind of gratuitous composition, unplanned yet right.

As she studied other shots of Roches Ridge, with the white mountains in the background and the electric-blue sky overhead, Clea felt her pulse speed up and her breathing quicken. Grabbing the remote control, she switched on the TV for distraction. But when the Waltons bowed their heads over Thanksgiving dinner while John-Boy asked the blessing, Clea's eyes flooded with tears. She cried for the rest of the program, head on her desk.

Clea's companion at a Sutton Place dinner party that evening was an attractive young editor from *Getaway* magazine, with whom Clea had been flirting for several weeks. There was talk of a long weekend together in Antigua to cover the carnival. They exchanged innuendos about the fireworks visible from the hotel room balcony.

In the midst of verbal maneuvers designed to elicit sexual histories so each could make an informed decision concerning the risk of fatal infection, Clea found herself yawning. For Jim at age thirty-two, an affair with an older woman was probably exciting, but for Clea even excitement had become boring. She'd been through this too many times. In her youth she'd thought passion was profound. Each new lover seemed to be whispering in her ear the combination to the lock on the portals of permanence and purpose. But each passion eventually waned, sputtered, flared, and died, like a Girl Scout campfire in a drizzle. So in time she learned to do a mental calculation whenever she felt an attraction brewing: Was present rapture worth eventual disappointment? Usually she ignored the answer and proceeded anyway. But she sometimes deliberately sidestepped a stroll down a moonlit beach with a lover because she knew its memory would distress her when they broke up. In more recent years she had come to regard men as dragonflies, and marveled at the gossamer wings when they alighted, without expecting them to linger. But tonight's courtship of Jim was feeling more like a gin rummy game—draw, play, and discard. Appalled to see herself in this cynical light, she pleaded a headache and departed.

As she entered her empty house and glanced around at the plush furnishings she'd selected and maintained so assiduously, she realized her current modus vivendi was moribund. New York City, so diverse and vital, had recently swiveled to reveal its shadow side. And her affairs, always diverting, had turned tedious. So steeled was she to let go that she couldn't even take hold anymore. And she thought she'd scream if she had to summarize her autobiography to one more new paramour.

That night Clea dreamed nonstop of the little Vermont village, white and silent under the winter sun, inhabited by a race endowed with droll good humor and rock-solid integrity. Waking in her king-size bed, Clea listened to the echoing house and the endless rain against the windows. Turner was in Brussels. Promoted to vice-president in charge of international marketing of Fresh-It toothpaste, he'd be away constantly now. Theo and Kate were ensconced at their respective schools cramming for midterms. Elke was no doubt working through the night on her new sculpture in her West Thirteenth Street studio. Jim was probably at Maxwell's Plum, chatting up some less world-weary younger woman. *And Clea was kneeling in Big Mac cartons, earlobes dripping blood, nostrils filled with the stench of rotting produce from a nearby garbage can, armpits wet with sweat . . .*

Switching on the light, she picked up the Roches Ridge photos from her nightstand and studied them, heart beating a restless tattoo. What had gotten into her? Small-town life, suffocating when she was eighteen, now seemed to proffer safety, continuity, and purpose.

By late afternoon Clea was in Roches Ridge, discussing local real estate over a cup of coffee with the bouffanted Loretta Gebo at Casa Loretta, Home of the Taco Pizza. Turner, Kate, and Theo could leave her, but she could also leave them. She'd keep the home fires burning still, but home is where your house is, and hers was going to be in Roches Ridge, on a spine of granite that wouldn't shift or vanish.

# 2  Calvin Roche

Calvin Roche stacked his VCR and his boxes of "Dallas" tapes in the back of his battered pink '64 T-Bird with its green tags reading TEX. He was pretty darn happy to be unloading this house on that flatlander from New York City. He'd been trying to get rid of it and move to Abilene, Texas, ever since Boneeta died of a stroke two years before.

As he hobbled toward the house in his pointy-toed cowboy boots, Calvin eyed the huge gray stone wreck. What the hang she wanted with this dog was more than he could figure. She turned up at his door one day looking like Mandy Winger on "Dallas" (plus crow's-feet and graying hair), so excited that she shifted from foot to foot like she had to pee. Some Roche built this place in the late 1700s, and it had been nothing but trouble ever since. The sills were all eaten up with dry rot, and the bathtub was about to fall into the cellar. But by the time Mrs. Shawn discovered this, he'd be living in Abilene, with no forwarding address.

Laying a couple of suitcases atop the VCR, Calvin reflected that over the years smart Roches had found reasons to leave—the gold rush, the Civil War, World War I. He himself went to Abilene during World War II to guard German POWs while they weeded colonels' flower beds. He spent his time off in the Silver Dollar Saloon, with disabled cowboys who talked about punching cattle all over west Texas. After the war Calvin meant to return to Vermont only long enough to break up with Boneeta and say goodbye to his parents. But he and Boneeta were next-door neighbors and sweethearts since childhood, and Boneeta won out.

Soon there were four babies. To keep mittens on their hands and Chef Boyardee in their bellies, Calvin worked in the McGrath quarry, cutting granite for gravestones. As he operated the forklift, he imagined he was throwing calves on the west Texas range. His co-workers called him Tex. When Boneeta put on sixty pounds, he started calling her Burrito. Saturday nights, in his red satin western shirt and string tie, he and Burrito (twice his width even without her crinolined skirt) did the Texas Schottische with the Fancy Steppers at Brad Bradbury's

Country and Western Colonial Inn on Route 7. Fridays nights were devoted to "Dallas." Calvin was convinced he'd fit right in at South Fork as one of Ray Krebbs' ranch hands.

Now Boneeta lay in the cemetery behind the Congregational church. The other half of her headstone already had his name on it, with a blank space for his death date. (Sonny Coffin tried to get him to burn Boneeta and bury her ashes beneath a brass plaque, but Calvin's pension depended on a healthy gravestone trade.) Calvin's children were working in the aerospace industry in Utah and on the assembly line in Detroit. It was true he'd roughed them up some when they were kids. But only when he'd been drinking too much Lone Star ale and recalled that their existence was preventing him from riding the range. He'd written trying to explain, but his children never answered. It was like being one of those transsexuals he read about in the *National Enquirer* who claimed they were women trapped in men's bodies: He was a Texan who'd been born a Vermonter.

Now, however, there was nothing to stop him from assuming his true identity. He pictured himself in leather chaps, vest, and boots, Stetson on his head and coiled lasso in his hand, loping across a prairie on a quarter horse. Or playing a guitar around a campfire, with a tin mug of coffee and a saddle by his side. At least he could sit around the Silver Dollar and swap lies. It beat the hang out of sitting alone in this old stone crypt, watching "Dallas" reruns on the VCR and waiting for the bathtub to sink into the cellar.

Calvin was shoving his olive army duffel bag into the T-Bird when Clea Shawn drove up in her ivory BMW. She got out, buttoning her plaid-lined trench coat.

"Hello there, Mr. Roche."

"Howdy, m'am. Just on my way out." He tried to conceal his impatience to leave. She might start wondering why he was in such a wicked rush. She might discover the rotting sills.

Clea was studying his embroidered cowboy boots and Levi's jacket. "Off to Texas right away, Mr. Roche?"

"Yes, m'am, sure am."

"Well, have a safe trip."

"Thank you, m'am. Sorry the place is such a mess. Eight generations create quite a clutter."

"Don't worry." She patted his bony shoulder, so low she could have rested a breast on it. "I'll take good care of your lovely house."

Calvin climbed into his T-Bird, thinking she ought to take his lovely house, burn it, and collect the insurance. Build a nice tight new split-level with all right angles and no rats. Waving his Stetson as though riding a bronco, he called, "Have a good one, Mrs. S.!" He'd picked up this valediction from Ishtar at the Karma Café. Ishtar came from California, changing her name from Barbara Carmichael while living in a tepee along Mink Creek with a dozen other lezzies, who called themselves the Boudiccas. Normally Calvin didn't have much use for weirdos, but he liked Ishtar because she explained that his love for "Dallas" proved he'd been a cowboy in a past life. Last week when he told her he was moving to Abilene, she looked up from the spider plant she was repotting to say, "We'll see each other again. If not in this life, then next time around. Have a good one, Mr. R.!"

Ishtar and Loretta were the only ones in town he'd miss. He ate at Casa Loretta and the Karma Café on alternate nights. But to be honest he despised Ishtar's "whole foods nouvelle home cooking." When Ishtar first opened, Calvin helped Loretta change her name from Loretta's Luncheonette to Casa Loretta. Taco pizza was his idea too. Loretta said he'd saved her neck. And he had. People used to call her place the Road Kill Café behind her back.

As Calvin drove down his driveway for the last time, in this life at least, he resolutely itemized his reasons for leaving. Bull dykes from California in tepees along Mink Creek. Crippled redneck Jesus freaks from Georgia in old yellow schoolbuses up to Granite Gap. Sonny Coffin turning his granddaddy's hay barn into a crematorium. Heating his home with human flesh, some were saying. One-eyed commie college professors trying to organize the farmers to burn down the Xerox factory. Roches Ridge wasn't what it used to be, and what it used to be wasn't much.

And Marshes next door. Never to see a Marsh again was in itself worth a move to Abilene. Even if Waneeta Marsh was Boneeta's twin. His outlaws, he called the Marshes. He passed their peeling frame house, windows plastered with stickers reading THIS HOUSE INSURED BY SMITH AND WESSON, front porch strewn with auto seats and rusted appliances. In summer, Marshes lay on those auto seats drinking Miller High Life and hollering till the moon went down. Calvin put up that stockade fence there, and Marshes tossed Miller bottles and skunk carcasses over it. Waneeta's kids showed his kids pictures from *Hustler* and forced them to play taxidermist in the back shed. The spotlight in their auto graveyard glared through his and Boneeta's bedroom window all night long. Their ultraviolet bug light sizzled and popped twenty-four hours a day, every season of the year.

"Rot in hell, you Marshes!" He gave their crumbling gray homestead the finger as he roared past in his crammed pink T-Bird, mud flying up from his rhinestoned mud flaps. The last Roche of Roches Ridge was finally hitting the trail!

# 3   Roche House

Clea stood in the rutted driveway, hand raised, watching droll Calvin Roche depart in a flurry of splattering mud. It couldn't be easy leaving behind both your personal and your ancestral past. But ever since she first saw his handsome stone house, on a knoll surrounded by overgrown lilac bushes, she knew she had to own it. She only prayed he'd arrive at his last roundup before realizing he'd sold his birthright for a bowl of pottage.

Face flushed, palms sweating, she turned like a maiden on her wedding night to inspect her new house. Simple, elegant Georgian lines. A leaded fanlight over a massive oak door. A Palladian window on the second floor.

But roof slates were falling off like guillotine blades. Chimneys were collapsing. Stones needed pointing. The wooden ell was swaybacked. Windows with unpainted trim and broken panes stared blindly. Turner refused to set foot in the place until it was finished. But he rarely had time to unpack between trips anyway. Upon returning to New York from Brussels and hearing about her purchase, he asked, "Is this your subtle way of filing for divorce, Clea?"

"I just want a quiet place to work when you're away, Turner," she replied, stretched out on their quilted bedspread, watching him unpack. "With some pleasant neighbors to drop in on."

"Looks like a mid-life crisis to me," he sighed, removing his shaving kit from his suitcase. "I thought you promised to love, honor, and obey me."

"But I didn't promise to go to Brussels, did I?" Turner thought he wanted her to play Penelope to his Odysseus. But when she tried staying home after the children were born, he began seeing her as Medusa instead, and fled into the arms of other less available, less threatening women. No doubt this movement away from him would increase her allure, but that wasn't her motive.

Inside, camera hanging from her neck, Clea inspected the mess

Calvin Roche had referred to—stacks of *National Enquirers* and *TV Guides,* grocery bags full of Lone Star ale bottles, rotting TV dinners in foil trays. The lower door corners had been gnawed off by rats. Wide pine floorboards were covered with many layers of floral linoleum. Walls bulged with peeling paper and crumbling plaster. Calvin had lived in just the kitchen. A cot with a moldy mattress stood in one corner. A blackened ladder-back chair lay in the walk-in fireplace. Clea began snapping pictures. She'd take the same shots after the renovation. An editor at *House Beautiful* had already expressed interest in "Roche House of Roches Ridge: Before and After."

As the sky outside turned salmon and mauve, Clea built a fire with the charred chair, pleased with her new adventure, undertaken while her peers were beginning to discuss living wills. She spread Theo's down sleeping bag on the cot and heated a Lean Cuisine Zucchini Lasagna in the gas oven. Sitting on the cot, eating from the foil tray, Clea listened to the crackling of the fire, the creaking of the house, and the hum of unfamiliar appliances. And she visualized the place as it would be soon—waxed and polished, painted and papered; crewelwork curtains, antiques, and Oriental rugs. She'd live here alone, working and reading Vita Sackville-West's *All Passion Spent.*

Lying down, Clea felt lonely. She missed Elke. They'd talked on the phone almost every day Clea was in the U.S. for seventeen years. Clea's experiences didn't come to life until she reported them to Elke. Elke would savor her description of Calvin Roche and his collapsing house, asking questions until she could picture it as vividly as Clea. Then she'd describe progress on her new sculpture (of a newborn baby hoisted on a bayonet) and encounters with bag ladies and greengrocers. She'd pass along bitchy gossip about mutual acquaintances. The phone wires crackled once Elke got going.

When Clea told Elke about Roches Ridge, Elke said nothing, wrapped in her gray wool shawl in the black plaid armchair in her studio, dull twilight visible out the streaky skylight. Finally she replied, "All I can say is that you've got too much energy for your own good, Clea. Or for *my* good, at any rate."

And it was true. Clea couldn't stay put. But Elke wouldn't budge. As Clea saw it, you kept moving or dropped dead. But for Elke, death was inevitable anyway, so why not get in practice? She'd lived in the same apartment and been married to the same man for over thirty-five years. Even her artwork exhibited a preoccupation with the same theme—suffering and long-suffering women and children, victims of war and violence. Graphics in the early years—drawings, etchings, lithographs, and woodcuts. Sculpture more recently, initially of clay, now of scrap steel. Brilliant but morbid, Clea felt. Elke was so skilled technically that her creations seemed almost to glorify destruction and romanticize victimization. Nonetheless, her work was very much in vogue, having been "discovered" by feminist art critics.

Elke attributed her love of stasis to an adolescence spent fleeing both German and Russian soldiers—across Germany to France, across the Channel to London. And to a young adulthood in Greenwich Village, under the gaze of HUAC, which eventually blacklisted her husband, Terence, now a political science professor at NYU.

"But you *will* come visit, won't you?" asked Clea as late-winter thunder rumbled through the skylight.

"My dear, you know I don't rusticate. I overdosed on haylofts and animal feed during the war." Elke's head lay against her chair back, and she studied a far corner of the ceiling.

In fact, disapproval of Clea's Roches Ridge venture had been nearly universal. (Excepting Terence, who was always delighted to have Clea far away, so he could monopolize Elke.) When Clea phoned Theo at Hotchkiss, he sputtered, "But, Mom, you can't just like *move away.*"

"Why can't I?" Theo was no doubt wearing his perennial silver astronaut jacket with the American flag patch on the sleeve and his blue Mets cap.

"Well, somebody's got to stay home to like take care of everything and stuff." He was permanently outraged with her for not being June Cleaver and meeting him at the door in an apron, with a glass of milk and an unquenchable interest in his days' pranks.

Kate, at Smith, merely said, "Honestly, Mother. Act your age."

Clea could picture her irritably twirling the long string-thin braid at the back of her neck. "How do women my age act?" Clea laughed. "That's what I'm trying to figure out." Her own mother had lain in bed in a frayed coral robe, pickled on Smirnoff's, during *her* menopause.

"Not like you, that's for sure," Kate said, half critically, half admiringly.

Clea realized all her near-and-dears wanted her waiting around Turtle Bay while they went out to play. But maybe *she* wanted to play too. While she still could.

Clea almost got up from Calvin Roche's cot to go into town and find a phone. Instead she closed her eyes and pictured Elke—high cheekbones and sharp chin, silver hair in a topknot, with wisps escaping all around like an aura, patient navy-blue eyes that focused with an unsettling intensity. After turning up at Elke's studio for the *American Artist* portrait, Clea had stayed all evening, hypnotized by those sorrowful eyes, which looked as though they'd witnessed every atrocity reported by the world press. Feeling a need to cheer her up, Clea regaled her during the photo session with stories about her babies, eliciting a few weary smiles. Eventually a tall, thin man with a slight stoop appeared from downstairs, holding the *National Review*. His dark hair was short on the sides and long and kinky on top like a Brillo pad. Black-framed glasses perched halfway down his nose. He asked Clea to leave so Elke could get her rest.

"My husband, Terence," Elke explained with an apologetic grimace after he left. "He's very protective."

"So I see," said Clea, gathering her equipment, spread out among stacks of copper plates, blocks of paper, chunks of stone, trays of paints, piles of what looked like debris. "I'm sorry I've outstayed my welcome. I had no idea it was so late."

"Please," said Elke with a helpless gesture of one hand. "I've loved having you here. Come back, won't you?"

"Sure. Call me when you're free. And thanks for the photos."

Riding home in the taxi along silent shadowy streets, Clea wondered upon what strange conjugal preserve she'd trespassed. Elke had made no move to contradict her rude husband. Clea would probably never hear from the woman again. But the next morning Elke phoned, and she had phoned almost daily ever since, whenever Clea was in New York.

Together Clea and Elke sparked like downed electrical wires. Once they tried converting this energy into sex, in a darkened seaside cottage on Saint John, beneath a slowly turning wooden fan. It was not a success. Blessedly, since Clea doubted she could have overcome her own technical fascination with the hydraulics of the penis. This desire to possess each other's bodies subsided, but their signets on each other's hearts remained inviolable. Sometimes Clea wished they could transform this charged connection into the more comfortable old-shoe camaraderie each shared with her husband. Perhaps this was partly why she'd moved to Roches Ridge—to escape the relentless mutual fascination neither had ever known what to do with.

Light from next door glared through the kitchen window, and the last leg of the ladder-back chair glowed in the fireplace. A sizzling sound, like a late-night fish fry, came from behind the stockade fence along the side yard. Clea glanced around the shadowy room at the disheveled stacks of magazines and the bulging walls. What had she gotten herself into? She thought about her Turtle Bay town house, its spotless beige wall-to-wall carpeting, its soft sofas ... its security system. Roche House had no locks, no curtains. Some itinerant marauder would look in, was probably looking in at this very moment, would see her alone and defenseless ... *She was kneeling among Big Mac cartons, the steel of a pistol barrel icy against her temple. The click as the man cocked it seemed to echo up and down the alley. Her mouth was parched, and her skin prickled with terror....*

Taking a deep breath, Clea reminded herself that there were no marauders in Roches Ridge. She sat up and turned on the bare overhead bulb. Searching her pocketbook, she found a spiral notebook and a Bic pen: "Elke—I'm longing to talk with you right now, my dear friend. Who've you seen, what've you heard? Our phone ritual, do you think it's an addiction? Maybe we need Dialers Anonymous. I'm sitting in the kitchen of my new house ..."

Clea looked up to see a large rat with red eyes sliding under the cellar door. Shuddering, she crossed her legs on the cot like a camper. "Elke, it's a gorgeous old place—Palladian window, leaded fanlight, pine floorboards 26″ wide. Only one family has inhabited it since 1790. Calvin Roche, who sold it to me, is a true New England eccentric. His children have moved away, so it's apparently my fate to rescue Roche House from collapse."

Suddenly exhausted, Clea put down the notebook and shoved her feet into the sleeping bag. Irritated by the glaring lights and crackling noises from next door, she fell into a restless sleep on the narrow cot as the embers faded in the fireplace. And she dreamed of her parents, as she still did in times of turmoil, searching aimlessly at the source for solace.

# 4  Elke

Sometimes the only way Elke could be sure she was still alive was that her fingernails kept needing clipping. She studied her blunt hands, veined and chapped and grimy, the tools of her trade. She was sitting in the black plaid armchair in her studio, missing Clea. New York seemed like a ghost town with her gone. It was easier when Clea was in Japan or Australia, because then she was unreachable. But to have her just five hours up the Northway was difficult. The anecdotes Elke saved up to amuse Clea with during their nightly phone conversations were going unheard. For instance, today a man in a pin-striped suit behind Elke in a long line at the cleaners pulled a .38 special and demanded his shirts ahead of everyone else.

Elke's innermost thoughts and deepest feelings were also going unexpressed. Surely Clea was finding this ridiculous new arrangement equally unsatisfactory. But she was in love with that squalid little town, Wretched Ridge. And the gusts of first passion would have to blow themselves out. Elke had watched the process time after time—the totally unworthy people, places, or projects that captured Clea, briefly but completely, so that she had no time or attention for anything else. Like her Zen meditation phase in Kyoto, when she was convinced she was hearing the harmony of the spheres, only to discover the high-pitched hum was tinnitus from an evolving hearing loss. Or her classical Indian dance seizure in Bombay, when she slipped a disk. Or Ryan Sullivan, the BBD&O account executive she seduced on Martinique, who gave her hepatitis. Clea claimed she was finished with obsession, but this rural solitude gig was merely her latest fixation. She always came back home eventually, however, sheepish and loving, like a house cat yowling in the alley who finds herself suddenly out of heat.

Elke felt wary of Clea's idealism. The search for purity sometimes involved the need to destroy perceived impurities, so that you brought about what you'd been opposing. Once Clea gave her a coral rose, to commemorate the tenth anniversary of their meeting. An outside petal was slightly withered, so Clea pulled it off. The entire rose disintegrated all over the studio floor. Elke tried instead to accept things as she found them, rust and all, like the scrap steel she used for her sculptures. Growing up in Nazi Germany, she'd been vaccinated early against idealism, having witnessed it running amok. But Clea was burdened with that implacable American innocence, believing life was meant to be a pleasant and meaningful experience. She'd never witnessed rivers flowing red with her countrymen's blood.

Just as Elke got her first menstrual period, the Russian sweep into Germany began. Tales of horror from Poland reached Elke's town on the Oder. As houses were searched, occupants were being gang raped. Girls were being requisitioned for use by Russian troops. Mothers were blackening their daughters' teeth, hacking off their hair, ripping their clothes, rubbing dirt into their skin. Elke's brother, a Luftwaffe pilot, had been killed the previous year in an Allied attack on a Tunisian airfield. A friend of his had sent them a photo of his grave, marked by a white wooden swastika, his helmet hanging from one arm. A few months earlier, Elke's father, a Wehrmacht medical officer, had been hanged by the Volksgericht in Berlin for his part in the bombing of Hitler's bunker at the Russian front. A thoughtful neighbor anonymously mailed Elke's mother a newspaper photo of his corpse, dangling by the neck. Entire families of some convicted officers were being executed as well. Elke and her mother had been waiting to be dragged off in the night. But the approaching Russians would make no distinctions. Germans were Germans.

Elke and her mother hit the road west, walking, hitching rides in farm wagons, sleeping in barns and on pine needles, gnawing turnips thrown to cattle. The woods and roads were crammed with refugees, army deserters, and escaped POWs. It was spring, so there were dandelion greens in the fields, and sometimes a cousin would share a scant meal. A Wehrmacht friend of Elke's father provided passes to France, and relatives in London got them through Allied lines and across the Channel. Everywhere they saw rubble and mutilation. The trip was a blur of fear and hunger, wet and cold to Elke. She carried a permanent record of this hegira in her rotted molars and her insatiable longing for safety.

In London, Elke wandered the blitzed city in a daze, making pencil sketches of charred ruins and hollow-eyed survivors. Drawing was her form of journal keeping. Getting down on paper the images she observed around her had always been her attempt, largely futile, to make sense of the world. She couldn't recall when she'd started this or why. But she did remember prowling her father's waiting room before the war, sketching his patients as they sat in the grip of injuries and diseases.

When Allied troops opened the concentration camps, Elke stared sullenly at her mother in their Camden Town flat and murmured, "But you must have *known*, Mother." The next day when she got home from school, her mother, having finally reached her limit, lay dead from a heart attack on the flowered parlor carpet.

An aunt in New York City arranged for Elke to attend Cooper Union. In the beginning she studied oil painting, but she quickly discovered she lacked a feeling for color. Nevertheless, the anatomy courses and drawing from plaster casts and live models engaged her. And she learned to etch her sketches of the blitz onto copper plates and to draw them in greasy crayon on lithography stone. Time after time, in different media, she reworked the cratered landscapes and limbless civilians.

At an art opening one evening she met Terence, a student on the GI Bill at City College, who lived in a fourth-floor walk-up in Greenwich Village. Tall and gaunt, he wore his dark hair curly on top and short at the sides. Having been among the first American troops in Germany, he was furious about the world bequeathed him by his parents' generation. To express this contempt, he joined the War Resisters League and the Communist Party. An intriguing mix of fire and ice, he was in constant turmoil beneath an aloof exterior. Almost from their first date he behaved like a guard dog, staking out her aunt's apartment and threatening her other dates, until she gave up and married him, moving to West Thirteenth Street, where she'd been ever since. She converted the attic above his apartment into a studio, outfitting it with a drawing table and a proofing press.

Soon she discovered that Terence sometimes woke up screaming at night. Over the months, he described what he'd seen in the gestapo prisons and concentration camps his commando unit had liberated. Although this confession eased *his* nightmares, it increased her own. So she struggled to exorcise his ghastly visions via a series of stark woodcuts, which enabled her to graduate with high honors from Cooper Union.

Terence was everyone's least favorite dinner guest. He had no small talk, and his large talk took the form of argument. In order to be truly content he needed to feel beleaguered. When the political climate of the country shifted leftward in the sixties, Terence, rather than feeling vindicated for his sufferings under McCarthy, became a supporter of the Vietnam war, insisting that anything 65 percent of the American people opposed must be okay. Elke could scarcely keep up with such a compulsive heretic.

"Why do you hang on to someone so quixotic?" Terence had demanded the night before, as Elke sat eating supper at their oak-pedestal kitchen table, in silent misery about Clea's defection to Roches Ridge. He was peering over his glasses, which perched halfway down his nose, with an expression indicating *he* was eminently practical and reliable, and therefore worthy of Elke's sole devotion. He liked her upstairs alone, working all the time, while he sat downstairs, reading the atrocities in the world press and protecting her from distracting intruders, like a eunuch at the portals of a seraglio.

"Because I love her."

"Then you're a bigger fool than she is."

"No doubt." It always amazed Elke that Terence was still jealous of Clea. It was obvious he'd won out in some ways—and never even stepped in the ring in others. The time when she considered leaving him for Clea was long past. She was his until death did them part, lucky fellow.

Running her thumbnail under her fingernails, Elke rested her head against her chair and gazed up at raindrops rolling down the streaky skylight. It was true. She *was* a fool, as obsessed by Clea as Clea was by Roches Ridge. Yet when Clea focused all her energy on you, you became a participant in her inner drama, which transformed everyday life into a Mardi Gras. Clea was a garish butterfly who flitted from garden to garden, searching for the perfect bloom. Elke herself was a termite, who munched away at rot in the dark. But Elke knew she could topple buildings, whereas Clea's blossoms, however perfect, inevitably faded and festered.

Although Clea never stuck around to witness decay. Even her photos were mostly hype. For instance, those she'd done of Elke for *American Artist,* using a soft-focus lens and backlighting, and retouching to minimize wrinkles and blemishes. Elke had never seen anyone who could travel so much and learn so little. So preoccupied was Clea with laying out glamorous vacation brochures in her brain that she didn't even notice the horrors staring her in the face. When the Shawns lived in Bombay, surrounded by limbless beggars starving in the streets, Clea had photographed the baroque relics of the British raj. This temperamental difference was a big factor in their attraction: Clea provided the flash, and Elke the pan.

Elke remembered first seeing Clea in her studio doorway seventeen years before, tall and lean, with long wavy black hair, dark eyebrows, and long lashes. She wore a black floor-length cape with a hood and a scarlet satin lining, reminding Elke of a flamboyant Clara Barton. The portrait session took hours, Clea constantly changing cameras, lenses, film, and lighting. While she assumed every imaginable posture—lying, kneeling, squatting, perching on a ladder—she talked about her children in a husky contralto Elke found mesmeric. Despite this flourish, the resulting photos showed a conventionally attractive woman with smooth skin and amiable expressions. Although mildly flattered, Elke had scarcely recognized the person who at that point was making woodcuts of terrorized Vietnamese women and children for antiwar posters. It made the session with Clea seem like casual sex—technique substituting for real contact.

In touch with Clea constantly after this, Elke began to experience pain whenever they parted, convinced from her experience with her mother that she'd never see Clea alive and well again. Clea and Turner were embroiled at the time in that tired old marital debate about monogamy. Both sides of it struck Elke as immature. These American Gothic ethics that regarded time-honored European traditions like tax avoidance and extramarital sex as "cheating" tended to get her down. Of course, she herself had never faced this issue. As far as she knew, Terence was compulsively faithful. Sometimes she yearned for him to distract himself from his concentration on her with some nubile undergraduate.

But Clea was suffering over Turner's "promiscuity," so Elke offered what comfort she could. Turner was sweet but flighty—a charming dizzy-blond salesman who made Terence seem like a troll. He had no interest in the convolutions of Clea's delicious psyche, wanting only a ready ear, willing body, and clean house when he returned from his journeys. Elke and Clea began to talk of fixing up a joint studio in a nearby loft, and Elke toyed with the notion that this might lead to a more total living arrangement.

But Kate and Theo were stumbling blocks. For an hour at a time, the babies were enchanting. Elke would sit on Clea's couch and sketch them at play, or in Clea's lap with their arms around her neck, insistently asserting a claim that surpassed Elke's. But twenty-four hours a day every day seemed a bit much. On the whole, Elke regarded her trips to Turtle Bay as visiting hours at the women's prison. Elke's work required her to stay underwater long enough for the squid to appear. This submersion necessitated confidence that no typhoons were brewing up above. Yet life with small children was a continual typhoon.

Meanwhile, the physical attraction was becoming so intense that Elke felt like a pile of nails being pulled to pieces by a magnet residing inside Clea. Elke tried to back off, calling less and canceling lunches, terrified of where her feelings were leading. She sequestered herself in her studio and struggled to distill her stacks of drawings of Clea and her children into an etching or a lithograph. But she felt so shy about the result that she didn't show it to Clea for a long time.

The strain of staying away from Clea began to take its toll. Elke developed migraines. Finally she could stay away no longer, so she went miserably with Clea to Saint John, to that bed beneath the slowly turning wooden fan.

And then Turner was assigned to Paris, and Clea was gone, as though punishing Elke for that tortured afternoon (which was punishment enough in and of itself). Clea's letters were briskly cheerful, and soon she was having an affair with a Belgian journalist, to whom she no doubt whispered sweet nothings in her atrocious French. Her attention, like a searchlight, had swiveled to illuminate someone else. Elke sought comfort from Terence, relieved to know she could count on his always being there to annoy her with his omnipresence.

That afternoon on Saint John still haunted her. Some days it seemed a missed opportunity, other days a lucky break. She had no wish to spend her days on the barricades of social change, but if she and Clea had been able just to act and let the chips fall, she might have left Terence for a life with Clea. Oh, she loved Terence; he was as replete with admirable principles as the U.S. Constitution. But Clea lifted her higher. Sometimes she felt like a hot-air balloon, Clea's fire inflating her, driving her skyward, Terence firmly restraining her with ropes of habit and domestic felicity.

But theirs was no simple triangle. It was a dizzy kaleidoscope of geometric forms involving spouses, children, other friends and lovers. Triangles were for the young. The middle-aged, with their complicated pasts and their hunger to devour life before the grave devoured them, were often enmeshed in networks as complex as the double helix. Just because "Little House on the Prairie" never portrayed such arrangements didn't mean they weren't common. The rootless Americans had their extended families, all right; but the bonds were usually emotional in origin rather than genetic.

Sighing, Elke glanced at her new sculpture beside a blue gas tank for her blowtorch. A screaming infant skewered on a forest of bayoneted rifles, held aloft by anonymous male hands. She'd named it "Suffer the Little Children." She liked the title, but the damned thing itself wasn't working. The balance was wrong, and the content was boring. She'd done infanticide. She'd also done rape and mutilation. She wanted to grab her torch and cut the jagged shards of metal to bits. Then she remembered it was evening. She always hated her pieces at that time of day, when her energy ebbed. Maybe tomorrow, recharged by rest, she'd once again be challenged to get the lines and angles right.

# 5  Astrid Starr

Astrid Starr's IGA was Roches Ridge's Mission Control. Astrid conducted the flow of rumors through town as Trooper Trapp did cars. It
was her form of public service. Although the high school boys stocking
the shelves could do the job, Astrid preferred to don her dark-blue
polyester jacket with the "IGA ♡ YOU" badge on the pocket and run the
register herself. As she rang up totals, she passed on nuggets of gossip
panned from previous customers. Every few months, like a fire drill,
she'd time on her Casio stopwatch how long it took for a customer to
come in and tell her something she herself had started up earlier in
the day. The town's record was forty-three minutes. (The record holder
was Sonny Coffin, who'd just come to Roches Ridge from Forest Lawn
with plans to build a crematorium in his grandfather's hay barn.)

Recently much news had concerned the woman in the green plaid
lumberjack shirt just walking through the glass door, camera around
her neck. A real estate speculator, some were saying, fixing up Calvin's
house for profit. The anxious mother of one of those dykes down by
Mink Creek, others said. A front woman for the born agains up in
Granite Gap, who planned to take over Roches Ridge for Christ, starting with Calvin's house. An FBI agent looking into Alvin Jacobs' communists at Camel's Hump Community College. Rumors were flying
thick as bats on a summer evening. But today Astrid hoped to get at
the truth, and then pass it along.

While Clea pushed her cart down the canned-fruit aisle, Astrid
hummed "Some Enchanted Evening" and flipped through the Royal
Viking Line brochure from the morning mail. She had the most complete collection of travel catalogues in town. Her current goal was to
sail from Vancouver to Anchorage. (Originally it had been the Greek
Isles, but when those Arabs pushed Klinghoffer overboard, she
switched oceans.) She pictured the rumba under the Big Dipper, the
aerobics on deck, the interesting fellow passengers from Iowa and
Alabama.

Two years ago, for their honeymoon, Astrid and Earl cruised the
Hawaiian Islands on the *Norwegian Star* with a group of Elks and Elkettes. The ship docked for side trips. You could bus into a tropical rain

forest to see rare orchids, or helicopter over an active volcano. But of course she and Earl weren't interested in that kind of thing. Earl's favorite stop was Pearl Harbor, because there weren't any Japs around. At a souvenir shop he bought his floppy Australian army hat, with an emu feather in the leather band.

Her own favorite stop was the luau. While the pig roasted in a pit, she and some Elkettes, leis around their necks, lip-synched the sound track from *South Pacific.* Upon her return, Astrid asked poor little Angela McGrath to play *South Pacific* on her harp, hoping it might distract her from her endless grief over her dead baby son. In spring and summer that harp music floated across the green and all over town. It was even better than Muzak.

If it was up to Astrid, she and Earl would embark for Alaska today. But despite being an heiress, she wanted to seem like an ordinary citizen. Her grandfather had traded groceries for farmland at the turn of the century, when crops had failed. Her father sold the land to developers. Alpine Glen ski area, Colonial Manor Estates, and the Xerox factory were all once Starr land.

This was a second marriage for both Astrid and Earl. Earl's wife ran off with the roofer who was replacing their slates with asphalt shingles. Astrid's husband Homer died of diabetes. He'd been popping sugar cubes by the carton for years while stocking shelves.

Astrid went to Mink Valley High with Earl Atkins back in the Dark Ages, and they'd never looked at each other twice. But once each was single again, something clicked. Earl used to hang around the register and help her bag after he'd been checked out. Finally she got the picture and invited him home for supper. That night his belly, which hung over his belt like a puffball mushroom, started looking cute. He said he'd loved her since high school and had been writing poems in secret. Pulling out some papers, he read: "Prettier than the month of June, / Brighter than the sun at noon, / More mysterious than the harvest moon, / It's you I love, Astrid." She began wanting to pat his belly, and one thing led to another, until here they were—Roches Ridge's oldest living lovebirds. Together they'd roam the globe. If they could just get out of town.

Earl sold his barbershop to Jared McQueen, who recently moved home after two years at the Yankee Clipper in Albany. Earl got upset when Jared took down the striped pole outside and changed the marquee from EARL'S BARBERSHOP to MANE MAGNIFIQUE. But Jared planned to run a unisex boutique like the Yankee Clipper. Alpine Glen skiers wouldn't patronize a barbershop. Say what you like, you couldn't fight progress. Now Earl was organizing the Miss Teenage Roches Ridge Pageant and devising a new shelf arrangement for the IGA. With the Grand Union right there on Route 7, with its salad bar, cracker barrels of carob-covered bridge mix, and monthly singles nights, you couldn't afford to stand still.

Waneeta Marsh plunked a six-pack of Diet Cherry Coke on the counter and reached for the Banquet Dinners in her cart. Astrid laid down the Royal Viking brochure. "Pretty day," suggested Waneeta, tugging with one hand at the forest-green Dior sweater dress that stretched tautly over her enormous breasts.

"Looks like spring, all right."

"Ayuh."

"Polly delivered the other night, did she, Waneeta?"

"Ayup. A baby girl. I love them when they're little."

"But then they get big," muttered Astrid, reflecting that Roches Ridge had too many grown Marshes as it was. Astrid punched the total button as though detonating a land mine beneath the Marshes' house.

"Yup, kittens into cats." Waneeta smiled, bright blue eyes shining like cat-eye marbles in sugar-cookie dough. She handed Astrid a booklet of food coupons.

Irritably Astrid tore some out. With three grown sons, why was Waneeta still getting these things? Some people had no pride and liked to steal their neighbors' hard-earned tax dollars. You could always spot Waneeta, looking like a round hay bale on legs, in line outside the town hall whenever there was a giveaway of government surplus cheese or butter or rice. It wasn't a pretty sight. Waneeta even wore the clothes of crash victims, salvaged from suitcases in wrecked cars her son Ray towed home from the interstate. Sometimes you saw her going off to clean houses in a designer dress. She flaunted her poverty just so Astrid would feel guilty that Starrs had made a bundle off Marsh land, forgetting that Astrid's grandfather saved Waneeta's from starvation during '92-and-Froze-to-Death, when it snowed every month of the year.

"Polly come up with a name yet, has she, Waneeta?" The Marshes had always had trouble naming their babies. When Waneeta had her twins, the nurse finally put her foot down and said she needed names for the birth certificates. Waneeta looked down at the tag on her housecoat and announced the girls would be called Polly and Esther Marsh. She named her subsequent sons Orlon, Rayon, and Dacron.

"She's thinking about April."

"That's a pretty name," Astrid said, bagging the Cherry Coke.

"I told her if she didn't hurry up and decide, she'd have to change it to May," said Waneeta, stuffing the remaining food coupons in her white plastic pocketbook.

"Well, May's a nice name too. Old Mrs. Murphy's a May. Heard from Calvin yet, have you, Waneeta?"

"I don't expect we will. Calvin's long gone."

"He's been a strange one, Calvin has, ever since Boneeta passed on."

"Well, Boneeta kept him civil. Once she departed, we never saw him from one month to the next. Sometimes he'd sneak over at night to shoot out our bug light." Waneeta loaded her bags into the cart.

"There's your new neighbor now. Over to the ant traps."

Waneeta craned her neck to see the tall, dark-haired woman in her stiff new green lumberjack shirt. " 'Twas a helluva crash over to Calvin's this morning. Guess his tub finally fell into the cellar. Must be a wicked mess. Calvin threw his trash down there whenever it was too cold to throw it in the yard." Waneeta was pushing her cart toward the door. "Well, we'll see you, Astrid."

Nodding, Astrid eyed the front window display as Waneeta passed it. Skates, a Yankee Flyer sled, scarf and mittens, with appropriate products grouped around them—Swiss Miss cocoa mix, Chap Stick, Vicks VapoRub. Past time for the sugaring display already. The seasons changed so fast Astrid could hardly keep up.

Clea Shawn was at the register with several Lean Cuisines, two bottles of lime Perrier, and some Liquid-plumr. She was on a diet; she wasn't a drinker; she wasn't expecting company for the weekend; her drains were clogged, but not enough to need a plumber. Show me a person's shopping cart, Astrid always said to Earl, and I could paint you their portrait.

"Pretty day," observed Astrid.

"Yes, very." Clea smiled.

"I'm Astrid Starr."

"Hello, I'm Clea Shawn. It's nice to meet you."

"Bought Calvin's house, have you?"

"Yes, and I guess you can see that I've got my work cut out for me."

"I *guess* so. Planning to vacation in Roches Ridge, are you, Mrs. Shawn?"

"No, I'm here to stay. My husband isn't convinced we should leave New York, but I'm working on him."

Husband, noted Astrid. New York. "Why Roches Ridge, if you don't mind me asking?"

"We were passing through after skiing at Alpine Glen, and I fell in love with the place. I've never seen a more beautiful spot. It's so peaceful and quiet. And everyone's been so kind."

"Ummm," said Astrid. It *used* to be peaceful before weirdos started moving in. The born agains and queers and coupon clubbers and communists. Used to be, you let your kids out the door and didn't see them till suppertime. Now they might come crawling home with AIDS.

"Of course, since you live here all the time," said Clea, taking money from her wallet, "you may not realize how lucky you are."

Astrid eyed her Royal Viking brochure. "To tell you the truth, Mrs. Shawn, I prefer my beautiful spots in a warmer climate, like Hawaii." Mrs. Shawn looked taken aback, but how could she be expected to know that a dinky little backwater like Roches Ridge could produce a woman who'd visited every state in the nation except Alaska and North Dakota.

"Hawaii is lovely. But give me green hills and clear lakes and maple forests and crisp blue skies any day."

"Whatever." Astrid ripped the receipt off the register and dropped it in Clea's brown paper bag, on which was printed JUST SAY NO TO DRUGS.

"Tub fell into the cellar out to Calvin's this morning, did it, Mrs. Shawn?"

"Yes. But how did you know?"

"Word travels fast in small towns."

"Remind me to behave myself." Clea laughed.

Astrid gave her a speculative glance, antennae quivering.

Maureen Murphy and her mother, May, were walking past the front display window in slow motion. May's aluminum walker had a large pink satin bow tied to the handle. She wore a heavy black overcoat despite the warm spring sun, and glitter socks over her boots.

"That woman's a living saint," announced Astrid, trying to be generous to her former rival for Earl's affections.

"Who is?"

"The daughter there. Maureen Murphy. I remember her coming to school with her clothes all in tatters. But she keeps her mother so nice. Always pretty new socks over her boots to keep the salt off. Every day on her lunch hour from the post office she walks May around the green. And she takes her on trips all over the world. She's always asking me for suggestions. Of course, May, the poor soul, wouldn't know California from Calcutta. She's got the Alzheimer's."

"That's a difference in small towns. In New York, the old woman would be sleeping on a subway grate and eating from trash barrels."

"Well, May deserves trash barrels. But Maureen is a saint. No doubt about it."

# 6   Pollyannoia

On her way out, Clea studied the signs taped in the front window of the IGA: housework wanted, hay for sale, a lost beagle, golden retriever pups for sale. Clea scribbled the address for the pups on her grocery bag. A poster featured a grinning adolescent in a bathing suit and high heels, rhinestone tiara on her head. MISS TEENAGE ROCHES RIDGE PAGEANT. TOWN HALL. APRIL 8, 8 P.M.

"You don't want to miss that," called Astrid from the register. "Everybody goes."

Clea nodded, taking a last look at Astrid, who resembled a sturdy corner mailbox in her dark-blue polyester jacket, her mouth the slot. This woman was her new neighbor, whom she'd be seeing week after week for the rest of their lives. This thought, stifling in Poplar Bluffs, now seemed comforting. Families kept disintegrating on her—first her Poplar Bluffs one, now her New York City one. But Roches Ridge would be her new extended family, one she had chosen with deliberation, one that would cohere through the decades remaining to her.

Clea nodded to May and Maureen Murphy as they labored up the sidewalk, to the thump of the mother's walker. May had glasses with lenses so thick her eyes swam, and hearing aids in both ears. Thin white hair revealed a pinkish scalp. The mouth was caving in like a rotting jack-o'-lantern's. Maureen had prominent frown lines and tightly clamped lips. Graying bangs were held flat to her forehead by a strip of Scotch tape.

So everyone in town already knew her bathtub had fallen into the cellar, Clea reflected as she crossed the road. She'd forgotten the lessons learned in Poplar Bluffs. In New York City, everyone was searching for someone to spill his guts to. Bag ladies stopped you in the street to detail their ruination. But in small towns you devoted your energies to *concealing* your guts.

So effective was this practice in Poplar Bluffs that Clea was over thirty years old before she realized her mother had died of alcoholism. An aged aunt, looking across the Ohio to the limestone cliffs of Kentucky, let the cat out of the bag by observing, "So tragic about your poor mother's drinking."

This explained much about Clea's ostensibly privileged childhood—muffled arguments late at night, missed meals and canceled trips, lamely accounted-for illnesses and injuries. Some days Clea's mother, dressed in a coral robe, would enfold Clea in her arms and hide her in a tent of long black hair. Other times she'd eye Clea with disgust and turn away. Clea would silently vow to keep the younger children quiet and to pick up the toys in the yard. Once she threw herself at her mother's feet, pleading, "Mother, I'll do anything you want if only you'll stop being angry." Mostly her mother stayed in bed with headaches. But when she emerged dressed for a dinner party in an emerald satin sheath to match her eyes, she was the most gorgeous creature Clea had ever beheld, dazzling guests with her charm and wit. And when the guests left, Clea's father would mix her mother a highball and help her up the stairs.

Clea's father was uniformly pleasant and aloof. As president of the Poplar Bluffs Farmers Trust, he went to work each day in a three-piece suit and wing-tip shoes. When loans for townspeople couldn't be arranged, he'd sometimes pull out his personal checkbook. Their back porch often had country hams from grateful farmers swaying from the rafters. Thanks to Ulla, the Swedish housekeeper, the house was orderly and meals were on time. On Sundays the entire family strolled in pairs down the block to the Presbyterian church, where the minister often lauded Clea's father from the pulpit.

Clea's mother, brilliant at college, had wanted to go to law school. Her lawyer father maintained that law was too cutthroat for a woman, so she trained as a librarian. But her husband insisted she remain home with her babies. And she adored each baby, nursing and fondling it all day long. Until it reached the age of two, and began walking and talking, with plans of its own. Then she lost interest and lay in bed with headaches until she became pregnant again.

Clea heard of each new pregnancy with despair, feeling she'd just gotten her mother through the last one, and that the next one was likely to be just as disappointing. Clea helped Ulla bathe her younger siblings, and watched "Ozzie and Harriet" and "Father Knows Best" with them. She read them "Little Lulu" comic books at bedtime and baked them peanut butter cookies topped with chocolate kisses. She taught them to ride bicycles and swim the crawl and play Kick the Can. They trailed along after her like ducklings to her friends' houses. And though she sometimes scowled at them and called them babies, they refused to go away. As they grew older, Clea advised them on playground protocol and took them shopping for bras or jockstraps.

Her six siblings, grown now, assured her she had been like Lucy in "Peanuts." When they played circus, she insisted on being the head trapeze artist. If they were an Indian tribe, she performed all ceremonial dances, the others watching and drumming. When they were a cavalry regiment, Clea was Colonel Courage, who got to enact all feats involving heroism. And she was always the father of their pioneer family in the backyard playhouse. On trips, Clea organized the seating— one up front between her parents, two lying on the rear floor on either side of the drive shaft, three sitting on the back seat, and Clea lying on the rear window shelf. At her command, she and those on the back seat would roll off and squash those on the floor. In short, her siblings now informed her, her need for control had made Stalin look like a wimp.

At school, Clea was valedictorian, and president of several clubs. She read almost every book in the library, rereading *Wuthering Heights* five times. During class she'd appear attentive, while in her mind she was riding a raft down the Ohio to Cincinnati, where she was greeted at the docks by a kindly older woman very much like Harriet Nelson, who offered to teach her how to put on eyeliner. Cincinnati itself was full of sophisticates who dined in restaurants where strolling gypsies played "Ave Maria" on violins.

When Clea finally made it to Cincinnati, with the Girl Scouts in junior high school, to swim in the indoor pool at the Y, she was deeply distressed to find it similar to Poplar Bluffs, only bigger. And Harriet Nelson was nowhere in sight.

After this, when Clea sat in class trying to visualize her escape from Poplar Bluffs, the raft would always capsize. So eventually this fantasy transformed itself into an escape on foot in the opposite direction—to New York City. She would live in a penthouse overlooking Central Park, where a debonair older man who resembled Robert Young on "Father Knows Best" would mix highballs on the terrace, while city lights twinkled below. Thus did her heart first reveal its palimpsest nature, fresh reveries quickly masking outdated ones.

· · ·

A Stop sign stood before Clea at a corner of the green. Beneath STOP someone had spray-painted STAR WARS. This was crossed out and replaced with RAPE. A pair of workhorses clopped past the War of 1812 cannon. A muscular young man in faded jeans and denim jacket stood on the wagon bed, holding the reins. Clea set down her grocery bag and used her zoom lens for several pictures. Clydesdales yet—this was amazing. What kind of town rituals occurred on this green? Fiddlers' contests? Band concerts?

Crossing the green, with the skeletal branches of the stately old elms swaying overhead, Clea saw two young women in down parkas on the steps of the Victorian bandstand, which sported a cupola, a railing with turned spindles, and a hatchwork skirting. One called to the man on the wagon, "Working hard, Gordon?"

"Hardly working!" he yelled, a sweet grin transforming his bearded face.

Three toddlers scrambled on and off the cannon and between the legs of the bronze Civil War soldier on its concrete pedestal. Raised lettering around the base of the soldier read: ROCHES RIDGE HONORS HER FALLEN HEROES. On three sides were lists of the dead from the Civil War, World War I, and World War II. The fourth side was blank, no doubt awaiting the results of World War III. Putting down her groceries again, Clea asked the women if she could photograph their children.

As Clea framed the scene and adjusted for the lighting, she thought about how this central green was a time capsule. The most recent generation used monuments left by previous ones as their playground. These children were probably descendants of original settlers. The houses those settlers built, which circled the green like covered wagons around a campfire, were still intact and in use. She noted with approval the angle of the shiny black cannon in relation to the triangular peak of the white town hall in the background.

The children were reaching heights of exhilaration as they jumped off the cannon. Clea began snapping rapidly, trying to capture them in midair with their jubilant expressions. The contrast of their ephemeral grace to the iron cannon and the stolid town hall would be striking.

As she strolled along the dirt road back to her house, early-spring sunshine warm on her shoulders, Clea felt satisfaction with the pictures she'd just taken. After all her years of training and experience, it had become almost second nature to juggle simultaneously the different elements—light and dark, background and foreground, lines and shapes, the surge of emotions. When she was younger, she relied more on a shotgun approach, shooting roll after roll with the hope of getting a decent picture via the law of averages. But by now she could often anticipate the "decisive moment," as Cartier-Bresson called it, when all the elements were in alignment. It suddenly occurred to her that these photos and others like them might make an interesting book. "1776 Revisited." Something like that. "Our colonial past lives on in this small Vermont village. . . ."

Clea had already published three books—on France, Japan, and India, where she had lived while her husband, Turner, supervised marketing for Fresh-It. He kept getting reassigned because he was being groomed for a vice-presidency. The fortunate timing of these transfers rescued him from the consequences of several indiscretions—with the wife of a French colleague, with a Japanese geisha girl. Clea and Turner had the original open marriage, in the days when it was still called infidelity. Clea first became aware of this one night when Turner returned from Amsterdam with crabs. After an inner struggle, she decided to play by his rules, so she took up infidelity herself. She also resumed photography, having dropped a free-lance career after Kate's birth. Through Turner she had access to the world of international business and diplomacy, and her travel books explored privileged sectors ordinary tourists never glimpsed. American snobbery made the books sell well. So maybe Karen, her editor in New York, might like her idea of "1776 Revisited."

At the bottom of the jagged hole in Clea's kitchen floor sat the cracked white bathtub on its claw feet. The odor of putrefaction wafted up from the dirt cellar. Darius Drumm, the contractor, a small, gaunt man in starched khaki work clothes, who sucked continually on an unlit wooden pipe, stuck a penknife in several exposed beams. "Bad news. Dry rot." Talking to Darius was like reading a telegram. Descended from a dynasty of Vermont carpenters, he used mostly hand tools, as had his father, grandfather, and great-grandfather.

"How bad?" Clea found herself replying in kind.

"Twelve, fifteen thousand bad."

"That's bad," sighed Clea. "But I have no choice, do I?"

"Nope. 'Cept to sell the dog." Darius sucked on his pipe.

"Okay. Go ahead."

Darius nodded.

Clea felt like Lady Macbeth, too far steeped in blood to turn back now. She'd seen enough of life not to be outraged anymore when things went wrong, rather to be grateful when they went right. This sill problem was probably just the beginning, but she hoped some surprises would be pleasant—like a hidden staircase, or stenciling, or a secret room for the Underground Railroad.

Clea had meant to make a sandwich, but her kitchen had been reduced to rubble. On the spur of the moment she decided to drive to New York. She could discuss "1776 Revisited" with Karen, drop in on Elke for the latest gossip, and see Turner before he left for Mexico City. When she returned, Darius would have the kitchen floor patched and an upstairs bedroom ready. After all these years of consulting the combined schedules of Turner, Kate, and Theo, it seemed odd to be able to suit only herself.

"Clea, are you sure about this?" asked Karen over trout cheesecake at Lutèce. Clea's romanticism was clearly making her nervous. Well, Karen should know, having been the object of it when they first met, over Clea's photo essay on France, in Karen's office overlooking the East River. Clea immediately decided Karen was the most wonderful person she'd ever encountered. Until she discovered Karen got bitchy before her periods, and loved Campbell's tomato soup, and wore wool socks and Lanz nightgowns to bed in winter. And all the other flaws Clea soon uncovered that made Karen less than the quintessential all-nurturing sophisticate Clea originally perceived her to be. And then Clea became disillusioned and moped around looking at Karen with mute recrimination. It was a couple of years before Clea could treat her as an ordinary flawed but lovable mortal.

"Karen, do you think I'd present you with this proposal if I weren't certain?" Clea picked a black olive from her salad, reached across the table, and popped it into Karen's mouth. During the course of this lunch Clea had felt her own internal engine, idling after only a few days of rural languor, begin to rev up again in response to Karen's.

"No, I don't." Karen smiled, chewing. "You're often wrong, Clea. But you're never uncertain. I mean, who would buy such a book?"

"History buffs. People who love Vermont. Vermont has a real mystique right now. With city people nostalgic for their rural heritage."

Karen nodded doubtfully.

"And people who admire my work. Some do, you know."

"Well, I can't dispute that."

In the end Karen reluctantly agreed to the proposal because she didn't want to lose Clea to another publisher, and because Clea agreed to a ridiculously small advance.

"Believe me, Karen," Clea concluded, sipping the last of her Pouilly-Fuissé, "Roches Ridge is as foreign to modern America as India."

"I am open to being convinced," said Karen.


Clea watched Elke blush violently upon opening her studio door, blowtorch goggles on her forehead. It was gratifying still to be able to elicit such a strong reaction. "I know you hate to be dropped in on, Elke. I'm sorry. I tried to phone, but I got your recording. And I'm only in town for another day."

"Come in."

Clea could tell Elke was poised between pleasure and irritation, glad to see her but annoyed she'd been away and would soon go away again. She always behaved like this after Clea's trips. By now each rarely experienced an emotion the other wasn't aware of.

"Darling," murmured Clea, wrapping her arms around Elke and feeling a surge of affection and obscure longing, as unremitting as ever.

"Darling yourself," said Elke, stepping back to study her. "Well, you haven't turned to granite yet."

"Damn it, Elke. I wish I didn't love you."

"It would be more restful, wouldn't it? All this coming and going. When will you be content to stay put?" Elke plopped down in her plaid armchair and removed her goggles.

"Why don't you come to Roches Ridge?"

"What a good idea. And immerse myself in everything I hate most— fields and woods and rural folkways." She unzipped her burnt-orange coverall to the waist.

"You really must overcome your aversion to the bucolic, Elke. There's an ell you could turn into a studio. I keep picturing you strolling the fields in tweeds and Wellingtons. I promise there are no Russian soldiers in my woods." Clea tossed her raincoat on a table and sank into the old rust corduroy chair opposite Elke. They had sat like this for seventeen years, experiencing toward each other every emotion in the human handbook.

"There are worse ways to grow old," added Clea.

"Name some. No, we'll have to make do with letters and phone calls. Until you sober up and crawl back home."

"Roches Ridge *is* my home." Clea placed her forearms resolutely along the chair arms.

"And Ryan Sullivan is your true love forever. Remember, I've heard it all before."

"This is different."

"Each one is *always* different. When will you acquire some perspective?"

"Never, I hope, if having perspective means settling into stasis."

"There are worse ways to grow old, to quote a valued friend. What are you doing here, by the way?"

"I wanted to get some film developed at my lab. And discuss a book idea with Karen. The past still flourishing in rural Vermont. Something like that."

Elke pursed her lips. The sounds of a revolving garbage truck seeped through the bamboo shades.

"So what do you think?" Clea asked, reluctant to expose her nascent idea to Elke's often withering scrutiny.

Elke sighed, knowing she couldn't escape the exigencies of candor. They always said exactly what they felt about each other's work. If not about each other's private lives. "I'm not sure I get the picture. What do you have in mind?"

"Well, here. Like this." Clea reached for a file folder on the table and handed Elke a print of the children jumping off the cannon. And another of the young farmer driving his team of Clydesdales.

Elke studied them for a long time. Then she looked up. "Clea, my dear, your work is always delightfully decorative, and technically flawless and well composed," she said, a faint German accent tincturing her BBC English. "You always show beautiful scenery and privileged people. But where is the pain and poverty and suffering and despair of real people? They are an illusion, your handsome pictures."

"And I suppose your escapees from Bosch are reality?" Clea was stung by the "decorative." She knew Elke considered her work superficial, but she'd never been able to figure out why.

"You and Turner belong together. He sells toothpaste in countries where people have lost all their teeth to malnutrition and disease. But we've had this discussion before." Elke rubbed her temples with the thumb and index finger of her left hand. Her hands, gnarled and rough from struggles with metal and stone, were unusually large and strong in contrast to her frail frame.

"It's the essence of all our discussions. I say you're paranoid, and you say I'm pollyannoid. But really, Elke, you don't have to flag down every ambulance that comes along the pike. You shiver like marsh grass in each passing breeze. Sometimes people need their cocoons of well-being."

"You don't have to flag down ambulances if they're headed right at you."

"Only if you insist on standing in their path."

"If we haven't resolved this dispute in the last seventeen years, I'm sure we never will," observed Elke. "So let's just drop it."

Clea shrugged. Secretly she agreed with Elke and regarded herself as a deeply shallow person. In Roches Ridge, though, without the distractions of a big city or a foreign country, she planned to slow down. "Chill out, Mom," Theo was always suggesting, glancing up from the "Leave It to Beaver" reruns he'd discovered on TV. The chaos would subside. In this new state of solitude and simplicity, Clea would get beneath the surface to whatever Elke felt her photos lacked.

Clea stood up and strolled around the studio, studying each new object since her last visit—piles of discarded notes and sketches, scraps of metal, blobs of clay wrapped in damp cloths, a mobile of bolts and bedsprings wrapped in glossy red cord, the disconnected limbs of a mannequin. Going on a walk with Elke was like shell-collecting on a beach. She was always stooping down to appropriate some urban treasure washed up on a curbstone.

Arriving at the bayoneted baby, Clea inspected it from every angle, saying nothing. Now it was her turn, but she couldn't bring herself to say that this piece lacked Elke's usual brilliance.

"I don't like it either," said Elke.

Clea grimaced. Neither could get away with a thing. Their boundaries were so fluid it was sometimes hard to remember who was who. "Well, it's not your best. Or not yet anyway."

"I'm thinking about calling it 'Suffer the Little Children.' "

Oh, give me a break, thought Clea, raising her eyebrows but saying nothing.

"But I may abandon it altogether. I'm fed up with evil."

Clea looked at her with surprise. "I can't believe these deaf old ears."

"The problem is, I don't know what to replace it with. I have a great horror of turning pollyannoid."

Clea laughed. "That'll be the day, you old curmudgeon."

# 7 Turner

"So how's Elke?" asked Turner, looking up from the stove as he sprinkled chopped chives on an omelet.

"She seems a bit subdued," said Clea, leaning against the refrigerator with her arms folded across her stomach.

"As usual." Elke was like the Grinch who Stole Christmas. Turner was certain she'd be able to find a down side to paradise.

"She says she's fed up with evil."

"Aren't we all?"

Clea smiled. "As a theme, she meant."

"Well, well," said Turner, flipping the omelet. "So Elke is having a mid-life crisis also?"

"Who knows? Wouldn't it be a shocker if she left that gloomy Terence?"

"It'd probably be awful for them both after all these years." He cut the omelet in two, dished up the halves, and handed one to Clea. Despite their separate lives, it would be awful for *him* if Clea departed for good. She was like a house cat—aloof when on the hunt, but fiercely protective of her kittens, and eager to see her mangy old tom when she was in heat. He only prayed she'd get this rural idyll out of her system and come back home soon. It unnerved him when he was in Mexico City or Belgrade to think of her alone in the woods. No doubt she could cope. After all, she'd survived a mugging without his assistance. But he liked to picture her sprawled on the sofa at Turtle Bay, babies crawling on the carpet and tugging at her skirt. This image was his St. Christopher's medal. He'd been worried about her lately. She'd burst into tears at the drop of a hat. The first time this happened was at her twenty-fifth Cornell reunion the previous fall, while talking to her erstwhile mentor and lover John Galmer. Their doctor said it was probably a combination of empty nest and menopause, that Turner should be patient and supportive. He was trying, despite his mystification. But it upset him to see Clea, usually so aloof, in tears.

"I suppose you're right." Clea sat down at the butcher-block table with her stoneware plate. "This looks delicious, Turner. Thanks."

"Kate called."

"Just to chat?"

"And to announce she's going to Saint Augustine for spring break. It's not fair: As soon as she recovers from being a repulsive teenager, she vanishes from our lives."

Clea laughed. "She wasn't that bad. Sex and booze and rock 'n' roll. Nothing we didn't do."

"No wonder your parents took to drink."

Clea nodded grimly. "Well, we've done pretty well, wouldn't you say, Pop?"

"Too soon to tell." He ripped apart his French bread. Actually he preferred business to parenthood. You could issue directives and get results, instead of dragging on year after year in the same old stalemates. And if people didn't perform to your standards, you could fire them. Kate and Theo lay around their rooms all day, listening to atrocious music. At their age he was mowing lawns, washing cars, saving for college. Clea slipped them money instead of making them earn it. Since she was the soft touch, he had to be the heavy. Of course, Clea and he could never present a united front because they were rarely in the same place at the same time. But this was why their marriage had endured for twenty-two years.

As Turner sat down, he studied this stranger, his wife. And if they stayed together another twenty-two years, he wouldn't understand her any better. Behind her surface élan lay a self-containment so pervasive that it frightened him. She didn't need him. He liked that. She came and went as she pleased. He liked that less. Especially when he observed the wives of his colleagues, whose lives revolved around their husbands and their husbands' careers. But when he looked more closely, he could see the strain on the wives' faces under their careful makeup, and the hunted look in the husbands' eyes as they struggled to carve out some private retreat the wives couldn't invade. Just like his father back in Milwaukee, fabricating union duties to keep him away from that apartment crammed with squabbling females.

Turner ran his hand over his balding head to check for new growth. Losing his thick crop of curly blond hair had been a trauma. He knew how a deciduous tree must feel in autumn. Thinking about Picasso and Yul Brynner and Telly Savalas, he comforted himself with the knowledge that excess testosterone was the culprit.

Clea's self-sufficiency had drawn him to her in the first place. He remembered watching her across the crowded barroom in the basement of the Cornell DU house at the freshman tea his senior year.

Her date had passed out on the make-out room floor. Clea, making the best of a bad situation, was singing alto on "Roll Your Leg Over," dark hair hiding one bleary eye. Turner offered to walk her back to the Tri Delt house.

"Why are you walking me home?" she asked as they shuffled along the sidewalk, while a full moon hovered like a cough drop on the lip of a gorge. "Because I seem pathetic—drunk, with my date passed out?"

He laughed. "Hardly. Because you looked like the most interesting woman in the room."

"Sorry to disappoint you."

"That's for me to decide, isn't it?"

At the crew races the next weekend, she stood in the grass along the lakeshore in her plaid pleated skirt, pearls, and raincoat, silent and aloof as the crowd chugged beer and cheered the rowers. When he tried to slide his arm around her waist, she shrugged it off. In the DU basement afterward, Turner was so drunk he mixed vanilla ice cream into the milk punch with his hands, squishing it as he had margarine during World War II to mix in the coloring. Clea watched and laughed and drank the punch anyway, and sang a wavering alto on "In China They Do It for Chili." All the things expected of a coed if she wanted to be invited back. But with Clea there was a difference, which stemmed from her air of amused detachment. When he walked her back to the Tri Delt house, she declined to kiss him good night.

This went on all spring, Clea reserved and evasive, treating him with a distracted tenderness that was almost maternal, even though she was three years his junior. She acted as if there was some guy back home, but when he asked her, she assured him there was no one else. He fell ever more deeply in love, unattainability being his favorite aphrodisiac, the result of that cramped Milwaukee apartment filled with clinging females. Soon he'd be graduated and moving to New York City for a marketing job. Clea's attitude indicated this would end it, but he felt they'd barely begun.

One hot afternoon toward the end of term they climbed down into a boulder-strewn gorge and sat on his London Fog raincoat in a rhododendron thicket, which was purple with blossoms and humming with bees. Clea allowed him to pull her down into his arms, where they lay still and silent, listening to water gurgling over rocks at the foot of the gorge.

"I want you, Turner," she finally said, in a voice husky with desire.

"Just like that?" he asked with a nervous laugh. This was the era when "nice" girls necked and petted their brains out but rarely went all the way, and certainly not as freshmen, unless drunk. But it required a more sterling character than he possessed to point out the drawbacks to her own well-being that this undertaking might entail.

In the past his penis, always capricious, had responded most reliably to female helplessness. One night driving to Syracuse he passed a woman on a lonely road beside a car with a flat tire, and he became hard as a jack iron. After he changed the tire, she invited him back to her apartment for a reward that had become ongoing. Now, faced with a woman who didn't need him, who suddenly simply wanted him, a coed from a prosperous midwestern banking family, he couldn't predict his wayward member's behavior.

But as his hands explored her willing body, he discovered his penis was cooperating. Swiftly tearing open the condom packet extracted from his wallet, he pushed into Clea before his penis could change its mind. As her head fell back and her dark hair lashed, he felt alarm, accustomed to his Syracuse waitress, who mentally drummed her long red fingernails on his back until he finished.

After a while, Clea asked, "Is that it?" He felt his already limp member wither, and it didn't recover for the rest of the term.

In New York City, he was so busy cutting a swath through the wild oats he was sowing in the typing pool at Green Gourmet Foods that he rarely got back to Cornell. Clea in any case was singing alto with assorted DUs; her shameful behavior in the make-out room, which they reported, would have sunk the reputation of any coed with less sangfroid. The last straw for Turner was a rumor that she was putting out for some jerk in the art department named John Galmer. When he confronted her at Homecoming, she would neither confirm nor deny the rumor. She showed no regret when he angrily informed her it was over—a shock to Turner, accustomed to women weeping when they contemplated a future without him.

He and Clea lost touch. Until one afternoon four years later when Clea turned up in a beige linen suit, dark hair falling across one eye, working as assistant on a photography session for Green Gourmet frozen peas, for which Turner was account executive. Clea gave him the famous warm, cool smile that had confused and enchanted him at Cornell, as she brushed vegetable oil on the peas, which sat on a Royal Doulton dinner plate under floodlights. Turner's penis, weathercock of his emotions, alternately swelled and shriveled all afternoon as he watched Clea fulfilling the photographer's requests, but with the detached bearing that made her seem scarcely in the room.

"So. We meet again," she said in the elevator at the end of the shoot, not looking at him. He detected the spicy scent of her cologne.

"And not a minute too soon." Taking her hand, he led her down the block to the Oak Room at the Algonquin.

"So how have you been for the last four years?" he asked over a round oak table so small their knees rubbed. Clea moved hers aside.

"Busy. And you?" She consulted the drink list.

"The same. Playing corporate ticktacktoe." The waiter took their order and departed.

"Where are you living?" Clea looked up from the menu and into his eyes for the first time all afternoon.

"On East Sixty-seventh at Second. A big ugly modern block that should have remained unbuilt. And you?" He'd forgotten how striking her eyes were—golden brown with flecks of green and yellow, framed by dark brows and long lashes.

"I'm on the West Side just off Riverside Drive. In an old building with parquet floors and fancy woodwork. With a view of the Hudson." Clea stirred her apricot sour with the swizzle stick, studying the miniature whirlpool.

"The West Side. That's brave of you." He willed her to return her eyes to his, but she didn't.

"It's all I can afford right now."

"Boyfriends?"

"A few. And you?" She looked up again, and into his eyes. He felt an absurd stirring in his heart, and in his lap.

"I date some, but I live alone." He signaled the waiter for another round—apricot sour for her, Johnnie Walker for him, on the rocks with a splash.

As he and Clea did an update on the whereabouts of each DU and Tri Delt from the classes of 1957 to 1960, he covertly inspected her, feature by feature, limb by limb, quick sips from the pool of sensual memory. The high, firm, round breasts beneath her silk blouse; the stockinged knees, slightly parted; the arches of her feet, in beige heeled sandals.

During their third round, they reviewed the activities of each member of their respective families. As he described the new ranch house his parents had purchased in a Milwaukee subdivision, fulfilling a lifetime dream after all those years of renting on his father's machinist wages, Turner recalled how Clea had surrendered herself on his rain-coat, golden eyes going bleary, head sinking back, dark hair lashing, mouth falling open with jagged gasps. Miraculous behavior from a mid-western coed. It was about the only time he'd seen her drop her cool reserve.

While Clea told about her younger sister Lou's acceptance to law school at Northwestern, her eyes locked with his. She stopped talking right in the middle of reciting the names and ages of her nieces and nephews. Studying the ice in her glass, she raised the glass to her lips and drained the last drops of apricot sour.

"Shall I get us another round?" he asked weakly.

She shook her head no.

"Shall I get us a room upstairs?"

"*Yes*," she said.

Later, holding the sheet across his chest, Turner murmured, "You've got to admit I've improved."

Clea nodded. "You've been practicing."

"You nearly destroyed my manhood that afternoon in the gorge."

"What do you mean?"

"Remember? You asked afterward, 'Is that it?'"

"I *didn't!* God, Turner, I'm sorry."

"It's okay. I've recovered."

"So I see." She nodded at the pup tent his erection was making of the sheet. Rolling on top of him, she murmured, "Let's see if I can make it up to you."

Afterward, he observed, "You've been practicing too, you dirty girl." He put his hands behind his head, elbows out, and looked at her questioningly. Her dark hair was damp around the temples, and fine beads of sweat glistened on her upper lip. He had never seen her more beautiful. He felt frightened of how badly he wanted to see her like this again. He forced himself to lie still and continue to meet her golden gaze, when he really wanted to escape into the bathroom.

"What? Did you expect me just to wait around?"

"I had hoped you might," he said, only half joking, breathing unsteadily.

"You've got the wrong girl, Turner."

"To the contrary. I think I've met my match," he was alarmed to hear himself say.

But the next morning she vanished at dawn. He couldn't figure it out. The sex had been hot, and she had seemed happy. When he phoned her later that day, she sounded pleased to hear from him. But she refused to go out with him again. Which predictably enchanted him, and confirmed his determination to win her over—which was finally achieved with the aid of kiwifruit.

"So how's it going up there in the woods?" asked Turner, wiping up the last of his omelet with a crust of French bread.

"Fine," said Clea, sitting back and lighting one of the two cigarettes she smoked each day. "There's a problem with the sills, but Darius is fixing them. That man's a gem."

Concentrating on his crust, Turner said nothing.

"Yes, I know you do," said Clea, smiling faintly.

Turner glanced at her questioningly.

"I know you wish I'd just stay home."

Turner smiled grimly. Clea often knew what he was thinking, but she usually had the sense to keep it to herself. But when she'd been with Elke, she forgot. Because that was how they conversed, voicing each other's thoughts and completing each other's sentences. Overhearing their conversations was unsettling because it forced him to recognize that Clea got from Elke a type of interaction he could never provide. Nor would he want to. This female capacity for self-abnegation appalled him. No wonder men used to burn them as witches. Yet it was disturbing to know Clea wanted this type of merging. Her combination of distracted tenderness and self-sufficiency made men fall in love with her constantly, and she sometimes responded. But Turner rarely felt jealous, since he knew their only edge was novelty, which would fade with time. Elke posed a more serious threat, though: She experienced aspects of Clea that he could never experience. Yet evidently the reverse was also true, since Clea had stayed married to him all these years.

"Well, why *won't* you stay home, then?" he asked playfully.

Clea toyed with her cigarette over the ashtray. "Look, Turner," she said, leaning forward, golden eyes troubled. "This madonna trip you think you want from me—it's just not on, darling. It never was. You thought I was a real drag when I quit my job after the babies were born. And now they're gone. If I hung around here waiting for you, I'd be a resentful bitch. Remember the fit I threw over those crabs you brought back from Amsterdam?"

Both smiled ruefully. In their early years Clea doted on their beautiful drooling babies, while Turner traveled and tricked all across the globe. He never mentioned the latter because it didn't seem important. Sex to him was like food, necessary but varying widely in quality, from junk food to the four-star Michelin meals Clea sometimes served up. In Amsterdam, a lovely blond Dutch woman named Marianne invited him back from an Indonesian restaurant to her tiny apartment, up many narrow steps to a converted attic. Following nights of enthusiastic calisthenics under the roof beams, they would breakfast on bread, cheese, and strong coffee in an alcove overlooking a bicycle-filled street with a murky canal beyond.

In their bed after his return, Clea began scratching, and eventually pinched something between thumb and index finger. She held it out to him. It was a crab. His flustered explanation, more comprehensive than it might have been without jet lag, involved several women and every continent except Antarctica. Clea said very little, golden eyes flaring, as he pleaded loneliness and assured her of the irrelevance of the acts and the women in question.

But he'd been ashamed to tell her the rest (although, as usual, she knew): How little she excited him now that he had her exactly where he wanted her. How much he resented finding an exhausted woman in a sweatshirt, with baby food in her hair, impersonating his sleek, self-supporting, linen-suited wife. How when he watched the babies nurse, he felt revulsion, knowing he had sucked there too. How he sometimes wanted to grab the babies away from her breasts and dash out their brains against the corner of the bureau. He felt utter despair watching his and Clea's love nest become transformed into a snake pit of need and emotion similar to the one in Milwaukee he'd clawed his way out of. And since he was bringing in the money to support this Turtle Bay crèche, he felt he deserved an uncomplicated screw or two. Particularly since Clea leapt out of bed to see if the babies were still breathing almost every time he managed to put all the foregoing aside and get turned on by her.

Within months Clea was free-lancing for her old boss Allan Barkham again, and sometimes working overtime on her back. A hired housekeeper had taken her spot on the couch to greet Turner's return from foreign parts. After initial panic, Turner had to confess that he liked this arrangement. To be with Clea was exciting again. Lovemaking became a process of reclaiming her, however briefly, from the embraces of strangers.

The truth was, Clea was his anchor. His affairs were merely the sails. And with the AIDS epidemic, he'd been trimming his sails lately and bagging his spinnaker. He felt sad and scared for Kate and Theo, coming of age when sex was associated with disease and death. Thank God he'd been in his prime during that charmed fear-free, post-pill, post-penicillin, pre-AIDS interlude. Clea claimed the epidemic was giving women a chance to express what they'd thought of semen all along. That women weren't as enchanted with the stuff as men assumed, that they in fact felt about as much enthusiasm for it as men did for menstrual blood. But Turner wasn't certain he wanted to know what women really felt about most things, and certainly not about semen.

Clea set a mug of coffee before him on the butcher-block table. He studied the streaks of gray through her glossy black hair. "Clea, I understand that you don't want to be in New York anymore. Or go on my trips. Or live overseas. But I'm not going to be in the U.S. very often. And when I am, *I* don't want to be in Roches Ridge, Vermont. So what are we going to do?"

"I'll come back when you're here, Turner. It's just a five-hour drive. Don't worry."

"But I *do* worry, Clea. It feels as though we're headed down diverging roads. Is that what you want?"

"No."

They sat sipping coffee in silence.

"But I guess I need something to hang on to," she finally said.

"You've got me. The kids. This house. Elke. The city. Dozens of friends. Your work. What more do you need?"

"Not more. Different," murmured Clea.

"So it *is* a mid-life crisis?"

"Call it whatever you like, Turner. But this scene isn't working for me anymore. It made sense when we were raising Kate and Theo. But now we've got to regroup."

"Regroup or disperse?" asked Turner glumly.

"Do you want to disperse?"

"You know I don't, Clea. But this new plan looks unworkable to me."

"I'll make it work. Give it a chance, Turner."

"Whatever." Irritably he ran his hand over his rapidly expanding bald spot.

# 8  The Party Chairman

Clea waved goodbye to Turner, who was making ridiculous faces as a guard frisked him at JFK security. Walking back to the parking garage, she reflected that Turner could still amuse her like nobody else. On their drive out here he'd ranted about Fresh-It pricing issues in the light of the falling peso. Guns or butter? Toothpaste or tortillas? She never understood how he could perform so competently tasks he described with such good-humored contempt. She didn't always admire his adaptability, however. Sometimes she longed for an ideologue like Terence, who was prepared to die for his convictions, even though they changed radically from one decade to the next. But Turner was profoundly pragmatic, not to say opportunistic, haunted by a meek father who considered himself a failure as a provider of the accoutrements of the American dream.

Climbing in her BMW, Clea thought about the many times she'd seen Turner off and welcomed him home at this airport, babies on her hips or toddlers hanging from her hands. As she headed up the Hutchinson River Parkway to the Tappan Zee, she began to cry, passengers in passing cars eyeing her with curiosity or indifference. She loved Turner. Why were they continually parting from each other? He could easily replace her with some fresh young thing eager to provide the comforts Clea denied him. Why did he stick around, in however attenuated a fashion? Probably because he had exactly what he wanted with her—an antidote to the enforced togetherness at the cramped Milwaukee apartment of his childhood.

The first time she ever saw Turner, he was standing on the DU bar in a curly blond woman's wig, stirring Canadian Club into the punch with a hockey stick. Then he squatted to ladle it out with a black high-top tennis shoe, singing a baritone that bubbled like perking coffee on "Roll Your Leg Over."

Turner was the DU party chairman, and for their first date he invited her to a crew race, where he oversaw the tapping of the keg by the lakeshore. Then he asked her to don a rabbit costume and join the DU Bunny Hop through downtown Ithaca, collecting Easter Seal donations in baskets. Next, attired in a tux, he escorted her to a candlelit cocktail party in a concrete drainage culvert. At the DU Spring Fling, Turner and Clea won the jitterbug contest, through their inspired use of settings, including the DU spiral staircase landing, the bar counter, and the roof of a Dodge station wagon in the driveway. Clea was learning to play. For the first time in her life, no small children trailed in her wake.

But then she heard through the DU girlfriends' grapevine that some girl with false eyelashes and long red fingernails came to visit Turner from Syracuse. One afternoon Clea ran into them near the library, Turner with lipstick smeared at the base of his neck, the girl clutching his arm possessively. And for the first time Clea glimpsed the elusiveness beneath his playful chivalry.

So she seduced him on their next outing—on his raincoat in a rhododendron thicket at the foot of a gorge, while shafts of hot spring sunlight pierced the cool shadows. Startled, Turner made love to her sweetly, if briefly, as water gurgled in the creek. Clea assumed this uninspired coupling united them for life. Turner would invite *her* to Manhattan next year. And eventually they'd live in the penthouse overlooking Central Park. But Turner seemed embarrassed and apologetic, and avoided a repeat.

Soon he was working at Green Gourmet Food Corporation in Manhattan, and she was incarcerated behind the grille at her father's bank for the summer, counting out bills to customers who insisted upon regaling her with tales about her father's goodness. She wrote Turner a letter that made many assumptions about their relationship. Turner wrote back, "... I care about you very much, Clea. But we're too young to get so serious. You have three more years at Cornell. So just relax and have some fun. I sure am having some here. Although of course I miss you and so forth." Clea cut this letter into tiny pieces and flushed them down the toilet.

Back at Cornell the next fall Clea listlessly dated other DUs. But being at the DU house served only to feed her memories of Turner. The jitterbug contest, "Roll Your Leg Over," and crew races by the lake. This was her first experience of how painful happy memories can be. Turner came up for Homecoming and grilled her relentlessly in the Tri Delt living room about a rumor concerning her and a professor in the art department.

"What's it to you?" she demanded. She was in fact flirting with Professor Galmer, but it outraged her that Turner should try to control her behavior even after they'd broken up.

"Nothing at all," he snapped, stomping out.

Professor Galmer had developed a special interest in her work. And in her breasts, where his eyes alighted when he thought she wasn't noticing. He summoned her to his office to show her his portfolio of nudes, discussing lines and angles, light and shadow, lenses and exposure times. He was in his Edward Weston phase, trying to make vegetables look like female bodies, and vice versa.

Even Clea was aware of the cliché when he asked her several weeks later to pose for him. At first he tried to make her hands resemble tree roots. By the end of the session she was sitting naked in a large sink in one of the darkrooms, stirring the water with her fingers as Professor Galmer tried to photograph her pubic hair swaying like seaweed.

As Galmer helped her out of the sink and carefully dried her body with a towel, he dropped his artistic detachment regarding her lines and angles. On the dark-blue corduroy couch in his office, with color photos of his blond wife and grinning teenage sons observing, Clea discovered that sex was more fun than she could have believed after her session on Turner's raincoat. It bothered her that one of the hands that elicited this pleasure wore a gold wedding band, but not enough to interrupt the undertaking.

Under Professor Galmer's tutelage Clea began to gain confidence in her photographic eye, as well as in the rest of her anatomy. Soon she was the only woman staff photographer for the student newspaper, breezing into sporting events and student government meetings with her press card and camera bag. Sometimes she photographed campus lecturers like Martin Luther King, Jr. and Madame Chiang Kai-shek. Eventually the yearbook staff asked her to shoot some familiar campus landmarks, slightly out of focus, as though already transformed into memories.

Her arrangement with Professor Galmer suited them both. They discussed their work and made love on his office couch. Then he went home to dinner with his family, and she went back to the Tri Delt house for dates with various DUs. Professor Galmer assured her that once she finished her B.A., his children would be in college and he'd be ready to leave his wife. He and Clea would build a cabin in the woods, with a photography studio and darkroom—and a huge loft among the trees with a king-size bed where they would rock all night in each other's arms, while the branches outside tossed and heaved and swayed. They would be a latter-day Stieglitz and O'Keeffe. He would finally make his breakthrough by recording the shifting moods and configurations of Clea's face and body. Gradually this vision replaced the Central Park penthouse. And John Galmer cradling her in his arms, pale hips pushing insistently into hers, replaced Turner mixing highballs on the terrace.

Professor Galmer had a show in the campus arts center that included a print of Clea's swaying pubic hair, and another of her nipples after lovemaking, tight and shriveled like raisins. At the opening Clea stood in a corner watching Galmer's blond wife eye a series of prints of Clea's limbs arranged at bizarre angles, in imitation of Cubist painting. The wife herself was dumpy and wrinkled, in contrast to the sleek, smooth flesh in the photos. Furthermore, Professor Galmer said his wife didn't understand him or his art. Clea felt sly triumph. In a couple of years *Clea* would be the one standing beside him at public functions and sleeping beside him in their loft among the trees. And that night in bed at the Tri Delt house, Clea realized she'd gotten through an entire day without once thinking of Turner Shawn.

During her senior year, however, talk of the loft among the trees began to recede. With dismay Clea watched both Professor Galmer and herself begin to cancel sessions in his office. Those first two years, not even an approaching tornado funnel would have kept her from his corduroy couch. One afternoon as graduation loomed, Professor Galmer urged her to take a job in New York City as assistant to a freelance photographer named Allan Barkham, a former student.

"But what about our cabin?" Clea asked. They sat fully clothed at opposite ends of the blue corduroy couch, a wall of awkwardness between them.

"Cabin? Oh, our *cabin.* The one in the woods."

"The one with the studio and darkroom and loft," she replied sullenly, not looking at him.

"Well, people spin a lot of delicious fantasies when they're first in love," he said gently, almost pleadingly. "But you have a brilliant career ahead of you, Clea. You'll go farther than I ever have. And I can't be responsible for holding you back. You need to be in New York."

Clea looked up from studying her hands. "But maybe I *want* to be held back?" This was a genuine question. She was appalled to discover that she felt almost relieved at the prospect of being exiled to New York.

"You don't really. You'll find a nice man in New York, Clea. And then you'll have it all—your career, plus a lover you don't have to share."

"You're trying to get rid of me."

Professor Galmer smiled sadly. "Don't be so silly, Clea. This is one of the most painful sacrifices I've ever made. Hurry up and take it before I change my mind."

"But who are you making it *for?* Not for me. For her. For *them."* She stabbed a finger at the blond wife and grinning teenagers on his desk. The younger children always came first. But what about her?

"Well, maybe for all of us," he said in a low voice, looking at his Kodachrome family. "Someday when you have children you'll understand."

Clea stood up, grabbed her book bag, and marched out. All the way back to the Tri Delt house she fluctuated among gratitude toward Professor Galmer for all he'd given her, anger at him for chickening out, agony over the loss of him, relief to be free, excitement over New York City, and frustration that she couldn't sustain the state of unalloyed misery appropriate to the situation.

The Central Park penthouse had been dislodged by the cabin among the trees. The question once she moved to New York became how to get rid of that cabin. Presumably some new image would have to supersede it.

One afternoon she ran into Turner at the shooting of an advertisement for Green Gourmet peas. As she brushed oil on the peas, she spotted him, tall, lean, blond, and amused in his pin-striped suit and silk rep tie. Her hand trembled so violently that she splashed oil on the plate and had to start over. It had taken over a year to recover from a few sunlit months with this DU party chairman. Only a fool would go back for more.

When Turner finally noticed her, a blush rose slowly from his throat to his receding blond hairline. Surrounded by their superiors, they couldn't speak personally until they stepped into the elevator at the end of the day.

"So. We meet again," murmured Clea.

"And not a minute too soon." Turner took her hand, as though nearly four years of water hadn't gone over the dam.

Clea considered extracting her hand, but she didn't. Fool! yelled her brain.

As they chatted over drinks at the Algonquin, Clea's emotions engaged in a silent struggle with her brain. But when Turner suggested taking a room upstairs, she heard herself saying fervently, "*Yes.*"

On the way up in the elevator she told herself she just wanted to show him what she'd learned since her dismal defloration on his raincoat, so he could eat his heart out. She also wanted to obliterate permanently John Galmer's damned cabin among the trees.

As they rolled and sweated and trembled between the sheets, she assured herself this was a grudge match, never to be repeated, designed to leave Turner full of remorse for refusing to claim her when she was already his. But as she awoke the next morning, Turner asleep in her arms, sunlight flecking his hair with gold, the vision of the Central Park penthouse greeted her, revived and vivid and leering. Shoving Turner aside, she scrambled out of bed and into her crumpled linen suit.

"Don't go," he said with a lazy, self-satisfied smile, squinting in the sunlight.

"I'm late."

"What's the rush? We've got the rest of our lives."

She looked at him ironically. "I care about you very much, Turner. But we're too young to get so serious. Although of course I shall miss you and so forth."

Turner looked blank.

"A quote from that letter of yours."

"What letter?"

"Your Dear John letter to me in Poplar Bluffs that summer."

"What are you talking about?" Shielding the sunlight with his hand, he looked at her blankly.

"When you broke up with me."

"We broke up at Homecoming your sophomore year," said Turner, scooting up to lean against some pillows, his muscled chest with its mat of fair hair looking alarmingly inviting. "I came up from Manhattan to see you, but you were involved with that creepy old guy in the art department."

Clea frowned as she bent over to fasten her sandals. "That's not how I remember it."

"Well, never mind. It doesn't matter now. The point is, I want you back in this bed. Please don't go."

"I'm already gone." She closed the door behind her, bemused. How could he not remember that obnoxious letter that drove her into Professor Galmer's arms in the first place?

Clea resolutely dated a series of product managers, law clerks, interns, and stockbrokers, searching for the one who would replace Turner at the rooftop bar in her mind. But sooner or later each revealed himself to be a little boy instead of Robert Young.

Meanwhile, Allan Barkham was giving her the education of a lifetime: One day they'd be at an estate on the Hudson, taking pictures of the gardens for the landscape architects who'd designed them; the next, in an operating theater, shooting illustrations for a medical textbook; the next, in southern New Jersey, photographing crops at a truck farm for a seed catalogue. She was learning to work with color film. And instead of appearing on a scene and trying to present what she found, as she'd done for the Cornell newspaper, she was learning how to portray things in the best possible light, manipulating details if necessary.

No doubt taking his cue from his mentor, Professor Galmer, Allan eventually began to indicate that Clea's job description included posing nude. She indicated she'd look for another job. So he reverted to a less draconian courtship, involving such tactics as praise, raises, and private darkroom time, which she used for her ongoing experiments with black-and-white film.

Turner was flooding her with charming notes and phone calls. She longed to respond, but was afraid this flood would recede if she did, leaving her high and dry among the flotsam, the penthouse fantasy her only lifeline. But why *not* respond, since she was miserable anyway? The grudge match between the Algonquin sheets had been a mistake. She was now stuck with that image of Turner sitting up in bed with sunlight across his bare chest. Merely the sound of his voice over the phone left her wet between the legs.

One evening she returned from work to find Turner in the lobby of her apartment building, entertaining the doorman in his moth-eaten maroon uniform by juggling three kiwis. Spotting her, he grabbed the fruit out of the air. "Hi. I was just passing by with a bag of this new fruit from New Zealand, and I thought maybe you'd like to try it."

"Kiwifruit," she said, trying to sound uninterested. "Thanks, but I've already tried it. It's delicious. Hope you enjoy it."

"Please can't I come in, Clea? Whatever I've done to offend you, I'm sorry."

The doorman looked at her pleadingly on Turner's behalf. Two of them she couldn't combat.

"Come on up." She tried to recall if her roommate, Jane, would be home that night. Half of her hoped so, and the other half prayed not. She left the matter in the hands of the gods.

The gods had sent Jane to her mother's on Long Island, and they sent Clea to the moon. She'd experienced much competent sex with Professor Galmer, but never the tenderness she felt for Turner as they lay in the dark with sweat drying on their bodies. His gradually slowing heart thumped against her cheek, and his jagged breathing rustled her scrambled hair.

"God, Turner, don't ever leave me again."

"But *you* left me," he insisted.

They studied each other quizzically in the moonlight through the window.

He bounced out of bed.

"*Now* where are you going?"

"To pour us some cognac. Come stand here by the window, and let's look down on all the poor jerks who aren't us tonight."

"I love you, Turner," she said, defeated, as he took her in his arms by the window, spilling cognac down her back. "Damn it, I guess I've been in love with you all this time." All the pain and loneliness, all the anonymous groping in the DU make-out room, all the passion on the corduroy couch, vanished like fog burning off on a sunny morning. Leaving only Turner and her, standing naked in each other's arms, looking down at the solitary dog-walkers on Riverside Drive and the full moon over the Hudson. Clea's Poplar Bluffs vision was finally fulfilled. She was in New York City in the embrace of the debonair older man who'd take care of her forever.

Turning down the road to Roches Ridge, Clea smiled with impatience at the silly young nitwit she used to be. Turner and she had been through the Crusades together since that night. He was not who she'd thought. *She* was not who she'd thought. And love and passion were not what she'd thought.

Pulling up beside her stone house, Clea felt a glow of satisfaction. After decades of wandering the globe among genial strangers, she'd at last come home. To a village that was a repository of all the tired old biblical virtues she'd spent her entire previous life trying to escape. The ground was squishy as she strolled down her sloping back field to the tree line, visualizing the stone walls, perennial beds, and ornamental trees that would eventually transform this meadow into a shrub-bordered garden. Patches of melting snow lay in the shadows.

To her dismay she discovered that Lone Star ale bottles and foil Banquet Dinner trays littered the field and woods, snow having previously concealed them. Shit. She might as well be on Forty-second Street. Still, she'd pick up the trash, and strangers wouldn't strew more.

She'd plant flowers, and no one would trample them. Resolutely she pictured the gardens behind English manor houses she'd photographed—Sissinghurst and Hidcote, Gravetye and Knole.

Hands in her tweed trouser pockets, Clea gazed through the bare birches down to Mink Creek. On a hillock near the bank, bathed in the golden light of late afternoon, sat two tepees, a house trailer, and several wooden sheds. Hunting camps? She studied the scene for a long time, without spotting inhabitants. The creek was rising from the thaw. Surely the site would flood.

Shrugging, Clea reflected that she'd been everywhere, seen everything, and done most of it. Turner, John Galmer, Elke, a dozen others ... She was tired of falling in and out of love. The process was as predictable as the flooding and draining of the locks in the Panama Canal. And she'd reached an age at which the fluctuations of her own inner life ought to be more intriguing than any external stimulus.

She tried to picture some of her less crucial lovers but could summon only exotic foreign settings—a shaft of moonlight across a futon in a Japanese teahouse, a pink sand beach beneath clashing palms, a Paris pension with accordion music out the window, a motel overlooking the sea in a small Australian beach town. She remembered baklava oozing honey in a Greek taverna and gray eyes gazing into hers on a train across the Nullarbor Plain. Maybe her recollections took this form because she was a travel photographer. Perhaps an accountant would recall his affairs in terms of what things had cost. Each love had been so intoxicating. Yet each had left no more lasting an imprint than a footstep in spring snow. All she really remembered anymore, apart from settings, was her own emotion, identical in each case, an intense wave of connection and purpose. While it lasted, it was glorious. But it had always ebbed, dragging in its wake a scow full of grief, remorse, and wounded relatives. Now she felt profoundly sleazy to have struck time after time at this same tawdry lure. But at least she'd finally had the sense to attempt a deeper dive.

Strolling up the yard as the setting sun laved the gray stone house in tangerine, Clea discovered through the maples on the opposite ridge a circle of derelict yellow school buses, surrounded by wisps of soft blue mist from the thaw. Off to one side was a huge white satellite dish with a giant silver cross painted inside it. Now that the snow was melting, junk was appearing everywhere. Once she finished cleaning up her house and yard, she'd have to start on the neighborhood.

Beginning with the house next door, which Clea eyed with distaste. The original structure, evidently an inn, was now a vast rickety tenement that might blow down in the next storm. Stickers on the windows read: THIS HOUSE INSURED BY SMITH AND WESSON. Auto seats and rusted washing machines cluttered the sagging porch. Antlers and wings from large birds of prey decorated one wall of peeling gray clapboard. A mountain of gutted auto carcasses rose up behind the house. When Clea bought her house, the piled autos had been covered with snow, and she'd assumed it was a foothill. In the driveway stood a blue tow truck with a winch and roll bars. A bumper sticker read: ATTENTION, HITCHHIKERS: GAS, GRASS, OR ASS—NO ONE RIDES FOR FREE. She'd noticed derelict cars and vans in this driveway, people with bad teeth, and children splashing in mud puddles. This house would have to go. It would destroy the effect of Clea's renovation. Maybe she'd buy it too, and create a compound. Lure Elke and Terence and Turner and the children here permanently.

In the kitchen, she heated water for tea on a gas burner. Sheets of plywood covered the hole in the floor, and the cracked tub now sat in the driveway. Darius Drumm's tools and supplies cluttered the downstairs, but upstairs a rear bedroom was ready for her habitation. She moved Calvin's cot up there until she should have time to order a new bed.

Sitting on the cot with her tea as the sun out the back window vanished behind the mountain range across the lake, Clea tried to figure out what she was doing. Her life decisions had always been propelled by white-hot emotion. And once the fervor faded, they would sometimes make sense and sometimes not. Which category would Roches Ridge fall into? Turner's and her primary goal had always been not to duplicate their parents' marriages—nightmares of midwestern monotony that drove Clea's parents to drink and made Turner's mother a hysteric in a housedress. However this venture turned out, at least Turner's and her union would not degenerate into the Ozzie and Harriet death grip she'd originally thought she wanted.

# 9   A Marital Maginot Line

During Turner and Clea's Manhattan courtship, Turner continued to function as party chairman. In summer they raced to Montauk Point for the sunrise in his rusting forest-green MG, or down the Jersey shore to buy peaches and tomatoes, or up to the Catskills to pick wildflowers.

One afternoon they rented a rowboat and made love on every island in Bear Mountain Lake. In winter they skied in Vermont and tanned in Florida. They attended night court and street festivals, art openings and TV game shows. As he wound the MG through Central Park late at night, she lay in his lap and gave him blow jobs. Eventually Clea was so exhausted from this regimen of play that she accepted his proposal of marriage. Hoping they could then just stay home and watch TV and be boring.

In the end it was Clea who stayed home and became boring. Whereas Turner continued his dizzying schedule, which would have felled any ordinary overachiever. Having parlayed his successes at Green Gourmet into a job offer from Fresh-It, he was now dazzling his Fresh-It superiors. They kept giving him raises and travel assignments. He and Clea bought the Turtle Bay town house on the strength of his prospects and her trust fund from her father's bank. It wasn't the Central Park penthouse, but it was close enough.

After a year of rolling around their living room carpet and king-size bed whenever both were home at once, Clea became pregnant, not planned but not regretted. As the delivery approached, she quit her photography job with Allan Barkham. Her mother was supposed to arrive from Poplar Bluffs for the birth, but was detained by a headache. In the taxi on the way home from the hospital, with infant Kate in a flannel blanket, Clea reflected that she had tended her mother after *her* babies arrived. She'd been assuming turnabout was fair play, but evidently she'd been mistaken.

Soon Kate was a toddler, and Theo an infant. Clea was delighted to spend her days sprawled on the living room couch watching her enchanting babies creep and totter around the wall-to-wall carpeting, barely avoiding collisions with end tables. She felt the same rush sniffing Johnson's Baby Oil that teenagers did over airplane glue. She was endlessly amused by Kate's insane enthusiasm for fitting puffy plastic doughnuts on a spindle—and endlessly bemused by her *own* insane enthusiasm for this "Brady Bunch" wet dream. One would have thought her career as a big sister would have purged her of maternal impulses forever. But it was not the last time she'd be bamboozled by her physiology.

Turner was behaving like a panda father she'd helped Allan photograph at the Washington zoo for *Natural History*. The panda sulked around his cage, glumly eyeing the mother, who was besotted with their new offspring. Turner interrupted Kate's baby talk at dinner, and ridiculed both children for getting food in their hair when aiming for their mouths. His face went blank with horror as he realized he and Clea could no longer roll naked on the living room carpet whenever they felt like it. He was appalled when she refused to go out to dinner or a movie, or when she leapt out of bed in the middle of lovemaking if she heard a cough from the next room. He started staying out late, and began to request overseas assignments. The party chairman was looking for less cloying venues. He'd breeze in after such a trip bearing exotic foodstuffs. But one day he brought home crabs as well.

Even now Clea couldn't think of those subsequent weeks of appalled disbelief without going numb. Turner, her tender protector, was nothing but a typical swashbuckling male who wanted a madonna at his hearth and a whore in every port. Her fortress, encompassing the sofa and carpet, her babies, and her strong warrior husband who sallied forth to defend them, lay in ruins. And all because of one lousy insect. Turner explained and apologized and begged for understanding, and Clea accepted the apologies and struggled to understand. But the damage was done.

At first Clea blamed herself: She'd fallen in love with her babies and formed a threesome, not a foursome. If she'd accompanied Turner on his trips, she could have fulfilled his sexual needs as they arose. She could have taken the babies to Turner's mother, or hired a housekeeper. It would have been worth it to save her marriage. Maybe it still was. So she mentioned this idea to Turner. Who seemed not to hear.

Hoping to be amusing, not wanting to nag, Clea bought outfits from several countries to which Turner had upcoming trips—a Macdonald tartan kilt, a silk sari, an embroidered dashiki. Each night at supper she'd wear one. Finally Turner said, "Okay, Clea. I get the message."

"So what do you think?" She'd put the children to bed early so she and Turner could share a quiet, candlelit, wine-washed dinner. She was wearing the sari, but was prepared to remove it for a roll on the carpet. If they could be finished in time for Kate's midnight trip to the bathroom.

"I think you've got two babies who need you here."

Three babies, thought Clea sourly. "But you need me too, Turner. And I need you. And so do Kate and Theo." She leaned forward and studied him intently. He looked troubled and exhausted, his tie loose around his neck like a noose.

"Look," he snarled, stabbing at his fish, not returning her gaze. "I'm perfectly capable of exercising sexual self-control without you there to police me."

"*Police* you? Listen, Sinbad, I suggested this because I love you. I miss you. I want to be with you."

"Oh, yeah?" He finally looked at her in the candlelight, eyes blood-shot. "Well, why now? Admit it: You suggested this because you don't trust me anymore."

"Yes, I do," lied Clea.

"Clea, when I'm on these trips, I'm *working*, okay? I don't have time to entertain you."

Clea said nothing, seeing herself through Turner's anguished eyes. Self-sufficient during their courtship, she was now simultaneously clingy, demanding, and rejecting. Always eager for sex before the babies arrived, she was now too exhausted or preoccupied. She remembered his parents—in their new tract house in a Milwaukee suburb with TV game shows blaring at top volume. His mother, aunt, and sisters, faces white with cold cream like aboriginal warriors, ululated all day long about the sale price on economy jars of Miracle Whip at the A&P. Turner and his father were expert at finding excuses to slip out the door and stay gone until bedtime. Clea suddenly understood Turner's horror of domesticity, his need for escape hatches. Poor Turner. Poor Clea. How had this happened? They had loved each other so completely on those islands in Bear Mountain Lake.

Later that week, after Turner's departure for Glasgow, Clea sat on the couch, hair disheveled, babies tugging at her crumpled skirt, and reviewed her options. Turner said he would change his behavior, and she knew he'd try. But Turner was Turner. To ask him to resign as party chairman was to destroy the person she'd originally fallen in love with. Besides, she'd been warned right from the start—by the Syracuse waitress at Cornell—and she'd pursued him anyway. Her options now were to leave, just opt out of this whole trite domestic scenario; or to accept the status quo, crabs and all; or to mount an offensive.

Never a pacifist, Clea hired a housekeeper and went to see Allan Barkham about free-lance work. Or perhaps he needed a darkroom assistant. During the course of this interview, she finally posed nude for him, on the floor behind his desk in a corner of his studio. Throughout the sex act she stared grimly at a steel I-beam overhead, feeling nothing. Allan kept pausing to inquire, "Are you okay? Shall I stop?"

"Please don't stop," she said without enthusiasm. If it took infidelity to save her marriage, then by God she'd be unfaithful. But she didn't have to enjoy it.

Reporting to Turner upon his return, she was delighted to watch his face go dark red. With the shoe on the other foot, he suddenly developed blisters. He began listening in on her phone calls and searching her desk for notes. Once she spotted him following her when she went out. He started lauding monogamy and warning about venereal disease. But by this time Clea refused to be dissuaded from seeing things his way, because she doubted his ability to return to the marital fold on a more than temporary basis.

Eventually Turner and Clea negotiated a modified cease-fire. Both would do as they pleased beyond the New York metropolitan area, defined as a circle with a forty-mile radius from their Turtle Bay town house. Within that charmed connubial compound, however, each could find sanctuary from the skirmishes of the dawning sexual revolution.

Clea's primary fear was that, as in any war, the main casualties might be the noncombatants—Kate and Theo. However, her devotion to them was beginning to seem smarmy even to herself. Theo had rejected her breast by this time, insisting on a cup. He was in love with Annie, the Barbadian housekeeper, bouncing in his crib every morning at dawn and yelling in a voice husky with sleep, "Ann-ee! Where *are* you?" And Kate was obsessed with the fashion statements of her play group. Perhaps it was time to open the musty castle keep to some fresh air. And surely seeing their nagging, downtrodden mother and resentful, deceitful father struggling to become whole people couldn't be all bad for the children, whatever Dr. Spock might say.

Clea quickly realized, though, that she'd been outflanked when she and Turner drew their marital Maginot Line: Turner was often away from New York, but she rarely left. She was unconcerned for the present, however, because her delicious children still consumed most of her free time and energy. The point had been to make a stand, so Turner would stop viewing her as a spider forever sitting at home in her web waiting to entangle and poison him; so she could stop viewing *herself* that way. Besides, Clea had by this time photographed Elke in her studio and was talking to her on the phone every night. She was madly, if chastely, in love.

# 10 Loretta Gebo

Loretta Gebo was sitting on a stool at the Formica counter in Casa Loretta, smoking a Virginia Slim and leafing through a *Woman's Day*, looking for more contests to enter. She'd already sent in her Publishers Clearing House sweepstakes form, and Ray Marsh was going across the border today to get Canadian lottery tickets.

She slapped the magazine shut, took a drag, and exhaled with a sigh. She didn't know why she bothered. She couldn't even win at Rescue League bingo at the grade school on Tuesday nights. In the last Tri-State Megabucks lottery she didn't get even one number right. The only thing she ever won, she lost. Her checkout tape from the IGA one week had the winning number for a free bag of groceries. But she didn't notice until after the deadline. Stubbing out her cigarette, Loretta unwrapped a silver Hershey's Kiss and popped it into her mouth.

Ishtar at the Karma Café said bad luck was Loretta's karma this time around. But Loretta was damned if she'd accept her karma sitting down. She'd go to her grave buying lottery tickets. Ishtar told her to go with the flow and not push the river. She told Ishtar to get stuffed. But she didn't know if that was how lesbians did it. She didn't like to think about it.

Ray liked to think about it, though. He was always trying to get Loretta to invite Ishtar over to the trailer so they could snort some coke and see what happened. Calvin Roche once showed Loretta some *National Enquirer* photos of two women mud wrestling in a vat of chocolate pudding. She told Ray that was the only way he'd get *her* to lick a woman. So the next time he drove to New Jersey for Orlon, he came home with a pair of edible chocolate panties. He said he'd buy her more if she'd eat them off Ishtar. But Loretta didn't want to share Ray with some karma-crazed lesbo. She had a hard enough time dragging him away from the lesbians on the videos he rented. Ray probably would have liked to be a lesbian himself. But as Ishtar would say, better luck next life, Rayon old boy.

Loretta went into the bathroom to check her hairdo. Jared McQueen from Mane Magnifique said it looked like an Italian cannoli. He was so good-looking, just like Don Johnson on "Miami Vice," that she couldn't think of anything insulting to say back. But there was more than one opinion on her hairdo. The first time she ever saw Daryl Perkins, he hoisted himself out of his yellow van with Bible quotations painted all over it and swung into the luncheonette on his aluminum crutches. He took a good long look at her coiled beehive, shook his bushy red head, and said through his full red beard in his cracker accent, "I swear, li'l lady, look like the good Lord give you a crown and a half!"

Calvin read in the *National Enquirer* that Crystal Gayle's hair was five feet long. When Ray measured Loretta's, it was only four feet three. She was determined not to trim it until she caught up. People said they didn't see how she could pile it so high without her head being cone-shaped. How she did it was known only to herself and to Ray. Ray loved to pull out the hairpins and watch it swirl over her breasts and shoulders. Which is nothing Ishtar could do for him, with that ugly crew cut of hers. She'd been growing it out since she left the Boudiccas, but her head still looked like the rear end of a dog with mange.

Poking at her lacquered spit curl in the mirror, Loretta itemized what she'd buy when she won the lottery. First off, a lifetime membership in Chocolates-of-the-Month Club. Second, a better assistant for Casa Loretta than Dylan Scarborough, so she could be at home with Ray in the evenings. A house for her and Ray in Colonial Manor Estates, on the road to the Xerox factory. But she'd never get Ray to move over there. She couldn't even get him to move into her trailer at Sunset View. Astrid Starr said one day from behind the IGA register, "Lord, you can't get a Marsh to leave home, you know it? That house of theirs is so wicked big can't none of them find their way outen it. Only way to live with a Marsh is to move in over there." Loretta had thought she'd prove Astrid wrong, but so far Ray said he wasn't ready for commitment.

"But your tow truck's outside my door every night of the week and all day Sunday, Rayon Marsh. You think everybody in town don't know we're as good as married?"

"I want you, Loretta, but I don't want no wife," muttered Ray from the couch, in front of the lesbians on the VCR.

"What if the only way to have me is as your wife?"

Ray stood up and hitched up his camouflage pants. "Then it's time for me to head on down the road, old girl," he said with an amiable grin, picking up his olive air force parka with the wolf fur hood.

"Sit back down, you big jerk." She pushed him onto the couch and straddled his lap. "You know I can't get along without you." Her current plan was to get him so used to coming home to a hot meal and clean sheets that he'd never want to leave, apart from any official piece of paper.

Loretta sat down and removed her white-framed cat-eye glasses. She'd also give Ray some sweepstakes money, so he could take it easy. People said Marshes were no 'count because Ray's mother, Waneeta, used food stamps and took government-surplus cheese and wore the clothes of car-wreck victims. But Loretta never saw anyone work harder than Waneeta's sons. Ray drove up and down the interstate in his tow truck, waiting for accidents and searching trash barrels in rest areas for returnable cans and bottles. He stripped the cars he towed home and sold the parts. He drove to Bayonne with crates of Orlon's pelts.

Orlon, the oldest, was determined to restore the Marshes to their former standing as a founding family of Roches Ridge. He ran trap lines down Mink Creek. During deer season he worked as a guide for rich businessmen up from Boston and New York City. If they had any luck, he'd mount the heads and butcher the carcasses. He raised night crawlers for his bait stand in town. Recently he'd been doing odd jobs for Sonny Coffin at his funeral parlor.

Dack, the youngest brother, helped skiers onto chair lifts at Alpine Glen in winter. In spring he trapped minnows for Orlon's bait shop, and in fall he cut wood. He helped Orlon with his trap lines and Ray with his junked cars. He was the helpingest kid that ever lived. And handsome too, with that straight dark hair falling into his eyes, and his copper Abenaki coloring. Waneeta had raised three fine sons, though how she did it without a husband, who can say.

Waneeta's daughters were another question. Looked like Polly and Esther planned to repopulate the state with Marshes. Their house was like a fish hatchery, swarms of babies in dirty diapers flopping around wailing, without a father in sight. Polly and Esther already had children named June, January, and April. Maybe their goal was one for each month.

Loretta spotted Clea Shawn in the doorway in a green plaid lumberjack shirt, tweed trousers, and Sorel boots. "Well, hi there. Come on in and pull up a stool. I was just planning how to spend my lottery winnings."

"Did you win? How marvelous."

"*When* I win."

"Why not? What will you do?"

"Number one, haul ass out of Roches Ridge." Loretta laughed.

Clea frowned and said nothing. Loretta remembered that Clea was thrilled to be in Roches Ridge and probably wasn't eager to hear from those who weren't. She liked Clea. It was a relief to see a fresh face where Calvin Roche used to sit, reading to her depressing articles from the *National Enquirer* about disasters and deformities and the extravagances of movie stars. "Things going all right over to Calvin's, are they, Clea?"

"Yes, fine. Darius has fixed me up a bedroom. But the tub in the kitchen fell into the basement the other day."

"Calvin was waiting for that."

"He *knew* the sills were rotten? He must have forgotten to tell me."

Loretta raised one eyebrow. Calvin Roche was a lot of things, but honest wasn't one of them. He'd been so hot to get to Texas he'd have found a way to sell a diaphragm to a lesbian. She felt bad not warning Clea.

"Things seem pretty quiet today, Loretta."

"We don't generally get too bad a rush except at mealtime and when the kids get off school."

"Loretta, yesterday I spotted some tepees on the creek below my house. You know anything about them?"

"I *guess* so. The Boudiccas. A bunch of women. Lesbians, actually. They don't like men. They killed their rooster."

"I didn't realize you had lesbians up here."

"We got everything you got in New York City, and then some."

"God, let's hope not." Clea laughed.

"The Boudiccas aren't so bad once you get used to them. But I admit it's weird."

"Are they local women?"

"One is. Prudence Webster. Morning Glory, they call her. It's her daddy's land. The others are from all over."

"Looks like they're about to get flooded out."

"Wouldn't be the first time. Ishtar at the Karma Café used to live down there. She says they're crazy. But she's not so normal herself. They're always turning up in their headbands, trying to get Ishtar to come back. They put WOMEN ONLY signs in her windows and scare her customers over here, so I got no complaints. But she says if she's not around for longer than a week, they've kidnapped her and I should call Trooper Trapp. Frankly, I don't know if I would, because there's not room in this town for two restaurants." She hooted, throwing back her towering hairdo.

The door opened and in walked Jared McQueen, in his brown

leather bomber jacket, tan suede jeans, and heavy Mel Gibson five o'clock shadow. His golden hair, with a patch of turquoise at the crown, stood on end like a startled porcupine. "Lunchtime, Loretta!" he announced with a smile that crinkled his blue eyes to slits.

"Hello, Jared. Decided to grace me with your presence today?"

"You know I take turns between you and Ishtar, Loretta."

"Lucky us." It annoyed Loretta that a true born-and-bred Vermonter would frequent a restaurant like Ishtar's, which served maple syrup over tofu. "Jared, this is Clea Shawn from New York City. She's bought Calvin's house." She looked over to Clea. "Jared runs Mane Magnifique next door."

"You're a brave woman," he said, taking Clea's outstretched hand. "Even roaches won't stay in that old dump."

Clea smiled politely. "It does need a lot of work."

"I *guess* so. Tub fell into the cellar, did it, Mrs. Shawn?"

Loretta watched Clea blanch as she realized her private disaster was already public knowledge. But she'd better get used to that if she planned to stick around. "Don't mind Jared," said Loretta. "He's so good-looking he never had to learn any manners." She ruffled his spiked mane with her hand.

He rearranged it with an irritated expression. "What's your special today, Loretta?"

"Spam burritos."

"Jeezum. Well, I guess you better fix me one. Tried Loretta's Hawaiian pizza yet, have you?" he asked Clea.

"Uh, no, but I'm looking forward to it."

"This woman cooks like she invented food."

Loretta simultaneously smiled and frowned. With Jared you never knew if a remark was a compliment or not. Shrugging, she unwrapped a Hershey's Kiss, put it in her mouth, and turned to the kitchen window, where Dylan Scarborough, in his gold ear hoop, greasy ponytail, and EAT THE RICH T-shirt, was bent over his guitar, practicing his latest country-and-western protest song, "The Anne Frank Waltz."

"Dylan honey, put down that guitar and slice Jared some Spam, would you, please?"

# 11  The Town That Time Forgot

Deciding to give the Spam burritos a miss, Clea entered the phone booth at the rear of the restaurant and dialed her answering machine at Turtle Bay. The usual messages about work assignments and social engagements. Nothing urgent. But no Elke. Clea had left her several phone messages before leaving New York, but Elke hadn't returned the calls. She wondered if Elke was punishing her for Roches Ridge. Refusing to participate in such childishness, she dialed Elke's number.

Following the beep, Clea hung up. The creep was no doubt sitting right beside her machine, turning up the volume to find out whom she was being saved from talking to. Clea refused to give her that satisfaction.

As Jared devoured his Spam burrito, Loretta tried to persuade him to place a bet on the outcome of the Miss Teenage Roches Ridge Pageant.

"I can't play favorites, Loretta," he insisted, mouth full. "I'm styling the hair of five contestants that day. It wouldn't be ethical."

Flipping through postcards beside the death penalty petition, Clea picked several of Roches Ridge at the turn of the century, with horse-drawn vehicles on a dirt road outside the building that was now Starr's IGA. Sitting at a corner table by the neon Wurlitzer, she wrote Turner in Mexico City: "Hi, sweetheart! You'll be amazed by the progress on Roche House when you get home. Make it soon 'cause I miss you like mad." To Kate and Theo at school: "Wait till you see this place! Twenty minutes from Alpine Glen, and hot cider by the fire when you get home." To Karen: "See? Didn't I tell you, O thou of little faith? The roads are paved and the carriages are cars now, but otherwise it's just the same. What about *The Town That Time Forgot?*"

Clea paused, pen poised, to regard Loretta with her beehive hairdo and white-framed cat-eye glasses, unwrapping a Hershey's Kiss as she assured Jared he could place his bet anonymously. Casa Loretta was itself a time warp. Patti Page and Eddie Fisher songs should be on the Wurlitzer instead of John Denver, who was currently singing "Sunshine on My Shoulder." Malted milk shakes should be on the menu. Soon the place would fill up with girls in bobby socks, who'd clear the tables for a sock hop. Clea put down her pen and reached for her Nikon.

Clea laid her Nikon back on the Formica table. She kept forgetting that you didn't just barge into other people's lives and start snapping. That was a good way to get your camera destroyed and your face disfigured. Once on the Li River in China she tried to photograph two peasant girls in coolie hats and bare feet, baskets hanging from wooden yokes across their shoulders. They scowled and stalked away, leaving her full of apologies to all the people whose lives she'd invaded with her Nikon over the years.

But of course her ability to suppress this awareness had made her successful. Sometimes when she anticipated lack of cooperation, she buttoned her raincoat over her camera, with just the lens peeping out, and snapped shots without the subjects' awareness. Elke insisted this was exploitative. Perhaps so, but it had yielded some startling photos. She'd leave to Elke the paralytic debate about when ends justified means.

A middle-aged woman with matted hair like a graying barrister's wig walked through the door. She wore a cashmere skirt-and-sweater set, with a huge black-checked kaffiyeh draped around her upper torso like a tablecloth.

Loretta swiveled toward Clea, saying, "Genevieve, meet Clea Shawn. Clea, this is Genevieve Paxton. She keeps us out of the loony bin."

"I run the Center for Sanity," explained Genevieve.

Clea nodded genially, with a quizzical expression.

"Wait till you've been here awhile," responded Genevieve. "You'll be amazed."

Clea smiled politely, stood up, and took her leave. As she passed the Victorian bandstand on the green, she heard the squeaking and clanking of swings behind the grade school, and the shouts of children on recess in the fresh spring air. Beyond the school rose the mountain peak that bore the Alpine Glen ski trails, still white, wisped with blue mist.

The etched-glass door of a handsome white Victorian house opened to let out a portly young man in a business suit. A few bars of harp music drifted across to Clea. In the front window, which was bordered with stained glass, sat the frail woman from Clea's first photos of Roches Ridge. Dressed in white, with white-blond hair down her back, she was playing glissandos on a large golden harp with a frame like an

Ionic column. Clea studied her with dawning excitement. That original photo might make a striking jacket for *The Town That Time Forgot*. She'd have to discuss it with Karen.

At the post office, Clea bought stamps from Maureen Murphy. Maureen's eyes didn't meet Clea's, nor did her tight mouth move in response to Clea's smile. In fact, the frown lines between her eyes deepened, freeing a few strands of coarse gray hair from the Scotch tape across her bangs.

"Hi. I'm Clea Shawn. I've just moved into Calvin Roche's house."

Maureen's eyes lifted. She nodded curtly, then looked back to the Dixie cup on the counter, with the sign reading: COMMON CENTS: HAVE A PENNY? LEAVE ONE. NEED A PENNY? TAKE ONE.

The famous New England reserve, Clea concluded. She shoved her postcards through the mail slot and began to study the posters on the bulletin board. The Miss Teenage Roches Ridge Pageant again. Some FBI Wanted photos. All she had seen of the man who stole her earrings were his eyes, burning through the holes in his leather face mask, and the camouflage fabric of his trousers as he stood over her, holding his cocked gun to her temple. Several sets of eyes on these FBI posters looked familiar. . . . But how ridiculous to hang such posters in rural Vermont. A criminal here would stand out like a vulture among doves.

Clea had intended to tell Maureen how much she admired the way Maureen cared for her mother. New England was not Esalen, however. Intimacy here would take time to develop. But like granite, it would endure. Clea thought of her own parents' last days, in a nursing home in Poplar Bluffs, largely unattended by their children. Their relationship with their children had not been hostile, just underdeveloped. Since they hadn't been much help to their children during the rigors of life, it didn't really occur to their children to help *them* during the rigors of death.

Clea wondered if Kate and Theo would behave as badly when the time came. Probably she deserved it, both for neglecting her own parents and for neglecting Kate and Theo. If she had. She was never sure. Her goal had been not to lie ill in bed all day, as her own mother had. Yet in the end she'd probably been just as unavailable—off pursuing photos and lovers while a housekeeper kept tabs on Kate and Theo. And her emotional life had been lived largely with Elke rather than at home. How this would affect her children remained to be seen. At the moment they were ringing all the usual changes on the adolescent carillon, at times shy and dependent, at other times bold and obnoxious. It was too early to separate what was her fault from what was to her credit, from what had nothing to do with her. But successful parenting was like log rolling, and she'd often landed in the drink.

Clea sometimes wondered what would have happened if Elke had insisted on coparenting Kate and Theo, as Clea had hoped she might that afternoon on Saint John. In the beginning Elke spent a lot of time perched on Clea's sofa, drawing the children and seeming enchanted with them. She showed them how to mold tiny animals from Play-Doh at the kitchen table, pinching it and making lines with her fingernails. Unlike their harried mother, Elke was invariably patient, loving, and uncritical. The children adored her. Except when they sensed the intensity of the connection between Elke and their mommy, and became monsters of jealousy. But when the crunch came, Elke consigned Clea to Paris with Turner.

Clea had never solved the Delphic mysteries of parenthood. Kate and Theo had simply outgrown them. Until here she was, missing them in all their successive manifestations, proud they were able to go, resentful at having been left, amused by this resentment, relieved to be free. In a sense she'd sacrificed Turner and Elke for her children. During their childhood she felt as though she were trying to do the tango while pushing a pram. One or the other had to go, so she'd stopped dancing. But the children in question were now vanishing. And she had to watch them go, and help them leave. Parenthood required the self-discipline of an anchorite. No wonder she and Turner, like their parents before them, had invented escapes.

Removing a blank postcard from her shirt pocket, Clea scribbled on it on the post office counter: "Elke—Sorry I couldn't reach you before I left. Or just now on the phone. There's still no phone at my house, so please write me. And I'll call you again. I miss you, darling. Don't ever think I don't."

Shoving the card through the slot before she could change her mind, she leaned against the wall of mailbox doors and congratulated herself for refusing to play these missing/not missing, needing/not needing games that had plagued Elke's and her entire relationship, as both struggled in vain to blunt the impact of their seventeen-year collision.

# 12  Saint John

Following the *American Artist* portrait, Elke and Clea feasted greedily on each other's pasts, and on the minute fluctuations of each other's current internal landscapes. In the beginning it seemed neither had an interest the other didn't share—art, gossip, good food, bad jokes. Their meetings took place in Elke's studio, in Village restaurants, or at Turtle Bay. In time they began to talk of renting a loft near Elke's as a joint studio. Clea pictured them working back to back, then relaxing face to face over cups of tea. In less disciplined moments, when she forgot about Theo and Kate, she even imagined each woman turning her portion of the loft into a living space.

Inevitably, though, differences began to poke up like crocuses in the spring. They revolved around Elke's reluctance to leave New York.

"Why?" asked Elke wearily one afternoon in her studio as Clea tried to persuade her to go to Montreal for two days on a photo shoot.

"Because it would be fun." Clea had some vague notion of wanting Elke all to herself, without Terence's appearing to ask her to leave, without Turner's arriving to entertain them with tales of the European marketplace, without needing to outshout the Cookie Monster.

"For you maybe. Not for me."

"Elke, I'm a free-lance photographer. My husband is in international marketing. Travel is my *life*."

"But not mine." Elke massaged her temples with thumb and index finger.

Clea paused. It was the first time either had acknowledged that their lives weren't conterminous for all time.

"Look, Clea, you do your work, and I'll do mine. You tend your family, and I'll tend mine. You manage your household, and I'll manage mine. And when we have time left over, we'll spend it together."

Clea sighed. "Let's not make a big deal of it, Elke. I'm not asking you to marry me. I'm just inviting you to Montreal. If you'd rather not, fine."

"I've *seen* the world, Clea. It appalls me."

Everything appalls you, thought Clea, lying back in her corduroy armchair. Elke poked at her psyche as though at a sore tooth with her tongue. All her graphics portrayed creatures in distress—dogs starving, prisoners emerging from concentration camps, orphaned babies. Elke insisted horror was the price of facing reality. Every event in the news, all behavior of friends and people in the street, was interpreted in the bleakest possible light. Elke mourned unbought Christmas trees and boiled eggs.

Then Clea recalled that this woman had seen a photo of her father hanged by his countrymen. Her uncle had suffocated in a collapsing trench in Flanders during World War I. Her brother lay beneath a white swastika on a North African desert. Elke herself had fled rapacious Russian soldiers as a teenager. She had stolen turnips from cattle and slept in haylofts. Her adored mother had died of a broken heart on the parlor carpet. The world held only terror for Elke, not the glamour it promised Clea, whose more quiet tortures had occurred in the sanctity of her Poplar Bluffs home.

"Okay. Never mind. It's fine," said Clea gently. "I'm sorry, Elke. I know you hate trips."

As the months went by, though, Clea began to chafe. Elke and she had fallen into a pattern. They talked on the phone every night after Kate and Theo were in bed and before Terence got home from his night class. They lunched every Wednesday in the Village, having eaten at most nearby restaurants several times. Elke invariably ordered a chef's salad with Italian dressing—and without a hard-boiled egg. Clea dropped by Elke's studio when she went to her photo lab on the next block. Sometimes Elke ventured uptown to sit on Clea's couch. But increasingly Elke was canceling these treks because of headaches. And talk of the joint studio was falling off, just as it had with Professor Galmer at Cornell before he exiled Clea to New York.

What had started out as fresh and exciting had become a routine. Elke loved routines. They were predictable. Clea loathed routines. They were suffocating. They reminded her of the households she'd been fleeing. Elke's rigor mortis precluded fantasy. Since change was not possible, what you saw was all you got. Yet fantasy was Clea's mental fertilizer. And after an entire childhood of it, here Clea was, trying hopelessly to cheer up yet another deeply loved woman who lay abed with headaches.

In desperation Clea began to cancel Wednesday lunches and to inspect people she met with a new availability, in the market for some interpersonal excitement to ameliorate the tedium of her unembellished daily reality. At this point, no doubt sensing Clea's intended defection, Elke invited Clea to her studio to see some new work.

Elke sat in anxious silence as Clea studied the print of a woman very much like herself, who held out her arms to a child with features taken from both Kate and Theo. The child, also reaching out but unable to bridge the gap, wore an expression of longing and panic. The mother's expression was agonized and helpless. The forces that kept them apart were unspecified. Clea was left with a vague sense of horror. Out of all the poses and expressions Elke had sketched during her months at Turtle Bay, she'd chosen this one to immortalize as a woodcut.

Taking a shaky breath, Clea finally said, "Elke, you are an immensely gifted woman."

"But you hate it, right?"

"No, I don't hate it. I admire it technically. But surely you don't expect me to *enjoy* it?"

"I guess that would be asking too much. By the way," she added, "when's your next trip?"

"In two weeks. To do a brochure for a new resort on Saint John. Why?"

"Would you like some company?"


When they arrived at the resort, built around the ruins of a colonial sugarcane plantation, Elke was groggy from the Valium and alcohol she'd consumed to assuage her fear of air travel. While she napped in their seaside cottage, Clea toured the place with the PR director, who wore safari shorts and a pith helmet. As she inspected the carefully groomed grounds and sports facilities and planned her photos, Clea tried to decide where to sleep that night. The cottage had only one bedroom, but two double beds. It seemed absurd to sleep on the living room couch, yet sharing a bedroom might be too much togetherness for Elke. Clea didn't want to give her a migraine. She was touched by Elke's effort to accommodate Clea's wish for them to travel together, and she was determined to show Elke a good time so she'd want to do it again.

Back at the cottage before dinner, Clea carefully turned away in the shadowy bedroom when Elke emerged from the shower and began to dry herself with a fluffy white towel. As Elke bent over to shake her breasts into the cups of her bra, Clea entered the shower and washed away the sweat from her afternoon tour.

Standing in the bathroom blotting her wet hair with a towel, Clea looked into the bedroom. And saw Elke standing there, fully clothed in a floral sundress, calmly studying Clea's naked body. Clea lowered the towel to cover her torso and stared at Elke indignantly. Elke grinned and said, "Don't worry. I've seen it all before. Don't forget, I went to art school and worked from live models."

"But I'm not your model," snapped Clea, confused.

The resort's dining room was a converted cane mill, with rolling ocean and distant islands visible out the picture windows. The candle flame highlighted Elke's prematurely silver hair and the shadows beneath her cheekbones. Her upper chest showed the pinkish beginnings of a tan. "You look lovely," said Clea coolly.

Elke, studying the menu, said nothing.

"I'm glad you're here," added Clea with more warmth.

"Me too."

"Is it as unpleasant as you anticipated?"

Elke smiled faintly. "Well, it's always odd to be away from Terence. I doubt if we've spent more than a couple of dozen nights apart in twenty years. Sometimes his devotion drives me crazy, but apparently I rely on it."

"Tomorrow we can rent a jeep and tour the island," said Clea, alarmed with herself for not wanting to hear about Elke's domestic bliss just now. "Maybe hire some snorkeling equipment. The PR guy here has an underwater camera I want to try. We could get the kitchen to pack a picnic. . . ."

"Clea." Elke laughed. "Slow down."

"But we're leaving in four days."

"Sweetheart, we just got here. Relax. I'm ten years older than you. You'll wear me out."

By the time the conch fritters arrived, Elke's geniality began to fray. And in the middle of her grouper steak, she put down her fork and began to rub her temples.

"What's wrong?" asked Clea.

"I'm sorry, darling, but I've got to get out of here."

"How come?"

"Can't you feel it?" she demanded, looking at Clea through anguished eyes. "The slaves who sweated and bled their lives away in this building. On this very stone floor."

"Oh, for God's sake," sighed Clea as Elke stood up and draped her fringed silk shawl around her shoulders.

The next morning Elke agreed to the jeep trip, a straw hat tied on her head with a scarf. She insisted Clea stop when they came upon some wild donkeys by the roadside. As Clea snapped photos, Elke fed them bread crusts from the picnic basket.

In a deserted cove they donned face masks and flippers and floated slowly over the reefs, Clea photographing the brilliant fish and bizarre forests of coral. Even when she couldn't actually see Elke, Clea could feel her beside her or behind her. Once when they spotted a young barracuda, Elke grabbed her hand to ensure that they'd be ripped apart together.

"Wasn't that fantastic?" asked Clea as they lumbered out of the surf in their fins.

"What about that poor coral reef that was being devoured by those crown-of-thorns starfish?"

Clea turned to look at Elke in her face mask. "Elke, don't. Just for today, okay?"

"I'm sorry."

They sat down on their blanket in the shade and ate crabmeat sandwiches. As they lay napping afterward, Clea's right arm rested a fraction of an inch from Elke's left one. Elke extended her little finger to clasp Clea's, and Clea's existence became focused on that finger.

That night Clea slept fitfully, waking several times to Elke's steady breathing in the next bed, the wooden fan overhead swirling the musky scent of Elke's perfume. As the taupe dawn turned to coral, Clea studied Elke's rough hand resting on the white sheet, the lace strap of her nightgown slipping off her shoulder.

The next day Clea trekked around the resort with the safari-attired PR director, taking staged shots of grinning black kitchen help behind bushels of perfectly ripe tropical fruit. Sweltering in her khaki skirt and garish Hawaiian blouse, Clea longed only for a swim and a cold gin and tonic.

Back at the cottage at the end of the afternoon, Elke lay asleep in the sun on a cushioned wicker lounge chair, face tanned and relaxed. Clea set her camera bag on the smooth coral terrace and looked through some sketches lying on the wicker table—of a chambermaid stooped over to change the sheets, exhaustion in the lines of her face; of a sweating groundsman cutting back brush with a machete. Clea glanced around at the bright tropical foliage and turquoise sea. From all this Elke had selected these particular images. No wonder she had migraines.

Raising her camera and adjusting the focus, Clea studied Elke through her zoom lens—the silver hair and high cheekbones, the sharp chin and slightly parted lips. Slowly she pressed the shutter release. The click resounded in the hot, still afternoon like a gunshot. Wishing she had a silencer, she continued shooting.

Retracting her lens, Clea could see Elke's entire body, in a skirted one-piece black taffeta Betty Grable bathing suit that made Clea smile. The oiled reddish chest rose and fell evenly. The large rough hands were clasped across the stomach. Clea zoomed in on those remarkable hands—veined and gnarled, with short nails and blunt fingers. The hands of a craftswoman. Until this trip Clea had never seen Elke asleep. Nor had she seen her so scantily clad. She looked younger and more vulnerable. It was no doubt unethical to be photographing her without her awareness. But she was so beautiful that Clea couldn't help herself. Clea's chest began to ache in the vicinity of her heart. She wet her sun-parched lips with her tongue.

Turning her camera sideways, Clea crouched, studying the legs, smooth and muscled, with no sign of cellulite, a legacy of Elke's marathon walks around the city and daily climbs up the four flights of stairs to her apartment. Cradling the camera in both hands and focusing on the background of bougainvillea, so that Elke's reclining form was soft and misty, Clea snapped again.

Returning to Elke's face, she discovered a faint smile. The eyelids opened to reveal the navy-blue eyes. As the mists of sleep burned off, the smile faded into an expression of anxiety and uncertainty. Gradually the intense blue gaze seemed almost to penetrate the camera lens. Finally Elke stood up and moved across the terrace, backed by the hot-pink flowers. Clea's view through the camera became blurred.

Carefully Elke took the camera from Clea's hands and the strap from around her neck and set it on the wicker table. "Clea, look at me without that damn thing between us."

As she stood up, Clea's eyes darted over the coral retaining wall to the shore, where a flock of shrieking gulls had just landed. Slowly she returned her eyes to Elke's, and felt awash in the sea.

"What are we going to do about this?" asked Elke.

"About what?" asked Clea, swallowing with difficulty.

"Don't be coy." Putting her hands on Clea's shoulders, she studied Clea at arms' length until Clea dropped her eyes and nodded. "After all, isn't this why we're here?"

Clea said nothing. She had wanted Elke to herself, but there was a reason Elke had so studiously avoided this—and here it was. With all their innocent talk of joint studios, they had both watched the locomotive approach, bound firmly to the tracks by desire. She took one of Elke's hands from her shoulder and held the wrist to her lips. Elke's pulse pounded against her lower lip.

"Yes, I guess so," replied Clea, poised somewhere between terror and elation.

Pulling her wrist away, Elke turned to look at the surf drive white foam across the pink sand. "I made the first move. You'll have to make the next. If there's to be a next."

The slanting rays of the sun burned into Clea's bare forearm. "Do you want there to be?"

"No fair," said Elke, studying the sea.

Reaching out, Clea took Elke's silver head in both hands and kissed her firmly on the mouth, marveling at the smoothness of the cheeks and the softness of the lips.

"Okay, your turn." Clea had begun to tremble like a malaria patient.

"You're not much use, are you?" said Elke gently, taking Clea's hand and leading her into the cool, dark bedroom. With her other hand she flung the woven cotton spread off the nearest bed.

Clea's trembling turned into a slow, steady shudder. Putting her arms around Elke, she felt their breasts press together. She returned her mouth to Elke's.

Eventually Elke disentangled herself and walked back to lean in the doorway, framed by white sunlight.

Clea stood on the carpet, breathing unevenly. "I don't know much about this, Elke. But I do know you can't just walk away once you've kissed someone like that."

Elke turned, face haggard. "I thought I could go through with this, Clea, but I can't. I'm sorry."

"Christ, Elke, what are you *doing?*"

Elke returned to sit on the edge of the bed. "Look, maybe we ought to talk this over." She began to massage her temples.

"What a good idea," said Clea sarcastically. Now Elke would get a migraine and spend the rest of the trip in bed, a damp cloth across her forehead. And it would somehow be Clea's fault. Removing her sandals, Clea crawled up the bed behind Elke and leaned against a couple of pillows.

"I love you, Clea," Elke said in a low voice. "I loved you the first moment I ever saw you. In your black cape in my studio doorway. I thought you were the most exotic creature I'd ever seen. I wanted to draw you, paint you, etch you, sculpt you, make love to you. Own you, so you'd never leave me."

"You do own me," murmured Clea fervently.

"Fine, but what do we *do* with each other? I tried staying away from you, but I couldn't. Now I'm trying to be with you, and I don't think I can do that either."

"You're not attracted to me?"

"I *am* attracted to you. Sexually and every other way. But I'm terrified of where this is leading. I can't handle chaos, Clea. I need Terence. I need my routines. They keep me sane. You have no idea."

Clea folded her arms across her stomach as though protecting her vitals. "You're stronger than that, Elke. Look at all you've survived."

"I think it would be best if we pretend this never happened."

"Whatever you say."

They sat in silence, the wooden fan swirling overhead. Clea could feel Elke retreating behind their everyday boundaries. Desperate to halt this withdrawal, Clea asked, "But who said you had to give up Terence or your routines? Can't we just be together now, and leave it at that?"

Elke turned to look at her, dropping the hand at her temples into her lap. "Could you do that? You got so upset over Turner's affairs."

"Could you?" asked Clea, brightening.

"I don't know. I have a few times."

"Really? With whom?" Clea felt a stab of jealousy that strangers should have glimpsed a facet of Elke that she hadn't.

Elke shrugged. "A museum curator in Washington. An art history professor in Boston. Just a night here and there."

"I thought you didn't like your routines disrupted."

"I don't. But it's very undemanding screwing a stranger. You know what most men are like. The only place they allow merger is on the stock exchange. I could have been a vanilla éclair for all they cared."

Clea laughed. "Then why bother?"

"Different reasons. Loneliness. Ego. Hormones. Once or twice I got sick of Terence's guard dog routine and wanted to prove I was a free agent."

"Doesn't Terence mind?"

Elke pursed her lips. "He doesn't ask me what I do when we aren't together, and I don't ask him. But of course I wasn't in love with *them*," added Elke, reaching for Clea's sweating hand.

"Maybe it would get it out of our systems."

"Maybe. And maybe not."

"Let's find out," said Clea.

Elke studied Clea for a moment, then tentatively stretched out beside her.

"Where did you get this funky suit, by the way?" Clea ran her fingertips along the wire stays.

"At a secondhand clothing store on Canal Street. I thought it might amuse us. But I admire your skill at sidestepping the issue at hand."

"Sorry." Clea clasped Elke's right hand and studied it carefully. The blunt fingers and enlarged knuckles, the blue veins and rough skin. Turning it over, she traced the creases across the palm with a fingertip—the head line, the heart line. The hand began to tremble. Clea had watched this hand sketch and etch designs with great skill and originality. She'd watched it assemble meals and fold laundry. She'd watched it reach out to touch Clea's forearm for emphasis during a discussion, and absently clasp Terence's hand for reassurance. She'd watched it pinch and twist balls of Play-Doh into miniature animals for Kate and Theo, and brush the hair from their eyes as they tried to copy her. This familiar and versatile hand was about to assume a new role. It was now going to explore the curves and crevices of Clea's body. As she kissed its palm, Clea abruptly pictured Kate and baby Theo being washed out to sea in a life raft, while she stood on shore in Elke's arms. She stiffened.

Elke looked at her questioningly.

Clea shook her head and slid her arms around Elke while the wooden fan stirred wisps of Elke's silver hair. She and Elke would be together for the next two days, Clea reflected. Back in New York, Elke would get on with her life and her marriage. Her ultimate loyalty would always be to Terence, the guardian of her sanity—or so she believed. Meanwhile, Clea would roam the streets howling for more, her own marriage in shambles, her children neglected, her career eclipsed.

Taking on its new function, Elke's hand reached over to unbutton Clea's Hawaiian shirt, which featured parrots in palm trees. But after the fingers slowly undid the top button, Clea rebuttoned it.

"Now what?" asked Elke with a sigh.

"What about Kate and Theo?"

"What about them?"

"I don't want to hurt them."

"Can it hurt them to have a happy mother?"

"And no father?"

Elke looked at Clea, fingers poised over the rebuttoned button.

"Do you really think Turner would stay married to a lesbian?" This label hadn't occurred to her until now. Lovemaking with Elke had seemed more natural and less frightening than with the men she'd loved. Yet she and Elke were respectable married ladies, who had no business doing what they were about to do.

Starting to laugh, Elke sat up. Shaking her head, she said nothing.

"What are you thinking?" Clea finally asked.

"Absolutely nothing. I'm dumbstruck by this image of your father-less children. But I thought you and Turner had an agreement to do as you pleased outside New York."

"With men. I don't think women ever occurred to him."

"Silly boy." Elke rolled off the bed and walked toward the bathroom. "What a pity you Americans so often regard sensuality as a disease."

"Wait a minute, Elke. We've started this. We've got to settle it."

Elke turned to look at her. "As far as I'm concerned, it's settled. You have a husband and two beautiful children. They need you more than I. However much I may want you."

Clea looked at her in silence, unable to dispute this, not even wanting to.

"You want me to offer to help you raise Kate and Theo," Elke suddenly realized.

Clea said nothing. She supposed this *was* what she wanted—assurances of a life with Elke, to replace the one she would jeopardize with Turner.

"I thought we were talking about making love a few times and then getting on with our lives," said Elke bemusedly.

"We were. But as we talk it over, surely you can see it's not that simple."

"Not for *you*, perhaps."

"Fine, Elke. Do your world-weary European number. Ridicule my midwestern earnestness. But if we make love, you're going to be more hung up on me than you ever dreamed possible."

"What is this, self-promotion?" Elke laughed from the bathroom doorway. "Look, darling, I love you. I lust after you. But I can't raise your children. I have to do my work."

"So I gather you're only interested in me sexually?"

"Screw you, Clea," snapped Elke from the shadows.

"Don't I wish." Clea stood up, Hawaiian shirt damp with sweat.

They adjourned to the terrace to watch a scarlet sun sink into the black sea. Elke put on a white terry-cloth beach robe, tying the belt tightly. Clea mixed gin and tonics. Handing one to Elke, she lit a cigarette and sat down in a striped deck chair, feeling the smooth pocked coral beneath her bare feet. Exhaling, she said grimly, "So now what?"

Elke shrugged. "We continue as before, I suppose."

They drank in silence while waves crashed on the beach. "We're missing dinner," observed Clea.

Elke shrugged again, gazing at the sky, where stars were just appearing.

Clea reminded herself that it probably wasn't too late to spend the night in Elke's arms. It was silly to fret about disasters that might never occur. Yet she could feel the machinery revving up that would transform her into a harridan who'd demand to know whom Elke was with and what she was doing whenever they weren't together. Who would require praise, presents, sex, and reassurance. Who would pace the floor on nights when Elke was making love with Terence. It was a dreadful thing to impose on a wonderful friendship. She envied Turner his ability cheerfully to share physical pleasure with other people and then return to his real life with scarcely a backward glance.

Elke was shaking her head in the twilight.

"What?" asked Clea.

"Did I ever tell you I had an abortion?"

"No."

"Early in our marriage. Terence was being harassed by the FBI. And we were both traumatized by the war, and couldn't imagine bringing an innocent baby into such a world. My career was just beginning, and it was fashionable at that time to believe a woman had to choose between her work and a family. I remember apologizing to the embryo as I stood on a street corner waiting to be driven by a stranger to some seedy apartment in Jersey City. I truly believed either it or I had to go. But I watch you cope. So I guess I was wrong."

"We have different standards. I just get by, as a photographer and as a mother."

"Nonsense. You're absolutely fine at both. Anyway, I was just wondering if parenting your children would make my abortion seem pointless and sordid. I mean, maybe I *could* be daddy for Kate and Theo, if it ever came to that. (Which I doubt, by the way.) Especially since I love their mother so much."

"Right now you do, on a terrace in Saint John after you've drunk too much gin. But what about in the middle of a winter night when a child crawls into our bed to vomit, and you're too tired to work in the morning?" The worries and responsibilities of parenthood, and the resentment they sometimes engendered, had driven a wedge between her and Turner, and they would between her and Elke too. Elke would no doubt do whatever was necessary to fulfill such a commitment, including slighting her work. Thereby ceasing to be the gifted, uncompromising woman Clea had originally fallen in love with. Clea couldn't accept such a sacrifice even if Elke offered. Which she hadn't exactly . . . But might, if pushed.

They smiled at each other warily, negotiations stalled. Clea stubbed out her cigarette and pulled on a cotton cardigan. "I guess we have to figure out some new way to be together, Elke. Some hybrid mix of lover and friend."

"There's nothing new about it. What do you think women have been doing with each other for centuries?"

Turner announced at dinner the next week that he'd been assigned to Paris.

"But, Turner, I can't," said Clea, fork suspended over her salmon. Theo was hurling squished peas at Kate.

"Why not?"

"Well, I mean, my life is here. My work. Our housekeeper."

"Staying here isn't an option for me right now, Clea. Not if I want to be vice-president. You can get free-lance work in Europe. And the kids aren't in school yet. It's an ideal time for us to go."

"But, Turner, I can't," she whispered. "My friends . . . "

"You have no trouble making friends, Clea. You'll make new ones in Paris."

Clea thought she detected a note of smug self-assurance in his voice. As though he understood the true source of her reluctance, and the impossibility of her refusing to go. She studied Theo in his high chair, red T-shirt wet with drool. And Kate sitting primly with the grownups, trying to pretend she didn't know the little boy who was banging on his tray with a fish stick. What would Harriet Nelson do? She'd move to Paris, smiling sweetly.

When Clea told Elke about the move in her studio the next evening, Elke made a sudden gesture with her arm as though warding off a blow. After a long pause she said, "Clea, I . . ."

"Yes?" said Clea quickly.

Elke began to massage her temples.

The door opened. Terence stood there with his glasses halfway down his nose, looking pointedly at his watch. Noticing Elke's temple massage, he said, "Elke, I hope you're not getting another migraine. You haven't had enough sleep lately."

Clea looked at Elke, outraged.

Elke said faintly, "Terence, please go away. Clea and I are talking."

Clea felt a flicker of hope. This was a first step. She waited.

Elke's breaths came shallow and jerky. Her eyes stayed fixed on the skylight for a long time, jaw muscles clenching and unclenching. Finally she lowered her gaze, resigned and anguished, to Clea's and said, "Well, I guess you'd better go with your husband, then."

# 13   Maureen Murphy

As Clea Shawn studied the FBI posters, Maureen Murphy slipped behind the partition, removed Clea's postcards from the mail drop, and read them. Alpine Glen ... hot cider ... *The Town That Time Forgot* ... Astrid Starr at the IGA prided herself on knowing everything that went on in Roches Ridge. She was always trying to pump Maureen about which people in town received dividend checks or sex aids. One day Astrid had said, "Oh, come off it, Maureen. Alone all day with a bag of postcards?"

Maureen replied, "Some people would never read other people's mail, Astrid. Or steal other people's partners."

"Earl Atkins was a grown man, Maureen. He made his choice. I didn't *have* to steal him. But I'm sorry it hurt you."

Maureen stuffed the postcards into a canvas sack. Peering at Clea Shawn through the thick glass door of a mail cubby, Maureen reflected that she looked like the kind of person who'd get lots· of certified letters, express mail, and special delivery parcels. Trouble, in short. Maureen sighed. As if she didn't have enough trouble, with an octogenarian mother who refused to die. If Maureen weren't convinced she could hurry it along and save money at the same time, she'd have put her mother in a home for the unpleasant long ago. But since her mother *wanted* to be in a home, Maureen was determined to keep her right here in the house on Elm Street where she'd made Maureen's early years a hell. She'd get drunk and tie Maureen to the bedstead and burn her with cigarettes. When boys arrived to pick Maureen up for dates in high school, her mother would be passed out on the hall floor. The boys rarely called back.

After Earl Atkins's wife ran off with the roofer, Earl turned up at the post office to help Maureen sort mail. If she ignored his belly, she could see a resemblance to Christopher Plummer in *The Sound of Music*. Earl was stern and manly, with a jaw like a leg-hold trap, but with a loving twinkle in his eyes. (By this point she'd watched her *Sound of Music* videocassette a hundred and ten times, and was listening to the sound track nightly. On her dining room wall hung a commemorative plate featuring a dirndled Julie Andrews in a field of edelweiss.)

One night Earl stopped by her house, awkward and blushing. Sitting on the living room couch, he told her he'd loved her since high school and had been writing secret poems to her. Reaching under his belly, he pulled some papers from his pocket and began reading: "Prettier than the month of June, / Brighter than the sun at noon, / More mysterious than the harvest moon, / It's you I love, Maureen. . . ."

During the part about the call of the loon, Maureen's mother staggered into the living room and fell at Earl's feet. Earl raced for the door, stuffing the poems into his pocket. Two months later he married Astrid Starr and cruised the Hawaiian Islands, returning in an Australian army hat with an emu feather. To add insult to injury, Astrid persuaded Angela McGrath to play *South Pacific* on her harp all day long, replacing *The Sound of Music*. Since Maureen's mother had ruined Maureen's chances for a normal happy family life, Maureen intended to return the favor.

Maureen emptied the cup of pennies on the counter into her pocketbook. Then she took the proceeds from shortchanging Clea Shawn out of her cash drawer and put that in her change purse. Every little bit helped. Travel was so expensive these days. She returned to the cubbies to sort mail for the rural route driver. Some more literature from Red China for Alvin Jacobs at Camel's Hump Community College. Deciding Trooper Trapp ought to know, she shoved the envelope into his slot. A postcard to Dr. Evans from a Xeroxer at Club Med in Guadeloupe: "Thanks for the suggestion, Doc. Rest and sun are just the thing. A Vermont winter takes it out of a guy. . . ."

Maureen had taken her mother to Guadeloupe last year, and dragged her up the volcano, and through the rain forest, and along the dusty roads of Îles des Saintes. But Dr. Evans said she had the stamina of a forty year old. At lunch on a bougainvillea-draped patio overlooking the turquoise sea, other tour members gasped, "Your mother, she's so pale. Shouldn't she rest? Shouldn't she take off that black wool coat?"

Since Maureen had her mother's hearing aids in her pocketbook, her mother couldn't verify their concern. Maureen said, "Oh, Mother's indefatigable. She wouldn't nap if her life depended on it." And the fellow tourists shook their heads and proclaimed her a remarkable old lady.

Ishtar at the Karma Café was always saying that people who were enemies in this life must have been antagonists in previous lives—Ajax and Achilles, Caesar and Brutus, Hitler and Churchill. Ishtar said if people could work through their issues with each other in this life, they wouldn't have to engage in the next. But Maureen had no interest in working through anything with her mother. She was taking revenge. She drove her mother to the shopping mall in Burlington and marched her along the crowded corridors in her wool coat, walker tips squeaking, until her mother was red-faced and gasping. Her mother knew if she didn't cooperate, Maureen wouldn't let her watch "The Young and the Restless" that afternoon.

One morning as her mother smiled at puppies in the pet store window, Maureen realized her mother actually *enjoyed* mall walking— the other shoppers, the piped-in Muzak, the seasonal exhibits in the center booths. So she began confiscating her mother's glasses and hearing aids on their mall walks. Nor would she return them when she watched *The Sound of Music*, ever since her mother referred to it as *The Sound of Mucus*.

Alarmed, Maureen rushed to her handbag by the desk. But her mother's hearing aids, eyeglasses, and false teeth, the phone receiver and the doorknobs, were all there. And yes, she'd remembered to hide the walker in the garage. She used to keep the walker in the cellar, but one day her mother managed to descend the steps on her rear end. She dragged the walker up and was trying to pry open the back door with a dinner knife when Maureen arrived home for lunch.

Was there anything she'd overlooked? mused Maureen. Her mother couldn't write notes because of bad eyes and arthritis in her fingers. Without false teeth, her speech was incoherent. Once she wrote HELP ME backward on a frosted windowpane. But Maureen was the only one in town who knew her mother didn't really have Alzheimer's.

Once Anita Perkins, the wife of that born-again preacher from

Granite Gap, tried to call on May to offer her salvation. As though the old bat wasn't irretrievably damned to hell. Anita came racing into the post office on her snowmobile boots, blue veil flying, to tell Maureen that her mother was dead, sitting motionless in her armchair while Anita beat on the door and windows. Maureen rushed home, but the old lady was alive as ever, having simply not heard or seen Anita. After that Maureen bought blinds to lower when she went to work.

Returning to her sorting, Maureen held up to the light an envelope for Astrid Starr containing a Xerox dividend check, and wondered where to take her mother next. She'd ask Astrid for someplace hot, mountainous, and insect-ridden. With bad water and the possibility of kidnappers. Mexico maybe. Or Peru. They could climb Machu Picchu. Thin air might do the trick.

The envelope drooped in Maureen's fingers. She could keep her hatred at full pressure only so long before it turned to sorrow. She always cried as she watched those poor children in *The Sound of Music*, motherless like herself. But at least they had Christopher Plummer to console them.

Hearing the door open, Maureen looked through the mail slot into the lobby, to watch Clea Shawn exit in her stiff green plaid lumberjack shirt. You could always pick out the flatlanders by their lumberjack shirts. You had to snub them repeatedly before they finally understood that your behavior was motivated by authentic dislike rather than by Yankee reserve.

Beyond Mrs. Shawn, Maureen spotted Daryl Perkins's yellow van parked outside Starr's IGA, painted all over with Bible slogans like VANITY OF VANITIES, ALL IS VANITY. Daryl's wife, Anita, and three other women in blue veils, long dresses, and snowmobile boots clambered out. Daryl sat inside the van, stroking his bushy red beard. Southerners, all of them, who hadn't yet learned to mind their own business and let other people worry about their own damn afterlives.

# 14 Daryl Perkins

Daryl Perkins sat at the wheel of his Dodge Ram van as the sisters climbed down with their grocery lists. Sometimes it made him furious that he couldn't do things for himself anymore. Before that land mine near the Cambodian border, he'd been the one to help everybody else. His mother's oldest son, he'd run the Georgia hog farm after his daddy died. But this was why the good Lord put that land mine in his path. He'd been arrogant, blind to the fact that *he* was the one needing help, needing to learn to lean on his Lord.

Anita shut the back door and stood by his window with lowered eyes and clasped hands. He knew the Lord liked her submission, but he himself didn't much care for it. Even though he'd made the rules about the sisters always looking at the ground, and speaking to men in whispers, and carrying a handful of dirt in their pockets to remind them of their lowly condition. A struggle was going on in Daryl's impure heart. The devil made him admire godless women who wouldn't know submission if they ate it for dinner. Like Loretta Gebo. The most wicked people in Roches Ridge hung out at Casa Loretta, eating taco pizza and listening to John Denver sing "Rocky Mountain High" after an evening of gambling at Rescue League bingo. But that beehive of Loretta's held Daryl in thrall.

Daryl first saw Loretta behind the Formica counter in Casa Loretta right after the Church of the Holy Deliverance arrived in Roches Ridge, fleeing Georgia, like the Hebrews did Egypt, because of the child abuse charges. Despite the fact that it says right there in Proverbs 23:14: "Thou shalt beat him with the rod, and shalt deliver his soul from hell." But you couldn't tell the godless nothing.

Right from the start, Daryl ached to pull the pins and watch Loretta's hair cascade over her shoulders. He tried to stay away from Casa Loretta, but some days the devil overcame him, and he found himself sitting in that den of Satan, eating Spam burritos with the godless. Afterward, he would wear barbed wire around his chest under his shirt for a day or two. But a few weeks later, sick of his congregation of goody-goodies, he would again be seized by the urge to look at that bleached blond beehive, and he'd be out the door on his crutches so fast that even Anita's plaintive "Please don't, Daryl. You know you'll be sorry in the morning" couldn't stop him.

"Go on, shop!" he said out his window to Anita. "What're you waiting for, woman?"

She continued to gaze at the ground. "*You* know, Daryl."

Irritably he pulled his Bible from his Eisenhower jacket pocket and placed his palm on it. "I swear by our Lord God, Ruler of heaven and earth, that I won't go to Casa Loretta while you're inside shopping. Okay?"

Anita nodded, turned, and glided toward the IGA on her snow-mobile boots.

Daryl knew that Loretta Gebo's beehive, like the Israelites' golden calf, was coming between himself and his Lord. It was like Samson and Delilah in reverse: Her long hair was sapping *his* spiritual strength. And hers as well, since she spent her entire life spraying her spit curls. Daryl flipped his worn Bible to 1 John and read carefully: "He that committeth sin is of the devil. . . . The Son of God was manifested that he might destroy the works of the devil." Well, that beehive was a work of the devil if he ever saw one.

Shutting his Bible, Daryl leaned back in his seat and closed his eyes. He pictured himself as a skeleton, flesh rotted off, organs collapsed into putrefaction, bones bleached white, a hot wind swirling sand through the rib cage. Daryl often did this when under temptation, to put life on this earth in perspective.

Abruptly he sat up and gripped the steering wheel, rigid with illumination. Staying away from Loretta wasn't eradicating her allure. But this was a message from the Lord: Loretta Gebo's soul was crying out to Daryl for salvation. He must go into the Casa Loretta wilderness and rescue Loretta like a little lost lamb, and bring her on home to the Holy Deliverance fold. In order to wear the blue veil, Loretta would have to lop off that vile beehive. And if she accepted him as her earthly lord and master, like the other sisters, she'd look at him with meek obedience rather than with mocking amusement.

But how to accomplish Loretta's salvation? Daryl flipped through his Bible for inspiration. Suddenly his eyes riveted themselves on the Stop sign in front of the van. It seemed like a crazy idea, but it just might work!

Daryl flung open the door, climbed down, grabbed his aluminum crutches, and swung over to the traffic sign. Lifting one crutch tip, he traced the STAR WARS the communists at Camel's Hump Community College had spray-painted beneath the STOP. Then he traced the RAPE the lesbians from Mink Creek had added. His answer to Loretta's salvation had arrived, praise the Lord! Daryl felt the peace which passeth understanding flow through him. "The Son of God was manifested that he might destroy the works of the devil," he muttered.

Daryl spotted Loretta watching him from the Casa Loretta doorway, evil beehive leaning like the Tower of Pisa. He had sworn on his Bible not to consort with her, but that hairdo drew him like a duck to a June bug. Cringing, he pointed his crutch tip at Loretta and called, "Get thee behind me, Satan!"

Loretta put her hands on her hips and gave him a perplexed smile.

Daryl swung back to his Dodge Ram van, eyes fixed on the quotation on the yellow van that read: EXCEPT A MAN BE BORN AGAIN, HE CANNOT SEE THE KINGDOM OF GOD. JOHN 3:3. Tossing the crutches in back, he climbed into the front seat. After slamming and locking the door, he sat back panting. Loretta shrugged with a puzzled frown and skulked back into her lair of licentiousness. Daryl heaved a sigh of relief. This was the first time he had successfully turned his back on that Delilah.

Yet Loretta's beehive was just the tip of the iceberg of evil here in Roches Ridge, Daryl reflected. He reviewed the many disguises the devil was assuming. There was that Catholic priest and his concubine housekeeper. And Dr. Evans in his white lab coat, with his little brown bags of drugs. And that one-eyed commie college professor who kept coming up to Daryl outside this IGA to tell him that religion was the Valium of the people. And that Avon woman in her old green Chevy who sold paint and powder to the Roches Ridge Jezebels. And those Boudiccas down on Mink Creek, wearing crew cuts and men's clothing. And that haircutter at Mane Magnifique. He was probably gay. And his faggot farmer brother, who ran that gay hayride last autumn. Cornholers were everywhere these days, like earwigs, turning Roches Ridge into a Sodom. Homosexuality was about as wicked as you could get. In Romans 1:27 the Lord spoke of "men, who leaving the natural use of woman, burned in their lust one toward another."

One day in Vietnam, Daryl hugged a fellow whose best friend had just been blown away by a sniper. As Daryl stroked the guy's arm, he started having unclean thoughts. He hadn't been with a woman in weeks, and it felt good to have strong arms around him and a head resting against his neck. The next day the good Lord saved him from losing his soul in the name of lust by putting that land mine in his path, praise the Lord.

But it took years of bitter gall to identify the land mine as a blessing. In the beginning he cursed the light. Anita, who tended him at the VA hospital in Atlanta, agreed to marry him. One night he became so enraged at his inability to get it up that he slit open their water bed with his army bayonet and tried to drown her. Once the devil let loose of him, he was aghast, and he revived her with mouth-to-mouth resuscitation.

Anita refused to stay with him unless he agreed to attend church. And one night under a revival tent outside Marietta, Georgia, Sister Evangelica healed him to where he could stand up from his wheelchair and walk with crutches, tears pouring down his cheeks. And the next week, while he was reading about the recommended treatment of women captives in Deuteronomy, he felt a stirring in his groin that turned into an erection, praise the Lord.

The Lord restored him so he could perform His work. Since then his life had blossomed like the acacia tree in the desert. He started preaching, and soon had a congregation he named the Church of the Holy Deliverance. Anita gave birth to a baby son, whom they baptized Deuteronomy. The Lord revealed to Daryl that Deuteronomy would lead the people of the Holy Deliverance in the post-holocaust world. Next year on Deuteronomy's third birthday the world would end. But the people of the Holy Deliverance would be saved, praise the Lord. How wasn't clear yet. Maybe by spaceships from another galaxy. An old hay barn in Granite Gap was being turned into a Welcome Center for the space aliens. A satellite dish with a huge silver cross painted inside it had been installed, and a TV was being monitored twenty-four hours a day for messages from Them. Mine shafts in Granite Gap were being converted into bomb shelters as Daryl waited to receive more complete instructions from the Lord. And the people of the Holy Deliverance were going house to house in Roches Ridge, sharing their joy in the Lord, recruiting new foot soldiers for the army of God, and accepting donations. Daryl only prayed that this vile and wretched world would hold together long enough for him to make it on network TV to warn all mankind about the End. He had more to offer than Bakker, Swaggert, and Falwell put together, plus which he had a purple heart from Vietnam. But unfortunately, Anita was no Tammy Faye.

Glancing up, Daryl saw a poster in the IGA window featuring a picture of a half-naked girl. The Miss Teenage Roches Ridge Pageant. Daryl made a mental note. The church would picket the pageant, confront the godless with their lust.

Over on the green by the post office stood a tall, dark woman Daryl had never seen before. A tourist probably. She had a camera around her neck and was staring at his van. In his presalvation days he might have rolled down his window and yelled, "What're you gawking at, bitch?" But he held his tongue nowadays because he knew he was but a tool in the hands of the Master Carpenter, and that gawking was the first step along the pathway that led to holy deliverance, praise the Lord.

# 15 Wilderness Survival

Clea stood on the green, trying to make sense of what she'd just witnessed. A man in a red beard plunged down from a yellow van covered with Bible quotations and lurched on silver crutches to the Stop sign. He yelled something to Loretta Gebo in her doorway. Then he raced back to his van, crutches flashing in the sun, leapt in, and locked the door. He was now slowly beating his forehead against the steering wheel. What was going on? She felt as baffled as she had once in Kabul before the communist coup, photographing the Afghan national sport, which involved a bunch of madmen on horseback dragging a dead calf up and down a pasture.

Clea crossed the green, pausing before the three-story white frame town hall, with the date 1830 above the door. Town meetings went on in this building the first Tuesday of each March, just as they had for a hundred and fifty years. Townspeople took charge of their community affairs behind this edifice. In contrast to New York City, where a citizen controlled nothing, not even his own heat supply. Attaching her wide-angle lens, she snapped several shots of the structure, from different vantage points. It was probably constructed in a house-raising. She'd read town records and find out. Possibly one of Darius Drumm's forebears had overseen the project.

As Clea headed down the road to the Congregational church, she noticed a young woman with a mangy crew cut on the deck of the Karma Café, a pot containing a spider plant in one hand. No doubt the renegade Boudicca Loretta had mentioned. Clea would eat at her restaurant soon. She hoped Loretta wouldn't mind. But as Jared McQueen pointed out, it was too small a town to play favorites.

Clea inspected the white church looming before her. It featured a square-tiered steeple very much like a wedding cake, with a cross where the bride and groom figurines would stand. Sitting down on the exposed root of a huge old elm, she changed her film. Below her stretched a wilderness of mossy headstones. And beyond that, a field with a few rows of sunken brass markers, as anonymous as tract housing.

Almost imperceptibly, conversation at Clea's New York cocktail parties had shifted from natural childbirth classes, private school tuition, and orthodontist fees to pension plans, retirement communities, estrogen replacement therapy, bypass operations, and burial plots. Instead of discussing their futures, her friends were now talking about how many years they had left. Until about last week, Clea could have counted on one hand the people she'd known well who had died. But recently she'd have needed a computer to update her list.

As she wound the film into her camera, Clea reflected that one aspect of aging evidently involved having more friends who were dead than alive. John Galmer, for instance, whom she'd encountered last October at her twenty-fifth Cornell reunion, for the first time since her graduation. He appeared alone across a crowded beer tent in a paisley ascot and a blue blazer. His hair and eyebrows were white, and his upper back was bowed. Clea stared at him, jolted, trying to recall what had been so aphrodisiac about him. She remembered his muscled white hips pounding insistently into hers on that blue corduroy couch. But now it looked as though any pounding might land him in intensive care. If they'd built their dream cabin in the woods, she'd now be tending him whom at age twenty she'd regarded as *her* protector.

When he spotted her, he smiled and shuffled over. "I wondered if you'd be here, Clea."

"Here I am." She pecked his creased cheek.

"You look marvelous middle-aged."

"Thanks. You too."

He raised her hand to his lips. "Very gallant, Clea. But we both know I'm an old man now."

"I've seen older," said Clea.

"You've made quite a name for yourself."

"Have I?"

"So I hear."

"Well, you certainly gave me a leg up, so to speak."

He smiled. Each stood in silence, gazing at their clasped hands. Clea noticed liver spots on his, which had once stroked her so expertly. She'd insisted for three years that this man was her sole reason for living. Yet she'd managed to survive the past twenty-five without so much as a glimpse of him. What was it all about?

"I missed you when you left," he finally said. "Badly. For a long time."

"Life is strange, isn't it?" said Clea, not wanting to rummage around in their shared past. Who knew what wraiths might get stirred up?

"The closer I get to leaving it, the stranger it strikes me."

"Still married?" Clea withdrew her hand from his.

"Yes. I have four grown grandchildren. And you?"

"One husband, two children—both off at school." Kate and Theo had just left, in fact, and she had spent an afternoon in bed crying over them. She was still feeling fragile, and she didn't need this reminder of yet another loss.

"Lovers?" He grinned, and she glimpsed the rakish man she remembered.

"A few." Clea laughed. "I've always blamed that on you, John. If you hadn't shown me such a good time, I'd never have had the incentive to stray."

"That's very flattering. Thank you."

"Thank *you*." Clea felt tears flood her eyes and overflow down her cheeks. What was the point, she wanted to demand of the gods, of creating an entire world full of wonderful people whom one came to love—only to have them all eventually snatched away by time and circumstance, leaving you feeling like a fool for ever having rested content in the solace of something so insubstantial as mere mortals? To allow yourself to love someone was to ask to be devastated. And yet surely the solution wasn't not to love at all?

Galmer handed her the silk handkerchief from his blazer pocket and studied her with surprise and distress. "I'm sorry. What did I say? Is there anything I can do?"

Clea blotted her eyes. "There's nothing *any* of us can do. It's just so damn sad, John—all the people I've loved and lost."

"I know what you mean. But of course then there are all the creeps you'll never have to see again."

Clea smiled. "My life has begun to seem like a wilderness survival test. And I'm getting stripped of all external support except a box of wet matches."

"I hate to tell you, Clea, but you've just begun. Trust me, it gets more grueling yet."

"I think I've had too much beer. Or maybe it's all these faces out of my past. Please forgive me for being such a bummer, as my children would say."

"There's nothing to forgive." He stuffed his handkerchief back in his pocket. "For three years you were the light of my life, Clea. And now you're a very handsome, talented, and successful middle-aged woman. I have no complaints about you, now or ever. Only gratitude to have had those happy years with you."

Their eyes locked, and Clea felt tears gathering again. But then Turner appeared, tall, genial, and balding. Sniffling, Clea held out her hand to him. "John, this is my husband, Turner. Turner, Professor Galmer from the art department."

"Emeritus," said Galmer, holding out his hand. "Very emeritus."

Turned grinned as he shook the hand. "I've heard a lot about you."

"I can imagine," said Galmer, studying Turner with interest. They exchanged pleasantries. Then Galmer excused himself. Clea didn't see him again. The most recent alumni magazine had contained his obituary.

Lichen-dappled headstones bore the names of Marshes, Roches, Drumms, Starrs . . . almost every name still current in town. As Clea recorded this phenomenon with her camera, she wondered what it would feel like to grow up in this town and live here all your life, knowing your ultimate destination was this graveyard beneath the elms, where eight previous generations awaited your arrival. She recalled in history class at Cornell being outraged to read Moreau de St. Méry's condemnation of the American character: "Indifferent in love and friendship, [they] cling to nothing, attach themselves to nothing." *The Town That Time Forgot* was going to send such supercilious European assessments packing.

Clea came upon a stone that read BONEETA ROCHE, 1918–1984. Beside it was carved CALVIN ROCHE, 1915–. As she prepared to photograph this, a face wearing a surgical mask popped out from behind the stone. The gargantuan man wore green work clothes and carried a spray tank labeled Tri-Die, slung from his shoulder on a strap. Clea jumped back with a startled gasp. *She was kneeling in Big Mac cartons, torn earlobes throbbing with pain, watching a rat slide behind a trash can while a pistol barrel caressed her temple. . . .*

The man nodded curtly and removed his mask, to reveal an unshaven face with a weak, cruel mouth like Caligula's.

"You frightened me," explained Clea.

He looked pleased. "Just spraying the church foundation there. The dang carpenter ants is swarming wicked."

"I'm Clea Shawn. I'm new in town."

"I know. I seen you."

Clea shuddered, picturing the dilated pupils and bloodshot whites of the man in the leather ski mask. *Where* had he seen her? Through her window as she undressed, from the looks of him.

"Zeno Racine." He took her extended hand, which had begun to tremble.

Racine. Clea had just seen that name on an entire grove of bleached gravestones.

"Well, we'll see you, Mrs. Shawn," he promised. She watched him turn around and start misting the stone foundation with his tank wand. She felt ashamed to have reacted to him with such city-bred paranoia. She had jumped to conclusions from his unattractive appearance. But Zeno Racine was just an ordinary hard-working Roches Ridger.

Next to Calvin's headstone was a memorial featuring the shepherd David in bas-relief, kneeling atop a dead lion with a rescued lamb in his arms. IAN MCGRATH IV, 1980–1983. Three years old. A toddler. What had happened? A disease? An accident? Someone had placed several stuffed animals, now soggy and mildewed, on the mound. Clea felt tears gathering. Good grief, she was turning into Old Faithful. She ought to hire out as a professional mourner. Impatiently shaking off the tears, she raised her camera and began to photograph nearby headstones. It suddenly struck her that a section of *The Town That Time Forgot* could include such photos, juxtaposed to portraits of the current generation who bore those same names. A comment on the interplay between continuity and change.

By the time she'd used up her film, Clea was so elated with her new idea that she began to speculate on whether she could persuade Turner and Elke to be buried here with her in this graveyard beneath the dying elms. But Terence would no doubt insist on coming too. And Kate and Theo. And probably some of Turner's old lovers. Some of hers too, perhaps. And *their* friends and families. In the end they'd need a plot the size of a football field. And who would lie next to whom? Maybe it would be simpler if they were all cremated and their ashes mixed. But she was damned if she was going to mix her ashes with Turner's mistresses'. It was hard enough having had to learn to share him in *life*.

# 16   Des Petites Aventures

Fresh-It maintained several apartments in Paris for visiting executives, and the Shawns' was located on the fifth floor of an art nouveau building on a side street near the Bois de Boulogne. The building looked as though it had been designed by an architect on LSD. The stone doorway had been carved into crashing waves and creatures of the deep. The wrought-iron railings across the balconies resembled vines, leaves, and overripe fruit. Little Theo cried every time they had to go in or out the front entrance: He insisted some stone ravens clinging to the facade were live bats.

The apartment interior had originally been decorated in keeping with the tastes of the French bourgeoisie. The walls were covered with paisley cloth in primary shades of red, blue, and yellow. A huge bookcase filled with leather-bound French classics spanned one wall. At the long windows were sheer lace curtains, cinched into scallops across the top of the moldings. But the furniture—leather, chrome, and glass, in stark modern designs—looked as though it had been installed by the visiting Americans, desperate to halt this descent into European decadence.

Other perks included a Portuguese *bonne* and an Algerian driver for their huge Citroën sedan. Conceição, the *bonne,* lived in an appallingly cramped room on the roof. Kate and Theo took to her instantly, and were soon babbling with her in broken French about nursery school politics.

Turner was still gone much of the time, overseeing Fresh-It operations in various European capitals. When he was home, he and Clea attended endless parties at which elegantly dressed people from all over the world ate exquisite food and drank expensive champagne in luxurious settings, while conducting witty repartee in several languages. Heady stuff for a girl from Poplar Bluffs.

Children and housework taken care of, Clea began to grasp the allure of imperialism. But she didn't know how to fill all the time that had been freed up by her houseful of helpers. Conceição had previously worked for a French family, and her standards were much higher than Clea's own. In fact, Clea's instructions usually appeared to fill her with disdain. To keep away from this apartment with its alarming decor and contemptuous servant, Clea arranged shopping excursions with other imperialist wives. They prowled through the designer boutiques on the Rue du Faubourg Saint-Honoré like jackals in search of offal. All these wives seemed to have played field hockey in tartan kilts at American finishing schools. Their married lives had been spent in luxury all over the globe, and Clea was soon au courant on handicraft bargains in Dar es Salaam and croquet clubs in old Rangoon. The women made each place they'd lived in sound like the Golden Door surrounded by the South Bronx. Clea entertained herself during their interminable three-star lunches by imagining the scathing remarks Elke would make.

Being only marginally interested in her wardrobe, and inhabiting an apartment that was already crammed with unnecessary objects, Clea soon tired of shopping as a raison d'être. She began to take solitary walks through the autumn afternoons all over Paris and its suburbs, trying to decide what to do with herself. Leaving New York had entailed leaving behind her free-lance contacts, apart from a few travel editors. She would do some pieces on Paris and its environs. But to tackle the rest of the continent would mean leaving the children. And although they were enchanted with Conceição, they were in a foreign country, far from everything familiar. They needed her, especially with Turner gone most of the time. But her career would evaporate if she didn't get moving.

Clea sprawled on the chrome-and-leather sofa in the apartment salon, with its view of the tennis stadium where the French Open was played. And she studied her adored offspring with affectionate frustration as they performed gymnastics on the Oriental carpet and parquet floor. When she escaped into her office to work, she felt guilty being away from them. But when she sat on the sofa and watched them cavort, she was resentful not to be able to work without interruption. There appeared to be no route through this maternal Scylla-Charybdis.

Eventually Clea began to conclude her solitary walks at a small café on Avenue Emile Zola, near the Pont Mirabeau, where she sipped coffee while waiting for Conceição to retrieve Kate and Theo from their nursery school. In the rear of the café was a row of pinball machines that lit up and bonged in a steady din. This din mixed with American country-and-western singers wailing about lost love, lost jobs, and the consolation of hard liquor and easy sex. The café reminded her of a roadhouse in Ohio where she and her high school friends, feeling daring and dissolute, had drunk Budweiser and smoked Lucky Strikes. She came to regard the café as a haven of normality amid all the cloying Parisian charm and chic that made her feel as awkward and unsophisticated as when she first arrived in the Ivy League from Poplar Bluffs. Surrounded by the clatter of pinball machines during the day, and by the pop of champagne corks at night, her life took on a faintly schizophrenic cast.

Sometimes, at a small marble-topped table in the café, she would take out her contact sheets of Elke, from the *American Artist* portrait and from the afternoon on the Saint John terrace. The former conveyed a conventionally beautiful woman, calm and unlined; the latter, Elke herself, tough and vulnerable, tender and ironic. Studying the sheets, Clea tried to understand the difference.

She missed Elke, missed her dour perspective on world events, missed her bitchy gossip and funny stories. She even missed their tedious routine of Wednesday lunches and nightly phone calls. Occasionally, she summoned the sensation from that afternoon on Saint John of Elke's lips on hers, Elke's breasts against her own. Apart from anything else, Clea's curiosity had been thwarted. What was Elke like when she made love? Clea had scrutinized her range of facial expressions, but she had never watched her dark-blue gaze go soft and yielding, or hard and hungry.

One afternoon at the café Clea opened a letter from Elke from the afternoon mail. It was sad and quietly accusatory: "Thanks for your brisk and cheerful note. I'm glad things are going well over there. You do understand it's harder to be left than to leave? Your days are filled with exciting new sights and people and activities, whereas all I have is your absence. Your chair in my studio stays empty, and my phone doesn't ring. My world has gone flat and gray. I hate to seem an urchin scuffling among peanut shells watching your carousel, but that's how I feel and I want you to know it. I hope you're pleased with yourself. . . ."

Draining her espresso, Clea felt a certain grim satisfaction. It served Elke right for not leaving Terence to make a life with Clea and her children. Inspecting this thought, she recognized its absurdity, so she took out a pen and notebook to scribble: "I have to laugh at your plaintive letter, Elke. You think I'm on a carousel? I guess I haven't told you about the hours I spend alone in a café studying your contact sheets and trying to conjure up your every expression—from your tight-lipped smile, to your grimace of irritation, to your malevolent grin when you're dishing the gossip, to your gaze of amused tenderness. Please don't think I'm forgetting you, or ever could. However much I may sometimes want to. You have burned your brand indelibly into my soul. I am yours, even though you don't know what to do with me, or I with you."

Why had she thought she needed Elke to be daddy for Kate and Theo anyhow? Clea wondered. Their real daddy was never around. Clea supported herself financially. She could have stayed in New York and taken Elke as her lover. Elke could have stayed with Terence or not. What did it matter? Why this conviction of Clea's that she needed a partner? Partly because parenting was the most demanding job she'd ever done, she supposed, drawing on reserves of patience and responsibility she never even knew she possessed. She needed someone to worry with. Yet what sane adult would be willing to take that on without some biological stake in the outcome?

A heavyset man with a full mustache and bushy sideburns was sitting at the next table, also writing. He wore a double-breasted pinstriped suit jacket and a tie with a loosened Windsor knot. Looking up, he caught Clea watching him. Smiling, he toasted her with his coffee cup. She nodded almost imperceptibly.

The next afternoon this man was writing at the same table when Clea arrived. Taking out her notebook, she jotted down some thoughts that had occurred to her as she strolled through the Montparnasse cemetery past Baudelaire's grave. Rather than several travel pieces on Paris, she could do an entire book. But the market was glutted with guides—Berlitz, Fodor's, Baedecker's, Michelin. She needed a gimmick.

Doodling in her notebook the next day in search of a gimmick, Clea found herself instead sketching Elke's profile. She paused to study her version of the high cheekbones, wispy hair, and dark, penetrating eyes. Jesus, you'd think she was in junior high school, lovelorn over a football star. At this rate she'd soon have no career left to worry about. She scribbled out the sketch.

Her sideburned neighbor arrived at his usual table, carrying his briefcase. An elderly couple from Dayton already occupied it. Glancing around and finding all the tables occupied, he gestured to the empty chair beside Clea. "Do you object?" he asked in English with a heavy French accent.

Clea forced herself to smile and removed her raincoat from the extra chair. Each wrote and sipped coffee in silence. When her second cup arrived, he insisted on paying for it. "Please," he said. "For consenting for me to share your table."

The next day, although his own table was free, the man again asked to sit with Clea, and she reluctantly agreed. As she pretended to make notes, she appraised the situation. She was unable to get on with her work because she was preoccupied with Elke. In the past she'd recovered from one person only by replacing the person with someone else—Turner with John Galmer, John with Turner, Turner with Elke. This Frenchman beside her with the sideburns halfway across his jaw, or her Algerian driver, or any of several men who eyed her speculatively at parties, would do. Why not immerse herself in this Paris adventure and stop clinging to a love with Elke she couldn't have? Yes, she was in love with Elke. But she could supplant her with someone of the proper gender if she decided to.

On the other hand, Clea reflected, she'd not had success with adultery. She had stared at the steel I-beam across the ceiling throughout her sessions with Allan Barkham. And she'd fled from Elke like Odysseus from the sirens. But this was 1970, and her fellow Americans seemed to believe that whatever they didn't like about the world or about their own personalities could be changed by a demonstration or a weekend workshop. Perhaps she could organize her own private encounter group here in exile.

Clea eyed her dark neighbor, who was scowling and scratching out a line on his legal pad. Could she take this fellow to bed and not become a maniac about it? Would that erase the image of Elke that burned in her heart like a child's night-light? If she could, it occurred to her she'd then be ready for Elke. But if she developed the ability to take sex or leave it, why take it, with all the attendant risks and turmoil? If she really mastered the art of unfaithfulness, though, there'd *be* no turmoil. In other words, if she could manage not to want Elke, she could then have her. Confused, she rested her chin on her fist and gazed across the sidewalk at an accordion player in a tattered U.S. army uniform beneath a chestnut tree.

"How do you say in America, a wooden nickel for your thoughts?"

Laughing, Clea looked over at her neighbor in his suit jacket and loosened tie. "A penny," she said, uncertain if the humor was deliberate. "A penny for your thoughts."

Grégoire was the Paris correspondent for a Brussels newspaper. He wrote his stories in this café rather than at his office because he felt the flavor of the city more keenly here. Clea learned this through a combination of his florid English and her schoolgirl French. Her French vocabulary from Cornell included obscure existentialist terminology, but she was hard-pressed when it came to asking for a toilet. His extensive English vocabulary resulted from playing Scrabble with a dictionary, and often included words more formal than everyday usage.

To Clea's relief, there were no immediate bedward maneuvers on either side. Instead Grégoire took an interest in her struggle to find a gimmick for her travel guide. In his free time during the ensuing weeks he escorted Clea to all the standard tourist sites. Then to sites off the tourist trail. Twice she took photos he was able to sell to his newspaper. He mentioned a wife in Brussels, with whom he played Scrabble, so Clea was not certain their connection would become physical. Which suited her fine, since she was beginning to find a route back into her work and away from missing Elke.

Elke in a letter urged Clea to go see Käthe Kollwitz's Memorial to the Fallen at the German World War I cemetery in western Flanders where her uncle was buried. Elke had been there with her parents as a child and vaguely recalled the imposing granite sculptures. She asked Clea to take some photos if she went. So Clea dutifully enlisted Grégoire to drive her up there in his Renault.

As they passed through the rolling pastoral landscape north of Paris, Grégoire informed her that 250,000 men had died during World War I near the small town to which they were headed. To say nothing of other towns and other wars.

"These fields of white crosses are our cash crop," said Grégoire with a grim smile. "We fertilize them with flesh, and irrigate them with blood. The tourists, they come from all over the world to find the graves of their men. They buy meals and lodging. Lace and chocolates. We Belgians are clever capitalists, yes?"

As they raced through gently undulating fields of hops, demarcated by hedges and rows of poplars, Clea tried to picture the vista slashed with trenches and stitched with rusted barbed wire. Swarming with soldiers who were lonely, horny, hungry, wet, sick, exhausted, cold, afraid. Each man some distant woman's son, husband, lover. She struggled to visualize curtains of smoke and whining shells from booming artillery. But her imagination, usually in overdrive, stalled out. Her eyes kept fixing themselves on quaint country cottages draped with clematis vines and placid herds of ruminating cattle partially veiled by wisps of drifting ground fog.

Grégoire parked in a gravel lay-by. He and Clea walked through an opening in a thick hedge. Spread out before them across the Flanders plain were tens of thousands of white crosses, in orderly rows that belied the chaos of the deaths. And watching over the graves, mourning on separate pedestals, knelt a mother and father of blue-gray stone, slightly larger than life. The mother's shawl flowed down her body like a river of tears. The father, dressed in a suit, wrapped his arms tightly across his chest in a futile effort to embrace and comfort his own numb heart.

Clea gazed at these grieving parents for a long time while larks sang in the hedgerow. The ocher turf beneath her feet was damp and squishy. Consulting Elke's letter, she and Grégoire walked silently down the rows of bland white crosses until they found the uncle's. A wild rosebush sprinkled with vermilion blooms grew atop his grave, one tendril winding itself up his cross. Clea found herself unable to take hold of the camera that hung from her neck. Instead she groped beside her for Grégoire's hand.

As they lunched at a redbrick café on the town square around which the 250,000 had been killed, Clea told Grégoire Elke's history in a low, stunned voice.

Shrugging, Grégoire replied, "Eight and a half million were killed during World War One. Forty million during World War Two. It would be an unusual European who was not touched by the carnage." He described centuries of invasion of his homeland by Normans, Spaniards, Germans. He told about his father and brother, who died in World War II, the looting of his family home, his own adolescence spent in uniform, dodging bullets.

He sounded so business-as-usual that Clea was unable to reply for some time. Finally she said, "But I just don't get it, Grégoire. Why do men seem to have this need to live in tents and kill each other?"

Pursing his lips, he replied, "Perhaps if you were circumcised as a baby without an anesthetic, you would want to kill too."

Clea gave a weak laugh. "But I thought you Europeans prided yourselves on being so civilized."

"Certainly. Which requires us to stockpile our uncivilized behavior for our nasty little wars, *n'est-ce pas?*"

As they hurtled back toward Paris, Grégoire pointed out the faint zigzag remains of a trench, and a sink hole left by a mine, and a pile of rusted shell casings in the corner of a meadow. Clea felt longing for Elke shoot through her like a bolt into a lock. She hadn't understood until now that while she herself was playing Kick the Can along the Ohio, Elke was darting like a hunted rabbit through woods and fields infested with men trained to murder each other.

Grégoire pulled up to the curb outside "their" café. The burglar alarm on a Peugeot across the street was whooping, though no burglar was in sight. Still gripping the steering wheel, not looking at her, Grégoire said in a kind voice, "Clea, you have not spoken for eighty kilometers. You are sad about your German friend in America, yes?"

Clea nodded numbly.

"Perhaps it would assuage your distress to arouse some ardor?" He spoke as offhandedly as though proposing a meal.

Clea studied her hands, which were folded in her lap, and said nothing. Several people leaned out of apartment windows to observe the whooping Peugeot, whose driver had not yet appeared.

"Your wife doesn't mind?" Clea finally asked.

Grégoire shrugged. "Marriage, it becomes so, how you say, ener-vative, *sans des petites aventures, n'est-ce pas?*" A teenage boy came out the door of an apartment building, an egg in each hand. He hurled them against the front windshield of the Peugeot while the people in the windows applauded.

Clea realized she didn't mind being defined as an *aventure*. She didn't care how Grégoire regarded her. Right now all she wanted was hard flesh pounding into hers, generating heat and light, dispelling those rolling acres of deliberate death. And Turner was in Oslo.

Clea and Grégoire threw off their clothes in a small room on the second floor of a nearby pension. Clea greedily clutched handfuls of the dark curly hair all over Grégoire's back as she pulled him down on top of her on the sagging bed.

Afterward, Grégoire went out to their café for a bottle of Pernod, while Clea lay among the chaotic bedding and studied the pressed-tin ceiling. Her grief and horror had given way to sorrow. She felt pro-foundly unfaithful. But to Elke, not to Turner. The emotions of this day had all concerned Elke, yet Clea had discharged them with an amiable stranger. Still, Elke wasn't here, was she?

While she and Grégoire sipped Pernod and smoked cigarettes, the accordionist from their café began to play in the street. Grégoire sang softly in French, ". . . the paradise in bed, remember that instead, in-stead of all these sorrows. So rest here in my arms, love, for we still hold tomorrow. . . ."

"How romantic," said Clea with a laugh. "Where did he come from?"

Grégoire rubbed his thumb and fingers together to indicate he'd procured him with francs.

Clea resolutely put away Elke's contact sheets and immersed her-self in those of Grégoire posing before French monuments, châteaux, and battlefields. The tourist trail and the café beside the chestnut trees were abandoned for the tin-ceilinged room in the pension, where they met a couple of afternoons a week before the children got out of school, to move together in time to accordion renditions of Jacques Brel from the street. Turner would return from Venice or Stockholm to find her languid and distracted, deeply uninterested in the state of his libido.

Finally one night after dinner, as they sat reading on the chrome-and-leather couch in the paisley salon, he asked, "Clea, are you seeing someone else?"

Recalling Elke's saying she didn't ask Terence what he did when away from her, she looked up from her edition of Pascal to reply, "But, darling, we're three thousand miles from Turtle Bay."

His face turned incandescent to the roots of his thinning blond hair. "Our agreement included anyplace we're living as a family."

"This is the first I've heard of this codicil," said Clea. "What about that young woman with the pouty lips who hangs around outside our entry when you're away? She makes nasty faces at the children and me when we go by."

Turner's eyes shifted from hers to the tropical orchids on the glass coffee table. "I don't know what you're talking about."

"Uh huh. Well, then, I don't know what *you're* talking about." As she concealed herself behind her book, she realized she was making progress with this adultery business. It simply wasn't necessary to discuss, explain, and justify your every movement. In fact, it was immature to do so.

In the meantime, love struck. It became clear to Clea that she and Grégoire should be a photojournalistic team, she taking the pictures and he writing the copy. One afternoon beneath the tin ceiling, her hands stroking Grégoire's buttocks as they pushed into her with delicious precision and restraint, Clea whispered in his ear her growing wish to forfeit family, citizenship, and native tongue. Her desire to learn Scrabble.

Grégoire looked as though she'd just offered him a stale baguette. He paused, pulled out of her, and jumped to his feet, explaining that he had to go to the café for more Pernod. After throwing on his clothes, he leaned down to kiss her gingerly and tell her never to forget that he "relished her resplendent anatomy."

When he hadn't returned in a half hour, Clea got up, parted the blinds, and looked down to the curb. In the spot where Grégoire had parked his Renault stood the accordion player in his tattered army uniform, looking up at the window for his customary francs.

The lighting of the streetlamp out the window finally convinced Clea that Grégoire would not be back. Elke was evidently not the only European who found her midwestern earnestness distasteful. Clea sank down on the crumpled bed and whispered in her fractured French the lyrics to the song the accordion was playing: "Don't leave me. I will no longer cry or speak. . . . *Ne me quitte pas, ne me quitte pas, ne me quitte pas.*"

Theo tried to console his mother during the weeks of numb despair that followed by standing in her lap on the chrome-and-leather sofa and transferring hard candies from his mouth into hers. She realized she had accomplished her goal: She was so busy suffering over Grégoire that the pain of Elke and the horror of Flanders faded into the background.

Turner also consoled her whenever he was home, assuring her she was infinitely gorgeous and desirable. Fulfilling his role of party chairman, he cajoled her into dressing up so he could drag her off to dinners and cocktail parties with the international business community. At one such function Clea realized she'd at last found her gimmick. Turner called her proposed book "France on $2,000 a Day."

In a weak postcoital moment that same night, Clea, fogged from Dom Pérignon, agreed to extend their marital Maginot Line to a forty-mile radius around any spot where they were living together.

"But you don't seem to really get the hang of infidelity, Clea." Turner, laughing, sat up in bed in their room overlooking the tennis stadium to put on his pajama top. "You've been in agony for weeks over this last guy, whoever he was."

"I know. I think I need a coach."

"I'll be your coach. I'll teach you how to be unfaithful to me."

"Why does this feel strange?" Clea laughed, laying her head on his chest and entwining her long legs with his.

"Lesson number one," continued Turner. "If you're just passing through, you can't afford to give your heart away. Because you'll need it for the rest of your trip."

Clea smiled at him in the wavering light from the candle on the night table. "You've got a big challenge ahead of you, Turner. I think I may be adultery-impaired."

# 17 Jared McQueen

Jared McQueen's ambition was to bring punk to Roches Ridge. He'd watched it sweep Albany when he was working at the Yankee Clipper. You had to convince only one influential citizen. Then everyone wanted spikes. His target person was Loretta Gebo. She had high visibility and was a trendsetter. This week she was serving Spam burritos as her South of the Border Special, and next week everyone in town would be making them at home. And Loretta needed a new hairstyle. She'd had that beehive since the Stone Age. He remembered marveling over it when he was in junior high.

Jared leaned forward to study himself in the mirror behind the styling chair in Mane Magnifique. He picked at the patch of turquoise spikes to one side of his crown. It wasn't as though he asked anything of customers that he didn't embrace himself. He rubbed the stubble on his chin. He shaved each day in late afternoon, stroking down instead of up. By morning it was just about right. Shaving off his beard and mustache a year ago had been a struggle. There was mystery to a beard. But beards were out. And Jared had to admit that stubble looked good on him.

That woman he'd just met at Casa Loretta, who bought Calvin Roche's house—would she come to him, or go to Albany? There was nothing in Albany hair care that she couldn't get right here at Mane Magnifique. She had a classy New York City cut, but he longed to get his hands on her gray. How would *she* look with spikes?

Jared began sweeping up the clippings from Bethany Wagner, who sat under the dryer setting her new body wave. She pretended to read *Redbook* but was actually gazing at him as he bent and stooped in his tight suede jeans. Oh, he supposed he was a pretty good-looking guy. Both men and women had whistled at him in the streets of Albany. But those looks had gotten him into a lot of trouble. With Regine, for one. Regine hired him right off the street as a receptionist for the Yankee Clipper upon his arrival in Albany with no money, no training, only the dream of being the best hairstylist Roches Ridge had ever produced.

At Mink Valley High, while the other boys played sports, Jared discussed outfits and makeup with the cheerleaders. He got into fistfights over his manhood on a weekly basis. (The irony was that his oldest brother, Gordon, was the one who turned out gay.) The other boys could never understand why Jared got more action than anyone else. More than he actually wanted. But fucking was a small enough price to be allowed to rearrange the girls' hair afterward.

After graduation Jared realized he had to go to a big city to gain experience in the hair trade, and he picked Albany because it was close to home. But he should have paid attention to his own alarm when

Regine, who had a magenta pompadour, said upon hiring him, rolling his eyes, "It's 'at times like this I wish I had a casting couch." And when Regine took him to a party that weekend at which the women were spiking the volleyball over the backyard net while the men copied each other's recipes in the kitchen.

He stood behind Regine and watched him cut, color, set, and comb out. Eventually Regine let him shampoo, and Jared felt as though he'd died and gone to heaven. When Regine insisted on sending him to the Albany College of Cosmetology at night, Jared knew his dream was coming true. Alone at night in his rented room after class, Jared reviewed the plot of *Shampoo*, with himself in Warren Beatty's role, wielding a dryer like a phallus.

Unfortunately, Regine was falling in love with him. Jared should have foreseen this. Regine made no bones about the fact that he was gay, and he often rolled his eyes in a swoon when he saw Jared leaving work in his leather bomber jacket. The Yankee Clipper staff wore sailor bell bottoms and skin-tight T-shirts, and sometimes Regine stroked Jared's butt as he checked the trousers during morning inspection.

After Jared had his own chair at the Yankee Clipper, Regine invited him out to dinner after work. Over stir-fried cashew chicken, Regine explained how he knew from the first moment he saw Jared, standing before the reception desk in his leather jacket, that Jared was gay too, and needed time to understand this about himself.

Jared replied, "Of course I love you, Regine. You've been so good to me. But I'm straight as the center line down the Northway."

Regine looked haggard in the candlelight. The quiet corner table, the expensive wine, the fresh rose, the linen tablecloth—dinner wasn't supposed to be taking this turn. Regine rearranged his face to convey amused indifference. "Suit yourself, dear. But I'll be needing your chair next week. I've got a new stylist arriving from Akron."

Jared's mouth dropped open. "But, Regine . . ."

"Surely you don't expect me to do a Jackie Kennedy mourning over you, Jared?"

"But I thought we were friends."

"Friendship is two-way. What's in this for me?"

"Well . . . but . . . I don't know, Regine. I'm sorry if I led you on."

"How about *dragged*, darling?"

Ishtar said Jared's parting with Regine was meant to be, and was part of the cosmic scheme that brought him home to Roches Ridge. And the catastrophe did appear now to be a blessing in disguise, because Mane Magnifique was the shop he'd always imagined—with complimentary Chablis and baroque concertos. Just the name had taken months to perfect, while that ugly Earl's Barbershop sign and striped pole outside scared off potential customers from Alpine Glen.

As Jared removed Bethany's curlers, he wondered if he had in fact led Regine on. He couldn't help it if he was friendly and good-looking. People were always coming on to him. Wasn't that their problem? He'd had only one serious girlfriend, Estelle, in Albany. He orchestrated their dates—what each would wear, eat, do, and say. During lovemaking he would sometimes halt to rearrange Estelle's cream-colored limbs on the mauve sheets, the way Ishtar arranged food on a plate. After three months Estelle said, "Let's face it, Jared: we're both in love with you." And a few days later he received in the mail the yellow Oral-B toothbrush he'd been leaving at her apartment.

He sometimes had affairs with women who picked him up in Albany singles bars. In the end they always let him punk their hair. Other men might vanish leaving swelling bellies, but he left behind indigo spikes.

These Xerox types, he thought as he combed out Bethany's perm. They all wanted the same hairdo, the Julie Andrews Special, he called it. They lived in identical houses in Colonial Manor Estates. They drove Saabs or BMWs or Volvos. Must be why they married men who manufactured copy machines. Maybe Alvin Jacobs at Camel's Hump Community College was right, and that factory ought to be torched.

"There!" He handed Bethany the mirror and twisted the chair so she could see the back of her head. Bethany maintained she'd once been Ms. Empire State. Buried beneath her current conformity beat the heart of a rebel. Maybe spikes were in her future.

"Perfect." As Bethany handed back the mirror, her arm brushed the front of Jared's suede jeans.

While Bethany wrote a check, Jared gestured to the hair care products behind him. "Anything else you need today, Bethany?"

She paused to look at him. "Is that a firm offer, so to speak?"

Jared laughed nervously and patted her shoulder, more muscled than it appeared. "Bethany, you're *bad*."

"Not nearly as bad as I'd like to be," she murmured. "Seriously, Jared, how about it?"

"Bethany, I'm trying to run a business."

"All night too?" She gripped his forearm as though it were a barbell.

Wrenching his arm away, Jared knocked a plastic bottle off the counter. He bent over and picked it up. "Ah, saved by the gel," he announced, handing it to Bethany with a winning smile and ushering her to the door.

Now, was that *his* fault, he wondered, as he watched Bethany climb into her silver Saab Turbo. He had such an odd relationship with people, touching their hair, studying their faces, and hearing their deepest secrets for an hour a month. Once business picked up, he'd hire an associate and switch over clients like Bethany Wagner. If she didn't bench press him into submission first.

Across the green he spotted Angela McGrath strumming her harp in her front window. Angela could benefit from a visit to Mane Magnifique almost as much as Maureen Murphy at the post office, with her Scotch-taped bangs. Sometimes he thought about sending them both anonymous gift certificates. Angela, stringy white-blond hair to her waist, appeared to be doing a Rapunzel trip. He'd like to get her alone in a room with a can of mousse.

Daryl Perkins' harem in their flowing blue head scarves, ankle-length dresses, and snowmobile boots came out of the IGA carrying grocery bags. They climbed into Daryl's yellow van, which was covered with cheery slogans like: THERE SHALL BE FAMINES, AND PESTILENCES, AND EARTHQUAKES. MATT. 24:7. Jared felt lost at sea looking at those be-scarfed women, unable to comprehend someone willing to cover up her single most compelling asset.

# 18  Ishtar

Ishtar was kneeling on the wooden deck of the Karma Café repotting a spider plant, in a hurry because she had to bake a tofu cheese-cake. Customers would be arriving by the carload in a couple of hours. She attributed her success to the three T's of whole-food cookery— Tofu, Tahini, and Tamari.

Although the café ceiling was already filled with spider plants, Ishtar was careful to pot each segment as she split clumps. Like cows in India, you never knew which division might be a relative in retrograde. Sometimes she rued the day she took that first cutting from Starshine. She hadn't realized caring for it would become her life's work. But it beat caring for Starshine. She did this swaggering bull dyke number, but get her alone on a futon, and she went all passive like a beached Portuguese man-of-war. From guru to goo-goo.

Ishtar first heard about the Boudiccas when, still known as Barbara Carmichael, she was waiting tables in Santa Rosa. During rebirthing she kept getting blocked in the birth canal. The rebirther suggested this had to do with being adopted, and he recommended she contact her real mother. So she wrote the Iowa City agency from which her adoptive parents had procured her. They said they'd keep her name on file in case her real mother contacted them. This unleashed a storm of pain and anger in Barbara toward the unknown woman who had abandoned her and not even tried to track her down since. Reading in *Amazon Quarterly* about the Boudicca Healing Intensives on woman-owned land, she hitched to Vermont in five days, her possessions in a Kelty pack.

At the Vermont border her ride left her off at a rest area. After brushing her teeth in the rest room sink, she watched a lanky man in camouflage pants extract some Coke cans from a trash basket on the sidewalk. He strolled over to a blue tow truck. Noticing her, he called, "Heading north, are you? Hop in."

As she did so, she said, "I see your bumper sticker—grass, gas, or ass—and I'll tell you right now it's got to be grass, 'cause I got no money and I'm a lesbian."

The man grinned. "I got no objection to lesbians."

"Maybe not, but *I've* got objections to making it with men. So if that's a problem, I'd better wait for another ride."

"Relax. Grass is cool. I got a woman waiting for me at home."

"Lucky you." Ishtar removed a Thai stick from her pack, then planted the pack between her feet. As the truck picked up speed, she rolled a joint.

After two joints, smoke was swirling through the cab, and she and Ray were gossiping like old pals. The center line disappearing behind them in the dark was exercising its hypnotic effect, loosening limbs and tongues. They'd never see each other again. They could say anything.

"I'm gonna tell you something, Barbara, something I ain't never told nobody before."

"I'd be honored, Ray. Shoot."

"Barbara, I've always wanted to be a lesbian. Do you think that's weird?"

"Well, it's probably not normal. But do you know anybody who is? I'm not the right person to ask about weird."

"So now you think I'm disgusting?"

"No, I don't. I can understand wanting to be a lesbian. It's wonderful. I wish you could be too." This was before she'd read Shirley MacLaine and realized that he probably would be, or had been.

"There's this bunch of dykes on a creek below my house. My brother Orlon runs trap lines down there, and I'm always offering to check them. So I can set up in them woods and watch those girls go at it."

Barbara studied him with glazed eyes.

"Well, they run around half naked. And they're always going off into the bushes with each other."

Barbara said nothing.

"I don't see that it's doing no harm if I just watch and appreciate."

"Where did you say you live?" asked Barbara uneasily.

"Roches Ridge." Ray glanced at her.

"That's where I'm headed. Roches Ridge. Down on that creek with those dykes."

"Jeezum crow."

Both giggled nervously. They looked at each other in the darkened cab, then began to howl with laughter, the truck careening from lane to lane.

"Looks like we're friends for life, Ray. I won't tell them, but you've got to stop it. Do you know what they'd do if they caught you? Those women are no joke."

"I've thought about that. The idea of them catching me is pretty darn exciting."

"Ray, if I ever see you out there spying, you're in deep shit. My loyalty to a man I've known for two hours can extend only so far. However much I may appreciate the ride."

Ray let her off beside his house, a huge rambling place with an auto graveyard behind it and a violet bug light to one side. As Barbara passed a shack out back, she smelled a disgusting stench. Light came from the windows, but the panes were painted over. Then she heard howling, chanting, and drumming from the valley below.

Descending the cliff, she could see a campfire through the trees, surrounded by several dozen naked women, who were pounding African drums and dripping with sweat. Throwing off her clothes, Barbara sat down. A dried gourd was passed to her, and the circle fell silent.

Barbara looked at the rattle. "I've come from California for the Healing Intensive."

Everyone opened her eyes to inspect Barbara. "It was last month," replied a woman with Buddha-like folds of flesh around her middle and a luminescent blue-and-yellow parrot on her shoulder. Starshine, the big cheese herself, Ishtar soon learned.

"But the *Amazon Quarterly* said this week."

"Sorry. A typo."

"Power to the People!" shrieked the parrot.

"This is Sexuality Week," said Starshine. "We're doing a sweat, then a masturbation circle."

"Whatever," sighed Barbara. She'd been counting on some healing. Her wounds of maternal abandonment were still running sores.

"Make Love, Not War!" screamed the parrot.

"So what's your preference?" asked Starshine.

Barbara looked at her blankly.

"The rattle. You're holding it. You can describe a fantasy, sing a song, or pass it on. Whatever you want."

"I guess I'll pass till I get the hang of it." Barbara handed the rattle to the next woman, Morning Glory as it turned out, who wore a red bandanna headband and a spiral little-toe ring. She asked for the drumming to resume.

During the masturbation circle Barbara fell in love. The other women were self-conscious or matter-of-fact, but Morning Glory really got into it, eyes closing and mouth falling open. Barbara wanted to know her better, so she became Ishtar.

Ishtar came to Vermont on a typo, and stayed out of lust. Sometimes she wondered if the whole thing wasn't one big mistake. When Starshine became aware of the attraction between Ishtar and Morning Glory, she canceled their nights of sleeping together, maintaining that the privatization of their emotions was interrupting group flow. Ishtar tried to accept this, but like a tamed wolf, she'd tasted blood and would have to be shot before she'd give it up. Morning Glory, however, was more docile and kept Ishtar at a distance.

Until one night on forest patrol. Ishtar and Morning Glory went into the barn at the top of the cliff and smoked a joint Ishtar had been hiding from Starshine's inspections in her parka lining. The scent of hay mixed with the acrid marijuana smoke. Ishtar puffed out her cheeks and mimicked Starshine, talking about her superior spiritual incandescence. Morning Glory was both horrified and titillated. Then Ishtar reached over and unbuttoned Morning Glory's flannel shirt. Morning

Glory gasped, "We aren't allowed to do this, Ishtar. Besides, it's my night with Foxglove."

"Who says we aren't?"

"You know the rules."

"Fuck the rules. Run away with me, Morning Glory."

Morning Glory said she would, and Ishtar kissed her little-toe ring and worked up, as the old barn swayed and creaked around them.

But when it came down to packing up and walking away from Mink Creek, Morning Glory backed out.

Meanwhile, Ishtar was having trouble with the Boudicca menu. Because of their refusal to harm any living creature, they were eating a lot of peanut butter and crackers. And because of a chronic money shortage, they were raiding the Dumpster behind Starr's IGA for spoiled produce. This deprivation no doubt explained why Ishtar opened a restaurant after her escape. Which came soon after she read Shirley MacLaine's *Out on a Limb* and realized that by hating men, Boudiccas were storing up some bad karma and might have to return in future lives as rapists.

Starshine instantly announced at a teaching session in the house trailer that she, too, was writing a book, *The Lesbian Book of the Dead*, about how to negotiate one's transition to a higher soul plane, where you could be absorbed into the goddesshead of pure female energy. Ishtar suggested that Starshine title it *Out of Her Tree*. Starshine proceeded to beat her up with karate kicks and punches.

The next day Ishtar was gone. And since then she'd seen Morning Glory only during Boudicca actions outside her café. While the others hassled Ishtar's bewildered customers, Morning Glory in her red bandanna headband would gaze at Ishtar with fear and longing. But it seemed unlikely she'd leave Mink Creek. Ishtar was heartsick. She could rejoin the Boudiccas, but it would be torture to put up with Starshine's guru nonsense.

Ishtar sometimes saw Starshine around town, dressed in a suit, heels, and panty hose, on her way to talk to Alvin Jacobs' Amerikan Gulag class at Camel's Hump Community College about gay rights, or to Conrad Bohring at Mink Valley Savings and Loan about her investments. Sometimes, with a guilty glance around the green, she'd duck into Casa Loretta for a Ridgeburger or a Spam burrito, while her troops in the valley ate peanut butter and crackers. Once when Ishtar ran into Starshine emerging from a taco pizza debauch, she asked, "Well, well. And how's the Imelda Marcos of Mink Creek?"

Ishtar picked up a spider plant, carried it inside, and hung it near the ceiling amid hundreds of identical plants. En route to the kitchen, Ishtar glanced at the poster on one wall that listed her past lives from 10,000 B.C. to the present. So far she'd identified twenty-six. Shirley MacLaine got in touch with hers via acupuncture with golden needles, but Ishtar had had to make do with sterilized straight pins. Some of her prior lives seemed to involve a place very much like Roches Ridge, and people who lived around her now—Father Flanagan, for instance, the Catholic priest in his tight white collar and gold Pro-Life lapel pin, who came to the Karma Café late at night and rambled on about his failings as though in a confessional. And his housekeeper, Theresa, in her funky forties housedresses with padded shoulders, and her veiled straw pillbox hat decorated with wooden cherries, with whom Ishtar sometimes chatted on the green.

At some point she must have been a vegetable, Ishtar reflected, judging from her allegiance to spider plants in this life. Before Calvin Roche left for Texas, she introduced him to reincarnation, explaining how customers who loved sushi had probably been sharks. Pointing to Ishtar's poster, Calvin asked, "But why stop at 10,000 B.C.?"

"You have to draw the line somewhere," she replied. But it was a good point. Where *did* you draw the line? When she wrote to ask Shirley, she received a mimeographed form wishing her well on her own inner journey toward the light. But if she didn't work through her obsession with past lives this time around, she might get to come back as Shirley MacLaine.

Looking out her front window, Ishtar saw a tall woman in a green lumberjack shirt, camera around her neck, walking up from the cemetery behind the Congregational church. This was probably the most striking woman Ishtar had ever seen in Roches Ridge, with streaks of silver through her dark hair and a slim but buxom body. Lest Ishtar in her current state of unwilling celibacy forget why she bothered being embodied this time around. Holy crow, who was she?

# 19   The Outer Parameters of Celibacy

Clea stood in the field behind her stone house, holding a green garbage bag, which was nearly filled with Lone Star ale bottles, Banquet Dinner trays, and Wonder Bread wrappers. But it was just the beginning. This afternoon she'd discovered several generations of trash beneath this stratum—bales of rusted barbed wire, rotting shoes, bald tires, smashed sap buckets and milk cans, bent pitchfork prongs, an obsolete plow, a broken floral chamber pot, cans of petrified paint, entire place settings of shattered china. All this was bound together like a tapestry by tangled wild grapevines and Virginia creeper. The truth was, Clea's sloping backyard, site of her proposed perennial gardens, was an Early American garbage dump. It had taken Roches two hundred years to assemble this moraine. There was no reason to expect it would take Clea and her heirs any less time to disassemble it. If she were an archaeologist, she'd be having a field day. But she wasn't.

Sighing, she resolutely pictured the gardens and orchard at Sissinghurst. She'd seen photos of the place when Vita Sackville-West purchased it, and Roche House was luxurious by comparison. Yet after many years of drudgery and large infusions of cash, Sissinghurst was now a showcase. She had to quell her impatience and accept that her renovation would take however long it took.

Clea resumed tossing junk into her garbage bag, working furiously, trying to exhaust herself. Celibacy was one aspect of life in Roches Ridge she hadn't allowed for. She felt anxious and irritable, in heat and on the prowl. On the one hand, she was grateful for her energy. It had allowed her to live and work all over the world. It had yielded three books, two wonderful children, several important friendships, and a satisfying twenty-two-year marriage. If the stone house behind her evolved into anything other than a ruin, it would all be owing to this energy. But she also cursed her energy, which had propelled her into complicated emotional messes her entire adulthood. Whenever she lacked a focus for it, a book or some other project, it grabbed her by the scruff of her neck and dragged her into adventures that often seemed pointless in retrospect.

One night in Paris, for instance, after Grégoire had left her. Conceição had put the children to bed, cleaned up from dinner, and gone to her room on the roof. Turner had phoned from his Frankfurt hotel before going to dinner. With a woman, Clea suspected, because of his hearty bonhomie. When she gave a couple of plaintive hints that she got the picture, Turner said sweetly but firmly, "Clea, you know you're the only woman I love. But no one gets out of this life alive. So let's enjoy it while we've got it. Together and apart."

As she hung up, Clea knew this made sense. It was the cornerstone of their long-distance marriage. She didn't want Turner to be lonely and miserable. But why did she feel as though Conceição had just taken a slice off her heart to sauté for dinner? Still holding the phone receiver, she wondered whom Grégoire was playing Scrabble with these days. If she'd had his number, she'd have called him, promising not to lapse into sweet nothings again if he'd just meet her for an hour at their pension.

She dialed Elke. It was midafternoon in New York, and Elke had just finished working. Together they struggled to bridge the three thousand miles of icy water with an hour of details about daily life that anyone else would have found soporific. Yet Clea avoided mentioning the affair with Grégoire, unable to gauge Elke's reaction without seeing her face. She wanted neither to hurt Elke nor to lose her. And after all, Elke herself had set this example of clandestineness, not telling Clea about her extracurricular dalliances until Saint John. Perhaps some matters were best kept to yourself.

No doubt sensing some important omission, Elke became withdrawn and irritable. Trying and failing to woo her back, Clea turned guilty and annoyed. As Clea's francs poured into the coffers of the central telephone exchange like quarters from a slot machine, she and Elke argued bitterly over the American role in NATO.

"Elke," Clea finally said.

"Yes?" she snapped.

"I don't give a shit about NATO. I just miss you. That's all. A plain stark simple human fact: I miss you."

"I miss you too, Clea," said Elke in a muffled voice.

They hung up, agreeing to stick to letters except when Clea could use Turner's office phone, since what it cost to disagree about NATO would have financed a flight to New York. Walking to the window, Clea parted the hideous lace curtains and gazed out at the floodlit tennis stadium, where a match was under way. Down in the street, a woman in an evening gown and furs and a man in a tux emerged from an art deco building opposite to climb into a Bentley. Clea reflected that she was alone in an alien culture, deprived of Elke, trapped here by her love for the two young children who lay asleep in their beds. And by her inexplicable love for their roving father.

This wasn't an unusual situation. It was a wife's job to generate from her vitals the current that created and sustained life. To allow her loved ones to take nourishment from her like birds at a feeder. But who performed this function for the wife? Traditionally, her mother, aunts, sisters, women friends. Lacking those, no one.

There were various solutions to this riddle of giving and not getting, wanting but not having. Her own mother resorted to Smirnoff's. Elke buried herself in work. The wives of the other capitalists about town shopped their brains out, but Clea had already abandoned that route. Her French wasn't fluent enough for her to lose herself in television dramas. And in any case, her relentless energy never allowed her the more passive routes to oblivion like alcohol, books, TV, or sleep.

Plopping down on the leather sofa and gazing at the garish paisley wallcloth, Clea felt restless and bored. She reached over to the coffee table for Pascal's *Pensées*, which she had extracted from the shelves of leather classics several weeks earlier. Since she was stuck in France, she might as well fill in the many gaps left by her French literature courses at Cornell. Stretching out on the sofa, she began to read. Maybe she should convert to Catholicism while she was in Paris. She could wear a black lace mantilla and join the ranks of devout matrons she'd seen kneeling in the Madeleine.

Tossing and twitching impatiently, Clea came to a passage that read: "Men's unhappiness is due solely to the fact that they are incapable of sitting down quietly in a room and relaxing." Pondering this, Clea realized it was in fact her problem. She couldn't sit quietly in a room. If she were a saint, she could have rested rapt in the Godhead. But since she was a mere mortal, there was boredom, loneliness, and sensual hunger where the Godhead, whatever it was, ought to be. Besides, she didn't *want* to sit quietly. If Pascal had been able to sit quietly, he clearly wasn't cursed with her hormones. She wanted to sing and dance and make love. She'd *have* to sit quietly in a room at a rest home soon enough, and lie quietly in a coffin.

Slapping Pascal on the coffee table, Clea jumped up and went to her desk, where a note lay from a Houston banker named Phil, who was working in Paris for the next several weeks without his family. She'd met him at a party the previous weekend. Phil was sleek and glossy, a broad-shouldered, narrow-hipped, unreflective animal on the prowl. They'd gone off in a corner together and made fun of the French fussiness about food.

"Hell, in Texas we eat anything the buzzards ain't got to first," he said with the self-mocking American humor Clea was hungry for.

His note had arrived a couple of days later, saying he'd love to take her café crawling if she'd give him a call. Seizing the phone, Clea dialed him and made a date for the next night.

At the end of the obligatory café crawl, they sat in Clea's café with the pinball machines bonging in back and American cowboys wailing from some hidden tape deck. Clea looked Phil in his sly but patient eyes and said, "Since no one gets out of this life alive, why don't we just enjoy it while we've got it?"

They enjoyed it extravagantly for a few weeks, Clea constantly reminding herself of Turner's advice not to give her heart away if she was just passing through. Or, presumably, if the other person was. She was proud of herself for feeling only mild regret when Phil returned to Houston, and relief when she didn't hear from him again. Despite unpromising Ohio origins, she had at last become a world-class sophisticate who could identify inferior champagne, and summon and dismiss lovers with aplomb. In the grip of hubris, believing she'd tamed the Minotaur, she propositioned Elke when she was next in New York. Elke, knowing better, merely laughed and turned her down.

As she tied up a green garbage bag of beer bottles, Clea remembered hoping as she began to skip menstrual periods in her mid-forties that menopause would put a halt to her urgent, if sporadic, wish to be held and touched. But to the contrary, separating sex from procreation had increased its allure. Turner had discovered that surefire foreplay nowadays was to whisper in her ear, "There is no point to this except pleasure."

But Turner was in Mexico City, and she had no wish to sully some innocent Roches Ridger with the complicated lusts bred by a corrupt urban civilization. The point of being here was to eliminate these toxins from her system. Part of this process would necessitate an exploration of the outer parameters of celibacy.

Clea paused unhappily, one hand on her hip, the other holding the garbage bag. Damn that John Galmer anyway. If only her knowledge of lovemaking had remained stalled at the raincoat-among-the-rhododendron stage. But he had to tackle her on his blue corduroy couch and make her feel sensations any sane person would want never to stop.

But this was finished. No more love affairs. She could write the entire libretto before the opera even began—from the besotted oblivion, through the disillusionment, to the indignation and despair, to the eventual indifference and disbelief. Elke insisted Roches Ridge was merely her latest love affair. But Roches Ridge was actually her detox tank. After a period of withdrawal, she'd finally discover a sobriety and serenity that would see her into old age and beyond. She would at last learn to sit quietly in a room and not make trouble.

Braced by this meditation, Clea studied her new neighborhood: the auto graveyard next door; the derelict yellow school buses on the far ridge. The afternoon sun cast slanting rays on the tepees at the foot of her cliff. Through the trees Clea could see lavender women's symbols on the beige canvas. A commune of lesbian hippies. It was hard to imagine such a phenomenon here in Roches Ridge, where the twentieth century hadn't yet fully arrived.

Sitting down to rest on a rib of granite that poked through her trash pile, Clea ran her fingertips along a crevice that had been gouged by a glacier ten thousand years earlier. Here in Roches Ridge, it was the early twentieth century. A few hundred miles south at the World Trade Center, it was the twenty-first century. And in the Nile Delta, peasants were farming at this very moment with implements designed in the days of the pharaohs. In Jerusalem, you could rub shoulders with Hasids in garb from seventeenth-century Poland and with Arabs in robes like those worn by the biblical patriarchs. She'd photographed them all in her day.

This was the kind of insight *The Town That Time Forgot* needed, Clea mused. Perhaps this global and historical perspective was what Elke had always felt was missing from Clea's work. As she stood up and dragged a garbage bag across the yard toward the house, she speculated on how to impart such dimensions to her book. The photos of living Roches Ridgers beside the graves of their forebears was a start. She hefted the garbage bag into the cracked bathtub by the driveway.

Heading for the back door, Clea recalled that she had experienced this same curious intimation of simultaneity around Kate and Theo when she'd last seen them, at Christmas. Kate's hair was maybe an inch long, with a pencil-thick braid emanating from the left rear side of her head. She wore a full cotton ankle-length skirt and several stretched T-shirts with strategic rips. She'd spent the vacation berating her parents about CIA involvement in Latin America. Theo, who for the last six years had worn a silver astronaut jacket and a blue Mets cap, turned up at Christmas dinner in a sports coat and tie. He even removed his Mets cap when he sat down at the table beside Terence.

As Clea served up the creamed onions, she studied her handsome children, over whom she'd wept so desperately that fall when they departed for school. As Elke teased Kate about her bedraggled holiday outfit, Clea suddenly saw Kate and Theo all at once as helpless infants, zany toddlers, timid preteens, and belligerent adolescents. And also as the harried but responsible adults they'd become, and as the wise and wizened elders, one incarnation superimposed over another. Once you'd drunk enough cider, you could no doubt see in an apple blossom the entire progression. Yet it had been a moving perception, one she hoped to find a method for incorporating into her book vis-à-vis Roches Ridge.

As she ran water into the teakettle in the kitchen sink, she wondered what Kate and Theo were up to this afternoon. Until she could lure the phone company into installing a phone, there was no way to find out. She'd told them to leave messages on her machine at Turtle Bay if they needed her. She checked it daily from the Casa Loretta phone booth. But so far she'd had only silence from them. It was unsettling after all these years of knowing where they were and with whom twenty-four hours a day. It was also a relief. At one point Kate was dating a drug dealer in the East Village, so knowing where she was had been less than no comfort. Parenting teenagers was even more harrowing than parenting toddlers, because you couldn't send along a trusted baby-sitter on drunken car chases up the Palisades Parkway as they gave each other hand jobs at eighty miles an hour. Which Clea knew about because she and Turner had done the same. Clearly there was a god whose assignment was to protect ejaculating teenagers in transit. But at least if Kate and Theo were endangering the fragile lives Turner and she had struggled so diligently to protect and nurture, she didn't have to know about it anymore.

But God, it had been fun, hadn't it, she mused as she rinsed out her china pot with hot water and spooned in tea leaves. Those frenzied years with those crazy creatures who'd emerged from her body. She smiled remembering Theo in Paris, sitting in the front seat of the Citroën with her in back. He wore the Algerian driver's blue uniform hat down over his eyes. Looking out from under the brim, he asked the driver man to man, "Did you know my mom has a vagina?" And Kate insisting that Clea buy her a fluffy yellow lamb's wool coat from the marché aux puces at the Porte de Clignancourt because she thought it made her look like Big Bird.

Clea had a sudden impulse to phone Turner in Mexico City and thank him for Kate and Theo. It was the most wonderful gift they'd given each other in a quarter century of mutual generosity. However bizarre their marriage might appear to outsiders, it had provided them both with what they needed—a tightrope of connection, in contrast to the nets that had entangled and strangled their parents. But Kate and Theo would never again crawl into her lap for comfort after a fight at their play group. Nor allow her to design elaborate hairdos as she shampooed them. Nor insist she read *Where the Wild Things Are* so many times that she was ready to become a wild thing herself. In the midst of straining her tea, Clea discovered tears on her chin and dripping into her cup.

# 20  Starshine

Starshine lay on her futon in the house trailer trying to meditate, hands atop her large belly. The other Boudiccas were in their own spaces, doing a juice fast, so the only distraction was an occasional squawk from the parrot in his cage. But try as she might to clear her awareness so the pure light could shine through, Starshine kept thinking about the rising creek. Should they be sandbagging the banks?

Frankly, it was one big pain being a guru. The others believed she was receiving guidance from the goddesses, but in truth she was winging it. When Ishtar turned up one night during Sexuality Week, stumbling through the white birches, the bonfire reflecting in her dilated pupils, Starshine was delighted because that gave her an even dozen disciples, just like you know who. Little did she know that Ishtar was to be her Judas.

Che, the parrot, shrieked, "We Shall Overcome!"

Starshine found him in the Boston Common in 1972 and named him Che because he kept repeating "Che Guevara! Che Guevara!" His language otherwise consisted of political slogans from the sixties. Some Boudiccas objected to a male parrot on the land, so Starshine had been trying to teach him "The Personal Is Political." But apparently you couldn't teach old birds new words.

When the Boudiccas first arrived at Mink Creek, a double rainbow appeared through the trees, and Starshine took this as a sign of approval from the goddesses. It was a perfect campsite, a bowl that would increase the natural ley lines of the valley. Unfortunately, it soon became apparent that this site of power was a swamp. Mosquitoes and deerflies bred on the green slime. And because of the Boudiccas' decision never to harm living creatures, the insects bit unhampered. With the spring thaw, the creek was rising and threatening their projected women-only graveyard. It pissed Starshine off. It wasn't enough that she be highly evolved spiritually; she had to be a hydraulic engineer as well.

There were other problems she hadn't foreseen on that double-rainbow day—their unevolved neighbors, for instance. The Marsh brothers set leg-hold traps along the creek banks, like those concealed Vietcong pits lined with sharpened stakes. Once the Boudiccas surrounded Orlon to complain. Feral eyes darting, tongue licking his narrow mustache, he said, "Listen, ladies, this is how I put food on my table. If you don't like it, fuck off. I was here first. By about two hundred years. Trapping is part of my heritage."

"So's incest," replied Starshine. "I wouldn't brag about it."

Orlon's brother Dack was somewhat less subhuman. In fact, a couple of times Boudiccas had seen him release animals from his brother's traps. But when they asked him to take the traps away, he gazed at them with his big black eyes, rubbing the BORN TO DIE tattoo on his forearm. "Can't," he finally replied. "Them's Orlon's traps."

One day last winter the Boudiccas were thrashing through a new snowfall, trying to identify dead trees. They'd run out of firewood but hadn't cut more because of their refusal to harm any living thing, and their inability to tell in midwinter which trees were living. Dack appeared through the bare birches on snowshoes, with only a down vest for a jacket, and pointed out a few dead trees. Later that afternoon he drove down the frozen creek in a huge blue tow truck, to dump a pile of split firewood in front of the trailer without a word or a smile.

Boudiccas went to Roches Ridge on food runs to the IGA Dumpster and water runs to the post office spigot, in addition to the Stop sign project and actions at the Karma Café. Starshine once saw several women in pale-blue head scarves and dresses to their ankles shopping in the IGA. They didn't talk or laugh, and their eyes were habitually lowered. Starshine asked Astrid Starr, behind the checkout counter, "Who are they?"

"Those born agains from up Granite Gap."

"How long have they been around?"

"About as long as you," said Astrid, grimly punching the register.

Starshine watched the women as they went through the checkout. The one in back riveted her attention. She was tall and thin, with a sallow complexion and dark unhappy eyes, like Cher before she dumped Sonny. She followed some differently-abled asshole on crutches out to a yellow van that had Bible quotations painted all over it.

Starshine hadn't been able to get that woman out of her mind. Her desperate mien was haunting. Starshine felt like Harriet Tubman. Somehow she had to penetrate the mountain fastness of that cracker fanatic and rescue that poor enslaved woman. Bring her down to Mink Creek and let her discover what freedom from male domination was like.

"Make Love, Not War!" squawked Che.

"Shut up, Che. I'm meditating."

"Che Guevara! Che Guevara!"

Starshine got up and put the cover over Che's cage.

"Black Is Beautiful!" cried Che from the darkness, in a last desperate attempt to charm Starshine.

Starshine thought about the upcoming action at the Miss Teenage Roches Ridge Pageant. It was obscene parading young women like prize heifers. Besides, attacking some outside enemy might ease tensions around Mink Creek. The others were beginning to resent Starshine. Because she was more highly evolved, she sometimes had to employ drastic techniques to combat her followers' destructive traits. Such as Ishtar's pride. Self-esteem, Ishtar called it, but it was actually just your garden-variety pride. Starshine, as her teacher, had had to humble Ishtar by decking her with karate kicks when she mocked *The Lesbian Book of the Dead*. It was essential for Ishtar's evolution. But Foxglove and Morning Glory had been grumbling ever since Ishtar's departure.

Starshine wondered if she was suffering from guru burnout. What had started as a mission had become just another job. But she wasn't trained for any other work. She'd studied piano at the New England Conservatory and had played some recitals in Boston. There was talk of a concert tour. After learning the tour idea had fallen through, she sat alone on a North Shore beach, her dreams in ashes. Listlessly watching a dog day meteor shower, she suddenly heard a voice from the heavens: "You are Starshine."

"What?" she asked.

Again the voice proclaimed, "*You* are Starshine."

Being a guru was easier than being a concert pianist, which required endless practice. A guru merely set up shop. Disciples were drawn to you by the magnetism of your aura. And once their eyes glazed over, soon they'd be begging to donate their trust funds and share your bed.

Starshine studied Foxglove's astrological, biorhythmic, and menstrual charts, on the wall over the dinner table with everyone else's, to decide if it was propitious to sleep with her that night. Gathering up the tarot deck, she laid out some cards on the table, seeking an answer to this compelling question. The Death card turned up in the middle, and Starshine shuddered. Usually she was delighted with that card, bespeaking rebirth as it did, but today it gave her the creeps.

She shook herself and stretched. Must be the fast. These fasts were exhausting. But they saved money. The Boudiccas' savings and trust funds were nearly gone, yet the plan of becoming a self-supporting farm hadn't materialized. Luckily, Starshine had set up a pension fund for herself with Conrad Bohring at Mink Valley Savings and Loan. She wouldn't always be young and brimming over with enlightenment. She needed to free her awareness from earthly concerns like social security in order to be an open conduit for cosmic connections. She added the fees Alvin Jacobs paid her to lecture his Amerikan Gulag classes on homosexuality in a homophobic society. Also the Boudiccas were advertising plots in their women-only cemetery in *Amazon Quarterly*.

A couple of Boudiccas were desperate to have babies. In their circles they were discussing how to father them. Foxglove favored artificial insemination, but Morning Glory wanted to ask Dacron Marsh, pointing out that he had Native American blood, had given them firewood, and sometimes freed animals from Orlon's traps. Starshine had consulted Gordon McQueen about his sperm count before she heard of AIDS, but she hadn't talked to him since.

So many problems and so little pleasure, especially now that Ishtar had gone away. Starshine missed the companionship of someone who would struggle with her. The other Boudiccas just passively gave themselves over to Starshine, which was about as exciting as eating tofu. She couldn't understand, though, how Ishtar could admire a whacked-out Las Vegas dancer like Shirley MacLaine more than Starshine herself.

Starshine went out the trailer door and ran through a karate kada by the creek bank, hissing and making claws of her fingers. Then she assumed a t'ai chi posture, balancing her enormous bulk on one size-eight foot. Craning her neck, she saw someone up on the ridge in a green plaid shirt, tossing things into a green garbage bag that trailed along like a slave's cotton sack. Ishtar, spying on Morning Glory? No, Ishtar would never wear a lumberjack shirt. Starshine shrugged, lowered her foot to the ground, and ducked into the menstrual hut.

# 21   Ida Campbell

Ida Campbell pulled her old green Chevy into the circular driveway of Bethany Wagner's large frame neocolonial in Colonial Manor Estates. All the houses here were identical structurally, with split rail fences out front, but you could choose any color on the Williamsburg chart. Also optional was the orchard of dwarf apple trees in the side yard.

Ida inspected the Bohrings' house next door, with its weed-free, insect-free, disease-free lawn you weren't allowed to walk on, and its foundation plantings of artificial flowers—crocuses, hyacinths, and daffodils this time of year—which Frieda Bohring was watering with a garden hose. Ida raised her hand in a greeting that went unanswered. Frieda had cut Ida ever since Ida dropped out of the Coupon Club. But Ida simply didn't have time for coupons, plus her Avon business, plus her family, plus her art.

Ida studied Bethany's silver Saab Turbo. Her own '72 Chevy had so many rust spots that it looked like army camouflage. But once her novel was published, life would be a horse of a different color. True, Harlequin had turned down *Sir and Her,* but there were other fish in the sea to fry.

Bethany threw open the door. "What a relief it's you, Ida! I thought you were a born again from Granite Gap. If I have to hear any more about the end of the world, I'll kill myself."

As Bethany fixed tea, Ida laid her new products on the wagon-wheel coffee table. Then she sat back in the overstuffed couch and looked out the mullioned picture window to the lake. Once *Sir and Her* was published, she'd sell her mobile home at Sunset View and buy one of these houses. God knows she'd never afford one on her Avon commissions or on her husband Chad's earnings from the quarry.

Most husbands in Colonial Manor worked for Xerox, and their wives could afford to buy skin care products in New York and Boston. But Ida came here anyway because she enjoyed sipping tea from Wedgwood cups and chatting about personal grooming with her future neighbors. When *Sir and Her* sold, Ida would associate with a better class of people than her current Sunset View neighbors, who watched porn videos and got into drunken screaming matches. Loretta Gebo next door was okay. Plus which, she bought hair spray by the carton for her spit curls. But the others were the pits. Ida had two children, and a husband who beat up on her and them when he drank. But there the similarities ended. What her neighbors failed to recognize was the shooting star Ida had hitched her wagon to. She spent her days dispelling the dreariness of trailer park life with products designed to bring excitement and glamour. And she wrote books to transform everyday routines into romantic adventures. In her own life she'd shifted from seeing Chad, when he came home from hunting covered with deer blood and a week's growth of beard, as a brutal bully who was neglecting his wife and children, to seeing him as a handsome, manly woodsman. She first learned this lesson on talk radio in Platts-burgh, and it saved her marriage. Now she used this discovery that you could see the glass as half empty or half full to guide her writing.

It was true that *Sir and Her* hadn't yet been published, but one day her ship would come in and find smooth sailing in a safe harbor. She'd gotten Chad to marry her when they'd graduated from Mink Valley High. She was the number one Avon saleswoman in central Vermont. She'd written a novel, even though Chad said she couldn't write a grocery list. (This was not true. She'd always had a special way with words.) It was simply a question of following your star, dreaming your dreams, staying on your toes, and not getting caught flatfooted.

Chad was afraid she'd lose interest in him once she was a famous author. But she assured him that just as he'd loved her when she was a nobody, so would she continue to love him even when she was a somebody and he was still a nobody. Because that was what real love was all about. It didn't alter just because of fame and fortune.

Bethany handed Ida a cup of tea and sat down. "So how have you been, Ida?"

"Not too bad. Busy. Selling products like hot dogs."

"Spring's a big season?"

"Every woman who goes south to the sun during mud season needs a whole new color scheme to complement her tan." Bethany's toy poodle, Poo, climbed into Ida's lap and, smelling the cat from the last house, began to explore her upper thighs with his nose.

"You know, I never thought of that." Bethany, dressed in a mauve velour sweat suit, sipped her tea.

"You don't, until you come in off that beach and put on your face for dinner and look like a corpse. So I try to warn all my clients." Smiling grimly, Ida pushed Poo's nose out of her crotch.

As Bethany flipped through the spring catalogue, Waneeta Marsh wandered in, wearing a Dior sweater dress and carrying a dust mop. Ida nodded, not wanting to appear acquainted with a Marsh in front of Bethany. She dug a fingernail into Poo's probing nose. Poo yelped and looked up at her with indignation.

"Why, hello there, Ida Campbell!" bellowed Waneeta.

"Well, hi."

"You two know each other?" Bethany looked up from the catalogue.

"Sort of," said Ida as Poo resumed ransacking her midriff.

"Ida went out with my son Orlon in high school," explained Waneeta.

"We *dated* a time or two," corrected Ida, shoving Poo to the carpet as Bethany studied a car deodorizer in the shape of a giant yellow daisy.

"Or two hundred." Waneeta chuckled.

"Everything all right with you, Waneeta?" asked Ida to divert a total exposure of her lurid past. Poo sat at her feet, snarling softly.

"Yup. Enough cobwebs this time of year to hang yourself with, though." Waneeta reached into a corner with her mop.

"We had a break-in here the other night. Did you hear?" asked Bethany. "This hulk wearing a surgical mask and green work clothes knocks at the door. I open it, see him, and try to slam the door. But he sticks his foot in. So I do a judo throw that lands him on the sidewalk. I may not look like Ms. Empire State anymore, but I've still got some muscles. Well, he jumps up, and Poo dashes out and sinks his teeth in his ankle. Conrad Bohring is out in his yard with a flashlight, poisoning night crawlers, and he sprays the man in the face with chlordane. The man runs for the woods with Poo hanging off his ankle."

"Zeno Racine," said Waneeta. "He's always trying to commit crimes. You get used to him after a while."

"I guess he won't be back here anytime soon," said Bethany.

"I wouldn't count on it," said Waneeta, Windexing the picture window.

"I've always wondered why they don't lock him up," said Ida.

"Oh, everyone knows Zeno. He don't mean no harm."

"What *does* he mean?" asked Ida.

"He's just dropped a few stitches, is all," explained Waneeta, rubbing furiously at the glass.

Bethany shrugged, muscles rippling under her sweatshirt. "You know who you ought to visit, Ida?" Bethany laid the catalogue on the wagon-wheel coffee table. "That woman who's just bought Calvin Roche's house. Your new neighbor, Waneeta. What's her name?"

"Clea Shawn," replied Waneeta. "I don't know if this is a good time to call. Her bathtub fell into the cellar the other day. Left a big hole in the kitchen floor."

"Loretta Gebo said I ought to look her up too. She seem like the makeup type?"

"I *guess* so," said Waneeta as she dusted Bethany's Ms. Empire State trophy. "Wonder why she's all the time wearing that camera round her neck? Looks like a pig snout."

"Your hair!" cried Ida to Bethany. "It's different. I like it."

"I've switched stylists. I'm seeing Jared McQueen at Mane Magnifique."

"Jared and my baby sister were at Mink Valley High together. All the girls were crushed out on him wicked."

"I can imagine," murmured Bethany, patting the hairdo his hands had shaped earlier that afternoon. "He's something to behold."

"Not my type," said Ida. "I want a man who'll protect me. Jared would be too busy gazing in the mirror."

Bethany laughed.

"Taking a trip this mud season, are you, Bethany?" asked Ida.

Bethany rolled her eyes. "Ken won't budge. He's afraid if he goes away from Xerox, someone younger will confiscate his office. How're the books going?"

"Silhouette has had *Sir and Her* for three months now, so I've got my fingers crossed." She lowered her eyes to Poo, who crouched by the coffee table, lifting his upper lip to reveal sharp white incisors.

"What's the new one about?"

"I'm superstitious. I'm afraid if I talk about it, it'll vanish," she confessed, thinking about *His Truly*, in which a secretary falls in love with her boss while taking dictation for a love letter to his wife.

"I understand," said Bethany.

Ida repacked her products, then stood up. "Well, I guess I *will* stop by Mrs. Shawn's. Thanks for the tip, Bethany."

"Could you drop off Waneeta, then? It'd save me a trip."

Ida and Waneeta sat in Ida's Chevy, Waneeta disappointed not to be in Bethany's Saab Turbo. Out the window was the brick entrance sign, on which pretarnished brass letters spelled COLONIAL MANOR ESTATES: COUNTRY LIVING AT ITS FINEST. A split rail fence enclosed the sign, and a staked sheep cropped wisps of hay. The sun was setting behind the Adirondacks in a blaze of color. As Ida and Waneeta waited to pull onto the highway, a steady stream of Volvos, Audis, Saabs, and BMWs driven by men in suits and ties turned in.

"Yonder's Kenneth Wagner." Waneeta nodded at a cranberry Audi. The Volvo in front of him paused to let a BMW from the other direction pass. Wagner roared around the Volvo, almost hitting the BMW. As he hurtled past, type A face dark red with rage, Ida caught her breath. With his steel-gray hair, bushy eyebrows, and carefully knotted silk tie, he looked exactly like Mr. Fenton, the boss in *His Truly*.

"What's he like?" asked Ida, shaken.

"Bethany never sees him. And when she does, all he talks about is Xerox. He don't hunt. He don't fish. Why, I wouldn't have him on a bet."

Ida realized she would. What did this mean, that a character she'd invented really existed?

"All this land," sighed Waneeta. "If my granddaddy hada held on to it, we'd be sitting pretty today."

"Your family owned this land?"

"Ayup. Farmed from here to Mink Creek for a hundred years. Until Granddaddy sold out to the Starrs for groceries during '92-and-Froze-to-Death. Where Wagners' house sets, 'twas all hayfield."

"Nothing left now but your house?" Ida was trying to figure out how to make herself indispensable to Ken Wagner. Why hadn't she taken shorthand at Mink Valley High?

"Yup. House used to be an inn. The main stop between Albany and Montreal. But then they built a turnpike on t'other side of the lake. Seems like Marshes wasn't meant to prosper."

"How's Orlon? I never see him." Ida pictured his dark darting eyes and narrow mustache, his pointed incisors and receding chin, his blunt hands with the missing little fingers. Clearly not *His Truly* material.

Waneeta glanced at her. "Not too bad. Though I don't know as he ever did get over you marrying that other fellow. Spends his time in the woods messing with his traps. Or out back to his shop. Or over to the funeral home with Mr. Coffin."

Ida felt a thrill at poor Orlon's carrying a torch for her all these years. "But that was nearly twenty years ago."

"Some people heal slow."

"Well, I'm sorry I hurt him."

"Can't be helped. You do what you gotta do."

Ida shuddered as she let Waneeta out before her huge crumbling house, with moose antlers and hawk wings hanging by the door. Yes, she'd done what she had to, and it was a good thing too. If she'd married Orlon, she'd be living in this dump eating squirrel, instead of writing novels and making plans to move to Colonial Manor Estates. Ishtar at the Karma Café was right: Things work out as they are meant to, despite turmoil along the way. You could call Ida a cockeyed optimist, but she truly believed that every cloud had a silver lining.

And what about Kenneth Wagner? Was it meant to be that he had driven out of her novel and into her life this very afternoon?

## 22  The Eye of the Hurricane

Clea sat before her walk-in fireplace, sipping tea and studying ads in the Roches Ridge *Gazette*. Beneath her feet, plywood stretched over the hole in the kitchen floor. "Deathworks (formerly Coffin's Funeral Home): Whatever your dying needs. Fully automated crematorium. Extensive line of brass markers. Come in and discuss your death goals with one of our trained counsellors. No obligation. We honor all major credit cards."

Dear God, thought Clea. What was wrong with what Roches Ridge already had—the graveyard behind the church, overhung by dying elms, full of mossy headstones carved with droll New England aphorisms? She wadded up the *Gazette* and tossed it in the fire.

Leaning back in her chair, she assessed the damage to her body from that afternoon's exertions. She'd filled enough garbage bags with beer bottles to form a small pyramid in the bathtub beside her driveway. The goal of sapping her lust had been accomplished, replaced with an aching lower back. Her ankle, site of an ancient skiing fracture, was also throbbing. Inhabiting a body nearly a half century old was like driving a car with eighty thousand miles on it: You kept wondering what was going to give out next, and patching it up with makeshift repairs, and wishing you could trade it in for a more reliable vehicle, and admiring the sleek newer models on the streets. Kneading her lower back, Clea recalled slipping her disk during classical Indian dance practice in Bombay, and being rushed sahib-style through the beggar-clotted streets to the English hospital by her driver.

Returning to Paris from New York after Elke turned down her proposed night of passion at the Waldorf, Clea finally accepted that

Elke and she were friends, nothing more. Their living together happily ever after as lovers was not in the cards. It was an every-woman-for-herself situation. Elke was saving herself via a new fascination with sculpture and welding. Clea had to find her own lifeline. So she grabbed a young Danish professor who was teaching at the Sorbonne for the year, whom she met in a library while doing research for her travel book on France.

Johannes, fair and lean, looked like an extra from a Bergman film. He was continually gazing off into the distance with a haunted look, as though hearing the faint howls of starving wolves in the tundra. As he and Clea strolled along the Seine past Notre Dame in the glow of the setting sun, Johannes recited mellifluous verses from Baudelaire and Rimbaud while Clea staggered under the armloads of fresh flowers he bought her from street vendors. He talked a lot about carrying her off to a whitewashed cottage by the sea in northern Jutland, wherever that was.

Too late Clea discovered that Johannes didn't understand the rules of the game Phil from Houston and Turner had taught her to play after Grégoire broke her heart. Johannes left his wife, assuming Clea would also leave Turner. Instead Clea left town, moving with her intact family to a rambling Victorian bungalow in a walled compound on a hill outside Bombay. Anguished letters from Johannes arrived by the bushel. Clea read them sitting on the rattan-matted veranda surrounded by pots of white geraniums. One afternoon, pausing in the midst of his latest suicide threat to gaze down to the palm-lined beach and across a murky bay to the Bombay skyline, Clea reluctantly acknowledged that Pascal had been correct: Her inability to sit quietly in a room had generated a mess.

In Bombay, Clea's situation was similar to what it had been in Paris, with Turner gone a lot, the children in school and tended by an English nanny, and the housework performed by a flock of servants who resented her democratic attempts to help. At first Clea tried long get-acquainted walks through Bombay, though her Indian driver insisted on following along behind in the Jaguar to rescue her when she tired. After one such walk, as she stood before the Victoria Terminus, astonished by the fantastical Venetian Gothic, Indo-Saracenic railway station, a leper, walking like a dog on four stubs, with a bucket for donations hanging from her teeth, chased her to the waiting Jaguar. But not before Clea discovered the topic for her next book—the architecture of the British raj.

Her book on France was selling well, and Allan Barkham had subcontracted to her commissions in China and Afghanistan. Another assignment from him involved a piece for *Smithsonian* magazine on Indian classical dance. So Clea enrolled in a class near the university and began to learn the complicated movements that conveyed the ancient mythologies. Bringing to it her customary excess, she concluded that if half an hour of practice was good, an hour would be twice as good. So she soon ruptured a disk.

During the subsequent weeks of bed rest, pleading letters continued to arrive from Johannes, in a Copenhagen mental hospital. After reading them, Clea was forced to lie immobile in her bed, gazing at a bad painting on the wall left by a previous occupant, a homesick Scot, of the dark brooding Highlands near Glencoe. All day long Clea studied this painting and thought about betrayal—of the Macdonalds by the Campbells, of Johannes by herself. An innocent flirtation in the library stacks, begun in fun and fervor, had ended for him in suffering. She believed she had tamed the Minotaur, but all she had really learned from Turner and Phil was how to ensure that the one who got hurt was not herself. Which she had accomplished by separating her body from her heart, and her brain from both. Yet this dissection wasn't entirely successful, because as she lay in her darkened bedroom behind louvered doors, the knowledge that someone she cared for was in pain caused *her* pain as well. She thought about his haunted Nordic mien, their strolls along the Seine in the soft spring twilight, the never-to-be cottage by the sea.

One night she consulted her coach about Johannes' breakdown. Wearing an open-necked sports shirt, tanned from a recent trip to Malta, Turner sat in a cushioned bamboo armchair beside her bed while she ate dinner off a tray. A wooden fan overhead stirred the muggy night air and the mosquito netting that hung around the bed like a bridal veil.

After listening to her litany of guilt and regret, Turner replied, "But, Clea, Johannes is a big boy. If he decided to leave his wife, that was his choice. You mustn't flatter yourself by regarding yourself as anything other than a handy excuse. If you toss a pebble into a pond, you aren't responsible for the ripples that reach the shore."

"But if I heave a brick through a plate-glass window, am I responsible for the flying shards?" she demanded. She had believed Turner had mastered the art of the civilized affair, but maybe he, too, left capsized lifeboats in his wake.

As the weeks of recuperation wore on, Clea could locate no solution to her dilemma. If she sat quietly in a room, as she was now doing, she felt bored and restless. If she went out and tried to erase these sensations, she created chaos, for herself and for others. Tedium or turmoil, all she could do was to pick her poison. And even being assailed by remorse over her irresponsible behavior with Johannes seemed preferable to lying alone in this dark room with nothing to do. Especially since every time she removed her eyes from the Glencoe painting, they fixed themselves on the slowly turning wooden fan at the ceiling, which reminded her with a sharp stab of loneliness of Elke and that tortured afternoon on Saint John.

One hot morning as Kate and Theo hung around her bedside complaining that *they* were bored, Clea recalled another Pascal quote that had stuck in her craw since Paris: "If a man were happy, he would be all the happier if he amused himself less." During these weeks in bed, Clea had perforce amused herself less. But she was not all the happier. She was confused, upset, guilty, and lonely. Therefore, the logical conclusion was that she was not a happy person, everyone else's opinion to the contrary. People equated her vitality and flair with happiness. Yet maybe these were screens to conceal unhappiness. But why would she be unhappy? She had everything a citizen of the twentieth century could covet—a charming husband, delightful children, devoted friends, good health (apart from her damned disk), talent and a satisfying career, money and all it could buy. The only thing she lacked was whatever it was that allowed a person to sit quietly in a room doing nothing. So she decided to devote her considerable energy to acquiring this quality.

Which she proceeded to do once she completed her photo guide to the citadels of the British raj and got her family settled in a Kyoto suburb the following year. For her next book she decided to catalogue the Zen meditation gardens of Japan. In the process she hoped to discover the secrets of Eastern serenity, which allowed the Japanese to sit quietly in their own rooms for extended periods. (Until the moment arrived to board kamikaze planes or grab hara-kiri swords.) So she spent many months photographing austere assemblages of sand, pebbles, bonsai, and boulders behind temples and pagodas throughout the country. But she remained plagued by restlessness, no nearer to nirvana than when she arrived.

One afternoon, in a garden behind a shrine on a hill outside Kyoto, Clea watched a priest with a shaved head and a belted black robe speak with a group of visiting Californians who were clamoring for something they called "the knowledge." The priest responded good-humoredly in an American accent, somehow maneuvering them back onto their tour bus and waving them goodbye. It was a revelation to Clea that you could approach these holy men and ask for what you wanted. She thought they had to select you from a crowd because of the luminescence of your aura or something. It was also a revelation that this particular priest was American. Perhaps she should enroll in a course of study here. Abandon her country and career and family if necessary.

Cornering the priest beneath an ancient maple, Clea demanded to be allowed to submit and obey.

He observed her with faint amusement. "And what exactly is it you want?" he finally asked.

"Answers."

"To what?"

"To my questions."

"Obviously," he said, evidently enjoying himself, to Clea's increasing irritation. "But what are your questions?"

Clea looked at him quizzically. If he was so spiritually gifted, shouldn't he know what she needed to learn without her having to tell him? "I want to know what to do to attain peace of mind."

"Oh, that's easy." He laughed. "Nothing."

She looked at him suspiciously. This was the same thing Pascal had said, and it didn't help one bit. "And what should I think about while I'm doing nothing?"

"Nothing," he repeated. "Look," he said, as though off the record. "It's not something you acquire. It's something you recognize." He smiled pleasantly. "But our goal at this monastery is to locate the eye of the hurricane, not to *become* the hurricane. So the best way for you to follow this path is to leave it."

At the time Clea had been insulted, concluding that the priest, with his bald head and black robes, was a fraud who fed on the gullibility of his fellow Westerners. In a huff, she invented her own spiritual regimen, chanting until she was hoarse, standing on her head until her nose bled, and meditating until her ears began to ring with the harmony of the spheres. (Her annual medical exam during Christmas leave in New York that year, prior to the Shawns' move to Sydney, revealed this to be tinnitus from otosclerosis.) But she now suspected that the priest was a man of insight. Because she had realized since that he had correctly diagnosed her true condition: All her undertakings became fire storms. They wreaked havoc, then rapidly burned themselves out.

Roches Ridge, however, largely unaltered for two centuries, was in it for the long haul. And this time so was Clea. Sitting quietly in her house in this little Vermont town, amusement at a minimum, Clea had cast her lot with all the previous generations who had lived out unremarkable, but irreproachable, lives within these four thick stone walls. Their ghosts would surround and support her. She would finally find peace and purpose, to replace the restlessness and boredom that had always plunged her into such turmoil.

Clea started at a knock at her side door, wrenching her aching back. Who would be at her door in early evening? *She was kneeling in a puddle of dirty motor oil among Big Mac cartons while a man with a gun to her head ran his hand through her hair. . . .* Getting a grip on herself, she stood up. There were no locks, and an intruder wouldn't knock. She opened the door on a mousy middle-aged woman with lank brown hair and makeup as thick as Tammy Faye Bakker's, who carried an imitation-leather briefcase.

"Hello, I'm Ida Campbell. Loretta Gebo suggested I stop by to see if you're interested in any Avon products."

"Oh. How nice. I'm Clea Shawn. Won't you come in? Be careful," said Clea as they skirted the plywood to sit down before the fire.

"Yes, I heard your tub fell into the basement."

"You did?" Clea's face took on a hunted look. "Please sit. Excuse the mess. As you can see, I'm renovating."

"Good idea," said Ida. "Another heavy snow and this place would've collapsed. So here's our new catalogue, hot off the press."

Clea took it. "I appreciate your stopping by, Ida. But I'm all stocked up on makeup right now. In fact, I'd planned to cut down on it now that I'm living in the country."

Ida considered this, apparently never having thought of Roches Ridge as "country."

"Compared to New York City," added Clea. "Where I've been living off and on for the past twenty-five years."

"We carry home care products as well."

"Once I've got a home, I'll be needing everything." Clea laughed.

"It'd be better if I come back later?"

"If you don't mind." To soften this, Clea added, "So you know Loretta?"

"Everybody knows Loretta. She buys her hair spray from me," said

Ida proudly, studying Clea's Nikon, which lay on the fireplace mantel with several lenses. "You're a photographer?"

"Trying to be."

"I know. It's a struggle staying true to your art with so many temptations to sell out." Ida looked down at her hands, folded in her lap.

"You're a photographer too?"

"An author."

"What do you write?"

"Novels. I'm working on number two."

"Would I have heard of number one?"

"It isn't published yet. But it may be soon."

"That's wonderful. I've done a couple of photography books. Travel books actually. But I wouldn't have any idea how to go about a novel."

"I'm self-taught." Ida stood up, extracting a business card from her briefcase and extending it to Clea. "But it's suppertime, so I won't keep you. Call me when you need some products. But don't wait too long, because once my book is published, I'm kissing Avon goodbye."

As Ida climbed into a dilapidated green Chevrolet, Clea chastised herself for not buying something. Her small-town manners were as rusty as Ida's car.


Clea lay awake in her shadowy second-floor bedroom, a spotlight from next door glaring through one window. A crackling sound came from the Marshes' backyard, punctuated by an occasional crash. Throwing on her wool robe, she went to the window. Across the stockade fence stood a violet bug light, which was emitting the ghastly frying sound.

As Clea was wondering whether she could ask the Marshes to turn it off this late at night, she glanced past the bug light to the mountain of wrecked cars in the backyard. Standing atop it with a crowbar was a muscular young man in work boots and dirty jeans, which hung on his pelvic bones. Although his breath was frosty, he wore no shirt, and his copper-colored chest was streaked with sweat. In profile his nose was aquiline. As he paused to toss straight black Prince Valiant hair out of his eyes with one hand, his dark eyes seemed to meet Clea's. Except that she was standing in shadows and was in fact probably invisible.

Back in bed, Clea wrapped a pillow around her head and resolved to speak with the Marshes the next morning about their late-night insect executions. She focused resolutely on Turner, wondering what he was up to in Mexico City. She pictured him in a sombrero, drinking tequila with a flamenco dancer. It was his unquenchable gusto for life, however unnerving on occasion, that had always kept her coming back for more.

Adrenaline pumping from irritation, Clea was still awake an hour later. She turned on her lamp, picked up her notebook, and wrote: "Dear Elke— Damn it, I wish I had a phone! I need to tell you about my book, and the renovation, and the people I'm meeting. But where are you? Sitting atop your garbage skiff, surrounded by psychopaths, when you could be up here surrounded by mountains and forests. No accounting for taste. The house is going well, apart from a complication with the beams. The book: I'm going to juxtapose my photos of Roches Ridge to archival ones, to demonstrate how little has changed. *The Town That Time Forgot.* So far I've met the grocer and the postmistress. I'll bet they've never even heard of Acuras or buffalo milk mozzarella or extra virgin olive oil."

She paused in her scribbling. Jared McQueen with his turquoise spikes, Ida Campbell with her briefcase of cosmetics, Zeno Racine with his tank of Tri-Die, the man with the red beard in the yellow Dodge Ram van . . . She quickly ushered them out of her head.

"Another idea for the book: photos of old gravestones, beside portraits of the current generation who bear the same names. But more later, my darling friend. I miss you more than you could ever possibly imagine. Love, Clea."

Lonely, back aching, Clea returned to the window to watch the young man next door bend, stretch, and stoop, muscles straining as he wrenched at an auto carcass with his crowbar. A brown van with its headlights off appeared on the road before the Marshes' house. It backed down the driveway alongside the stockade fence. Printed on the side door was ORLON'S BAIT AND TACKLE. The van stopped beside the back shed. A rodentlike man wearing olive coveralls hopped out and nodded curtly to the young man, who climbed down from his tower of rusted steel. The two men carried something bulky from the van into the shed. The doors blocked Clea's view.

Standing outside the Marshes' side door the next morning, Clea could hear the sound track from a Flintstones cartoon. An unpleasant pungent odor floated on the breeze from the backyard. Battered snowshoes sat on their tips to one side of the door. To the other side were three old auto seats and a couple of rusting Maytag washers. On the clapboards hung some large wings and antlers. The door itself was scarred and pocked, as though someone had been chopping it with an ax. The young man from the previous night opened the door, feet bare, filthy jeans hanging on his hipbones. Tattooed on the forearm that held the door was BORN TO DIE in crude blue lettering. On the wall of the cluttered room behind him was a large rough-hewn wooden cross on which hung the bleached skeleton of a rodent, a crown of barbed wire encircling the skull. Several small grubby children lay on the floor before a TV, eating handfuls from a Kix box.

"Hello. I'm your new neighbor, Clea Shawn."

The young man nodded. Clea waited for an additional response. Getting none, she said, "I'm afraid your bug light keeps me awake at night. Would you mind turning it off after, say, ten o'clock?"

An indignant burn came to his dark eyes, though his face remained impassive. "Can't."

"Why not?"

"Skeeters bite the babies."

"There are no mosquitoes this time of year." Clea felt her back stiffen.

The young man continued to gaze at her, hand on the door.

Rarely had Clea elicited such dislike so quickly. But she'd ceased to care about her surly young neighbor's opinions. She just wanted a full night's sleep. "Will you do that, please?"

With a curt nod, he closed the door in her face.

# 23  Dacron Marsh

Jeezum, thought Dack as he flopped into an armchair with a raccoon-fur cover and resumed watching "The Flintstones." Flatlanders were taking over the whole dang state. Oughta restrict them to ski areas, like wildlife reserves. They did look like some kinda rare fowl, strutting around Alpine Glen in bright parkas and neon astronaut boots. His job was to sweep snow off the chair lift seats with a broom. Girls looked him over in his wool trousers and suspenders, plaid shirt, and mud boots, and giggled as they rode off. Sometimes the word "woodchuck" floated back to him. And that Jacobs guy in the eye patch who asked him to help burn down the Xerox factory kept calling him a peasant. He rubbed the BORN TO DIE tattoo on his forearm, which he'd etched with a pocket knife and filled in with a ballpoint pen during a Vermont history class at Mink Valley High.

But he didn't really care what some Connecticut cunt or asshole one-eyed college professor thought of him, because he'd be leaving Roches Ridge soon anyway. He wanted to be one of the ski troopers who trained on the Alpine Glen slopes. Dack couldn't figure out why they wore jungle camouflage on ski slopes, though. In a war they'd be sitting ducks. They probably had white coveralls they were saving for a war. Or hadn't anyone noticed that green wouldn't cut it on snow? Whoever was in charge seemed like a real dipshit.

He read about Arctic scouts in a library book at school. They defended America's northern borders from saboteur attacks on DEW stations and from missile-armed Soviet submarines, using ice knives and single-shot Lee-Enfield .303 rifles. They could repair a Ski-Doo with their bare hands at sixty-five degrees below zero, build an igloo in a gale, dig a fishing hole in five feet of ice, and find directions without maps or compasses.

As Dack tossed a handful of Kix into his mouth, he enumerated the problems standing between himself and ski trooping. One was that he couldn't ski. Joanne, an Alpine Glen instructor, gave him a couple of lessons, but he always ended up in a heap at her feet. The army would train him themselves if they accepted him, though. And they'd probably accept him if he really was part Indian, because most Arctic scouts were Eskimos. Everyone all over town said his father was an Abenaki who worked at McGrath's quarry for a while. His mother, Waneeta, wouldn't confirm this, but she didn't deny it either.

The second problem was homesickness. His brother Ray took him to a Red Sox game, and they stayed overnight at the Koala Motel outside Boston. Dack was awake all night, missing his mattress in the big drafty house in Roches Ridge. If he felt that bad in Boston with Ray, how would he feel in an igloo with a bunch of strangers?

But there was lots he *wouldn't* miss, like hunting season and Orlon's trap lines. When he was a boy, Ray and Orlon used to take him to deer camp near Mount Abraham. During the day they'd sneak through the woods with their rifles, and at night they'd drink Miller's and hold target practice by flashlight. He learned the need for a killing shot, since a wounded animal had more blood in its muscles when it

died, which gave the meat a gamy taste. And the need to guard the
antlers and the nose from breakage or puncture if you wanted to mount
a head. He watched Orlon field-dress carcasses, splitting them along
the stomach, belly downhill so he could pull out the innards intact.
Orlon also taught him how to remove, scrape, and salt hides.

One day his brothers decided it was time for Dack to kill his first
deer, and they stationed him beneath some maples by a cliff. Then
they flushed an eight-point buck in his direction. He raised his rifle
and found the buck in his sights—but he couldn't pull the trigger.
Orlon ran toward him, calling him a fucking fool. Dack started crying
and flung the rifle to the ground. "I can't," he sobbed.

"Why the hang not?" Orlon's dark eyes flashed contempt, and his
tongue darted out to lick his narrow black mustache.

"Because I don't *want* to," he blubbered.

Ray patted his shoulder. "Well, why didn't you say so in the first
place, baby brother? I never cared much for hunting myself. Let's go
home."

Orlon called them fairies, but Dack didn't care. And when Orlon
sent him to check his traps, Dack set the animals free if they weren't
hurt too bad. If they were, he cut their throats, which pissed Orlon off
since he wanted Dack to club them so his precious pelts wouldn't be
harmed. Dack tried to make it up to the animals he killed by using
their bones and hides to construct memorials. "Dack's messes," Orlon
called them.

Dack glanced up at his best mess, hanging over the TV. A wooden
cross with a muskrat skeleton on it. Orlon said it was sacrilegious and
kept taking it down. On the opposite wall was a rib cage and skull,
some leg bones and bits of fur. He didn't see how he could kill caribou
at Hudson Bay when he couldn't even kill a deer at Mount Abraham.
But Arctic scouts lived off the land, and he guessed that without Starr's
IGA down the road, he'd be blasting caribou with the best of them.

Maybe the army would make a man of him, something Orlon insisted he needed. But if Orlon was an example of a man, Dack would
rather just forget it. Money, for instance, did not slide easily through
Orlon's deformed hands. He was one cheap bastard, all the time talking about restoring the Marsh family fortune—while he let his own
mother, Waneeta, wear clothes from suitcases in wrecked cars Ray
dragged home, and clean houses for those rich Xerox bitches over at
Colonial Manor, and stand in line outside the town hall for free cheese,
and buy groceries with food stamps.

Ray said Orlon was so dumb that whenever he drove downhill, he thought he was headed south. And then there was his missing little fingers. He cut one off while mounting a deer head for some Boston businessman. When he was demonstrating to Ray how he cut it off, he cut off the other by accident. And his latest scam with Sonny Coffin in the back shed was going to get the whole family sent to prison.

Dack's third problem about ski trooping was Prudence Webster. Morning Glory, she kept telling him to call her as they sat on the banks of Mink Creek and watched tadpoles grow. They'd been at Mink Valley High together, but she'd hung with the jocks and class officers. He'd hung across the road from school with the smokers and druggies. But now that she was down to Mink Creek, she kept turning up in her red bandanna headband when he was working the trap lines. He'd started arguing with Ray over who got to check the traps.

Although she was living with those dykes, Morning Glory sure didn't seem like no lezzie when she came sauntering out of the woods in her tight faded blue jeans. So far all they'd done was talk. She said how sick she was of hearing a lecture every time she put food in her mouth. And how the bosswoman, Starwars, kept telling them to be brave women warriors, but all Morning Glory wanted was to get away with being a coward. How Starwars insisted all women of the world were one, but that some made Morning Glory want to puke. How the one she liked best, Ishtar, had left to run the Karma Café and wanted Morning Glory to elope with her. How Morning Glory was afraid of Starwars because she had nearly killed Ishtar with karate kicks. Dack wanted to assure her that he'd take care of Starwars, but he wasn't actually certain he could. She was one big motherfucking bull dyke. Well, he didn't know exactly what Morning Glory had in mind, but he sure as hang didn't want to miss it by going off to no basic training in the snow.

# 24  Nonaggression Pacts

As Elke walked toward the Italian restaurant on Morton Street, she thought how strange it was to be seeing Turner Shawn alone after all these years of family birthdays and holidays. They were bound together by their love for Clea, yet kept apart by faint envy of each other's hold over her. At more than one point, though, it had been Elke's decisions that had maintained Turner's ascendancy.

After the Shawns moved to Paris, Elke wandered the Village past restaurants where she and Clea had ordered meals that remained uneaten, their appetites being for each other. She tried to convince herself that Clea's departure was a good solution to an impossible situation. She had no wish to be a home breaker. And whatever Clea claimed, she had a conventional streak a mile wide that required an ordinary American household and a father for her children. Despite her frequent self-portrayals as a midwestern hick, she was a very elegant ruling-class woman who knew all the right things to wear and say and serve. It would mortify her to earn her society's contempt. She'd despise living in bohemian squalor with a woman lover, and she'd no doubt eventually take out her chagrin on Elke. Yet the armchair in Elke's studio where Clea usually sat mocked her with its emptiness. And Clea's chatty letters about multinational life on the Continent didn't help.

Elke began to have nightmares about her previous losses—her father dangling from a noose, her mother cold and blue on the parlor carpet, her brother blown to bits on a Tunisian airstrip, the house of her childhood a charred ruin, her homeland a charnel house, her countrymen maimed zombies. Everyone and everything Elke loved eventually vanished, and so would Clea. So *had* Clea. Elke would wake up at dawn, sweating, shivering, and weeping. Terence would hold her stiffly and reassure her, without conviction. The terror of her nights yielded to the bleakness of her days, which she spent doggedly sketching the images of loss from her nightmares, in an attempt to exorcise them.

But finally, in response to a desperate letter from Elke, Clea wrote a real reply, detailing her true feelings, which included missing Elke badly and studying her contact sheets of Elke in a café near the Pont Mirabeau. Elke kept this letter in her shirt pocket above her heart, rereading it whenever the demons threatened. Unlike the other losses, Clea's abandonment wasn't permanent, nor was Elke's pain one-sided.

Bolstered by this knowledge, Elke made a halfhearted foray into early seventies collectivity, on the lookout for someone to take Clea's place. Just because Clea was a captive of the capitalist dream didn't mean Elke had to be too. She joined a group of women artists called Arts Alive, whose goal was to bridge the gap between visual artists and their community. Their first project involved clearing a junk-strewn lot in the East Village, planting sunflowers, trucking in hay bales, and erecting painted wooden silhouettes of cows and trees. Elke enjoyed the sweaty physical labor and the clear-cut goal, a relief after the nebulous experiments her solitary work usually entailed.

Next, the group spread white bed sheets across Seventh Avenue. Bikers, truckers, and motorists drove through puddles of paint and across the sheets, making a labyrinth of tire treads. The women hung this colorful piece of communal art inside a popular bar.

For an Arts Alive antiwar show Elke found a cast-off cloth doll in the street, torn and dirty, its stuffing coming out. She bought some wooden toy soldiers and arranged them in a blitzed landscape around the supine doll. Their bayoneted rifles plunged into the doll's wounds.

During these months various women, no doubt sensing Elke's simultaneous attraction and resistance to their world, extended hands to help Elke hop up on the tribade bandwagon. She kept thinking that if only Clea and she had been younger, they'd have belonged to this insouciant generation for which a lesbian interlude was obligatory. Having explored female bodies visually from every angle during art school and since, Elke had to confess, at least to herself, to an urge to explore them with her other senses as well. Self-confident and humorous, these women appealed to Elke very much. This, plus the fact that most lived within blocks of Elke's own apartment, would make it impossible for Elke just to walk away after a night or a week or a month. Clea was right: An affair with a woman would not be so simple as Elke had tried to portray it on Saint John. But if she refused to disrupt her safe, orderly life for Clea, she certainly wouldn't for some stranger, however alluring. Elke found herself distressed and confused, since sexual fidelity was not a virtue she valued, and especially not fidelity to someone with whom she'd never slept in the first place.

When the collective voted as their next piece of performance art to squirt Super Glue in the door locks of all the uptown galleries, Elke reluctantly parted company with them, realizing her real work required the isolation she'd been avoiding. And once she resumed it, she understood why. The sketches she'd done of Clea with her children, her glimpses of Clea naked in the shower on Saint John, and the antiwar tableau of the doll and the toy soldiers combined with the contents of her recent nightmares to yield a new image—of a full-breasted pregnant woman, dead atop a bombed-out building, legs sprawled open as though from a gang rape. Elke did dozens of studies of this image, in ink, pencil, charcoal, crayon, and watercolor. She tried etchings, lithographs, woodcuts. But none satisfied her.

Then one day Clea wrote about seeing, at Elke's request, Käthe

Kollwitz's granite mother and father at the war cemetery where Elke's uncle lay. She apologized for being too stunned to take any pictures. Sitting in her studio reading this letter, Elke thought about seeing those sculptures as a young girl. They had towered above her in a field of white crosses and crimson poppies, heavy and solid, almost like a natural rock formation. She recalled thinking she, too, would like to make objects that would cause people who looked at them to feel what she felt.

Visualizing the stone figures, Elke realized this was what was lacking with her pregnant woman: She needed to stroke and shape the mounds with her own hands instead of merely sketching them via lines and shadows. Drawing on what she remembered from art school, she tried out the image in plaster, then clay. Clay provided the fresh-grave effect she needed for the belly and breasts, but not the molten jagged look she wanted for the ruins. She molded some walled structures from clay and baked them in a friend's kiln. In the studio she dropped lithography stones on them until she achieved the necessary rubble. But still the lines and angles she'd envisioned eluded her. So she enrolled in a welding course at a trade school and began to experiment with scrap steel.

In the midst of this Clea returned to New York to arrange publication of her book on France. She arrived in Elke's studio doorway one night in a mahogany leather jacket and jeans, cheeks ruddy from the winter wind. Elke drew a sharp breath. Immersed in the new sculpture, she had believed herself immune to Clea. As they kissed, she realized that she wasn't, and probably wouldn't be this side of the grave. Whenever Clea appeared, it was for Elke as though someone had turned up the rheostat. The hairs on her forearms felt as though they were standing on end.

Clea unzipped her jacket, to reveal a tight black turtleneck over the full breasts Elke had visualized so thoroughly for her pregnant woman. Dropping into their usual armchairs, they began to cover the gossip that had failed to cross the Atlantic in letters. Clea seemed a bit agitated. There was an odd gleam to her eyes, and a tremble to her lips when she smiled. Eventually she looked at Elke and said, "So, Elke! What's new? Or rather, *who's* new?"

Elke felt a lurch. There was always this moment when, bullshit out of the way, one of them dodged beneath the other's verbal matador cape and plunged for the heart. Elke subdued her lurch by considering why Clea seemed unable to make an equivalent plunge in her work—get beneath visual chitchat to real substance. Her photos for the book on France, which Clea had just shown her—of wine festivals at châteaux on the Loire and sunsets off the Brittany coast—were utterly compe- tent, and utterly pointless. And Clea had avoided shots Elke would have deemed essential, like Käthe Kollwitz's mother and father keep- ing watch over the field of white crosses.

"That's a safe question, as you very well know," replied Elke. "No one is new for me. What about for you?" She felt a stab of anxiety, not really wanting to hear with whom Clea had replaced her in Paris.

Clea studied her, head to one side. "I had affairs with a couple of men."

"Yes?" Elke gave a pained smile. To her alarm and surprise, she felt a visceral revulsion at the image of a coarse black beard scraping across those smooth, firm breasts she'd appropriated for her woman of clay.

"Yes. And now I'm ready for you."

Elke started, having thought this topic settled on Saint John.

"My first affair was pretty painful. But the second was fun. I've finally learned how not to make a big deal of it. So I was wondering if you'd like to take a room at the Waldorf with me tonight." Clea blushed, belying her pose of blasé sophistication.

Elke grimaced. She'd created a monster. Shaking her head with amused disbelief, she tried to drag herself out of the haze of concen- trated distraction in which she resided while working on a new piece. She had disciplined the emotions Clea had unleashed in her, and was now pouring them into her new sculpture. Since she could control its whereabouts, it seemed a safer receptacle.

"I can see this idea really appeals to you," said Clea, tense, not looking at her.

"Clea, it's been over a year since Saint John. I've done a lot of thinking. And I've realized you were right that afternoon. You and I could never have a cooled-out, fun-loving roll in the hay. Perhaps we can mess around with men. But never with each other. What's be- tween us goes too deep."

"Couldn't we at least try? I've been looking forward to this for a long time."

"That just proves my point, doesn't it?"

"Well, let's not mess around, then."

"And what? Have a passionate love affair that would blow our mar- riages sky high? Because if you have an ounce of honesty left, darling, you know that's what would happen."

"And why not?"

"You *know* why not, Clea. Our work, your children, our husbands, our mental health. We've been over this before." Elke's desire for Clea had become almost interchangeable with the passionate intensity she needed for her sculpture. There was no longer enough left over to lure her into upsetting their applecart. "Just hang in. This phase between us will pass. Everything always does."

"I'm not sure I want it to pass," murmured Clea, throwing one long leg over the chair arm.

"If we don't stop this, we're going to drive each other crazy," warned Elke.

Clea sighed, sails luffing. "I think maybe you and I need a Maginot Line, Elke. Like Turner's and mine."

Elke nodded.

"So I won't ask you again, if you won't ask me."

"It's a deal." Elke extended her hand across the space between their chairs.

Clea took it, patted it, and smiled resignedly. "But God knows I love you, Elke. In every way that God invented."

They had kept this nonaggression pact for over fifteen years now, gradually shifting from star-crossed lovers to devoted confidantes. The fever had broken, leaving behind only a low-grade infection. Yet even so, Elke suffered for weeks when Clea, back in Paris, wrote mentioning a new affair with some Danish professor. She made several trips uptown to the Met, where she sat for hours on a wooden bench before Georgia O'Keeffe's *Black Iris,* studying the velvety black petals folding back to reveal the rust-colored stamen, and feeling ill with desire for Clea's body.

Back at her studio after one such pilgrimage, Elke began a series of sketches of two women making love, in many different postures, with every conceivable facial expression. Because she had studied anatomy and drawn from live models so thoroughly at art school and since, she no longer needed models. All the details were already in her head. If only they hadn't been, this aspect of her life might have been easier to bear. But she had concluded androgyny was an occupational hazard. The "masculine" energy that made her hunger for Clea sexually was the same energy that allowed her to pursue her work with ruthlessness, and to fill vacant space with the pictures in her head.

Like the tree falling in the woods with no one to hear it, if you didn't act on your attraction to women, were you nevertheless a lesbian? Was this why she always seemed to disappoint Terence, who yearned for some perfect union she couldn't comprehend, and which she regarded with impatience and irritation? Yet she was doing her damnedest to discharge her love for Clea into her work, while keeping her libido here at home with him. What more could he ask for, apart from her being a different person altogether?

Unwilling to destroy her erotic drawings, she filed them in a bottom drawer. If Terence took to snooping, he might be in for an unhappy surprise.

In time, it became clear to Elke that no new lover was going to take her place in Clea's heart. Clea mentioned various men with a bravado Elke found unattractive. And she dropped hints when she was living in Australia that she was investigating some rather dubious sexual practices. Elke half expected to hear that she'd been snuffed in a seedy Queensland motel. But Elke never gave Clea an opening to describe these investigations. Her Clea was invariably earnest, tender, and whimsical. Elke didn't want to hear about her more callous shadow side. During those years Clea appeared to require the tension of the hunt, and the excitement of sex before habit and familiarity diluted it. But Elke eventually realized that she was Clea's pole star, the fixed point of reference around which Clea's zodiac spun.

A few times Elke tried to even up their dance cards with tales of listless flirtation with Terence's graduate students. But Clea's real rival was Elke's work, which was now consuming most of her time and attention, yielding one startling piece after another—angular, jutting tangles of torn and tortured steel that echoed her memories of a world at war.

So Turner owed her one, thought Elke grimly. She'd preserved his marriage. The irony of great life dramas, however, was their ultimate irrelevance. Here fifteen years later Turner and Clea's marriage appeared to be dissolving anyway, as the children for whom it had been safeguarded departed. And Elke, so protective of her work as to refuse even one night of passion with Clea, had gone stale. Her bayoneted baby was an abomination, and she had no fresh ideas to take its place. Perhaps if she'd accepted the upheaval and risks inherent in a full-scale affair with Clea, her work would now be vital and innovative rather than clichéd and fatigued. Fate had a way of thumbing its nose at even your most tortured and conscientious decisions.

Turner stood up from a corner table with a red-checked cloth to greet her with a peck on her cheek. "It's good of you to come," he said, drawn and weary from his Mexico City flight.

"It's good of you to ask me."

"No, it's not," he sighed, pouring her some Burgundy. "It's totally selfish."

"Not totally. I'm worried about her too, you know."

Turner looked at her sharply, not having stated Clea as the reason for their dinner, and loathing it when his womenfolk second-guessed him. Though why else would either be willing to spend an evening in the other's company eating mediocre Italian food? "So tell me, Turner, are the Mexicans brushing after every meal?" Elke sipped her wine.

"Not enough to satisfy my sales curve. I had some of the great unbrushed lined up against a wall and shot, so maybe that'll help."

"Sounds like effective product promotion. I see you're growing a beard." She nodded approvingly at his mangy stubble.

"I'm trying to detract from the absence of hair on my head." He ran his hand sheepishly across his expanding bald spot.

"Very manly. You look a bit like 007."

"Elke! I had no idea you were so up on American pop culture."

"Oh, I'm full of surprises."

"So my wife tells me."

Elke eyed him. He always managed to slip in little reminders of his status as Clea's husband.

"So what's going on with Clea up there in the woods?" Turner asked, glancing at his menu. "Do you know?"

"She seems somewhat depressed to me."

"Depressed?" He sounded as though he were examining a cockroach. "Over what?"

"Who knows? Shifting hormones. Aging. Death. The children's departure. Her work. That mugging. If you're depressed, everything contributes."

"But it's not a bit like Clea."

Elke suppressed a smile. "Believe me, she's had her moments."

"She's never gone around bursting into tears," Turner insisted.

"No. She just goes numb. I'd say tears are progress."

They gazed at each other, locked in combat over who knew Clea better.

Lowering his eyes to his menu, Turner said, "I've always been glad that Clea has you in her life, Elke. She loves you very much, and I'm grateful for your devotion to her."

Feeling patronized, Elke continued to gaze at him ironically. No doubt this was one of the conciliatory tactics that had won Turner a

Fresh-It vice-presidency. She wondered what he really felt about her and Clea's relationship. She'd prefer anger and accusations to smarmy sentimentality.

"Oh, I suppose you're right, Elke," Turner said, laying down his menu and sitting back in his chair. "I remember first meeting her parents in Ohio. They drank Bloody Marys at lunch and had highball glasses in their hands all afternoon. Her mother kept talking about her happy, healthy, successful children. And her father kept delivering lectures on the virtues of America's heartland. When I asked Clea if they always drank that much, she claimed my being there was a special occasion. But I remember thinking at the time that Clea's aloofness, which I'd always admired, was at least partly a facade. That she was shell-shocked from such a confusing childhood. Everything lovely on the surface, but rotten underneath."

Elke nodded agreement. Turner had just answered her perennial question about Clea's difficulty in getting beneath appearances with her photos. Clea might possess an instinctive knowledge of, and aversion to, the underlying decay. Elke was moved to speechlessness. This was perhaps the first genuine exchange she and Turner had ever had in all these years of bonhomie.

"I need your advice, Elke."

Elke nodded, feeling illuminated: She'd just glimpsed the Turner that Clea loved, the sweet, serious man beneath the dizzy surface self-absorption.

"Do you think she's okay up there alone in the woods? Should I take time off to stay with her? Or insist she come back here?"

Elke thought this over, slowly turning her wineglass by its stem. "As much as I wish she'd stay here, Turner," she finally replied, "I think she's okay up there. If what she needs is to make a break with you and me, then it's just too bad for us." She was offering Turner solace. He and she were in this together, both tottering as one side of their elaborate polyhedron removed herself.

A look of contained panic came into Turner's eyes. "Do you think that's what she's doing?"

Elke shrugged. "It looks that way to me. Of course, she's always fallen in love with a thud. Perhaps she'll recover from Roches Ridge one of these days."

"How could someone fall in love with a dump like Roches Ridge?"

"People fall in love with anything. Look at nuns and their crucifixes."

Turner smiled.

"I suppose those of us who want to be involved with Clea have to accept a state of permanent transition," Elke said. "Because she won't sit still." Elke thought how in her own case they'd gone from the excitement of an infatuation, through passionate sexual desire, into familial affection. Unwilling to play father, husband, or lover, Elke had become aunt, sister, and friend. But now that the ties that blind were loosening, what would replace them? With a stab, Elke realized nothing might. And that the self-protection she was exercising by not returning Clea's recent calls and letters was not only understandable but necessary. She'd thought a lot about Clea's insisting, on her last trip home from Roches Ridge, that people needed their cocoons of well-being amid the chaos. But no doubt Clea never intended Elke to employ this advice against *herself*.


Turner crossed Washington Square, savoring the walk after his flight from Mexico City. He'd logged so many hours on planes it was a wonder his posture hadn't assumed the lines of a comma. He was distressed by Elke's assessment of Clea's current situation as her "making a break."

He had always regarded "intimacy" as one of the great therapeutic boondoggles of the seventies. To him the term promised only the cloying suffocation he'd experienced in that tiny Milwaukee apartment with his strident aunt, mother, and sisters, and his passive, cowed father. The intimacy he'd experienced during his years of coming and going with Clea had been about as much as he could stand. Yet the idea of doing without their occasional talks, in which she skillfully extracted his true thoughts and feelings, was horrifying. Almost more horrifying than not having occasional access to her magnificent body. Fetching female bodies he could acquire as needed, but not Clea's instinctual understanding and ready sympathy. She knew him more thoroughly than anyone else, yet accepted and admired him nonetheless. And you couldn't buy that on the streets or seduce it at parties.

Elke was looking more handsome with each passing year, as her features sharpened and her hair silvered. No wonder Clea loved her so much. He envied their connection. Not because it deprived him in any way, since Clea always had as much time for him as he could endure. Had until this move to Roches Ridge, at any rate. In fact, in some ways Elke had taken the heat off him, feeding Clea's fires with emotional tinder he didn't possess. But he suspected that what the two of them shared had a savor he was incapable of tasting.

He smiled, remembering Clea in Paris begging him to coach her in the art of the casual affair. He let her believe it was a gift he possessed, rather than a disability he was afflicted with. Oh, he was an asset at a cocktail party or in a boardroom. He could charm a crowd or close a deal. But he had no talent for sitting down, looking people in the eye, and finding out what was on their minds and in their hearts. For years he'd studied Clea's connections—with Elke, with himself, with Kate and Theo, with dozens of casual friends. Like any virtuoso, she made it look easy. But for him it wasn't. And if Clea withdrew from him for good, she would take that skill with her, leaving him to empty affairs, cocktail party banter, and the babble of vying businessmen.

But maybe Elke was mistaken. She was depressed all the time herself, and she often created other people in her own image.

# 25   Gordon McQueen

As Gordon's lips met Randall's, he felt desire pump through his veins like maple sap through plastic tubing on a warm March afternoon. Stepping back, he held Randall at arms' length. Each other's mirror image—jeans, flannel shirts, down vests, work boots, short dark hair, closely clipped beards and mustaches. Narcissism, pure and simple. Randall smiled. When they were first together, each was certain the other would fade back into the night. There had been such awful urgency to drain the cup of passion to its dregs. But after several years, they were beginning to trust that it would continue to happen, whatever else might happen in the meantime.

Three stanchioned cows munched grain while the automatic milking machines sucked milk from their udders and conveyed it along plastic tubing to a refrigerated tank. Gordon glanced toward the front window of the concrete milking parlor—and saw a woman with dark hair, camera around her neck. "Don't look now, but we have guests," murmured Gordon. Randall pulled back. "Relax. I don't think she saw us."

"Hi," said Gordon, stepping out into the sun. "Didn't see you there.

Kinda noisy with the milking machines and all." The woman wore a trench coat, collar turned up.

"Hi. I'm new in town. Clea Shawn." She extended her hand. Gordon gave her his own.

"Something I can do for you?"

"I saw your sign in the IGA. About the golden retriever puppies."

"Oh. Right. The puppies."

"But I don't want to interrupt."

"No problem. Just a sec." Opening the door, he called, "Randall, I'm going to show this woman the puppies. Keep an eye on Maude, will you? She's almost done."

They picked their way through thawing mud toward a redbrick colonial with a long white frame ell that connected to a white barn, behind which stood a mountain of manure and two blue Harvestore silos. One had an American flag decal near the top. On the other was spray-painted LONG LIVE THE GANG OF FOUR.

"I guess you must be Jared's brother," said Clea. "I saw you driving your wagon along the green the other day."

"You met Jared, did you?"

"Yesterday. At Casa Loretta."

"He's just moved home from Albany. Now all us kids are back in town."

"Uh, excuse me," said Clea, gesturing to the spray-painted silo. "But what does that mean?"

Gordon laughed. "Got me. I woke up one morning and there it was. There's this guy at Camel's Hump Community College, name of Alvin Jacobs, my baby brother's political science professor. Always trying to organize the farmers around town to burn down the Xerox factory."

"But isn't the Gang of Four already dead?"

"Beats me."

As Gordon approached the ell, dogs within began howling and hurling themselves against the door. "Sorry no one's around. My mother's gone to Burlington."

"Shopping?"

"No. We just heard my brother Dan was hurt playing hockey at Camel's Hump. My mother went up to the medical center."

"Badly hurt?"

"Don't know yet. Could be. Got flung headfirst into a wall. Unconscious, last I heard."

"That's gotten to be such a rough sport. I'm sorry."

"Me too. He's a good kid. Oughta be. I raised him up right."

"You're the oldest?"

"Yup."

Clea knelt to play with some wriggling auburn puppies, the mother emitting faint warning snarls. "They're beauties."

"Nothing like a puppy for cuteness."

As Clea carried her chosen puppy to her car, she studied the cinder-block milking parlor with the patient black-and-white cows lined up outside. "So I guess you put the whole family to work during milking hours?"

Gordon looked at her with amusement. "Most have jobs over to Xerox now. So it's me and whoever I can hire."

"Do you mind if I take some pictures?" She put the puppy on a blanket in the back seat and reached for her Nikon. Gordon ran his fingers over a deep scratch down the side of her expensive car.

"Help yourself," he said, wondering why someone would want pictures at this time of year. The roads and barnyard were a sea of mud, and cluster flies and wasps crawled all over the sunny sides of buildings. Carpenter ants were swarming around exposed beams. Poor old Zeno Racine was man of the hour, racing around town with his Tri-Die. Gordon watched Clea angle her camera to exclude the mud and LONG LIVE THE GANG OF FOUR, focusing on the old brick house and the sugar bush on the hillside.

As the woman drove away, the puppy's terrified yapping drifted out her window. Sorel boots, a trench coat, and a lumberjack shirt. Well, the more queers around town, the better. Might help take the heat off him. Soon everyone was going to know. If they didn't already, after Daryl Perkins mistook Gordon's friends for space aliens and crashed the Gayride last fall. Gordon smiled, remembering Perkins ducking his red head inside the horse-drawn wagon as they stopped in Granite Gap for a pee break.

"Is it you?" demanded Perkins.

"Who?" asked Gordon, looking up from smooching with Randall.

"Have you come for us?" Daryl shone his flashlight at the piles of embracing men, then backed down the road on his aluminum crutches, holding them off with his flashlight as if it were an M-1. Since then Daryl had painted some new Bible quotations on his yellow van. One read: THE WOMAN SHALL NOT WEAR THAT WHICH PERTAINETH UNTO A MAN, NEITHER SHALL A MAN PUT ON A WOMAN'S GARMENT: FOR ALL THAT DO SO ARE ABOMINATIONS UNTO THE LORD THY GOD. DEUT. 22:5. So Gordon and some friends dressed in drag on Halloween night and went trick or treating at Daryl's yellow school bus.

Gordon walked back through the muck to the milking parlor. All his life Gordon had tried to be a good boy. He'd taken girls to movies in Rutland, held their hands, and covered his erection with his jacket. He'd kissed them and touched them until they demanded commitment. He'd committed, and come, and gone away in a flood of reproaches. But he loathed this hypocrisy, calling lust "love." It demeaned both. And his thoughts were always of nights at deer camp when some drunken friend would blow him or jerk him off, and never let on the next day. The rest of the year, excitement with these pals consisted of drinking a six-pack, then driving their dogs through the automatic car wash to watch them freak out over the swirling brushes. Or sitting in Casa Loretta holding up fingers to rate the sexiness of girls who walked by. Or watching the sheets of ice that floated down Mink Creek in spring shatter as they swept over the falls.

And then one night Gordon drove to Montreal and walked into a bathhouse on Saint Denis, and his years of turmoil fell away. Getting his rocks off without condemning himself to a lifetime of PTA meetings had seemed incredible. And the excitement of the pursuit: spotting a muscled body through the steam, making eye contact, maneuvering an encounter, ducking into a cubicle, knowing no heart would be broken when you left without a phone number.

But of course the price was proving higher than anyone could have imagined, now that all those glorious years of chicken were coming home to roost. AIDS seemed like the invention of a sadist. Constructing people with overpowering drives, then killing them off if they tried to discover harmless ways to discharge them. What a choice: You could burn, marry, or die. Most of his childhood pals were now married, with several kids, and jobs at the quarry or the Xerox factory. In their spare time they butchered small animals in the woods and brutalized their wives and children in their Sunset View trailers. Yet it was Gordon who was considered abnormal. When he ran into these friends around town, they acted nervous and departed quickly. Maybe they also remembered how much fun those drunken nights at deer camp used to be.

Gordon walked up to a workhorse standing by the pasture fence alongside the milking parlor and stroked his velvet nose. The horse shoved Gordon's hand to signal his wish for oats. "You old slugabed," said Gordon. "It's not even noon yet."

Gordon felt like a walking time bomb. Two friends had already died. He and several other friends had tended one in shifts, and watched the disintegration of the man they all loved, remembering his gusto for life, watching his skin go yellow and stretch tautly over his bones, listening to his tortured breathing, wondering who would be next. But death by AIDS sometimes seemed preferable to death by the monotony of monogamy. "Safe sex" was a contradiction in terms. The whole appeal of sex lay in its wild unpredictability.

Once Gordon stopped by the Karma Café to chat with Ishtar, and she described her agonized struggle with Starshine and Morning Glory. Who said what to whom. Who slept with whom behind whose back.

"But why don't you and Morning Glory just go for it until you're sick of it, and not worry about all this other stuff?" he finally asked.

Ishtar looked at him as though he were a Neanderthal. He knew men were retards at relationships, but love between women looked like a quagmire of tears and bile and menstrual blood. He feared his sisters in Sodom often equated intimacy with emotional collapse. That Ishtar had time to run a pretty good restaurant was a minor miracle. Ishtar assured him that if he didn't shape up, he'd come back in his next life as a dyke. But better a dyke than a het. As far as he was concerned, there were three types of human beings—men, women, and real people.

"The man of the house," his mother used to call him, as they stood over his drunken father. His father would stagger to his feet and beat the shit out of him. No one was sorry when Gordon's father moved out, and Gordon had been running the farm ever since. His father married some masochist in Burlington, attended AA, joined the Baptist Church, worked at GE as a security guard, was doing the whole recovering-alcoholic trip, complete with letters of amend. More power to him, but he'd left his trail of tears.

Even now Gordon sometimes lashed out at Randall for some imagined slight, leaving Randall bewildered and offended. Gordon wanted the tenderness with a man he'd never had from his father. But when he achieved it, it was so unfamiliar that he found ways to interpret it as the hostility he was accustomed to. He'd learned this in therapy with Genevieve Paxton at the Center for Sanity. She said the metaphor for it was the dog who drowned while attacking its own reflection in a pool. But Randall stayed, determined to convince Gordon that he really loved him, and wasn't trying to hurt or humiliate him. Whether Randall's mission would be successful remained to be seen.

Gordon's father kept buying his kids VCRs and microwave ovens.

Jared went to visit him the week before and came home in tears. His father had ridiculed Mane Magnifique and ordered him to shave properly. Maybe his new young wife fell for Jared. People always did. He was sweet as well as gorgeous. A fatal combination.

Gordon opened the door to the milking parlor, walked in, and draped his arm across Randall's muscled shoulders—accomplices in the crime of loving their fellowman.

# 26  A Can of Worms

Clea squatted among the weeds in her backyard with her new puppy. After initial distress at being separated from mother and siblings, he was now hurtling around the yard, yapping at sluggish flies. Because of the puppy's auburn coat, Clea had decided to call him Brandy. He was reminding her of Kate and Theo. He'd race off into the brush, sniffing. Suddenly he'd realize he was all alone and would rush back to her side for pats and reassurance. Once he'd had his fill, he'd scramble down and race away again, pursuing some elusive winged insect.

This was not a role she performed with grace, Clea realized, standing up and brushing the mud off her tweed trousers. Witness her departure for Roches Ridge once Kate and Theo left for school. She loathed waiting around like a pillar for her loved ones to pee against when they wanted to reclaim home territory. When Kate and Theo were babies, they required, and gave, total devotion. But once they were toddlers and wanted her to stay on the sofa while they explored the upper reaches of the Turtle Bay town house, her enthusiasm dimmed. It reminded her too much of their father.

Nevertheless, she'd always done her best. Wherever her family was living, she tried to be home after school. And to eat supper with the children and read to them before bedtime. She diligently monitored their emotional and physical health, their wardrobes, schoolwork, and playmates. Whenever they displayed the slightest interest in any topic, she procured books and arranged lessons to develop it. On weekends she corralled Turner for family outings to historical monuments and cultural events. Although it wasn't always possible, she tried to arrange work trips during school vacations so the children could accompany her. Looking back, she had no idea how she'd managed. Because at the same time she was also pursuing a demanding career and undergoing continuous emotional upheaval over a variety of lovers and other projects.

Following a long Christmas vacation in New York, the Shawns arrived in Sydney in 1980 in the middle of the sweltering Australian summer. Their rented house was in a suburb on a bay across from Sydney harbor, with its shell-like opera house. One afternoon not long after their arrival, she sat on a blanket on a nearby beach with Kate and Theo, discussing with horrified fascination the shark net across the mouth of the bay. Each was eating a meat pie into which the attendant at the snack counter had squirted mashed peas and ketchup.

As Theo dribbled ketchup down his chest, Clea noticed a tuft of coarse black hair near his throat. His voice had already started to crack. His sturdy boy's body looked as though it had been stretched in traction to twice its original length. The flesh now seemed barely to cover his painfully apparent rib cage and knobby joints. And Kate, wearing a microscopic bikini, suddenly had breasts and periods. She was demurely eyeing a Muscle Beach tableau a few yards away, which featured blond teenagers with golden tans, frolicking to a blaring rock radio station amid Frisbees and beer cans. This had all happened so gradually that Clea hadn't really put it together until now: Her babies had grown up. She glanced back and forth between them with alarm as Theo handed half his mango to Kate.

At Christmas the children had begged to live with Elke and go to a New York high school, or to attend an American boarding school. *They* might have been ready for this separation, but Turner and Clea weren't. So here they sat, disgruntled at having to make yet another group of friends they'd soon be leaving. But at least this time they weren't faced with a new language or a totally incomprehensible culture.

Still, Clea realized, as Kate and Theo raced across the sand to the water to rinse off the sticky mango juice, it was time to return to America for good. The children ought to be hanging out with their peers, not with their mother. When they first moved to Paris, she'd had no idea this exile would extend to three more countries and ten more years. But now Turner had conquered the globe and could return to New York in triumph, to assume the vice-presidency Fresh-It had been grooming him for so assiduously. She only hoped this nomadic life hadn't been too hard on the children. Turner's and her goal had been to turn them into citizens of the world, who would be free of narrow local prejudice. But perhaps they'd overdone it and failed to give the children a stable fulcrum. Neither she nor Turner, growing up, had had a model of parenthood that inspired emulation. Both had invented their style from scratch, and who knew if it was viable? Kate and Theo were test cases, poor darlings.

That evening some of Turner's colleagues arrived for a barbecue at the Shawns' rented house, a glass-and-wood contemporary set in a jungle of subtropical foliage. Clea, dressed in a floral cotton kaftan and sandals, performed her hostess function with élan. The requirements for making her guests comfortable and herself charming were so familiar by now that she could have sleepwalked her way through this party. And the guests were so similar to Turner's colleagues in all the other countries that she could have spoken their lines for them.

She watched with affectionate exasperation as Turner talked animatedly to a woman in white rayon trousers and a silver silk undershirt that displayed pert breasts to advantage. The poor man couldn't help himself. He was a congenital flirt. It was probably as hereditary as his receding blond hairline.

After the guests left, she and Turner wandered around the floodlit yard collecting cups and plates, while unfamiliar insects rasped among the intoxicating frangipani. Turner paused to take her in his arms and kiss her tenderly. "Thanks, wife."

"No problem, husband."

"So what do you think of our companions for the next year?"

"I gather you have plans for the woman in the silk undershirt?" Clea backed out of his embrace to inspect his face in the shadows. He grimaced and said nothing, hating as usual to discover that his deepest secrets were completely obvious to Clea.

"Turner, are you sure this is what you really want?" she asked with a fond smile.

"It's not a question of what I want. It's what we've got."

"We've got our current arrangement because it's what ... we want." She nearly said "you." But she'd participated in this circus for many years, so presumably it was what she wanted too, since she'd never been noted for docility. "If we wanted something different, we could find a way to do that."

"What are you saying?"

"We could switch jobs and stay home in New York with each other. Or we could agree to do without sex when we're apart."

"Clea," said Turner earnestly, holding her by the shoulders at arms' length. "One more year and we'll be back in New York for good. In the meantime, the past is over and the future may never arrive. The present moment is all any of us has got, so let's just enjoy it."

Clea sighed and smiled faintly. "Okay, Zorba. But just remember that you asked for it."

"What does that mean?" he asked with alarm.

"I don't know." Clea was alarmed herself, having no idea where those words came from or what they were forecasting.

A few days later she drove down the coast between Sydney and Melbourne to photograph the sweeping white sand beaches for Allan Barkham. The success of her picture books had enabled her to line up several jobs in the antipodes when she was in New York at Christmas. Though she stayed away from home overnight as little as possible because of Kate and Theo, this time she got stuck at nightfall several hours south of Sydney in a small beach town called Ulladulla. She phoned Turner and then checked into a motel on a cliff above the ocean. After unpacking in the unadorned little room with its painted concrete floor, she went out into the tepid night air and strolled across a lawn decorated with plaster elves.

Looking down the cliff to pale sand that stretched out of sight in both directions, she thought about the thousands of miles of sea before her and the thousands of miles of desert at her back. She thought about time and eternity, the vanished past and the uncertain future. She thought about acres of white crosses, and women in silk undershirts. She thought about rasping night insects and the fleeting nature of the present moment. And about Elke on Saint John beneath the slowly circling wooden fan. And about the bald Zen master in his black belted robe.

In town, after a supper of beer and greasy fish and chips, she wandered around the sidewalks watching children browbeating parents into buying inflatable plastic sharks, and teenagers dancing barefoot on a sandy wooden deck. She bought a postcard of a naked woman emerging from a giant conch shell and mailed it to Elke in New York. Then she bought a pack of prelubricated condoms without really wondering why.

Pulling into her parking space at the motel, she noticed a middle-aged man in blue gym shorts and a green Great Barrier Reef T-shirt carrying a suitcase from a Ford Escort into the next room. He had fashionably styled gray hair and a trimmed mustache to match. Going into her room, Clea switched on "Dallas" and sat on her bed to contemplate the long hot lonely night ahead. In Kyoto she had tried to learn how to sit quietly in a room and be happy, but she had failed. Now she felt the dreaded, if familiar, state of restlessness begin to creep up on her. But Turner was in Sydney. John Galmer was in Ithaca. Allan Barkham was in New York. Grégoire was in Brussels. Phil was in Houston. And Johannes was in Copenhagen. Besides, she'd finally recognized the script her affairs tended to follow: After an initial rush of giddy oblivion, reality set in and complications began. Sleeping with someone was like opening a can of worms.

However, it occurred to her as she watched Sue Ellen Ewing drink herself into a stupor over J.R.'s infidelities, what if there was no affair? What if you were driven only by your own needs, rather than being drawn by the other person's charms? What if there was only the impersonal friction between interlocking body parts? Perhaps then there would be no complications, and therefore no pain for anyone. Maybe she could beat men at their own game, using them for her purposes and then dismissing them. She could purchase lacy lingerie and become a lascivious creature of the night. These thoughts, and the one that followed of the tight buttocks in the blue gym shorts next door, generated enough titillation in Clea to blot out any lingering awareness of ethics, metaphysics, or public hygiene.

Knocking on his door, Clea asked her pleasantly surprised neighbor to fix her toilet, which wouldn't stop running. As the man walked ahead of her into her room in his flip-flops and plunged his hands into the toilet tank, she studied his green T-shirt, which clung to his muscled back in dark patches of sweat.

When he finished, he turned around and said, "There you go, mate. That ought to fix you up."

She slowly and deliberately ran her eyes down his T-shirt to his blue gym shorts and let them rest there, watching in silence, while moisture dripped off her toilet tank into a puddle on the linoleum floor. She returned her eyes to his, which were startled and hopeful. Untucking her shirt and beginning to unbutton it, she backed into the bedroom and turned off "Dallas."

An hour later the man left, at her request, and she lay on the damp sheets and reviewed her behavior with amazement. This was a new face to the many-headed Hydra called sex. That one word had to describe a variety of dissimilar sensations—from domestic affection, through breathless passion with all its conviction of connection and purpose, to the temporary oblivion of tonight's impersonal coupling.

Since she didn't even know her neighbor's name and he had called her Noreen, any fantasies in operation had been solitary. There was none of the delicious exhilaration of finally devouring forbidden fruit with someone you had desired for a long time. There was, however, a kind of lurid excitement, to do partly with the danger of the unknown. It had blotted out for a time all awareness of her surroundings or her companion. But as that jittery, jangling sensation faded, Clea felt vague distaste. And there was still the rest of this hot, heavy night to be gotten through. She went into the bathroom and tried to scrub her flesh clean under the shower.

Chalking it up to an interesting experiment, Clea stretched out on her bed and pulled up the sheet. As she lay in the dark, with the cries of night insects pulsing in the yard, she wondered how she could shift in the course of a single day from being a patient, adoring mother, to an attentive wife, to a lavish hostess, to an exacting photographer, to a driven sensualist who had just lain panting and moaning with a stranger like a wild animal in estrus? Maybe she had multiple personalities. Yet she, whoever that was, was able to catalogue these incompatible personae, so presumably she hadn't yet crossed over into the realm of psychopathology.

As time went on she perhaps *did* cross that threshold. What started as an experiment in Ulladulla became almost as compulsive as an obsessional's hand-washing. It was not difficult to find accomplices on the nights when she was away from home, in that country where men still regarded themselves as hunters. And during these sexual rites she first glimpsed the answer to the question she had asked Grégoire at the war cemetery in Flanders, of why men wanted to live together in tents and kill each other. It was an alternative to sitting alone in rooms and wanting to kill *themselves*. Evidently some people, herself included, preferred even unpleasant activity to none.

Every culture she'd ever read about or observed had its techniques for achieving an intoxication that lifted members out of their daily rut of boredom and suffering, and gave them an illusion of participation in some larger, purposeful whole. African tribes had their drumming and dancing. Mexican Indians had their peyote. Modern males had their wars, and Clea had sex. But like any narcotic, this anonymous sex quickly lost its punch for Clea, so that she required it more as she enjoyed it less. And she began to awake in the morning with a hangover of self-disgust.

Her body evidently possessing a graver sense of self-preservation than her brain, she developed chronic cystitis, which put a halt to her debauch. And soon the Shawns returned to New York for good.

Once home and healed, Clea, always a reluctant learner, tested polluted waters once more, seducing a young advertising executive on Martinique, who gave her a hot weekend and a long bout with hepatitis. As she lay in her sickbed at Turtle Bay, she finally realized that she'd been approaching relationships like a chain letter, recovering from the last person by passing her need to the next. Until the recipients had become indistinguishable. It was past time to break this chain and endure whatever calamities might ensue.

Which she finally accomplished that night at Sutton Place when she walked out on Jim from *Getaway* magazine, gave up her drug forever, and cast in her lot with Roches Ridge.

As Brandy yapped frantically from the vicinity of the Marshes' back shed, Clea reflected that during these years Elke had provided the psychic glue that kept Clea's conflicting personalities from flying apart like an exploding supernova. Her steady love had burned through Clea's chaos like a fog-shrouded sun. She listened to tales of Clea's exploits without encouragement but without condemnation. Her witty, insightful letters followed Clea around the globe. And when the Shawns were on leave in New York, she appeared at birthdays and holidays with wonderful gifts and appropriate remarks. She met each family member at airports any hour of the day or night, and her guest room was always available. She listened to the complaints and confessions of both children when they were hating their parents. She arranged with the cleaning service to prepare the Turtle Bay house for the Shawns' arrivals, and she kept an eye on house-sitters. She fed pets and watered plants. She consistently assured Clea that Kate and Theo were not going to become mass murderers just because Clea took them to live in foreign countries and sought assistance from housekeepers. In short, Elke was the doting aunt Kate and Theo otherwise lacked, and the patient older sister Clea had never had. Thus did Elke and Clea resolutely turn down the wick of the passion that had threatened to burn up both their houses, retaining from the conflagration a soothing blaze.

Meanwhile, Elke was producing one stunning sculpture after another from scraps of rusted steel. Since some featured a stylized woman or child or both in some ghastly situation engineered by men, Elke enjoyed eventual lionization by feminists. But her aversion to travel and her apparent indifference to honors allowed her to resist the impedimenta of her growing fame—speaking engagements, workshops, shows, and interviews. All her energy went into her work. And as her career flourished, Elke gained self-confidence, if not optimism. So evidently, Clea reflected, Elke's and her decision not to attempt a shared domestic life had been the right one.

Yet recently something had gone awry. "Suffer the Little Children" was a misstep. Not a misstep, a marking of time. Elke appeared stalled. And she hadn't returned Clea's calls and letters from Roches Ridge. Clea felt her backing away. Then Clea recalled she herself was the one who'd left town.

Brandy came tearing around the corner of the house as though pursued by a wolf pack and flung himself against Clea's knees, nearly knocking her over. She bent down and scooped up the wriggling ball of auburn fur, holding him before her so his writhing rear legs hung down to expose his fuzzy belly.

"Relax, Brandy." She laughed. Trying to cuddle the squirming creature in one arm, she walked toward the house. The sun was going down, and the air was chilly. Time to get cleaned up for the Miss Teenage Roches Ridge Pageant, whatever that might be. But she was accustomed to attending such incomprehensible local ceremonies as Guy Fawkes bonfires in England, to indicate her goodwill and her wish to participate in the community. Of course, those other forays were temporary. Whereas Roches Ridge was for real and forever.

Atop the wrecked autos in the Marshes' backyard stood the surly young man who'd shut the door in her face that morning. He was sweating over his crowbar, jeans dangerously low on his hips, back muscles straining and rippling. Noticing the puppy, he gave a curt nod. There was something almost Heathcliffian about this young man. Clea suspected a loyalty and sweetness lurked beneath all that surface belligerence. She felt a sudden challenge to tame this wild mountain man, stroke the black hair off his forehead, unzip those disgusting jeans. . . .

Assessing these thoughts as she kicked open her door, Clea was appalled. One of her former personalities was attempting to assert itself. For God's sake, the poor boy wasn't much older than her own children. Besides, she'd done enough taming of others. It was time to tame herself.

# 27 Miss Teenage Roches Ridge

The main room in the town hall was festooned with crepe paper. The basketball goals had been raised to permit a clear view of the stage backdrop, a painting of a marble staircase and railings, which was framed by moth-eaten maroon velvet curtains. A dozen young women in bathing suits were lined up, striking poses and looking terrified.

In the front row sat Astrid Starr, squat and bejeweled, giving her husband, Earl Atkins, hand signals about the sound and lighting systems as he peeked through the curtains from backstage. Jared McQueen in his leather bomber jacket, spikes of golden hair a tawny forest, was scrutinizing each girl's clip as though judging a dog show. Beside him sat Ida Campbell, briefcase of Avon products in her lap for last-minute touch-ups on contestants.

Across from Clea sat Loretta Gebo, her beehive periodically illuminated by the spotlight so that its tilted shadow appeared on the marble staircase mural. Ray Marsh, in camouflage pants, with a hooded air force parka in his lap, sat beside Loretta. Halfway down that row was Jared's farmer brother, Gordon McQueen, who'd sold Clea the puppy that morning. Brandy was probably shredding Calvin's stacks of *National Enquirers* in Clea's kitchen at that very moment. The man beside Gordon looked like an identical twin, with closely cropped dark hair, beard and mustache, plaid wool shirt and jeans.

Toward the front Clea spotted surly Dack Marsh, with his dark straight hair, high cheekbones, copper coloring, and Roman nose. Clea pictured that bizarre cross with the crucified rodent skeleton on the wall above his TV. It exhibited a savage artistry that made her want to know who had assembled it and why.

Beside Dack sat several others Clea had seen around the house next door: a rotund older woman with frizzy gray hair, who wore a mauve Chanel suit; the small, dark man with the pencil mustache who drove the van to the back shed the night before (his head was shaped like the rodent skull on that cross, with the same prominent feral teeth); and to his right, a woman with a blond bouffant that resembled a fallen soufflé compared to Loretta's. Diagonally across the gym Clea spotted the lapsed Boudicca from the Karma Café, in an overgrown crew cut, with several tiny hoops and cuffs on her ears. Although she'd lived here only a couple of weeks, Clea already recognized a dozen or more faces in this room. Yet after twenty-five years of New York City, she rarely recognized anyone at public events.

Clea's eyes returned to Dack Marsh. She pictured him atop his mountain of cars, hacking and ripping with his crowbar, copper chest glistening with sweat. She wondered if he'd keep her awake again that night with the spotlight through her window. She wondered if she'd again be drawn to her window to watch him. Something about all that primitive vitality was compelling.

Father Flanagan was trying not to watch the girls in their bathing suits. Stiff white collar chafing his chin, he kept stretching and twisting his neck. Lou Ann Asher stalked across the stage in black patent-leather spike heels and a glossy turquoise suit with leg holes to her waist. Father Flanagan remembered christening her, a tiny squalling baby in a long white gown. How these little girls grew, insisting on turning into magnets for male lust.

His first years as a priest had involved a South Boston parish, where he was adopted by the huge families. But then he was transferred to Roches Ridge. He remembered looking out the bus window at a bleak little settlement perched atop a precipice overlooking a swamp. Father Flanagan spent his days ministering to farmers and laborers, migrants from remote Quebec towns who spoke very little, and then only a stammering patois. He spent his nights in the lonely rectory on the green, struggling with his rebellious spirit, which demanded friends and family and fun such as he had enjoyed among the gregarious South Boston Irish.

Theresa, the widow from next door, came in to cook and clean, wearing a straw pillbox hat decorated with wooden cherries and a housedress with padded shoulders. One night after drying the dinner dishes, she came into his book-lined study and said, "I could sit with you for a while, Father."

"That won't be necessary."

"I know it's not necessary, but I'd like to. You seem so lonely."

So she began spending an hour with him. And then the evening, mending his vestments. After she went home, Father Flanagan would pass the night on his knees in his study, pleading with God for guidance. When he wrote requesting a transfer, he received no answer.

And then one night Theresa didn't leave until dawn, returning under the gaze of work-bound Roches Ridge to cook his breakfast as though nothing had happened.

He informed Theresa they'd sinned, and that it must never happen again. But the next morning he awoke in the blood-red dawn to find her curled beside him like a stealthy cat. Stroking his face, she maintained that loving God's creatures enhanced love for their Creator. Father Flanagan knew this was sensualist theology unworthy of a priest pledged to love all God's creatures without favoritism. But the problem for which seminary had not prepared him was that he loved Theresa. And he loved what they did together in his bed after the fire in the study died down and they took that long climb hand in hand up the stairs.

He finally found some relief by redefining his vow of celibacy, excluding only a liaison that might distract him from his duties to all God's family. But *this* liaison was making him more effective, his new happiness communicating itself, so that his parishioners laughed and joked with him as never before.

And then one night at the dinner table, Theresa told him she was carrying their child. He stood up, rushed to his study, locked the door, and fell to his knees.

Theresa went to an aunt's in Iowa. She named the baby Barbara before giving her up. He informed her they'd been heaping sin upon sin and that she must come to his bed no longer. Tears running down her cheeks, she insisted this was his worst sin yet. That was over twenty years ago. Now she left after the supper dishes, and he sat in his study alone, watching "The Cosby Show" and "Murder, She Wrote."

Roches Ridge was his purgatory. He often recalled a quote from seminary: "From our vices God makes whips to scourge us." To watch Theresa stroll across the green to chat with Ishtar at the Karma Café, to see her at the stove cooking his supper and at the railing partaking of the host, but not to be able to touch her ever again, was a torture worthy of the Inquisition.

Theresa, still wearing a straw pillbox, sat two rows down the gym from Father Flanagan, beside Dr. and Mrs. Evans. The doctor had probably delivered most Miss Teenage Roches Ridge contestants. He had confirmed Theresa's pregnancy all those years ago, but he never let on to Father Flanagan by so much as a raised eyebrow. Once Father Flanagan called on him to complain about the bags of Valium Dr. Evans was dispensing. Father Flanagan's flock was ceasing to experience the anxiety that could propel them into the embrace of the Holy Mother.

Dr. Evans, in his white lab coat and wire-rimmed spectacles, studied Father Flanagan from behind his desk, on which sat the bags in question. Finally he replied, "Let's face it, Father: You and I are in the same racket—relieving human suffering. It's just that *my* wafers work."

Had he done right, Father Flanagan wondered, to pick his duty to God over his duty to Theresa and their child? Or had he taken the coward's way out, fearful of public derision and the loss of his livelihood? Some days he saw himself as a noble steward of the Lord, renouncing personal pleasure for a life of service; other days, as the most pitiful creature who ever prayed to God for forgiveness.

As Daisy Wagner tap-danced to "Me and My Shadow," Father Flanagan touched his Pro-Life lapel pin with his fingertips. Two tiny gold footprints the size of a ten-week fetus's. At least Theresa had allowed their baby to live. If people performed irresponsible sexual acts, they should bear the consequences, just as he and Theresa had all these years.

Across the aisle Father Flanagan spotted Loretta Gebo and Rayon Marsh, Loretta's beehive towering over the audience like a lighthouse. The spotlight kept sweeping across it to cast a phallic shadow on the stage backdrop. When Father Flanagan's loneliness became intolerable, he strolled to Casa Loretta for a chat with Loretta about her latest lost lottery. She had a big bet riding on this pageant. He used to tell her she couldn't lose if she bet on the Lord, because if the afterlife was a reality, she'd partake of it. And if it wasn't, she'd never know the difference. But lately he had ceased trying to impart this faith to anyone. When he stood at the altar now, carefully removing the embroidered cloth over the communion chalice, he felt like a failed magician with no rabbit to display.

Some nights he went to the Karma Café for herb tea with Ishtar in her jungle of spider plants. Ishtar had some heretical notions about eternity, feeling she'd already lived many different lives.

Once she ridiculed his lapel pin: "What makes you think the fetus isn't running the show? Whispering its preferences into the mother's ear. Choosing a U-turn before emerging on a dead-end highway. Pushing the eject button on a doomed flight. Give a fetus a break, Father!"

He stretched his neck out of his stiff white collar like an agitated turtle.

"I mean, I'm adopted. Maybe my mother would have done me a favor to set me free to try again with a mother who really wanted me. Instead of condemning me to a lifetime of feeling deserted and excluded. And pursuing people who turn around and reject me all over again."

"Don't say that," pleaded Father Flanagan.

"Why not, if it's what I feel?"

Earl Atkins peeked out from behind the curtains, belly first, like Alfred Hitchcock. Father Flanagan remembered Earl's coming to confession in pieces after his wife ran off with that roofer. Now that Earl had found Astrid, he was full of energy and optimism. How could an abstraction like God compete with a warm-fleshed woman? Lowering his head into his hands, Father Flanagan prayed to God to restore his belief in Him.


Bethany Wagner was filled with pride as her daughter, Daisy, tap-danced to "Me and My Shadow," playing tag with her actual shadow from the spotlight. The spotlight kept projecting Loretta Gebo's bee-hive onto the backdrop as well. But surely the judges wouldn't hold that against Daisy. This act might take Daisy to the Miss Teenage America nationals in Dubuque. Daisy would take over where Bethany, shanghaied into motherhood on the brink of the big time, left off.

Bethany O'Toole was a Las Vegas cocktail waitress with a nineteen-inch waist and a thirty-eight-inch chest. She loved watching men drool as they stuck dollar bills down the top of her silver lamé body suit. Ken Wagner, newly divorced, on vacation from Syracuse to gamble for the first time, was fresh-faced, boyish, and naive. To her he was just another tourist, but for him their nights together were apparently profoundly meaningful, instigating a series of trips, presents, phone calls, and memos. Bethany eventually acquiesced when he insisted on rescuing her from her degradation.

But life in his suburban Syracuse ranch house wasn't what Bethany had bargained for. Obsessively attentive during courtship, Ken was absent once they wed, leaving her at the mercy of awkward tea parties with the other Syracuse Xerox wives.

In desperation Bethany began lifting dumbbells at the Gloria Stevens figure salon in the neighborhood shopping mall. Soon she switched to barbells at Steve's Gym in downtown Syracuse. Eventually Steve himself began spotting for her. And one day he asked her to be his partner for a mixed body-building contest.

Bethany became a real gym animal, going under the iron three times a day, seven days a week—biceps, chest, abs and calves one day;

triceps and thighs the next; then calves and abs, back and shoulders. When she wasn't tossing iron, she was practicing posing routines with Steve or working on her tan. Her training schedule left no time for Ken, who was so busy scaling the Xerox ladder that he scarcely noticed.

Bethany posted Arnold Schwarzenegger's photo on their refrigerator door. Her plans for her body exceeded anything then regarded as feasible for a woman. Her Las Vegas wasp waist was now twenty-four inches of hard-packed muscle, her voluptuous breasts a rock-solid forty-two inches, her biceps fourteen and a half inches of pure protein. Steve and she eventually became Mr. and Ms. Empire State. They posed for photographers, conducted body-building seminars, and began looking into endorsements. There was talk of a world tour, ending in Nice, where Steve would compete in the World's Strongest Man event. He'd begun preparing by lifting boulders onto trash barrels behind the gym, and turning over cars in the parking lot, and bench-pressing an oak crucifix.

When Xerox transferred Ken to Roches Ridge, Vermont, Bethany found herself facing the most poignant decision of her life—whether to be Mrs. Ken Wagner or Ms. Olympia. She'd just about decided on Ms. Olympia when she discovered she was pregnant.

Bethany studied the product of this pregnancy as Daisy twirled and tossed her cane, which was striped red and white like a candy cane. Bethany caught the eye of her cleaning lady, Waneeta Marsh, who was seated across the aisle with her son Orlon and his wife, Penny. Orlon and Penny's daughter, Crystal Sue, was also a contestant. Bethany smiled and nodded at Waneeta in her mauve Chanel suit.

Life in Colonial Manor Estates with a baby and a Xerox third-level-management husband turned out to be no picnic. Before dinner parties, Ken would take her body-building trophies from the dining room shelf and hide them in the linen closet. Her twenty-four-inch waist was now a spongy, stretch-marked thirty inches. Years later, Angela McGrath would mope around the Roches Ridge cemetery in her white Edwardian gown, lamenting the loss of her baby son. But back then, Bethany would have liked nothing better than to be freed of little Daisy in a socially acceptable fashion like death, so she could return to the muscle game.

Ken began traveling a lot, expecting Bethany to pack his suitcase, and calling from New Orleans in a rage if she had forgotten his toothbrush. Bethany became a recipient of Dr. Evans' little brown bags of happiness. But then one day she discovered Daisy posing before a mirror in Bethany's spike heels and a Burger King crown covered with aluminum foil. She put her daughter on a regime of dance, voice, and trumpet lessons. She took her shopping every weekend to malls all over the county (where they often ran into Maureen Murphy and her mother, May, marching to the thump of May's walker).

Daisy was now playing "Me and My Shadow" on her trumpet as she tap-danced. The crowd was cheering. Needless to say, Ken wasn't present. He'd promised, but a last-minute report came up. As usual. But Xerox Corporation was his mistress, and even Ms. Empire State couldn't compete with a multinational.

Bethany spotted Jared McQueen down front, assessing the contestants' hairdos. Jared was so damn gorgeous, despite his weird patch of turquoise spikes, but he just wouldn't give Bethany the time of day. Sometimes she wondered if he was gay. But his indifference probably had more to do with her thirty-inch waist. He'd started blushing when she ran into him around town, however. And where there's a blush, can a crush be far behind?

Jared probably thought she wanted sex, but sex was just the bait. She wanted to take his balls and run with them. First he'd work his pecs—six sets of ten to twelve reps with dumbbells, five sets of incline presses with a barbell. Then abs, quads, deltoids . . . It was hard to say how he should be shaped until she got his clothes off. But he was a natural, with his tawny hair, white teeth, and sturdy build. She pictured him and her built, tanned, shaved, oiled, flexing for a screaming audience to the theme from *Chariots of Fire*. Jared in hot-orange wet-look posing trunks with a tantalizing bulge out front, herself in a matching bikini, the Couples Green Mountain State first-place trophy on the stage before them. . . .


Clea was deeply impressed by the self-confidence of these young women on stage. Her own children fluctuated between agonizing timidity and obnoxious belligerence. They lacked what these young people had in abundance—a tight-knit network of relatives and neighbors who had known them since birth and who accepted them without qualification. Perhaps she and Turner had overdone their efforts to combat American insularity in their children.

At Christmas, Theo had sat hunched over on her office couch, watching his perennial "Leave It to Beaver" reruns. It still astonished her that someone who hadn't grown up on Wally and the Beav could find them remotely interesting, much less hypnotic. Her own son was retro.

As she walked past, he had muttered, "Did you know I'm the only kid at Hotchkiss who's never been to Disneyland?"

"But you probably have more visas on your passport than anyone else."

"Big fucking deal. What's for dinner?"

"Couscous."

He looked up disgustedly. "I'm sick of all this curry and couscous and sushi shit. Can't we just eat meat loaf and baked potatoes once in a while, like normal Americans?"

But maybe it wasn't too late to make it up to Theo. After all, she'd just bought a puppy, a golden retriever at that. Theo could spend the summer in Roches Ridge, ride a bicycle, play baseball with the local boys. Perhaps some of their small-town self-assurance would rub off on him.

Orlon and Penny Marsh watched their daughter, Crystal Sue, sing "Moonlight in Vermont." She was dressed in a mink coat she'd made in home ec at Mink Valley High, from furs Orlon had trapped on Mink Creek. "You ain't got no chance against all them rich Xerox bitches," he told Crystal Sue when she came home that winter wanting to enter this contest. But here she was a semifinalist. She wanted that scholarship something fierce, to study business administration at Camel's Hump Community College. Orlon liked the idea of a Marsh being a college graduate. But he didn't want any daughter of his lording it over him. Besides, he'd heard that college was full of pinkos, and he didn't want Crystal Sue running off to Red China.

Penny squeezed his hand with excitement. When he'd asked her to marry him during basic training at Fort Polk, Louisiana, he explained how things were in Roches Ridge: Ducks in September. Quail in October. Deer in November. Perch in the winter. Trout in the spring. Bass in the summer. Fox in the fall. Turkeys spring and fall both. Rabbits all year long. There were lots of things that needed killing. Not much time for a woman. But Penny said a man had to do what a man had to do.

So how come she was always nagging him to stay home now and eat Lay's potato chips beneath Dack's crucified muskrat? He'd yell,

"Jeezum crow, Penny, why the hang would I want to watch 'Bonanza' reruns with a bitch like you?" And she'd carry on about going home to Louisiana, and he'd stomp out wishing she *would* go.

His mother, Waneeta, always talked about how a Marsh and a Roche from Connecticut founded Roches Ridge over two hundred years ago. The Roche beat the Marsh in a fistfight and got to name the town after himself, so Marshes and Roches had hated each other ever since. During a recent lull, Calvin Roche next door married Waneeta's twin Boneeta. But once Aunt Boneeta died, the feud resumed, Calvin sneaking over to shoot out the Marsh bug light, and Orlon shining the spotlight over Ray's auto graveyard into Calvin's bedroom window all night long.

Upon realizing he was now head of the Marsh family, Orlon announced that his sisters Polly and Esther would have to move out if they got knocked up again. Polly called his bluff, however, and he backed down. Hell, you couldn't throw your own sister out in the snow with a new baby. Besides, all the Marshes deserved to be out in the snow together, including his own mother. Look at her sons. He himself was short, with sharp white teeth and a receding chin. Ray was fair, lean, and lanky as an old rag doll. And Dack had copper skin, straight dark hair, and a nose like an eagle's beak.

Orlon kept urging his younger brothers to make something of themselves. But Ray still refused to marry Loretta Gebo, and drove around the interstate in his tow truck, picking up Coke cans. As long as he kept making runs to the medical supply house in New Jersey, though, Orlon couldn't complain. Ray never questioned why a medical supply house would want animal pelts, but brains were never Ray's strong suit. As for Dack, he was mooning around over a dyke down to Mink Creek, which didn't speak too good for *his* brains either.

Shifting in his seat and kneading the stub of his missing left finger, Orlon spotted Astrid Starr down front, gesturing to her husband, Earl, who was ducking out from behind the curtain like a cuckoo in a Swiss clock. Waneeta talked about Astrid making fun of her in grade school when she arrived on a workhorse. And Astrid was still at it fifty years later, looking at his mother's food stamps like they were pornographic playing cards, and glaring out the IGA window as Waneeta collected cheese and butter at the town hall. As though it wasn't Starrs who'd hounded Marshes into poverty in the first place, seizing their land during a famine and selling it to developers. One day Orlon would buy the Grand Union on Route 7 and put that Starr bitch out of business.

A few more years with Sonny Coffin at the crematorium, and Orlon might even buy back whatever Marsh land was left, to breed race horses or something. Sonny assured him things would start hopping once the town accepted cremation. Ian McGrath was throwing a fit because his tombstone business was going bust. McGraths were decent people. Orlon had stuffed many an animal for them. But the rule around this town had always been eat or get eaten. Sonny said Orlon had been acting like a blade of grass on the putting green of life, bending over and getting balled. It was time he stood up like a real man and took charge of his destiny.

Orlon glanced around the gym for Sonny. Then he remembered it was planting time, as Sonny called it, when the ground thawed enough to bury bodies stacked up over winter, bodies he hadn't been able to convince families to cremate.

Orlon spotted Ida Campbell up front next to that fairy hairdresser. Orlon's heart broke all apart when she married Chad Campbell after high school. But Ida drove around town now in an old rusted Chevrolet, peddling cheap face powder, whereas his wife, Penny, had class. Her family had a magnolia tree outside their trailer in Baton Rouge. Ida used to bitch that he didn't have enough get-up-and-go. How would she feel once he bought out the Avon franchise for central Vermont?

Across from Loretta Gebo he spotted his new neighbor, Mrs. Shawn. It was so nice to have Calvin gone that he didn't care who took his place. As long as she minded her own business. But Dack said she was already complaining about the bug light. And her new puppy was yapping and sniffing around the back shed this afternoon. If it got too curious, it just might get its face rearranged with a shotgun blast.

Zeno Racine felt like everybody in the whole dang place was watching him, wondering what he was doing here in his green work clothes, since he didn't have any relatives or neighbors in this contest. But it was a fucking free country, and he had as much damn right to be here as the next fellow. He studied Crystal Sue Marsh as she sang "Moonlight in Vermont" and removed a mink coat to model a lime-green evening gown. You could see her tits clear to the back, where Zeno was sitting. You could slide your dick between those tits just like into a cunt, and come all over her neck and chin.

Muriel kicked him out. But hell, if their daughter wanted an affair with her old man, that was her own damn business. And if he wanted to drown the Barbie doll he bought her in the toilet, or hang it from a noose in the doorway, that was *his* business. "I spray ants all day long for you and that kid, Muriel. I'll do whatever I damn please when I get home." Over my dead body, she said. "Okay," he said, punching her in her fat gut. She got a damn court order. Said he couldn't get no closer than one hundred yards. And they called it a free country.

All day long he watched ants swarm out of walls and lie twisting on the floor. What was he supposed to do with his hard-ons if he couldn't get near his wife or daughter? He'd hide in the bushes behind Orlon Marsh's bug light. The zapping sound sometimes got him off. Other times, Calvin Roche shot out the light before Zeno was finished. But not before he saw Orlon Marsh doing some pretty sick things in that back shed.

People crossed to the other side of the green when they saw Zeno coming. The same thing at Mink Valley High. Sitting alone in the lunchroom while cheerleaders squealed at the basketball players. Until they needed him. Then they came over acting all sweet, like he was their dream man. Would he please anchor the class tug-of-war team? Like it was some kinda honor. Like he didn't know it was just because he weighed two hundred and fifty pounds. And they won, and the cheerleaders pounded him on the back for five minutes. Then he was back in the corner, alone again. Goddam fucking bitches.

Crystal Sue Marsh. Her daddy would cut his balls off and fry them for supper if Zeno got near her. Spying through the window of Orlon's ice-fishing shack, Zeno watched him slit perch wide open while they was still flopping, and rip out their egg sacs. Fry 'em up in butter, and wash 'em down with Miller's.

His mother playing with his thing. Her eye swollen shut, the side of her face purple from his daddy's work boot. Tying his wrists to the chair. Pointing at it and laughing. Eight years old, what did she expect, a telephone pole? It sure as hang wasn't small now. He felt it stirring alongside his thigh beneath his belly. She named him Zero. His first-grade teacher taught him to write Zeno instead.

Earl Atkins was announcing the winner. Daisy Wagner. Zeno had been watching her outside the high school. She was a cheerleader. He offered her a ride home one afternoon in his pickup with his Tri-Die in the rear. She backed away like he was a rattlesnake. Some ass-holes in maroon letter jackets yelled, "Go on, get out of here, you old pervert!"

He drove to Burlington that night, picked up a drunk college girl hitching to her dorm at Camel's Hump. Hit seventy on the side street out of town. She started screaming. Zeno snarled, "Shut up, bitch. This is your lucky night."

Seizing the gearshift, she threw it into reverse. The truck ground to a halt with a horrible clank. As she hurled open the door, he grabbed her arm. She sank her teeth into his hand. He yelled and pulled it away. She ran to the nearest house and pounded on the door. He had her teeth scars across his hand. Fucking bitch. Doc Evans looked at him real weird when he taped it up.

Daisy Wagner. When he sprayed the Congregational church the other day, he passed an open grave and thought about Daisy lying at the bottom of it. He'd climb on top of her. She'd let him. She'd have to. She'd be dead. As long as it took. In and out all night long. Sometimes with Muriel nothing worked. He pounded into her until she got fed up and went to the kitchen for Doritos.

He followed Daisy home to Colonial Manor Estates the other night. Put on his surgical mask and knocked. Her mother answers. He puts his foot in the door. The fucking bitch grabs his arm and flips him to the ground. A dog charges out and bites his calf. Some guy starts spraying him with chlordane. Finally he kicks the dog loose and escapes into the woods.

Back home at his Sunset View trailer he watched "Mink Valley Crimestoppers" for a solid week, expecting them to dramatize his break-in and ask viewers for information. Then he'd phone in and give a lead on himself. If they caught him, he'd receive the reward. He'd buy a handgun. . . .

At work around the church foundation one afternoon, Zeno spotted Angela McGrath kneeling beside those rotten teddy bears. She hung around talking to her dead son every day. In rain, sleet, or snow, like some goddam postman. He popped up from behind the headstone, surgical mask concealing his true identity, green work pants unzipped. She looked up and said, "That's too bad, Zeno, but if you keep pulling on it like that, it might grow."

That night he went to an interstate rest area and sat in his pickup, waiting for a woman alone stopping to pee. It was late, dark, no other cars. Up she drove, fucking bitch, in a white BMW. Raincoat and heels, middle-aged, dark hair with lots of gray. Nice-looking. Rich-looking, fucking bitch. She went inside. Zeno got out, looked in her BMW. A camera on the seat. He opened his passenger door, loaded and cocked the rifle in his gun rack, put his ax on the front seat. This was the one, fucking rich bitch thinking she could ride around alone at night without no man to protect her.

A blue tow truck pulled in. Out climbed Ray Marsh, who started poking through the trash barrel. Then he straightened up and looked at Zeno. "What you up to, Zeno? Heading home, are you? Ain't no point setting out here in the dark." He stood watching and waiting, so Zeno had to go back to his truck. But when he walked past the BMW, he dug a big long scratch down its side with his truck key.

Driving home, he thought, Fuck him, fuck that Rayon Marsh! I'd have killed the bitch. Shot her, fucked her dry, chopped her up, buried her in the woods. They'd have put *that* on "Crimestoppers." They'd have caught him, filmed him for TV, interviewed him for the *Gazette*. Put him on the cover of *People*, like that kid who murdered the Beatle.

Prison. A bed, three hot meals a day, no more ant nests or bats or cockroaches. Not so bad. A big strong criminal standing over you, making you kneel so he could shove his cock up your asshole, like his daddy used to do. Taking care of you, buying you cigarettes, making the others be nice to you because you belonged to him. Not so bad.

Zeno had seen that woman since. Sneaking around the graveyard snapping pictures with that camera from her BMW. And he saw her now, sitting halfway down the gym, smiling and clapping. Some kinda spy or something. One day if she kept snooping around the graveyard, he'd give her a grave of her own.

The winner, Miss Teenage Roches Ridge, Daisy Wagner. A crown on her head, a sash across her chest, flowers in her arms, a trophy at her feet, matching luggage, and a color TV. A scholarship to college. She was squealing and crying. The audience was cheering. But Daisy was still nothing but a snotty little Xerox bitch, and now Zeno simply had to kill her, to put her in her place.


As Clea's gaze swept the room, she felt excited by the notion of being part of this remarkable little town. In the centuries since Roches Ridge was founded, townspeople had come together like this on a regular basis. The reasons for the meetings had shifted in response to local and national events. The dead of one generation had been replaced by their heirs. But the families in attendance had remained constant. And Clea could foresee the day when she, too, would have her place in this mesh.

The crowd was on its feet, cheering Daisy Wagner and the runner-up, Crystal Sue Marsh. Earl Atkins was yelling into the microphone about "the brightest flowers of Roches Ridge young womanhood!" Clea kept reaching absently for her camera as she clapped. She longed to record this moment in all its endearing, good-humored simplemindedness. Life didn't have to be as grim and as complicated as it had often seemed in the urban centers of the world.

As Clea turned to leave, she saw behind her a gray-haired man in a clerical collar and black suit. He had the baffled, horrified, resigned look of a soldier who'd just missed the last helicopter out of Saigon. Probably this display of female flesh had offended his religious scruples.

Edging out the back door was Zeno Racine, the exterminator from the cemetery, in his green work clothes. He was no doubt mildly retarded. But he wasn't shut away in some filthy overcrowded institution. He was performing a necessary service and was an integral part of his community. It was pretty impressive, especially in contrast to the homeless of New York City.

Clea reached the rear and Dack Marsh pushed past her out the door, a brooding expression on his dark face. As his shoulder brushed hers, Clea felt a jolt of electricity down her arm. Bracing herself against the doorjamb with one hand, she drew a shaky breath. Good God, what was that?

The parking lot was jammed with cars and people. Headlights glared, puffs of exhaust drifted skyward, and car horns blasted. Clea found the sidewalk blocked by a man in a tweed jacket and a brown suede eye patch. Holding a Tupperware bowl, and a poster on a stick reading PLAYGROUNDS FOR PEACE: PLEASE GIVE GENEROUSLY, he studied her intently.

Clea stared back as he explained, "For a sister city in the People's Republic of China."

"Excuse me?"

"For the little children of the world."

"I see." Clea assumed this made sense to Roches Ridgers, of whom she wanted to be one. So she searched her pockets for change. Past him was a row of placards held by women in blue veils, with dresses to their ankles: MISS TEENAGE ROCHES RIDGE: YOU ARE AN AFFRONT TO YOUR LORD. Clea watched the red-bearded man from the yellow van lurch toward Loretta Gebo on his aluminum crutches. A veiled woman grabbed his arm, so that he tottered and almost fell. He turned back to her with a sheepish shrug.

Dropping a couple of dollars in the Tupperware bowl, Clea wove through the crowd. People were signing petitions, or arguing with those who held them. The woman from the Karma Café was looking longingly at another crew-cut woman, who wore a rolled bandanna around her forehead. The bandannaed woman was talking to Dack Marsh, who kept tossing the straight black hair out of his eyes with one hand. Clea didn't allow her eyes to linger on him.

Behind Dack she spotted a cluster of crew cuts, above which waved an entire armada of placards with such messages as REAL WOMEN DON'T EAT MEN and WOMEN ARE PEOPLE NOT HEIFERS. A heavy woman with an iridescent parrot on her shoulder yelled to Clea's neighbor, who was walking alongside Crystal Sue Marsh, "Orlon, how can you let your daughter do this?"

Orlon halted, tongue darting out to lick his mustache. "You girls just won't give me a break, will you, Starshine? First it's my traps, now it's my daughter."

"If you really cared about your daughter," said Starshine, studying the beautiful young woman in her low-cut gown, "you wouldn't let every man in town look her up and down."

"Che Guevara! Che Guevara!" screamed the parrot.

Crystal Sue gazed at the woman and her parrot with fascination.

"That's for me to decide, in'nt it?" said Orlon. "But I wouldn't worry about no beauty contest if I was you. Won't nobody come signing *you* up." He grabbed Crystal Sue's hand. She looked back over her bare creamy shoulder at Starshine in her I KNOW WHAT GIRLS LIKE T-shirt. Starshine smiled at Crystal Sue, then surveyed the crowd, blanching when she spotted a sallow blue-veiled woman who held a poster that read: THE BODY IS THE TEMPLE OF THE HOLY SPIRIT. Beside her stood the man on crutches. Starshine scrutinized the woman, whose eyes were fixed on the ground.

"Make Love, Not War!" shrieked the parrot.

The veiled woman looked up, saw the colorful bird, and smiled. But her eyes returned to the ground without meeting Starshine's.

As Clea reached the outskirts of the crowd, she saw the man in the clerical collar and suit coat, a tiny gold pin on his lapel. He clutched a clipboard to his chest and watched a small woman in a straw pillbox hat walk across the green.

As Clea headed toward the green herself, she began to realize that she didn't understand a lot of what was going on that night. It was like being deaf in a hearing world. But she reminded herself that it would just take time. In the foreign countries where she and Turner had lived, there had been an initial breaking-in period before she'd been able to decode cultural differences. She hadn't anticipated this here in her own country, however.

In the front window of the Victorian house across the green, a shadowy form fluttered around the golden harp like a trapped bird, as "Some Enchanted Evening" floated on the night air. So intent was Clea on the harp runs that she almost ran down Maureen Murphy and her mother, May, who marched up the sidewalk, walker skittering rhythmically on the concrete.

"Excuse me," said Clea. "I didn't see you. It's Clea Shawn. How are you this evening?"

"Not too bad," said Maureen, not looking at Clea from under her Scotch-taped bangs.

"Did you go to the pageant?"

"Mother has the Alzheimer's. Can't sit quiet in a crowd."

"I'm sorry. I didn't realize."

"She's an old lady. She's had a full life."

"Yes, of course."

The mother gave a caved-in smile and reached out to Clea. Clea took her hand and patted it. As they continued on their way, Clea realized the woman had deposited a slip of paper in her palm. Opening it under a streetlight, Clea read in a wavery scrawl: HELP.

II

## 28  Ism Gism

Elke shifted her goggles to her forehead and regarded the remains of her bayoneted baby on the studio floor, simultaneously bereft and relieved. At a standstill for months, she'd been unable to contemplate anything new without somehow resolving this piece. So now it was resolved.

Laying her blowtorch on the floor and unzipping her coverall to the waist, she plopped down in her black plaid armchair. As she looked at the forlorn scraps of rusted steel, she apologized to them for having promised them glory. But they hadn't managed to express how she really saw life. They expressed how she'd seen it in the past, and what buyers, critics, and friends *expected* her to see now. What she really *did* see now, however, remained fog-bound. For some reason, Clea's advice about not shivering like marsh grass in every passing breeze kept recurring to her.

She just hoped this decision to abort would make sense in the morning. Prior to menopause, her moods had had a reliable rhythm.

The days she felt like wreaking havoc usually heralded a menstrual period. For the last three years, however, periods had appeared so sporadically that her fits of destruction were impossible to chart. Today's action had beckoned consistently for weeks, though, so probably it was necessary.

But now came the dark. No bayoneted baby, and nothing to take its place. She was familiar enough with her creative process to recognize what she called the four D's—the Despair, the Dawn, the Delight, and the Drudgery. But recognizing the stages made them only minimally easier to bear. Besides, she felt cheated having to return to Despair without fully tasting Delight. It was like having to proceed directly to jail without passing Go in the Monopoly game she used to play with Kate and Theo. Clea refused to endure either Despair or Drudgery, and her work showed it, lacking both depth and craft. But Elke allowed herself no shortcuts.

Other visual artists had their movements, teaching positions, and colleagues, but Elke had generally shunned such padding, heeding solely the dictates of her unconscious. At Cooper Union and since, she'd listened to the debates about impressionism, realism, naturalism, expressionism, surrealism, minimalism, conceptualism—linked through the last century like a chain gang. And when her turn came, she usually had nothing to say. In the early years, when she ventured out in search of a gallery, she was unable to defend her work against the withering theoretical critiques of dealers. (Luckily, with Terence largely supporting her, she didn't have to subject herself to this sadomasochistic rite too often.) And now that she had a reputation and was pursued by those same gallery owners who'd once shown her the door, she felt equally unable to respond to their enthusiastic championing of her "post–abstract expressionism," or whatever corral they tried to herd her current tangles of tortured steel into.

Likewise, when critics and scholars enumerated the influences on her work in books and journals, she could only shrug. She had studied the various movements and the work of many individuals, and she had no doubt plundered what she needed from each. But her work left her mute. If she could have put its intended impact into words, she'd have perhaps been a writer instead, since a computer was so much less messy than paints and clay. If required to name the movement she most identified with, it would have been "anti-ismism."

The truth was, Elke felt out of it in this highly intellectualized New York art scene. Apart from her brief foray into collectivity with Arts

Alive in 1970, she avoided groups and rules, having observed the Hitler Youth closely while growing up. She did what she had to, for her own internal reasons. Her work constituted memos from a layer of herself that was unreachable during daily living. That these memos were sometimes meaningful to others was a wonderful by-product. Her working assumption was that something opaque to her was often also opaque to others, and that to clarify it for herself would clarify it for others if her presentation was adequate.

But Elke's work was also a drug. The only time her internal agitation eased was when she was passionately engaged in her search for the meaning of the suffering she observed around her. Yet much current art in galleries and museums seemed designed to thwart, obscure, and mock both engagement and passion, substituting novelty and whimsy, alienation and absurdity. After all, it was easier to declare that there was no meaning than to spend your free time searching for it.

So in reality, Elke concluded as she stood up, she *was* out of it. And pleased to be so.

There was a knock at her door. Terence called, "Better wrap it up, Elke. We're due at the Shawns' in an hour."

Elke glanced irritably at the door. He thought she couldn't tell time? That man was driving her crazy with his need to take care of her. It concealed the true situation—which was that Terence was very dependent on her emotionally, always hanging around the apartment longing for her to take a walk with him, or to praise his latest position paper on the Sino-Soviet split. All these years she'd listened admiringly to his struggles with capitalism, communism, fascism, socialism, Maoism, anarchism, Marxism, monarchism. He was so intelligent and articulate, so in command of information on world affairs. But it had all begun to seem like mental masturbation. She felt disloyal to have recently told Clea that his latest journal article was "ism gism." But the only system that really appealed to her anymore was democracy, if only because it didn't end in "ism."

Elke resolutely reminded herself that Terence was a fine person— kind and principled. Always bringing troubled students to live in their spare room. And when they first got together, she not only appreciated his caretaking, she required it. So this current marital gridlock was partially of her own making. She just hadn't anticipated that their relationship was going to have to make up to Terence for the failure of international communism.

As Elke wearily tossed chunks of steel into a garbage can, she bid her baby farewell, sad the outgrown had to be shed for the new to emerge. With any luck, this was what she and Clea were doing with each other. When Clea phoned the night before to invite Terence and her to this last-minute Easter dinner, Clea tried to chat cheerily as though nothing were wrong. Elke heard herself give terse replies, not wanting to, but unable not to. Because she was profoundly annoyed. Clea expected her to drop everything whenever she turned up. But Elke was tired of it. It would probably be painful sitting across from her today at the dinner table where they had spent so many festive family holidays. But maybe this new estrangement was just another phase in their seemingly endless interaction. And maybe not.


As Terence descended the steps from Elke's studio, he tried to figure out what was going on with her. She seemed so brittle lately. Usually she became calm and focused in the middle of a piece. With Clea gone most of the time now, she had one less distraction. She refused to define Clea as a distraction, but that was what she was, breathlessly barging in unannounced and bouncing off the walls until well past Elke's bedtime. Elke was always flushed and agitated when she left, sometimes succumbing to a migraine. Why did Elke subject herself to such a chaotic person?

Terence recalled first spotting Elke at a friend's art opening in a small gallery off Bedford Street. Recently mustered out of the army, Terence was studying political science at City College, intending to construct social blueprints that would lead civilization away from war, poverty, and injustice. Elke stood studying a still life of empty wine bottles, coat collar high around her cheeks, hands in a fur muff.

"So what do you think of it?" he asked.

"Dreadful," she murmured. Realizing he might be the artist, for all she knew, she blushed. Then she explained what she saw as the technical problems with the painting, and they looked at the rest of the exhibit together.

Upon offering to see her home, Terence learned she lived with an aunt in Washington Heights and commuted daily to Cooper Union. After persuading her to meet him for coffee the next day, he stalked the miles back to his apartment, heart flapping against his ribs like a wild bird in a cage.

Terence was twice surprised when Elke arrived at the Village café the next afternoon. First by her slight frame when she removed her bulky fur coat. And second by her unusually large, strong hands when she withdrew them from her muff. As they sipped coffee, her dark-blue eyes kindly but relentlessly extracted his entire life history. How his parents had died in a car wreck when he was twelve. How their best friends had raised him in Brooklyn Heights. How he had marched through a ravaged Germany, and been present when Bergen-Belsen was opened. How he was devoting his life to ensuring that something like that would never happen again.

Before they parted, Terence pointed out how much they had in common—both orphans, she German and he half German-Jew, both students. He informed her he was able to talk to her as to no one else since his mother's death. Flustered, Elke departed, agreeing to meet him again later that week.

Soon Terence began to follow Elke home from Cooper Union without her knowledge. Sometimes she took detours, stopping off in the Bowery or in Spanish Harlem to sketch people on sidewalks and in doorways. Or to inspect objects picked up in the street—a rusted muffler, a bedspring, a broken teacup. Terence was appalled. She'd evidently been exposed to so much horror that she'd lost her instinct for self-preservation. He longed to protect her. So, separated by a block or a subway car, he trailed her around the city. Terrible things were always happening to people he loved. He would make sure nothing happened to Elke.

Terence lost weight, and his grades began to slip. He had to resign from his War Resisters League committee because he kept missing meetings. Elke commented on the circles under his eyes and the hollows in his cheeks. Realizing he couldn't keep this vigil up much longer, yet needing Elke near him at all times so he could know she was safe, he decided they must marry immediately.

When Elke declined his proposal, Terence began to camp out in the doorway opposite her aunt's neo-Gothic apartment building. Whenever a date arrived to pick her up, he would appear, to announce that she was ill, or newly married, or had returned to Germany. When Elke learned this, she was outraged. But in time Terence's relentless devotion won her over.

They were quite a pair in their early years. He'd jerk awake yelling from replays of nightmares he'd witnessed—of a gaunt prisoner in Bergen-Belsen, too weak to stand, reaching through the barbed wire to grab blades of grass to stuff in his mouth; of a woman in a gestapo prison in Frankfurt his commando unit had liberated, entirely covered with scabs and fresh wounds, whom he had held in his arms so she could watch through her cell window as American troops marched down the street below. And Elke continued to wander New York in a kind of shell shock, dazed and unaware of present danger. Hand in hand, they had tiptoed through the minefields of their own war-torn psyches. Terence supported and protected Elke, and she provided him with the continuity he craved. Except on rare trips to an opening or a workshop, she was in their apartment when he got home, or in the neighborhood on errands, or upstairs working in her studio.

Yet something had always been missing. Elke got annoyed when he said so, but it was true. When she demanded to know what, he was unable to articulate it. As elusive as a faint star seen from the corner of an eye, it disappeared when he looked directly at it. It had to do with the intensity and absorption Elke brought to her artwork. She experimented restlessly all the time. On a walk, only half listening to him, she scanned the streets for junk to tote home. At night she'd bake liquid rubber in muffin tins in the oven to test its properties. He wished she'd bring some of this fervor to their relationship, to match his own. Early in their marriage he'd been relieved when she chose to have an abortion, because he hadn't wanted to share her with a child. But in the end he'd had to share her anyway, with a rival that would never grow up and go away. They exchanged intellectual observations and physical intimacies, but she kept her heart out of his grasp.

Usually when Clea was away, he and Elke came closer. She'd be sad, and he'd comfort her and counsel her to get rid of Clea for good. Since Clea's move to Vermont, however, Elke had been distant and irritable. But why?

In the early days Terence's fervor for his work had paralleled Elke's own. The only way to render the mayhem of the twentieth century acceptable, the only way to appease his haunting image of Europe in rubble and its people, his people, stacked in mass graves, was to view it as a clearing away of old exploitative political systems, to make way for a new era of peace and equality under world communism. Throughout the McCarthy period, when he and his friends were hounded like treed coons, this credo sustained him. These ideals in practice, however, had yielded Stalin's Gulag, the invasions of Hungary, Czechoslovakia and Afghanistan, the Red Guard, the Vietnamese boat people, and the killing fields of Cambodia. And the much-vaunted New Man looked alarmingly similar to the old one. He still wrote analyses of Soviet foreign affairs, since it was his job, but from a jaundiced perspective. The fire of his belief had long since guttered and died out.

Sitting at his desk eyeing his draft of a piece on the Afghan resistance, Terence envied Elke her ability to express outrage at human suffering without feeling she had to do something about it. He himself still yearned to discover the system that would eliminate it. Yet his middle-aged knowledge of human nature made him doubt such a system could ever survive in a world like this. So his goal had been shifting lately, from wanting to change the world, to wanting to depart from it when his time came with some modicum of decency intact. After having finally achieved with Elke a union, not just of their bodies and their daily lives, but of their souls as well. A union that Elke seemed increasingly determined to flee and subvert, for reasons he couldn't understand.

# 29  The Resurrection

Clea stood in the kitchen doorway in her apron, watching Turner in his wrinkled striped shirt carve the ham. Terence, buttoned into a three-piece suit, was pouring the wine. Six people. A sorry excuse for a holiday feast. In the past she'd had to use all the leaves for the dining table, plus card tables. Setting the places had required her everyday stoneware as well as her Wedgwood. But she'd been so carried away with Roches Ridge that she'd forgotten about Easter.

On the other hand, she thought as she bent down to remove a spinach soufflé from the oven, these people at her table today had sat here on many a Thanksgiving, Christmas, and Easter. What was to stop one of them from organizing Easter this year? How did she get stuck with being Grey Owl? They saw her as powerful and competent, someone to lean on or butt heads with. But none was interested in her needs or vulnerabilities.

"Vouvray." Terence scowled, wine bottle poised over Elke's glass. "Really, Clea. After how the French treated us during the Qaddafi thing, we ought to at least boycott French exports." Terence had felt his need for a wrangle building ever since Elke snapped at him for holding her elbow to help her into the taxi up here. He remembered her as a timid, traumatized girl in a fox coat and muff. Just as her German accent had faded over the years, so had this timidity. He'd watched her develop her talent, acquiring money and recognition along the way. On the one hand, he was pleased and proud; on the other, frightened, as she ceased to need his ministrations. When he asked himself what she wanted from him, the grim answer came back: "Nothing." However, he was more than just Elke's courtier. He was also a respected political analyst. And this Vouvray gave him a chance to remind her.

Elke, elbow on the table, covered her dark-blue eyes with one coarse hand. "Just pour the wine, Terence."

"I thought it was great," bristled Kate, leaning forward eagerly in her layers of torn T-shirt. "Who does Ronald Reagan think he is, John Wayne?"

"Sweet Jesus. Liberals," muttered Terence, gratified someone had picked up his gauntlet. "And she used to be such a sensible young woman."

"Here we go," moaned Theo, heaping scalloped potatoes on a plate from Turner.

"No politics," requested Clea, setting the soufflé dish on a silver vine-leaf trivet. "We're supposed to be having fun. It's the Resurrection." She glanced at Elke, whose face was tense. She had merely extended her jaw to meet Clea's lips when she arrived. What was going on? Something to do with Terence, judging from his eagerness to argue politics with a college freshman. Yet on the phone yesterday Elke had been curt with her too.

"Magnificent, Clea," said Turner of the puffy soufflé, pausing in his carving.

Clea smiled at him, feeling bad about his wrinkled shirt. She hadn't been here upon his return from Mexico City, and he'd run out of clean shirts. But damn it, he knew where the laundry was. Also the iron. Did he really have to wear such a crumpled shirt to Easter dinner? It was one of his passive-aggressive reprimands. Well, despite her days of Lean Cuisines in Calvin Roche's gas oven, at least she remembered how to cook. Removing her apron, she sat at the foot of the table in her Sheraton side chair and picked up a serving spoon for the soufflé. Detecting the faint stale odor of marijuana smoke from Theo's direction, she looked at him sharply.

"Theo," she said in a measured voice. In her absence the liquor cabinet had been ransacked and a hole, now concealed by a potted plant, burned in the living room carpet. Because she was trying to live in Vermont, her son would become an alcoholic drug addict, keeping pace with his father, the disheveled derelict of Turtle Bay. "I have a bone to pick with you."

"Look, Mom, if this is about condoms, I don't want to hear it."

Kate choked on her wine, and Elke laughed softly. Turner grinned, and Terence cleared his throat and looked uncomfortable.

Realizing she was about to precipitate a clash, Clea backed off, saying, "Never mind. It's not important."

From the corner of her eye, Clea could see Brandy gnawing the leg of the living room coffee table. He needed to be outside, roaming the woods and fields. Every time she sat down with someone else, he came bounding over, whimpering to be patted. Which in turn made Theo jealous. This morning he said, "Jesus, Mother, you treat that damn dog like he's the fucking Dauphin of France."

It reminded her of a supper at this table when the children were small. Turner was just home from Bogotá; and he, Kate, and Theo were battling with each other to tell her about exploits at the play group and in the boardroom. Sitting in the living room afterward, she realized she would start screaming and never stop if one more living creature demanded her attention. The cat came gliding across the carpet and wound around her legs. Then he leapt on the couch and curled up on her lap, purring and blinking slowly. She hurled him halfway across the room. Horrified, she stared at the poor startled cat as Turner and the children crowded around asking what was wrong. To call her a matriarch was to dignify the situation. She was the leader of the pack.

"Psyched," said Theo. "Let's not spend the Resurrection picking on Theo, okay?"

Clea studied him. As far as she knew, he hadn't yet had a long-term girlfriend. This was her fault for dragging him around the globe and subjecting him to a shifting array of caretakers, so he got the idea nothing was lasting. He had no hobbies, no plans for his future, and mediocre grades. Since her return from Roches Ridge, he'd been watching his wretched "Leave It to Beaver" reruns on the VCR non-stop. Finally this morning she'd said, "Theo, you do realize that June Cleaver is an actress? She's not home baking chocolate chip cookies for her *real* children. She's on a set, doing take after take under hot lights and getting paid big bucks for it."

Terence was gloomily observing his ham, chin on his Windsor knot. For him, Clea reflected, a dinner without a political argument was like a Resurrection without the corpse. Elke kept glancing at him, no doubt trying to conjure up some noninflammatory topic to placate him. Clea studied Elke, in the navy-blue silk dress that matched her eyes. She plucked at the bodice with a powerful hand. Her bayoneted baby was a parody of her earlier work, like a late Hemingway novel. Even the blinders of devotion couldn't conceal this from Clea.

Kate rolled a cigarette while waiting for Turner to finish serving the plates. Brightening, Terence asked, "Did you read that the original Marlboro man just died of emphysema?"

Kate regarded him evenly. "Do you mind if I smoke, Uncle Terence?" God knows the pleasures were few enough at this dinner table, surrounded by maggots who fed on the body politic. Her own father was nothing but a capitalist carpetbagger. Uncle Terence had reportedly once been a communist, but he was now somewhere to the right of Ferdinand Marcos. Even Aunt Elke, whose work Kate respected, sat here in a silk dress surrounded by silver and china and enough food to feed an Ethiopian village for a week. Striking a match on the zipper of her jeans, she lit her cigarette.

"On what level shall I answer that, Kate?" asked Terence.

"Fuck it," said Kate, stubbing out the cigarette and giving him a look more deadly than a lifetime of cigarettes.

"Could you please light the candles, dear?" asked Clea, to sidetrack Kate. As Kate struck another match on her zipper, Clea got up and turned off the chandelier. The dark closed in around them. For a moment the only sound was tires hissing on the wet pavement outside.

"Well, we've really separated the sheep from the goats this time," observed Turner, sitting down and putting his linen napkin in his lap. "We're down to the hard-core celebrants." He ran his hand over his head, studying Theo's carefully combed and parted rug of wavy brown hair.

Poor Turner, thought Clea, watching him stroke his bald spot. She hadn't bolstered him lately with assurances of his excessive testosterone. She was a lousy wife.

"Feels like shit," muttered Theo, eyeing his potatoes with dissatisfaction. "Where is everybody anyhow?"

Elke looked across the table at Theo as he sat there wearing like a badge his need to assert his uniqueness and depart from this fold. Before dinner he'd done his best to voice every narrow-minded prejudice he could think of, to thwart his parents' hopes of having produced a citizen of the world. Only a mother could love him right now, and even Clea appeared to find it a challenge.

Elke sighed, reflecting that Theo and Kate would go through years and years of disappointment, pain, failure, and suffering. They would watch all their fondest ideals and favorite friends get chewed up and spat out by life. And all for what? Elke hadn't a clue. For twenty years the existence of these offspring had determined the shape of Clea's life, and, through her, that of the other adults at this table. But now, just like Elke's bayoneted baby, this polyhedron was breaking up, falling apart, dispersing. The molecule was setting its individual atoms adrift in the void. Glancing past the candle flame to the shadowy living room where she used to sit sketching Clea and her babies at play, Elke shivered.

"Can I say grace?" asked Theo with a defiant smile.

Everyone looked at him. Grace had never before been uttered at this table.

"Why?" asked Terence, cheering up finally to locate his argument for the day.

"It's part of my religion."

"What religion is that?" asked Turner with alarm.

"I've joined the Baptist Church. I was baptized last month."

Silence billowed around the Sheraton table like a mushroom cloud. Clea eyed the white dress shirt and tie, where Theo's blue work shirt and silver astronaut jacket used to reside. She should have realized that something was going on *inside* as well.

"Jesus," muttered Kate.

"Well," explained Theo, directing his innocent gaze at his mother, "everyone needs *something* reliable to hang on to."

"I'm glad you've found something, Theo," replied Clea, wincing. She saw Elke glance at her sympathetically for the first time all afternoon. A born again, a hobo, and a depressive, all at one table and all Clea's fault. Keeping everyone happy and healthy was a big job. What made Clea think she could renovate a tenement and write a book as well?

They bowed their heads while Theo conducted a chat with his Lord about the upcoming meal, the people who lacked enough notice to be present, and the selfishness of unspecified adults who insisted on pursuing their own interests at the expense of loved ones.

"Amen," said everyone doubtfully. As Clea reached for her fork, she couldn't decide whether to throw it at Theo or to march from the room. Instead she passed Theo the raisin sauce. Their web was tattered and frayed, she reflected. She could feel the misery, like a fog over the table.

"They're having a contest to name these things," said Theo, spooning the sauce on his ham.

"What things, my darling boy?" asked Elke, coarse hand holding the elegant silver fork delicately.

"You know those raisins on TV that dance to 'I Heard It Through the Grapevine'?"

Elke drew a blank. She recalled her delight as she became enmeshed in Clea's family to learn about normal American phenomena like dancing raisins. Clea was her first friend from the heartland, complete with children, pets, and a backyard climbing frame.

"It's an ad," explained Kate contemptuously.

"I see," said Elke.

"Anyhow," said Theo, "there's this contest to, like, name the raisins. You can win five thousand dollars and a trip to Hollywood."

"Why didn't you say so in the first place?" asked Turner. "Surely with so many creative intelligences at one table we can name a few lousy raisins. How about Raisin Cane?"

"Raisin d'Être?" suggested Elke, buttering a roll.

"Too intellectual." Terence smiled. "We're dealing with the average American consumer. We need a nickname like Studs or Spike or Butch."

"Randy Raisin suggests an interesting image," offered Clea.

Theo laughed. "You guys are really out of control."

As this discussion became increasingly ridiculous, Clea sat back laughing and feeling relief as the entire group joined forces to reweave their web. She could have sworn she detected a faint shimmer in the air above Kate and Theo. Like glossy young animals, they were exuding the arrogant self-confidence that physical vitality breeds. Poised on the shore of sexual passion, all senses alert to detect the partners with whom they'd plumb the depths, they were about to immerse themselves in the most compelling element in nature's arsenal. As she passed Theo the rolls, Clea offered up a silent prayer that this force, which had propelled their mother into so many messes, would caress and buoy her poor innocent children. Their current splendor suddenly struck Clea as a remarkable joint achievement for the four battered adults at this table.

The hazy spring days in Roches Ridge seemed no more than a dream. She'd made the whole thing up—a village on a granite ridge, lake below and mountains in the distance; an antique stone house on a lilac-covered knoll; crusty Yankee villagers full of wit and integrity. In reality Roches Ridge was a bleak outpost overlooking a swamp, full of bizarre strangers. The red-bearded preacher in his yellow van, the exterminator in his surgical mask, the hairdresser with his turquoise spikes, lesbian tepees and Christian satellite dishes and Maoist silos— none of it fit her original *Vermont Life* script.

To say nothing of May Murphy's note reading HELP. The day after receiving it, Clea went to the post office to ask Maureen if her mother was in trouble. Maureen replied that her mother had Alzheimer's, and Loretta Gebo and Astrid Starr confirmed this. So Clea dropped the matter. But it reminded her of what she already knew from Poplar Bluffs: Even Eden had serpents.

All of a sudden, as Terence stood up to refill the wineglasses, Clea realized Elke was right: Clea had been on another binge in Roches Ridge, unavailable to loved ones, blind to the complexities of real life. The progress away from obsession she thought she'd made was an illusion. A fantasy addict, she was no different from her alcoholic mother. Roches Ridge was her Smirnoff's. The people at her table right now, making up names for dancing raisins, were the ones who really mattered.

When Turner was instructing her in the art of the casual affair in Paris, one lesson concerned the need to make it clear from the beginning that she would not allow a new passion to disrupt either her work or her family. She almost always writhed in the grip of these restrictions, but she adhered to them. And Roches Ridge had already reached this crisis point. It was coming between herself and her family, so it had to go. As she sliced the fat off her ham, she resolved to sell Calvin Roche's house and stay here in New York where she belonged. That house was a ruin anyway, which would cost more than it was worth to restore. The backyard and cellar were full of garbage, and the neighborhood was dominated by junked cars. She'd traded in the rat race for a rat's nest.

"Maybe they should put dreadlocks on one raisin, and have him dance to reggae music, and call him Rasta Raisin," suggested Theo.

Everyone laughed, and Theo looked pleased. Clea felt glad to be sobering up so quickly this time. She jumped up, turned on the light, and picked up her Nikon from the sideboard. While she focused, she called, "Smile, everybody!"

As Elke tried her best to smile, she realized this pretty much summed up Clea's approach to life: Here they sat, each in the grip of private misery, their shared past terminating, and Clea orders them to smile. She observed Kate ignoring her mother and trying to roll a cigarette with trembling hands, her brow furrowed. She'd been a sunny little girl, always climbing onto Terence's lap to unknot his necktie. Today, in her torn T-shirts and ripped jeans, she looked like a refugee from the dust bowl. Accepting defeat, Kate dumped the tobacco back into her pouch, braced her hands against the table edge, and announced, "I have something to tell you. Something you're not going to like."

They looked at her, still searching their minds for raisin nicknames.

"I'm a lesbian."

No one responded.

"Look, I know you think it's weird and sick and all that, but it's who I am, okay? And now that I've accepted this about myself, I'm a much happier person."

"Gross," muttered Theo.

"It's *not* gross," said Clea sharply as she sat back down. "It's fine, Kate. Is there anyone special?"

"Mother, do you have to be so bourgeois?" asked Kate. "Not everybody aspires to living happily ever after with Mr. Right, you know." She looked contemptuously at her father. "Besides, you're such a hypocrite. You don't really think it's fine. You've been propagandized by the media, just like every other American."

Grinning, Turner said, "I don't mean to steal your thunder, my darling, but your mother *is* the media."

Elke and Clea exchanged a look, and their eyes locked for a long moment. Elke was suppressing one of her smiles that made her look even sadder than a frown.

"Fine, Dad," snapped Kate. "Be witty and urbane. Don't confront your anger and sorrow. But it's not going to change my mind. I love women, and that's that."

"So do I," said Turner. "It makes perfect sense to me. Women are a superior race. They deserve your love."

Clea watched Kate become increasingly agitated as everyone blessed her choice. To satisfy her, Clea knew she should dredge up some disapproval, so she considered the topic of grandchildren, and whether she would mind if hers were nonexistent, or fatherless. Given all she had gone through to assure that Kate had a father. And she realized she was envious of Kate for being aware of options and choosing among them, rather than being bushwhacked by them. Both children had this luxury, of trying on an entire wardrobe of roles like Halloween costumes. And once they'd cast off every outfit on the ready-made rack, they could get on with figuring out who they really were.

At their age Clea had been offered only an apron, and Turner a three-piece suit.

Theo was saying, "If nobody else in this family can identify sin, at least *I* can, Kate. But Christ teaches us to hate the sin, not the sinner. So even though I hate what you're doing, I still love you."

"Where do you get off, laying your patriarchal Christian trip on me, you little turd?"

Later, as Turner and Terence went out in the rain in search of a taxi, Elke and Clea stood by the front door. Unable to gauge Elke's mood, Clea felt shy and wary, so she said nothing. Elke was silent too, except for a hurried thank you as a taxi pulled up out front. Clea stood watching Terence help Elke into the cab. She extracted her arm from his grasp and grimaced with annoyance. He looked hurt and bewildered.

As the taxi pulled away, Turner waving on the sidewalk, Clea observed the play of the streetlight on the puddles and felt forlorn. In the end, Elke always departed with Terence, however irritably. Throughout Elke's and her years of devotion, Clea had known that in a crunch Elke would invariably put Terence first. After all, he was her husband. Whereas Clea was just her primary emotional support and sole source of optimism and amusement.

In bed, Clea asked Turner, "So what do you think about Kate's announcement?"

He lay curled around her, chest against her back. "I don't care whom my children sleep with, so long as they don't get AIDS. But I wish they wouldn't insist on telling me about it. After all, I don't ask their approval for *my* sex life."

They're not your father, thought Clea. Turner had always had this difficulty differentiating between the children and the adults in this family. He often seemed like one of her younger brothers, for whom she was responsible. "I thought it was sweet she felt she could tell us. It shows she trusts our love."

"She was just trying to get a rise out of us."

"Ostensibly. But not really."

Turner groaned. "There you go playing sibyl again. Knowing what people intend better than they do themselves."

Clea wished she were talking this over with Elke. They'd have omitted this portion of the discussion, taking what Clea said for granted and addressing more arcane aspects. It was like requiring a physicist to do simple sums.

Turner buried his face in her neck. "But you'd have to be a fool not to love women. And our daughter's no fool."

Sighing, Clea rubbed his cheek with hers. "Turner, I've decided to abort this Roches Ridge project."

"But, darling, that's marvelous!"

"I realized that the people at our table tonight mean more to me than anything in this world. I need you all."

"And we need you," murmured Turner.

"I also realized New York is where I belong. You can't imagine how dreary a village full of dour Yankees is. I might as well have never left Poplar Bluffs."

"Exactly."

Clea could feel Turner's prick stirring against her buttock.

"I'm proud of you, Clea, for seeing this before throwing away a lot of time and money."

Slipping on a condom, Turner whispered, "Welcome home, sweetheart." He entered her from behind, moving slowly and tenderly, hands holding her hips.

With dismay, Clea found herself visualizing Dack Marsh atop his wrecked cars, copper chest sweaty as he thrust and pried with his crowbar, muscles straining and quivering.

# 30 The Eighth Circle

Clea awoke, stretching luxuriously amid sex-stained sheets, delighted to have her brief excursion into celibacy terminated. Turner had already departed for the airport, leaving on the nightstand a loving note that congratulated her on jettisoning Roches Ridge. Theo and Kate had gone back to their schools. She'd do errands, then meet Elke for lunch in the Village.

Dialing Elke, she got her machine. Damn. She was probably trying to salvage her bayoneted baby. Clea was miffed Elke hadn't phoned before setting to work. For all Elke knew, Clea was about to return to Roches Ridge. Was she punishing her for that, unaware of Clea's repatriation? Dack Marsh's appearance during lovemaking with Turner the night before had merely reinforced this decision. She wanted no more such entanglements, and certainly not an unrequited one with a redneck scarcely older than Kate. Apparently one aspect of solitude was hallucinations. She was pleased to discover she'd finally developed the ability to snuff out these sparks of delusion before they turned into holocausts.

When Elke opened her studio door, she looked fatigued and annoyed. She didn't initiate a hug or kiss, so neither did Clea.

"Okay, Elke, so what's up?" Clea demanded, dropping into the corduroy armchair. She was feeling like a yo-yo, with Elke jerking the string.

"What do you mean, what's up?"

"You know perfectly well what I mean. We haven't really talked in weeks. You don't return my calls or answer my letters."

Elke started to speak, then fell silent, gesturing helplessly.

"What does that mean?" asked Clea, mimicking the listless gesture.

"It means I don't know what's up. But I agree: Something is definitely up."

"Are you angry with me?"

"A bit." Elke sat down in the black plaid chair opposite her.

"About my move to Roches Ridge?"

"Perhaps."

"Well, you can cheer up, then. Because I'm selling the house and moving back home."

Elke shrugged, evidently uninterested.

"Clearly I flattered myself to imagine you'd be pleased." Clea recognized this fugue state in which Elke became supremely indifferent to everyday life, had no thoughts or feelings she was willing to express. Elke sulked when Clea went away, apparently unaware that she, too, went away sometimes, while sitting in the same room with someone. Her concept of creativity entailed such psychic thumbscrews. But for Clea, if something wasn't fun, she did something else.

"Where's 'Suffer the Little Children' gone to?" asked Clea, glancing around the studio.

"In there." Elke pointed to a metal garbage can.

Clea stood up and walked over to it. Raising the lid, she discovered a jumble of jagged steel. The smooth oval skull was cracked apart like an eggshell. Looking quickly at Elke, she said, "God, Elke, I'm sorry. I didn't realize." This alone could explain her weeks of unpleasant behavior. It was no small sacrifice. Elke spent months, years, on a sculpture, preceding it with studies in several media, and casts in plaster or clay.

"I had to. It just didn't have it."

"But you're such an extremist, to appear so mild." Clea laughed uneasily.

"It bored me."

"How about me? Do I bore you too? Is that why you're trying to toss our friendship into the trash heap?" joked Clea halfheartedly.

Elke smiled faintly. "You pain me sometimes, Clea, but you never bore me."

Elke's tone was bland and matter-of-fact, but it masked despair. Yet Clea was disturbed to note how uninterested she was in alleviating the despair, as though that capacity in her had shut down now that she was merely a mother emeritus. Mostly she wanted to get the hell out of this stuffy room. So she stood up.

Even though she'd just arrived, Elke regarded her without surprise or objection, saying wearily, "Take care, Clea."

Clea leaned over and kissed her cheek. They looked at each other. Clea walked to the door, her heart numb. Something felt final about this leavetaking, despite all their prior trial runs.

Walking up Fifth Avenue, Clea kept picturing that broken skull in Elke's garbage can, with its torn, jagged edges and terrified eyes. There was something so implacable about Elke when it came to her work. She allowed nothing to stand in its way—neither society's conventions nor her own. Faced with a choice between creation within her womb and within her psyche, she'd picked an abortion. And on Saint John she'd picked her messy studio over Clea's messy kitchen and nursery. This ruthlessness was perhaps a source of her brilliance, but in human terms it was frightening. You never knew when it might be directed at you. Maybe it had been. Maybe that was what was going on between them now.

But Clea's spirits began to revive despite Elke. They'd been through rough patches before. Elke would recover once she began a new piece, and Clea would be living in New York to welcome her return. Meanwhile, Clea felt elated to be back where she belonged. At her elbows she could have identified people of a dozen different nationalities. The air crackled and buzzed with energy. This was what she loved about New York—the variety and vitality. In contrast to Roches Ridge, which was so laid back you'd need a crane just to hoist the place to its feet. Yes, she was smart to cut her losses and come back home.

A freak overnight snowstorm had turned the crosswalk at Forty-first Street into a gray swamp. Smog, cab exhaust, subway steam, and smoke from chestnut vendors had combined in a dank gust that swept up the street, swirling a Snickers wrapper and a *Times* editorial page.

Head lowered, hand holding up her black cape, Clea tiptoed through the mire, wishing she hadn't left her Sorels in Roches Ridge. A man in a Chesterfield overcoat bumped into her, and she stumbled into a puddle to the ankles of her black suede boots just as the light changed. A truckdriver bore down on her like a *Ben-Hur* charioteer, blasting with his horn. He rolled down his window to yell, "Whadaya want, lady? A bridge?"

Regaining the sidewalk, Clea squished on, enumerating her errands, increasingly energized by the pulsing city. She'd break the bad news to Karen about *The Town That Time Forgot*. She was pleased she could renounce Roches Ridge so effortlessly. Yet the credit wasn't entirely her own. Becoming middle-aged was like climbing into a cyclotron. An entomologist she once bedded while photographing a butterfly hunt in Tasmania explained that metabolism slowed as one aged, causing perceived time to shrink. With more responsibilities and less time, detachment became a necessity. Clea scarcely had time to fold the laundry anymore, much less to brood over recent slights or ancient grievances. So many details hurtled past her these days that she simply had to ignore most. So the heralded wisdom of age was actually a physiological inevitability.

As Clea entered the revolving door to the Atrium, an eager shopper wedged in behind her and hobbled on her soaking suede boots. This was Clea's favorite store. An art nouveau mall, it contained everything any self-respecting yuppie could want, in four floors of specialty boutiques that opened off a central tiled and domed atrium. As she passed a plant-festooned fountain, smiling young women in business suits popped out from behind potted palms to wave atomizers of sample Je t'adore like censers. Clea inhaled the sweet mist and began to sneeze.

Eyes watering, Clea stood on the escalator, consumers with bulging bags pushing past her up the steps. Entering the gourmet shop, Clea leaned against a pillar, sinuses throbbing from the Je t'adore. A throng of gourmands clutching cooking implements waved credit cards before the cash register like brokers bidding on pork belly futures.

Retreating to the promenade, Clea conceded defeat before even joining the fray. As she looked over the railing at the spray thrown up by the ground-floor fountain, she heard a familiar voice say, "Clea! Hi!"

Turning, she saw Jim, the *Getaway* editor with whom she'd not gotten away. Their aborted flirtation had helped propel her to Roches Ridge. He was blushing above his tweed overcoat collar. "So how's the yeomanly life?"

"I've come back, actually."

"That was quick."

"Well, at my age it's hard to change. I've got so many friends and responsibilities here."

"Well, well. Good news for us."

Clea wondered if she detected a flicker of renewed hope in his eyes. But a reversion to her former behavior appealed almost as much as cleaning out Calvin Roche's cellar.

"Thanks," she said coolly. "What are you up to these days, Jim?"

"The usual. Trying to make our debtor nations sound glamorous to my readership."

Clea smiled. At least there had been a trace of logic in her attraction to him. "Let me know if you've got any assignments for me. I'm back in business."

"But no Antigua?"

"No Antigua," she said firmly. "Well, look, take care of yourself, Jim."

"You too, Clea. Such a pity." He shook his head as he walked away.

Down in the central atrium, shoppers wove in chaotic formations among the potted palms like a marching band on amphetamines. A hum like a bee swarm rose to the stained-glass dome.

Clea felt exhausted. Deciding her blood sugar needed a boost, she went to the café on the other side of the promenade and ordered coffee and a croissant. Had she lost the knack for city living? In order to exist happily amid so much sensory input, you had to shut down your senses—not see trash, not hear squealing tires, not feel crowding. But her senses were wide open from taking in all the new people and natural beauty in Roches Ridge. She visualized the equivalent errand-performing journey up there—strolling across the green under the stately dying elms, nodding at everyone you passed.

As Clea sipped her coffee, a model strolled in wearing a suit the color of Key lime pie, followed by a dozen models in similar brilliant spring outfits, with iridescent feathers at their ears and in their hair. Vivid eye shadow extended to their eyebrows and temples, causing them to look like high-fashion raccoons. The line wove among the tables, pausing to answer questions and refer shoppers in their damp wool overcoats and head scarves to the appropriate boutique. Several women downed coffee, tossed change on the table, picked up shopping bags with splitting seams, and left in search of garments that would transform *them* into tall, lean, angular birds of paradise.

"Interested?" the head bird asked Clea, striking a posture out of *Vogue,* with a hand on one overcocked hip and the other shoulder twisted back as though she were about to hurl a discus.

"Uh, no thanks."

The woman looked at her in her dingy black cape and wet suede boots, then lifted her bright red lip to observe, "Well, you ought to be." As though launching the discus, she spun around and marched away, followed by her gaudy disciples, leaving behind a pall of Je t'adore.

Sneezing again, Clea decided she wasn't up to shopping today. She descended the escalator. En route to the revolving door, she passed the line of models, posing motionless in grotesque postures that resembled the Stations of the Cross. The business-suited women flourished their atomizers like handguns.

Out in the street, Clea gasped cool gray air. Her heart was pounding. She had to get home. Turning to walk crosstown, she tripped over a bundle of rags. Glancing down, she discovered the bundle was a man passed out in a puddle of vomit, mouth lolling open. Shoppers stepped over and around him. So did Clea, hurrying through the shadowy abyss between rows of towering gray stone and steel. A woman in a toboggan cap and several sweaters was arranging objects from a shopping cart on cardboard over a subway grate. She grinned at Clea with broken blackened teeth.

A speck of soot flew into Clea's eye. As she tugged at her lid, tears began to trickle down her cheek. Her nostrils picked up the sulfurous odor of hot tar from a pothole behind a barricade of sawhorses and orange caution cones. She passed a video shop with posters in the display windows featuring bare breasts, whips, boots, and bulging male muscles.

At Third Avenue, Clea heard police sirens, squealing brakes, and screams. On the sidewalk lay a writhing mink coat, an expanding pool of red under the collar, shattered glass everywhere. Pedestrians were pointing several stories up. Cars were abandoned at bizarre angles. Revolving blue flashers from squad cars tinted the yellow smog an algae green. Voices crackled on police radios. A mounted cop struggled with his snorting horse, trying to hold back honking traffic. A siren joined the din. Soon an ambulance appeared, its throbbing red flasher turning the muck in the crosswalk to a river of blood.

The cop gestured for pedestrians to cross. As Clea did so, again to her ankles in slush, three men in reptilian leather face masks approached her. As they came closer, she could see their bloodshot eyes. *She was on her knees among Big Mac cartons, earlobes dripping blood, the shattered skull of a newborn infant before her.* . . .

Clea broke into a trot and dodged through the crowds toward her empty Turtle Bay town house. Resolutely she pictured Roches Ridge. Where fluffy puffs of springtime clouds were even now scudding across sunstruck skies, and harp music was wafting about the green on gentle zephyrs off the clear blue lake.

# 31   The Merry Month of May

Clea sat at the desk in her Roche House bedroom, writing in her journal for *The Town That Time Forgot.* Brandy lay asleep in a shaft of sunlight on a hooked rug on the polished pine floorboards. The desk looked out on the Marshes' junked cars. She could have chosen a more scenic view, but it was soothing when she was stalled with her writing to watch Dack heaving at the autos with his crowbar, sweat coursing down his copper chest. All that fierce vitality was energizing. Dack Marsh was the real thing, an untamed mountain man, so different from the effete sophisticates Clea had associated with most of her life. Poor old Turner wouldn't know which end of a crowbar to pry with, and he had no interest in learning. In fact, he'd been so disgusted with her return to Roches Ridge that he refused even to visit. But he'd no doubt relent once he got lonely enough. Other women could provide sex, but evidently none was willing to endure monologues about his safaris through the corporate jungle.

Elke, equally disgusted, was another matter. She and Clea had snapped at each other when Clea phoned to announce she was returning to Vermont after all. Elke said she was fed up with providing Clea with a base camp, from which she scaled her heights. Clea replied she was sick of enduring Elke's dreary moods and rescuing her from her self-generated doldrums. Each was left speechless, feeling totally misperceived by the person who knew her best. They muttered farewells and hung up.

Clea, refusing to dwell on it, had immersed herself in her new town. New York City was finished for her. Her vacant town house and the teeming metropolis frightened her. She would never live there again. Yet Elke wouldn't leave. No doubt they'd stay in touch in some attenuated fashion, but their preoccupation with each other would gradually fade away. In time Clea would recover from Elke as thoroughly as she had from all her lovers. Only a few isolated memories would remain—of a wooden fan slowly circling on a sultry tropical afternoon, of a sad smile and wisps of silver hair.

Yesterday as Clea was bagging debris in her backyard, she spotted Dack Marsh in his driveway, leaning on his crowbar. Strolling around the stockade fence, she asked him about the wooden cross bearing the rodent skeleton, which she'd seen above his TV the morning she met him. He said he'd made it. When she expressed enthusiasm, he invited her inside and showed her more wall hangings, on almost every vertical surface in the crumbling old house. And they were stunning—femurs, hanks of fur, bleached rib cages and skulls, hooves and antlers. Combined to form eerie abstract designs. There was a totemic quality to them.

Her first impulse was to urge Elke to come see. But it was useless. Elke wouldn't budge. Besides, Dack's hangings were actually more powerful than Elke's sculptures. Both described devastation, but Elke left it at that, whereas Dack created striking new forms from the spoils. It was the difference between the city and the countryside.

A huge forest-green garbage truck backed down Clea's driveway to the pile of lath and heaped trash bags and the cracked bathtub on its claw feet. Above its maw was painted SOONER OR LATER. Clea stared at this slogan for a long time before returning to her diary: "Today the junk man is carting the bathtub to the landfill. A pity it couldn't be salvaged, but a tub that won't hold water isn't much use. In my absence Darius has replaced the rotted sills and the kitchen floor. It's slow work with mostly hand tools. When I asked him if he could speed things up, he just kept sawing a 2 x 4 in half lengthwise, pipe in his mouth, and said, 'Nope.' But I guess the old ways are appropriate for this gem of a house."

Clea became aware that she was dawdling at her desk, hoping for a glimpse of Dack. Which she knew was ridiculous. Just because she'd returned to Roches Ridge didn't mean she was prepared to succumb to another attraction, and certainly not one for a teenager. She could appreciate the primitive fury of his art without seeking a more personal involvement.

Clea reprimanded herself for her lassitude. She had a dozen chores before heading to the town hall for the first meeting of the bicentennial festival committee. During a recent perusal of town records for her book, she'd discovered that Roches Ridge was chartered in 1787, following a winter in which the first settlers subsisted on dried pumpkin. Asking the town clerk, she found no birthday celebration in the works. So Clea was organizing one, seeing it as an opportunity to involve the entire town, thereby bridging rifts apparent among different factions the night of the Miss Teenage Roches Ridge Pageant. It seemed presumptuous for so recent an arrival. But *because* she was still an outsider, she had the objectivity to see what was needed. She envisioned a crafts show in the town hall. Folk dancing to fiddlers on the green. Rides for children on Gordon McQueen's horse-drawn wagon. A concert in the bandstand. Three-legged races and a tug-of-war on the soccer field.

Gazing out the window, Clea saw Crystal Sue Marsh, runner-up to Miss Teenage Roches Ridge, slip out the side door of the Marshes' house dressed in skin-tight faded Levi's, T-shirt, and jean jacket. Tying a rolled bandanna around her forehead, she trotted alongside the wrecked cars to the path down to Mink Creek.

Ishtar was lying on the bed in her tiny apartment above the Karma Café, twirling the needle in her Third Eye. The wand of moldavite on her heart chakra was vibrating. Of extraterrestrial origin, it assisted interdimensional communication. The spider plants filling the eaves were swaying in the breeze through the window.

Suddenly Ishtar was a newborn baby in a pioneer cabin. Her parents had expressions of horror on their faces. Her mother seemed to be Father Flanagan's housekeeper, Theresa. She wore a straw pillbox decorated with wooden cherries. But why this hat from her current life, in a pioneer cabin?

Ishtar wasn't alone. No, she evidently had a twin. Two heads, four limbs apiece. But something was wrong. They were Siamese twins, joined at the heart chakra. And Ishtar's twin was Morning Glory! The father slipped a hunting knife from its sheath on his belt. He was slicing them apart! Blood, pain, screams from the mother, then blackness . . .

Ishtar blew out quick rhythmic breaths to calm herself. This explained why she and Morning Glory were so drawn to each other in this life. But who was the father who'd hacked them apart, killing them in the process? Perhaps it was Starshine, with her need to keep them separate.

Plucking the needle from her Third Eye and setting the moldavite on the floor, Ishtar walked to the window. It was so odd being able to identify people from past lives but not her own parents from *this* life. She breathed deeply of the fresh spring air and gazed down the cliff toward Mink Creek and her former twin, Morning Glory (as she called herself this time around).

Where did Rayon Marsh fit into her previous lifetimes, Ishtar wondered, always hanging around her café, convinced he was a lesbian trapped in a man's body? Ishtar had lent him her moonstone, to help him explore his feminine aspect. And what about the connection she felt to Father Flanagan? He denied feeling any such thing when he drank tea with her late at night under the spider plants, but that denial was no doubt part of their recurring scenario, which they ought to be working through in this life. However, his Catholicism wouldn't allow him to entertain such pagan notions.

Ishtar spotted Angela McGrath crossing the green in her Edwardian gown. Angela glanced around nervously, then slipped through the Deathworks door. Now, why would Angela be spending time with her husband's competitor, Sonny Coffin?


Astrid Starr stooped down in the IGA window, belatedly replacing the sugaring display with the spring planting one—seed packets, bags of potting soil and fertilizer, a hoe, shovel, and rake. All things you sure as hang couldn't purchase at the Grand Union on Route 7. Plus snack items—candy bars and cookies, honey-roasted peanuts, Miller's and Diet Coke. And a new touch this year—flower and vegetable catalogues, open to colorful pages. You had to feed the imagination as well as the body.

And frankly, Astrid's imagination was skin and bones at the moment. Earl had finally confessed that he didn't really like to leave Roches Ridge, and that she'd have to visit her remaining two states and six seas alone. Plus which, his belly had started looking fat again, instead of cute. So apparently the honeymoon was officially over. Astrid had joined the Women's Oppression Workshop at the Center for Sanity to deal with her grief. Genevieve Paxton in her checked *kaffiyeh* told her it was time to switch from being in love with Earl to truly loving him. Genevieve claimed that what Astrid sacrificed in excitement she could make up for with depth. She said the metaphor was waterskiing versus scuba diving.

Angela McGrath was crossing the green to her son's grave, fringed silk parasol shading her from the warm spring sun. But no. Angela looked around anxiously, then vanished into Deathworks. Astrid stood up straight in her dark-blue polyester jacket, perplexed. She surveyed the empty green, one hand with its huge zircon engagement ring on her ample hip, the other spanning her several chins. Sonny Coffin and Ian McGrath were in a death grip over cremation vs. inhumation, brass plaques vs. granite headstones. So what was Angela up to? Astrid felt alarmed. What if Sonny Coffin knew something she didn't? Then she realized Deathworks could never replace Starr's IGA as Roches Ridge's solar plexus. For one thing, Sonny wasn't a native. Nevertheless, what she'd just witnessed had the potential to blow the town's record of forty-three minutes sky high.

Frieda Bohring, in her blue-rinse coiffure, arrived at the checkout counter with a cart of purchases, including sixteen-packs of white Charmin. Shoppers deserted their baskets in mid-aisle, and employees left shelves half stocked, to cluster around the register as though around a Las Vegas blackjack table. As Astrid rang up each item, Frieda extracted a coupon from her Aisle file and flung it down like a bridge player trumping tricks.

Astrid gathered together the coupons, added them up, and subtracted the total from Frieda's bill. The audience whispered, aware they were witnessing a master shopper in concert. Eyes flashing, Frieda punched figures into her pocket calculator. "Sixty percent off," she announced calmly. The crowd burst into applause. Someone called, "Bravo!"

Astrid scowled. Coupons gave her a pain. Besides, Frieda was not a loyal person. She also shopped at the Grand Union. Wherever buys were best, there was Frieda Bohring, rifling her Aisle file. She had a bumper sticker on her Rabbit that read I BRAKE FOR DOUBLE COUPONS.

Returnable cans and bottles also gave Astrid a pain. As did the seasonal displays in her front window. In fact, Astrid's whole life felt as stale as day-old bread. If someone didn't do something to break that forty-three-minute record pretty darn quick, Astrid might have to take matters into her own hands. Meanwhile, her hopes were hanging on Angela McGrath, who hadn't yet exited from Deathworks.

. . .

Man cannot live by death alone, mused Sonny Coffin, leaning back in his swivel chair, hands behind his head, feet propped on his shiny walnut desk. On the wall behind him hung a chart of upcoming funerals, next to a Norman Rockwell print of a country doctor sitting beside a patient's deathbed. Sonny's goal was to become the McDonald's of the funeral trade, with franchises all across the nation. He was already well on his way to the Big Board. Everything he touched turned to mold.

Sonny had come to Roches Ridge every boyhood summer to visit his grandparents in their apartment above Coffin's Funeral Home. In a field alongside the graveyard, he played Babe Ruth League baseball with town boys like his cousin Ian McGrath. Sometimes he dove head-first into a freshly dug grave while catching a fly ball.

For a brief time he wanted to pitch pro baseball. But he was cut during tryouts at college. Unlike his dear dumb cousin Ian, who went on to become an all-American shortstop. After college Sonny went to work at Forest Lawn, first maintenance, then sales. When his grandparents passed away, they left him their funeral home in Roches Ridge.

Vermont was virgin territory, mortuarily speaking. You could provide all kinds of innovative services for the modern dead Vermonter. Such as the coffin showroom downstairs, where customers could see anything from a composition-board model retailing at $390 to a seamless burnished copper one with cloud-soft satin interior at $25,000.

In olden times Coffins handled caskets and burial, and their McGrath cousins provided headstones. But times change. For instance, pyramids were now obsolete. And hacking stone slabs from a cliff and carving them with a chisel went out with hieroglyphics. Was it Sonny's fault if his cousin Ian clung to outmoded ways? Customers at Deathworks simply didn't need his headstones anymore. They needed urns for loved ones' cremains, and markers for the urns, or sifters for spreading the ashes. Poor old Ian's star was setting, as Sonny's rose to the midheavens.

Sonny refused to be alarmed that American life expectancy was on the rise. With the aging of baby boomers, death would soon become a real growth industry, and he was determined to hang ten on this upcoming wave of fatality. He'd utilize the ecological awareness of baby boomers, pointing out that bodies were biodegradable. Why seal them away in metal caskets when you could return all those valuable trace minerals to the ecosphere? But until the tide of deceased baby boomers swept in, there were other ways to keep your board afloat. For instance, Maureen Murphy had just contacted him about a possible trip to Colombia with her mother. . . .

Sonny switched on his intercom and asked his secretary to usher in his dear cousin Ian's lovely wife, Angela.

Clea glanced around the town clerk's office in the town hall. Astrid Starr, Loretta Gebo, Father Flanagan, and Conrad Bohring had shown up, but no one else, despite posters around town asking for volunteers. Clea was disappointed, having anticipated widespread enthusiasm for the upcoming bicentennial.

"It seems to me," began Clea behind the town clerk's cluttered desk, "our first item of business ought to be expanding this committee."

"It's hard to get people out to meetings," explained Astrid listlessly. "Everyone's so busy during the day and so tired after work. And Thursday nights is 'The Cosby Show.' "

"But this is the two hundredth birthday of our town we're talking about," said Clea.

Astrid shrugged, fiddling with her ring.

"I'm here," announced Conrad Bohring with a yawn, "because a festival would mean business for retailers, who are customers at my bank." Conrad had a steel-gray flattop, rigid as a fakir's bed of nails.

"I'm here because I promised you I would be, Clea," said Loretta. "But let's make it quick, because I left Dylan Scarborough running my kitchen, and he may have burned the restaurant down by the time I get back. I swear, that boy's so laid back I'm gonna have to lay him off."

They all looked at Father Flanagan, in his stiff white collar. His sad smile told them he had nothing better to do than come to this meeting.

"Well, I think we need more members," insisted Clea. "For instance, the Roches and the Marshes founded this town. No Roches are left since Calvin went to Texas. But there are lots of Marshes, and one should be on this committee."

Loretta hooted, throwing back her beehive. "Tonight's 'L.A. Law.' You won't get a single Marsh away from the TV."

"What about Ray?"

"It'll have to be Waneeta or Orlon," she replied. "They run that clan."

By the end of the meeting they'd agreed to invite the Marsh family, the Boudiccas, the Church of the Holy Deliverance, and Colonial Manor Estates to send representatives to sit on the committee, plus all area business people. Clea felt pleased, despite the poor turnout. She'd begun the process that would bind this town together. It was a skill left over from motherhood—the ability to identify and address each individual's needs, so that the individuals could temporarily drop their uniqueness to participate in a larger unit. Although Roches Ridge might not be the tight-knit community she'd originally envisioned, it *would* be by festival time.

Zeno Racine was sneaking through the woods by Daisy Wagner's house. The upstairs room with the light on was hers. He crept over to the rose bed alongside the house foundation. Carefully avoiding thorns, he climbed the lattice, slats cracking beneath his bulk. Grabbing Daisy's sill, he pulled himself up so his chin rested on it.

Inside, at a dressing table with a pleated skirt, sat Daisy in a bra and bikini panties, gazing into a mirror as she plucked an eyebrow with tweezers. Her curly blond hair spilled over her shoulders like a head of beer down a mug. Zeno was transfixed. Never before had he seen a more gorgeous creature, tawny skin set off by white lace underwear. She looked deeply into her own eyes, puckered her lips, and blew herself a kiss.

Zeno heard a growl. He spotted the miniature poodle on the carpet by the canopied bed just as it hurled itself at the window. Zeno lurched backward, tearing the lattice loose from the house. Grabbing at the sill, he hauled himself back in so fast that his head shattered the window glass, setting off the alarm system. Daisy, whirling around, gazed wildly at the window and gasped, "Danny, is it you?" Poo's bright white snapping fangs came at Zeno, and he lurched backward again, lattice peeling off the house like a scab. Zeno clung to it as he fell in slow motion to the lawn.

The alarm was shrieking, and floodlights were sweeping the yard. Zeno scrambled to his feet and raced for the woods, stumbling over a mound on the ground.

Ida Campbell lay in the leaves, feeling as though she'd been trampled by a warthog. Lights, auto horns, and shouts were everywhere. She staggered to her feet and sprinted for her Chevy, parked on the next block. What in the world had happened? She'd been minding her own business, watching through Ken Wagner's den window as he sat in his recliner, talking into a transistorized Dictaphone. Bethany was hefting dumbbells in the next room. Ida was wondering if Bethany realized how lucky she was to have a husband who kept his shoulder to the wheel, his nose to the grindstone, his head on his shoulders, his ear to the ground—when all hell broke loose.

Back in her Chevy, Ida revved the mufflerless engine and raced for the highway. As her heart steadied, she realized this could make a powerful scene for *His Truly*. Eva, her secretary heroine, could experience calamity while striving to get a glimpse of her boss's home life. It was wonderful how even life's tragedies became grist for your mill if you were a true artist. A thorn in your side could become a feather in your cap.

Ida's career was really taking off now. All signals were go. Silhouette had turned down *Sir and Her*, but she had found a publisher to print the book for a small fee. Ida was writing a press release for distribution with review copies. She would also circulate an autographed photo to all major periodicals in the country. It was truly amazing what could happen if you were just willing to branch out on a limb.

Once Ida was a best-selling author, Ken Wagner would know who she was. She was studying shorthand at night school, and trying to figure out how to get past the Xerox security gates without an identification badge. It wouldn't be long now before the man of her dreams would have to wake up and smell the coffee. Sometimes she felt guilty toward her husband, Chad. But although she wanted to be Ken Wagner's gal Friday, every other day of the week would belong to Chad.


As he drove home to Colonial Manor Estates from Mrs. Shawn's bicentennial meeting, Conrad Bohring, president of Mink Valley Savings and Loan, noted two suspicious things. One was a battered Chevrolet without a muffler speeding toward the highway. The other was a huge creature hunched over like a giant armadillo, lumbering across Route 7. The neighborhood was lit up like Christmas from searchlights and the flasher on Trooper Trapp's cruiser. Neighbors clustered on the sidewalk in front of Conrad's house, carefully avoiding his perfect lawn. Before realizing that the activity centered on the Wagners' house, Conrad had a brief moment of panic that that damn Poo might have defecated on his lawn again. Something was going to have to be done about that dog. He was a menace to tax-paying, law-abiding citizens like Conrad, who had fought the Huns and the Japs on land and sea and air in order to protect property rights that damn dog kept violating with his fecal matter.

# 32 June

Gordon McQueen lay under a willow in his cutoffs and red muscle shirt, yelling instructions to Starshine, who was plowing the site of her women-only graveyard with his workhorses. Her luminescent blue-and-yellow parrot perched on his knee. Men weren't supposed to be on this land, but apparently faggots didn't count. Shirtless, rolls of flesh burned red and dripping sweat, Starshine kept swatting at deer-flies and spooking the horses, who were snorting and tossing their heads. The ground was still wet from flooding, so the clods were huge and lumpy.

The other Boudiccas, plus Crystal Sue Marsh, all shirtless, were in a clearing, doing roundhouse karate kicks under the direction of Foxglove, in her white karate pajamas and brown belt. Gordon had been shocked to see Crystal Sue. Orlon would go on a rampage if he found out she was down here. But he was so busy doing Sonny Coffin's dirty work that he probably had no idea where Crystal Sue spent her days.

Gordon and his mother might have to be dealing with Deathworks before long. Dan had been in a coma at the Burlington Medical Center for weeks, ever since his hockey accident at Camel's Hump Community College. Gordon visited weekly, and it was torture to see his happy, active baby brother lying still as death, face battered and broken.

"How do you stop these things?" yelled Starshine, stumbling along behind the plow, mud-caked bare feet the size of ski boots.

"Pull back on the reins," called Gordon. Usually the challenge was to keep the horses moving. They stopped immediately and stood impassively, ears and tails twitching at circling flies.

Starshine collapsed beside Gordon. "Goddess, Gordon, get a tractor." Che hopped off Gordon's knee and onto Starshine's red belly.

"But the horses make me feel so manly, dear," he sighed.

"Not your problem, so I hear."

"*What* do you hear?" He broke off a blade of grass, arranged it between his thumbs, and blew on it to make a squeaking noise.

"That you're a slut, darling."

"So that's why you've stopped coming to my door asking to borrow a cup of semen."

"That, plus the fact that we're brimming over with buckets of the stuff. It feels like *Moby Dick* down here right now. Ray Marsh has been begging to provide stud service, and Dack has been sneaking around, mooning over Morning Glory."

"Must be something about those Marshes. I almost dropped my teeth when I saw Crystal Sue. Orlon'll kill you."

"She's as pure as the day she first appeared," said Starshine, sitting up and moving Che to her shoulder, where he made kissing sounds in her ear.

"I'd send her back home. You could get yourself in big trouble."

"It's like trying to keep an ant from honey."

They stood up and strolled toward the karate workshop.

"Power to the People!" screamed Che.

"What should we plant in that field to make it look nice, Gordon? We've got to sell off some burying plots fast, or it's curtains for Mink Creek."

"Try annual rye. It comes right up and is bright green. Just the sod under which you'd want to bury loved ones."

Foxglove was describing compliance techniques for rapists, pretending to be turned on, then ripping off the man's lower lip with your teeth, or blinding him with your thumbs, popping his balls like ripe plums between thumb and middle finger, or sending a sliver of bone into his brain by smashing his nose on your knee.

"Well, guess I'd better be running along," said Gordon weakly.

"Relax," said Starshine. "Pussy's not your thing, so you've got nothing to worry about."


Starshine sat on her futon, Che on her shoulder, reading the assignment for her correspondence course in word processing. She practiced once a week on Conrad Bohring's computer at Mink Valley Savings and Loan. Conrad traded computer time for investment advice. He said she had a gift for equities. The Boudiccas were going under. Call her a rat deserting a sinking ship, but once she completed her course, she'd resign as guru. She was sick of taking care of everybody and then having them resent her for it. She'd thought they'd become stronger and wiser watching her example, but they had instead turned into cases looking for a basket. Evidently, successful guruhood wasn't as simple as it seemed.

After Gordon left, the Boudiccas had called a goddess circle under the willow tree.

"You always take all the glamorous jobs like plowing, Starshine," said Sumac.

"But we've been talking about the need to plow that field for weeks, and none of you did it," pointed out Starshine. "It's almost too late to plant."

It was another example of on-the-job sex discrimination: If Starshine were a male guru, her disciples would go jump in Mink Creek without hesitation when she told them to. Well, they could all rot in this swamp as far as she was concerned. She'd withdraw her pension fund from Conrad's bank and skip town. Hopefully with the blue-veiled woman from the Church of the Holy Deliverance in tow. This part of the plan was still in its visualization stages.

"Make Love, Not War," announced Che.

Starshine smiled. Whatever happened, she'd never be lonely. Che would outlive her by several decades. *He* was the one who needed a pension fund.


Clea watched as the folding chairs in the town clerk's office filled up with a true cross section of Roches Ridge citizenry. She and Conrad Bohring had agreed he'd open each meeting with some town history— colonial lore tonight, maybe prehistory next month, flora and fauna and geology, the town's role in various wars. Conrad said he'd always planned to be a history professor but had gotten sidetracked into banking. Clea hoped having him chair these meetings would derail any criticism should a newcomer like herself preside. She was content to be the brains behind Conrad's throne.

Clea was pleased with herself. She was making a contribution here in Roches Ridge, something she'd never felt in New York despite her quarter century there. She was bringing this town together. She was rescuing from collapse one of its most stunning architectural landmarks. New windows and storms had been installed in the old stone house. The lath was off the inside walls. New plumbing and wiring were going in, one of Darius' few concessions to the twentieth century.

Her notes for *The Town That Time Forgot* were mounting. Once she got the back field cleared of debris, she'd landscape with trees, bushes, stone walls, vines, and flower beds. Her new life was satisfying and purposeful. She rarely brooded anymore over the chill between Elke and herself. Abandoning New York had definitely been the right decision, despite her Easter lapse.

Conrad was snoozing quietly by the black door of the walk-in safe. Clea nudged him with her Reebok. He jerked awake and gazed around wildly, hand ruffling his stiff gray flattop.

"Sorry to disturb you," whispered Clea, "but it's time to start."

"Right!" Conrad sat up straight and peered over his Ben Franklin spectacles. "Let the meeting come to order, please." The townspeople gradually fell silent. "It's good to see all you folks out tonight. As you know, next year Roches Ridge will be two hundred years old. We need to decide how we want to celebrate. But first I'd like to say a few words about the history of our town. Mrs. Clea Shawn, who first notified us of the upcoming birthday, has been kind enough to provide me with some data, which I'll now pass on to you."

"... the migration patterns of early European immigrants ...," Conrad Bohring was saying in his intriguing monotone.

Loretta felt her eyes cross. She bit the inside of her cheek hard to stay awake. Then her drooping eyes settled on Ishtar. Instantly they uncrossed, and Loretta sat straight up. On a chain at her throat Ishtar was wearing a milky polished stone pendant exactly like the one Loretta had found in the pocket of Ray's camouflage pants last night. It must be a pledge of some kind between them. She was losing Ray, she knew it. His obsession with lesbians was taking over. He'd move down to Mink Creek with the Boudiccas.

Standing in the window of Casa Loretta the night before, Loretta had spotted Ray emerging from the Karma Café. It was Ishtar's tofu French fries night. Loretta knew for a fact that Rayon Marsh had no use for tofu, French fried or otherwise. Later, as he slept in her bed in the Sunset View trailer, he was dreaming about something that was giving him a hard-on. Loretta was wide awake, searching her mind for some way to regain his devotion. She remembered Calvin's reading from the *National Enquirer* about a company that would coat you in chocolate for your Valentine for one hundred dollars. But *she* was the one who adored chocolate.

Stymied, she mused on into the night, while Ray tossed and sighed in his sleep. In a burst of inspiration, Loretta raced to the kitchen and heated some semisweet chocolate over the burner, adding a cube of paraffin. After the mix cooled, she took it into the bedroom and dipped Ray's erection into the saucepan. The chocolate hardened around him.

Loretta knelt over Ray and began to lick and suck the chocolate. Ray sighed Ishtar's name. Opening his eyes, he looked down to find Loretta poised over him, smeared with chocolate. His penis went limp. In quiet despair, Loretta removed the chocolate casing like an outgrown locust shell. Studying it, she shrugged and took a bite, while Ray turned over and returned to Ishtar.

Toward morning, Loretta rifled Ray's pockets for clues to what was going on with him. And she discovered that milky stone. Now she saw it was identical to Ishtar's. What did this mean? Christ, she loved Ray so much. Why did he have to be so strange? If she could just win some contest, she'd spirit him away from Ishtar. She had high hopes for the Monopoly game at McDonald's on Route 7. You could win a thousand dollars a week for life. You got a game piece every time you went in, so she was urging all her regular customers to go there instead and to bring her their game pieces.


Clea studied Waneeta Marsh, whose enormous bulk was engulfing her flimsy folding chair. Her arms were folded across her chest, and her facial expression suggested that she was almost as interested in Conrad's description of boat traffic on Lake Champlain prior to the French and Indian War as she was in the gross national product of contemporary Madagascar. It was hard to believe she was the mother of the sensitive young man next door who had created those dazzling wall hangings from scraps of dead animals. Clea had taken slides of the hangings and sent them to Anya, the owner of Elke's SoHo gallery. A sixties hippie who'd made it big, Anya decked herself out in Navajo silver and turquoise. She'd flipped over the "Abenaki totem sculpture," as she called it. Having had a last-minute cancellation, she scheduled a show right away. Clea was driving Dack to New York for the opening. She imagined escorting him around town and enjoying his amazement at all the city sights. They would stay at Turtle Bay. Her king-size bed floated into her head. She irritably ushered it back out again. She was giving a talented young folk artist a career break, nothing more. In any case, she'd sworn off new attractions. Evidently, her capacity for celibacy was modest, but she could make do with occasional bouts with Turner, once he recovered from his pique. Kate was right: It was time she acted her age.

". . . as a port for timber for masts for the British navy. . . ." Conrad was feeling pleased with himself in this tutorial role. He'd had to drop out of his history Ph.D. program to marry Mrs. Bohring when she became pregnant back in '35. It had seemed like the end of the world. But here he was in '86, seventy-two years young, president of Mink Valley Savings and Loan, decorated fighter pilot from World War II. Their five children had blessed them with eight lovely grandchildren. He and Mrs. Bohring had received a card from President Reagan last year for their golden wedding anniversary. Mrs. Bohring was the premier coupon shopper of central Vermont. He kept the best lawn in Colonial Manor Estates, despite that damn pooping poodle from next door (and he'd figured out a plan for Poo). In fact, Conrad had to confess that his only regret in life was not flossing more as a young man. . . .

"Hey, Bohring," called Waneeta Marsh, "can we wrap this up pretty quick? I got to get home for 'L.A. Law'."

# 33  July

Elke sat in the Spanish restaurant on Twelfth Street, watching Clea's noble savage try to figure out paella. The mussel shells mixed in with the rice were clearly too much for him. Clea beamed beside him like a new father. Her crushes were getting younger and younger. Soon she'd be seducing schoolchildren.

Elke was miffed with Anya for giving this goon a show, especially without consulting her first. But Anya was apparently as besotted with this surly young Native American nitwit as Clea herself. Clea's days and nights had been devoted to squiring this bumpkin around New York in his dirty Levi's and BORN TO DIE tattoo, watching his smoldering black eyes bug out over skyscrapers, seven-course French dinners, and subway rush-hour crowds.

Elke slapped her napkin on the table and pushed back her chair. "I'll leave you two to your carousing."

Clea looked up, surprised. "So soon, Elke?"

"I have to work in the morning."

"Have you started something new?"

"Not really. I don't know. Maybe."

As she walked home along familiar streets, Elke focused resolutely on her work, and off Clea and Squanto. She and Clea had come to the end of the line, and there was nothing more to be said about it. Sad but true, and it was no good pretending otherwise. As for her work, all she knew for sure was that she'd exhausted brutality as a theme, and herself with it. But what else remained for someone who'd seen her father hanged, her mother ice-cold on the parlor carpet, and her countrymen's corpses stacked like logs? She had no idea. But she longed to be able to work in order to shed this mantle of bleak futility that currently enfolded her. Every day she stood at her drawing table under the skylight, pen, pencil, chalk, or crayon poised. But nothing happened. She'd try to get her hand moving with doodles, but nothing would take on any life. And any faint images that did appear vanished quickly like reverse Polaroids. She'd spend her afternoons walking the city, hoping for a flicker of inspiration. But inspiration never arrived when you were searching for it. Rather, it seeped in when you were fully absorbed with scrubbing the bathtub. So she'd return to her apartment and perform every chore she could think of. But there were still no stirrings in her heart. All she could do was wait, hands extended, a midwife unable to locate the fetus.

Until tonight she'd managed to stay clear of Clea's vortex since Easter. No phone calls, no letters, no visits. The less Clea, with her compulsive need for chaos, invaded Elke's vacuum, the better. Elke was still miffed to know from their phone conversation after Easter that Clea saw herself as having had to put up with Elke all these years. When Elke's reality was the reverse. The only way to break the spell was to stay out of Clea's Enchanted Forest. If you strayed into her orbit, her gravity captured you like an asteroid.

Clea had always rummaged around in the psyches of her friends and lovers, searching for something she never found. But her own psyche was a walled fortress. One of the appeals of becoming her lover had been to discover what lay within those battlements. But over the years Elke realized that as a friend she'd been allowed more of a glimpse behind the armor than any lover, which wasn't saying much.

Later that night, as Elke lay in bed beside Terence, reading Albert Speer's diaries, the phone rang.

Clea said, "All right, Elke, what's wrong?"

"What do you mean? Nothing's wrong."

"You don't like Dack, I gather?"

"What's to like? He's a child."

"Well, it's not as though I'm trying to seduce him." Clea laughed. "In fact, he's sleeping the sleep of the just in Theo's bed right now."

Elke said nothing, jaw clenched.

"Oh, God, is that what you think, Elke? That I'm after Dack?"

"What I think is irrelevant."

"Not to me it isn't. Please tell me."

"Well, I think it's a pity you can't stay home, and do your work, and love your friends and family."

"At least, when I die, I'll have really lived."

"Meaning I haven't? That all depends on how you define 'real life.' You know what you are, Clea? An excitement junkie."

"Well, I'm in the wrong place, then. Roches Ridge is as sleepy a little backwater as you'll ever see. It's right up there with Poplar Bluffs for excitement. If you'd come visit, you'd know what I mean."

"No place is sleepy with you in residence, darling," murmured Elke in a half-critical, half-admiring voice. Damn. Clea was beginning to cajole her out of her irritation, as usual.

Terence looked up from his journal to give her a disgusted look. She'd told him at dinner that her friendship with Clea was over.

"You *will* come to the opening tomorrow, won't you, Elke?"

"I suppose so," sighed Elke.


Dack stood in a corner, clutching a plastic cup of white wine and looking surly. Only Clea knew he was scared to death. At least she'd persuaded him to run his Levi's through the wash. And he'd agreed to wear one of Turner's old polo shirts beneath his down vest. Clea, dressed in a gray-green silk shirtwaist with pearls at her throat, was circulating, eavesdropping on reactions to the show. The wall hangings looked spectacular on the white walls, illuminated by track lighting. Most people in the room seemed to agree. The *Voice* critic was whispering something to her companion as Clea passed about "uncompromising virility," alternately eyeing the hangings and Dack's aquiline profile. Dack was stammering something to Anya, who wore a silver-and-turquoise squash-blossom necklace that dominated her upper torso.

The only thing marring the evening for Clea was the fact that Anya had never given *her* a show. She'd included some of Clea's photos in group shows but had always sidestepped Clea's requests for a solo event. That, plus Elke's opinion that her work was "decorative," had gnawed away at Clea over the years. And especially tonight, with Anya so eager to make room for a young unknown out of the north woods.

Cup in hand, Elke was staring at the muskrat crucifix.

"So what do you think?" asked Clea, kissing her cheek.

"Powerful," said Elke reluctantly.

"Do you really think so?"

Elke nodded.

"Well, praise from Caesar, and all that."

Elke smiled grimly. "Caesar's headed downhill."

"You always believe that when you're starting something new."

"And one of these days it'll be true."

"But not yet," Clea assured her, feeling unsure. It remained to be seen if Elke's work would have lasting significance, or would seem dated as feminist concepts were absorbed into the mainstream. Clea had lived long enough to know that exciting innovations sometimes seemed clichéd a decade later.

Stanley Stoddard, a colleague of Terence's from the NYU art department, joined them. "Astonishing," he said, gesturing around the room. "As far as I'm concerned, this young man of yours has single-handedly raised the dialogue on holocaust to a whole new level of discourse."

Elke frowned and shrugged irritably, whether because she disagreed, was envious, or, like Clea, couldn't figure out what Stanley was talking about, Clea couldn't say. Clea often worried about her intelligence around academics, who always presented opinions with such conviction that she assumed they must be correct, even when they sounded incoherent. In any case, Stanley apparently liked Dack's work.


Clea watched the *Voice* critic flirt shamelessly with an oblivious Dack in the cellar of the Village Gate. On stage, a multiethnic West Berlin jazz band was playing "What a Friend We Have in Jesus." A Chinese man with a flaccid handlebar mustache was singing the lyrics in close harmony with a heavyset bald man in a Hawaiian shirt. Gradually the harmony began to slip. The Chinese man started pounding the piano with his fists. The drummer, dressed in camouflage gear, banged a hubcap with a tire iron. "People Who Need People" and "Teen Angel" had already received similar dressings down.

Stanley Stoddard leaned across the table to observe in a low voice, "It's marvelous, isn't it? These chaps are deconstructing American popular music before our very eyes."

The *Voice* critic removed her eyes from Dack's aquiline profile to nod and add, "It's deliciously witty. So European."

Elke was rubbing her temples with thumb and index finger. She probably longed to be home in bed. Clea wished she were too. Her sardonic presence was a drag. If they talked tomorrow, Elke would deride the whole event. In contrast to Dack, who regarded everything about New York with wonder. It was exciting to teach such an enthusiastic neophyte about the world. Clea felt like the aging Gandhi, rejuvenated by this proximity to the vitality of youth.

The Chinese man began to sing "Wish I Could Shimmy Like My Sister Kate" with a Mississippi sharecropper's accent, accompanying himself with honky-tonk piano. The man in the Hawaiian shirt improvised on a clarinet. Slowly the music disintegrated, until the drummer was beating the drums with his elbows. The clarinet player honked a bicycle horn and shook a carbine belt. The piano player began to tune a synthesizer to emit an ominous whining hum, punctuated by machine gun volleys. The stage became a battlefield.

Clea glanced at Dack to see how he was enjoying this send-up of hallowed American icons. His dark eyes were alarmed, and his head was swiveling, searching wistfully for an exit.

Observing his contained panic, Clea realized that this performance constituted an assault on Dack. Its black nihilism was a product of Berlin—a divided city poised on the brink of nuclear extinction. It had nothing to do with Roches Ridge, Vermont, where integrity and optimism still prevailed. She'd unwittingly exposed an innocent to contagions bred in a slurry of effete decadence. She'd been viewing herself as Dack's mentor, but in actuality he had things to teach *her*. In the taxi back to Turtle Bay, she apologized to him.

As Clea lay in her king-size bed that night, she became aware that Dack was standing outside her door. She could see the shadows of his toes in the hall light beneath the crack. Her heart began to beat like the machine gun volleys at the jazz concert. Probably he had a question about their trip back to Vermont in the morning and was trying to figure out if she was still awake. She willed him to open the door and come in. She tried to recall if there were any condoms in the nightstand drawer. But surely someone from the Vermont woods wouldn't have been exposed to AIDS. Rabies maybe, but not AIDS.

Then she reversed herself and willed him to go away. She and Turner had a deal that involved no third parties in the nuptial bed. That was their peculiar form of faithfulness, and she'd honored it for nearly a quarter of a century. But if Dack came anywhere near that

bed, she couldn't guarantee her behavior. With relieved disappointment, she watched the shadows vanish and heard Theo's door click
shut.

Climbing out of bed, she stood at the window, breathing unsteadily
and looking into the branches of the maple in her courtyard. Was Elke
right? Had she been hoping to seduce Dack? It was true she'd have
had a hard time turning him down just now. But that was different
from actually pursuing him, wasn't it? She couldn't deny an attraction
to him, but it involved primarily his youth and vulnerability. Kate and
Theo wouldn't allow her to mother them anymore. Kate was assailing
her from the left for being too conventional, and Theo from the right
for not being conventional enough. And by next week they might have
swapped places. The stated issues were unimportant. The real issue
was that they had to make a break. And she had to turn them loose.
But her maternal capacities, honed by years of relentless motherhood,
remained. And they were evidently seeking a new target in Dack. He
was temporarily inhabiting her empty nest. But that seemed harmless
enough . . .


Dack sat in Clea's BMW with eight hundred dollars in his pocket
and a review from the *Village Voice* that began: "The untrammeled
American wilderness, in all its fierce uncompromising savagery and virility, came to the crowded streets of SoHo last night. . . ." The whole
thing was like a fairy tale, and Mrs. Shawn was his fairy godmother.
Dack couldn't figure out how to repay her, or whether she even wanted
to be repaid. He offered her part of the cash, but she waved it away
with a laugh. Last night he climbed out of her son's bed in that fancy
house and stood outside her bedroom door for a long time, curling his
toes in the wall-to-wall carpet, trying to decide whether to go in. She
said her old man was gone a lot. If she wanted him to ball her, he'd
be glad to, after all she'd done for him.

At Alpine Glen, if he went in the bar for a beer after work, a rich
bitch would sometimes ask him back to her condo for a "drink." She'd
roll a condom on him and ask him to do all kinda weird things. Sometimes they were really old like Mrs. Shawn, and had had babies and
stuff, and you could've driven Ray's tow truck into them. But they
usually knew how to tighten themselves around him and suck at his
dick like a mouth around a nipple.

Mrs. Shawn kept apologizing in the taxi home from that band last
night. It was true that they weren't any good. They couldn't carry a

tune or keep the beat. But that wasn't her fault. He didn't know why she kept making such a big deal of it. She said he had things to teach her. This was what made him think maybe she wanted him to screw her. But he wished she'd come out and say so. How was he supposed to know?

"So who's your girl?" Mrs. Shawn asked with a sidelong smile as they hurtled through the Catskills.

He blushed and shrugged.

"Oh, come on, Dack, I bet they're all after you."

He did feel an obscure longing to talk to this nice lady about Morning Glory and tell her how he planned to spend the money. He'd rescue Morning Glory from Mink Creek and take her someplace where Starwars would never find them. Morning Glory wanted a baby, and he wanted her to have whatever she wanted. The ski troopers would have to wait. You couldn't take a girl to the Arctic Circle and feed her caribou meat. "Well, there's this one."

Mrs. Shawn stopped smiling. "Oh, yes?"

"Lives down to Mink Creek."

"A Boudicca?" She resumed smiling.

"Whatever. Calls herself Morning Glory. I went to high school with her. She was a cheerleader and stuff."

"Have you been together all this time?"

"Ain't never . . . been together." He rubbed the BORN TO DIE tattoo on his forearm.

"But you want to be?"

He nodded. "She wants a baby. But this head dyke down there, name of Starwars, tells her where to go when. So I don't hardly ever get to see her."

"I don't mean to discourage you, but leopards don't often change their spots."

"You mean she's a dyke for good?"

"That's how it looks to me."

"Not to me."

"Well, good luck," said Clea cheerily.


Clea studied Alvin Jacobs in his brown suede eye patch and Harris tweed sport coat. He'd just proposed to the festival committee that Roches Ridge sponsor a sister city in China.

"Ain't they commonists over there to Red China?" inquired Wa-

neeta Marsh, who wore a Guess? stone-washed denim skirt and matching bomber jacket with leather shoulders and collar. Apart from her
wardrobe, she reminded Clea of the waitresses in Munich beer halls
who carried four pint mugs in each hand, black tape wound around
their thumbs to prevent blisters. Dack's mother. Clea had noted with
alarm her own relief at learning that the current object of Dack's affections was a Boudicca. What was it to her?

"They're human beings, Ms. Marsh," replied Alvin with hauteur.

"*Mrs.* Marsh," snapped Waneeta.

Everyone in the town clerk's office looked at her. She shrugged
sheepishly.

"We could send over carpenters and supplies to build a Peace Playground. What better way to celebrate our bicentennial than by helping
the babies of the third world?"

"Baby *commonists*," clarified Waneeta.

"I move we table this discussion," said Astrid Starr. "There are
more pressing projects. Such as replacing the dying elms on the town
green."

"I second the motion," said Maureen Murphy, nodding her head
until her Scotch-taped bangs swayed.

"It's been moved and seconded that we table the sister city proposal," said Conrad. "All in favor?"

As everyone in the room said, "Aye," Alvin Jacobs stood up, glared
around, and stomped out.

"Commonists don't believe in democracy," explained Waneeta.

"I think we should replace the elms with birches," said Astrid.
"Birches are real New England."

"You can't get much more Vermont than a sugar maple," maintained Maureen.

"Birches turn a lovely yellow in autumn," said Astrid.

"Maples turn scarlet and orange," said Maureen. "And you can tap
'em come spring."

"Perhaps we should consider some of each," suggested Father
Flanagan, palms upraised in a St. Francis of Assisi imitation.


As Jared McQueen tried to assess the merits of birches vs. maples,
he thought what a much finer world it would be if people, like trees,
changed their hair color with the seasons. How could men war against
each other if they all sported indigo and chartreuse spikes?

Jared shifted his gaze to Bethany Wagner and caught her staring at him. He smiled and looked back to Astrid Starr. Bethany had been toying with him, letting him cut her hair shorter and shorter, but not actually allowing spikes. If he agreed to go to bed with her, she'd probably let him punk her. But he hated to think of himself as that kind of guy. Besides, he was still holding out hope for Loretta Gebo, who *wouldn't* require him to fuck her as well.

Jared glanced at his brother Gordon, in his tank top and Levi's jacket. Gordon was looking haggard behind his close-cropped beard. His friends were dropping like flies from AIDS. And rumors about Gordon's sexual orientation had been circulating around town ever since the Gayride. And then there was Dan, lying in a coma in a hospital bed. Dan, the baby, was everyone's favorite. He emerged from the womb with a grin on his face, and hadn't stopped since. Until now. He'd even allowed Jared to give him a magenta Mohawk. Their father kept turning up at Dan's bedside, reeking of sobriety, mouthing platitudes like "Let go and let God." Everyone departed quickly when he appeared, overflowing with amends.

That afternoon when Jared arrived at the hospital, Father Flanagan in his stiff white collar and gold Pro-Life lapel pin was standing by Dan's bed. Poor old guy, he always turned up in a crisis, but he never had anything helpful to say. Daisy Wagner was holding Dan's hand and whispering to him, tears running down her cheeks. Jared hadn't known they were seeing each other. She said it was on the sly since her father didn't approve of Dan, because of his Mohawk and because he smelled of manure from barn chores. Which outraged Jared. How would Daisy's fancy Xerox father feel if he knew his own wife was about to get punked to a fare-thee-well by Dan's older brother?

Swearing Jared to secrecy, Daisy told him Dan had often hitched from Camel's Hump Community College to scale the rose lattice up to her window and spend the night in her bed. They would both wear earphones to her Walkman and make love until dawn to Grateful Dead tapes. Jared was happy to know Dan had tasted the joys of the flesh before departing his own.

In an attempt to distract Daisy, Jared discussed her hairstyle for the upcoming Miss Teenage America pageant in Dubuque. If Daisy would let him punk her, she might become the first punk Miss Teenage America.

"I don't know if I can face the pageant," Daisy sighed, kissing Dan's large hand, which she held in both of hers.

"Daisy, you have to. It's what Dan would want."

"Do you think so?"

"I *know* so. Just imagine how proud Danny will be when he comes out of this coma and learns his girl is Miss Teenage America."

"I guess you're right." She gazed tenderly at Danny's handsome face, his magenta Mohawk resting limply on the white pillow.

"I think you'll find," Astrid was saying, "that most Roches Ridgers prefer birches to maples for their green."

"That simply isn't true," insisted Maureen Murphy. "Astrid Starr, you think you have your fingers on the pulse of this town, but I see into its heart."

Everyone looked at Maureen with surprise, impressed by her eloquence. The most anyone usually got from her was a curt nod and incorrect change.

Clea studied the two embattled women—the grocer in her blue polyester jacket, the postmistress with her bangs Scotch-taped to her forehead. The fervor with which they championed their respective trees made Clea realize something else was going on here, but she had no idea what. This realization made her lonely, because everyone else in the room no doubt understood the silent struggle beneath the words.

"We could perhaps take a poll," mediated Father Flanagan.

"I ain't paying taxes for no trees," announced Waneeta Marsh, smoothing the denim skirt over her lumpy lap. "You want trees, go to the woods."

"What do you prefer in the middle of your town, Mrs. Marsh, a desert?" asked Conrad Bohring.

"What's wrong with grass?" asked Waneeta. '

"When was the last time you paid taxes anyway, Waneeta?" growled Astrid.

"I move we table this discussion for now," interjected Clea, to stave off a brawl. These meetings weren't progressing as she'd envisioned, with townspeople crossing party lines to form a jubilant throng and extol the traditions of their venerable community.

"So far we've tabled everything," pointed out Loretta, removing and replacing a stray hairpin in her beehive. "At this rate it'll be the tricentennial before we've got a plan."

# 34 August

Loretta Gebo sat in her Sunset View trailer, on the horns of a dilemma. Daryl Perkins had lurched into Casa Loretta that night on his silver crutches, claiming to possess the winning number for the week's Tri-State Megabucks lottery. The Lord revealed it to his son, Deuteronomy, at his second birthday party, he said. And Daryl would reveal it to Loretta if she'd meet him somewhere private and allow him to take down her beehive. That was supposedly all he wanted.

Loretta tried to sort out her thoughts and feelings. McDonald's Monopoly was going poorly. She was four stamps short of the thousand dollars per week for life. Plus which, business at Casa Loretta was taking a beating because she'd sent all her customers to McDonald's to bring her their game pieces. Daryl Perkins was holding before her a Megabucks victory. But who was to say he wasn't lying, or self-deceived? However, what if God *had* given Daryl the winning lottery number? What if Loretta became set for life and could lure Ray away from Ishtar? But if there really was a God, would He be likely to spend His time composing lottery numbers for Daryl Perkins?

At this very moment Ishtar was acupuncturing Ray in her apartment above the Karma Café. So he could get in touch with his past lives and discover the origin of his obsession with lesbians. It was so farfetched that it could only be true. Ray insisted Ishtar just wanted to help him recover from herself, so he could be more available to Loretta.

On the other hand, Ray was the only man who had ever let down Loretta's beehive. By allowing Daryl to, however pure her motives, wouldn't she be betraying Ray? She had to decide tonight, or Daryl would submit the number at Starr's IGA on behalf of his church tomorrow. If she wanted the number, she was to leave her lights on and her curtains open. Daryl, waiting in the woods, would know.

Loretta leapt up from the sofa, frantic with contradiction. She needed some chocolate to clear her mind. Desperately she searched the kitchen cupboards and drawers. Then she crawled around the living room, looking under furniture and behind cushions. All her usual stashes were depleted. Jumping up, she raced to the bedroom and looked under the mattress and on the closet shelf. Opening the dresser drawer, she plowed through her underwear.

Suddenly her hand closed around a small cellophane package. Gamboling into the living room, she perched on the sofa, ripped open the cellophane, and drew out the edible chocolate bikini panties Ray had brought her from New Jersey in hopes of luring her into eating them off Ishtar. She tore away a large mouthful. As she chewed the panties, she felt pervaded with peace and clarity.

Daryl sat behind the wheel of his Dodge Ram van on the dirt road behind Loretta's trailer, forehead dripping sweat. He'd made a pact with the devil, and he was damned for all time. He'd had a clear-cut choice. He could have won the Megabucks lottery for Christ, and put his plan for Loretta Gebo's salvation into operation. He could have gone on national TV to warn of the impending cataclysm. Or he could have offered the winning number to Satan.

In a feeble attempt at self-vindication, Daryl told himself that one session alone with Loretta's beehive might free him from his private Hades. But in his heart he knew it would only tighten the chains of his captivity. He was lost. And glad of it. And forever damned to hell. Gripping the steering wheel tightly with both hands, he beat his forehead against it. He was sacrificing his church, his wife, his son, his calling, his TV career, and his Lord, all for a beehive hairdo.

When Daryl looked up through wild, reddened eyes to Loretta's trailer, he saw her beehive silhouetted against the curtain as she drew it shut. Then the silhouette vanished as Loretta turned out her light.

"Praise the Lord!" cried Daryl. He gazed at the darkened trailer with amazed disbelief. *Satan* had saved *him*. What did this mean? Theologically at sea, Daryl started up his van and rolled slowly down the road, through shadows of pointed cedars cast by the moonlight.

"I swear to you, Bethany, that I will come to your house at any hour, day or night. I will wash out the color and give you your usual perm if you don't like punk. Free of charge. And I won't charge you today if you'll let me do it." Jared stood behind the styling chair at Mane Magnifique, scissors poised, armpits wet.

"This sounds like an offer I can't refuse," said Bethany, mind working fast as she sipped her complimentary Chablis. "Okay. Go ahead, Jared."

"Really?" he gasped, scissors trembling.

"Go for it."

As Jared lost himself in a frenzy of clipping, coloring, and moussing, to the accompaniment of Bach's Brandenburg Concerto No. 5, Bethany hatched her plot. Ken was in Albuquerque. Daisy had a slumber party tonight. Bethany could give Poo a tranquilizer. Conrad Bohring was the only problem. He was always out spraying his lawn for night crawlers. She'd have to put off phoning Jared until Conrad went in.

When Jared finished, he handed Bethany a mirror and patted his heart, saying "I'm so nervous, Bethany. This could be the making of Mane Magnifique." He twisted her chair so her back faced the large wall mirror.

Holding up the hand mirror, Bethany was appalled. She looked like a mutant unicorn, stiff spikes of magenta, vermilion, and emerald sticking out all over her head. It was just as well for her plot that she could truthfully say, "Uh, well, Jared, I don't know. Let me live with it for a while. And if I can't, I'll give you a call."

Jared was rubbing his indigo hands anxiously. "I think it looks fantastic, Bethany. It's really you."

Late that night Bethany sat in her raincoat by the front door of her house in Colonial Manor Estates, awaiting Jared. He'd been deeply distressed to hear she wanted her old Julie Andrews hairdo back, but he was a man of his word. She felt guilty toward Ken over what was about to occur, but he wouldn't know the difference, since he was never home anyway. And with Daisy in mourning over Jared's comatose younger brother, and perhaps refusing to leave his side to compete at the Miss Teenage America pageant in Dubuque, Bethany simply had to have something to fill the emptiness of her life.

Bethany opened the door to let Jared in with his suitcase of tools and products. He smiled wanly and said, "Well, I think your spikes look wonderful."

Slowly Bethany unfolded her raincoat to reveal the body of a former Ms. Empire State, clad in an orange wet-look posing bikini. "And how do you think *this* looks, Jared?" she asked softly.

"Uh, very nice."

She extended one foot and flexed her quad at him.

"You don't really want me to unpunk you," Jared realized as they stepped over a barbell on the living room floor, Poo lying in a stupor of tranquillity on his corner dog bed.

"Not if we can find something else to do," negotiated Bethany, bending over to stretch out her hamstrings.


Clea stood in her backyard, Brandy at her side, watching a falling star streak across the black sky like a spark from a fire. The night air was tepid, and bullfrogs were croaking in the swamps around Mink Creek. An orange glow from a Boudicca campfire backlit the birch trees on the cliff. The Boudiccas in the valley had each other. The people of the Holy Deliverance on the hill had their Lord. The Marshes next door had their clan. The houses around the Roches Ridge green, and their modern counterfeits in Colonial Manor Estates, huddled together to form enclaves. Each star in the sky had its constellation. Even the bullfrogs in the valley had their bass choir. Only Clea was alone tonight. During the frantic years of corporate family life she'd longed to be free from the needs of others. But now that she *was*, she felt frightened and lonely. Having spent her entire life reluctantly learning how to accept responsibility for others, she now had to learn how to let them go their own ways—Kate, Theo, Turner, Elke.

Her plan to meld Roches Ridge into a harmonious whole that included herself wasn't working. Every festival proposal so far had been voted down. The town couldn't even agree on maples or birches for the green. Clea was no recluse. She saw townspeople constantly. But she was always on guard to do and say the right things, with the hope of fitting in. There was no one here to whom she could impart the heretical thoughts that drifted through her brain on a regular basis— as she used to with Elke, Turner, Karen, half a dozen other New York friends. But she'd seen Turner only twice all summer, on brief weekends in New York, when he was distant, irritable, and full of scathing remarks about Roches Ridge.

"Jesus Christ," he muttered at one point, "what kind of marriage is this? What kind of marriage has it *ever* been?"

To which she replied, "Give us a break, Turner. We're just two damaged mortals who've always done our best to conform to an impossible ideal."

Kate was protesting Cruise missiles at Greenham Common for the summer with friends from Smith. Theo was working at a Christian summer camp in Georgia. Elke pretended to be away, utterly transparent since they both knew she never went anywhere. It was a sorry way to end what had been a very important friendship. Nothing dramatic, just a gradual dwindling and withering of their love.

Brandy began whimpering, expressing Clea's emotions. She dropped to her knees in the damp grass. "I'm sorry, Brandy. I forgot about you. I'm not alone after all." Hugging the puppy, she picked him up and carried him to the house, his big paws waving in her face. He was getting nearly too big to carry.

After removing her work clothes, Clea stood on the hooked rug in her bedroom and looked down at her pale body in the spotlight through the window. With her fingertips she traced her appendectomy scar. Then the silver stretch marks around her nipples and down her hips. And the crow's-feet and frown lines on her face. A time-battered body, but still attractive. In the past men had marveled over it around the globe. But today it was a holding action: Her gums were going. She'd recently gotten reading glasses. Her hearing was fading. Her hormones were in turmoil from menopause. Her lower back and fractured ankle ached. She ran her hands down her chest, over her breasts, down her belly and upper thighs.

Out the window she spotted Dack in frayed cutoffs and work boots, ascending his pyramid of steel. A taut young body with all the parts working. And those supple copper muscles. She traced with her eyes the bulge of his pecs, the corrugation of his rib cage, the feathery arrow of pubic hair down his firm abdomen, the faint outline of his genitals beneath the denim. She imagined an erection straining against his jeans. And herself unfastening the snap, unzipping the zipper . . . As he hacked and pried with his crowbar, she began to tremble. Her breathing became shallow and jagged. Sweat popped out on her upper lip and at her hairline. God, she wanted him so much. And she felt stupid for wanting him. And old and ugly knowing he didn't want *her*.

As her hand moved between her thighs, she caressed Dack's sweaty chest and slim heaving hips with her eyes. She imagined pulling him into her, a hand on each buttock, her pelvis pushing up to meet his. With a long, slow shudder, she closed her eyes, sank to her knees, threw back her head, and gasped, "Oh, God, Dack!"

Clea lay on the hooked rug for a long time, crying silently. Eventually Brandy wandered over from her bedside, wagging his tail. Pushing him aside, Clea got to her feet, pulled on her nightgown, and climbed into bed. This was absurd. She had taken and dismissed lovers with aplomb, had turned down more male overtures than there were junked cars in that damn heap. That she should be reduced to pedophilia, voyeurism, and masturbation, like some dirty old man in a Forty-second Street cinema, was appalling. She was well on her way to becoming a Mrs. Robinson figure. She was incapable of sitting quietly in a room and being content. It wasn't even sex she wanted, she realized. She'd just proved she could provide that for herself. And it hadn't helped. She was still agitated and unhappy.

She missed Elke, who would listen to even her dumbest ideas with interest. But Elke and she hadn't been in touch for months. On her better days Clea told herself Elke was in the throes of creation. On the other days Clea suspected she'd been cast off as punishment for crimes with Dack she wasn't even committing.

The next morning Clea sat in her bathrobe at her desk, sipping tea and writing in her journal: "Darius has put batts of insulation in the walls, with lath on top. It feels as though this plastering has been going on for years, like Michelangelo's fresco on the Sistine Chapel ceiling. . . ."

Glancing through the window, she saw Dack stumble out of his door and around the stockade fence. She jumped up, tying the belt on her robe more securely. Descending the steps and opening her back door, she confronted Dack, whose left eye was swollen shut. In fact, the entire left side of his face was purple, and a front tooth was broken off halfway.

"Who's done this to you?" gasped Clea, gingerly touching the bruised cheek, restraining herself from taking him in her arms. She stood aside so he could enter and sit at her kitchen table.

"Don't matter."

"It matters to me," she said softly, aware of Darius' listening presence in the dining room, where he was troweling plaster.

"You said I might get some more money from my messes?"

"I'm sure Anya will sell some more. Why?" She went to the refrigerator for ice.

"Could you ask her to send *you* the money?"

"Yes." Clea wrapped a dish towel around the ice. "But why?"

"And could you hold it until I ask for it?"

"Certainly. But why?" She held the ice pack against Dack's cheek with both hands. Irritably he took it from her and held it himself. "So I gather someone took that other money from you?"

Dack nodded, eyes sullen. "Orlon said them was his bones and hooves and all."

"But they were worthless scraps until you put them together."

Dack shrugged.

"Did he really have to beat you up?" Clea was astonished such a creepy little man could have done such damage. Dack was a good foot taller and far more muscular.

"He didn't hit me till I got smart."

"What did you say, for God's sake?"

"That I'd tell Astrid Starr what he does in that back shed and he'd be run out of town. He hit me across the face with a femur. So hard it cracked."

"Uh, what do you mean?"

The wind shifted abruptly, and Dack's confiding demeanor became hard and secretive. "About what?"

"About Orlon's shed."

"What about it?"

"What does go on in there?"

Dack shrugged. "Nothing much. Taxidermy. He's just pissed today because he found Crystal Sue hanging down to Mink Creek." Dack stood up and laid the ice pack in the sink. "We'll see you, Mrs. Shawn."

"Clea, please," she called to his retreating back.

Clea sat at the table over her mug, going mad. Dack was not much older than her children. Every bone in her body quivered to rescue and protect him. And yes, all right, she might as well admit it after her passion play on the hooked rug the night before: She burned to take this lad to bed and teach him what she'd learned in a lifetime of licentiousness. Yet Dack was in love with a woman his own age. Who was a lesbian and would give him nothing but grief.

Please God, let there be some way to get this boy out of her head and keep him there. She simply couldn't handle the crazed oblivion of a fresh sexual passion. It was a disease, one she'd had the hubris to think she'd been vaccinated against.


As Astrid Starr bagged Ida Campbell's groceries, she said, "Heard about Angela McGrath, have you, Ida? Playing her harp for Sonny Coffin at Deathworks? She plucks your loved one's favorite song while the box rolls into the oven."

"What about her husband's tombstone business?" asked Ida anxiously. "Chad works over there. We need that salary. At least until *Sir and Her* is a best-seller."

"Angela never did have much use for tombstones," said Astrid. "That shepherd for their son's grave was Ian's idea."

"Well, but if it's your husband's business and all. I mean, the most beautiful thing a woman can do is to stand by her man through thick and thin, come what may, in sickness and in health. . . ."

"Tell it to Angela," interrupted Astrid, not wanting to hear about impossible dreams. First her husband, Earl, refused to travel. Now he was insisting the nuts go in the same aisle as baking supplies, instead of with the candy. WOW pointed out these were all ploys for seizing power. Maybe so, but Earl could *have* the damn power. She thought sadly of nights in his arms on the *Norwegian Star*, rocking on the ocean swells, with a warm sea breeze blowing through the porthole.

As Ida pushed her cart out the door, Astrid set her stopwatch, to time how long it would take for someone to come in and tell her about Angela McGrath's harp at Deathworks. After all, records were set to be broken. The current forty-three-minute one also involved Sonny Coffin's crematorium. That man was a small town's dream.

Glancing at the beach chairs and sand, shovels and buckets, cooler and picnic foods in the front window, Astrid realized it was time for the autumn leaves display. She couldn't keep up anymore. She felt old and unattractive now that Earl no longer admired her shelf arrangement. Time was when he thought she had each product exactly where it belonged.

Alvin Jacobs, in his suede eye patch, appeared at the next festival meeting, just as though he hadn't stomped out of the last one when his Chinese sister city project was tabled. His next proposal for the bicentennial was to engrave a plaque for the fourth side of the Civil War monument on the green with the names of all the Vietnam draft evaders and deserters from Roches Ridge.

The entire room fell silent and stared at Alvin in awed disbelief that anyone could be so consistently out of step with the cadences of the town.

"Why, Alvin, I suspect that proposal doesn't even merit a vote," mused Conrad Bohring, decorated World War II fighter pilot. Most committee members nodded agreement. "All in favor of not voting on this proposal say aye. The ayes appear to have it. . . . The ayes *do* have it. You have just voted not to vote on Alvin Jacobs' draft evader plaque for the town green."

Again Alvin stood up, surveyed the committee with his remaining eye, and marched from the room, to the beat of his different drummer.

Next Conrad regaled the committee with details of Roches Ridge's involvement in the War of 1812. Afterward, Waneeta Marsh raised her hand and described how her great-grandfather mounted cannons on the bluff to attack British warships heading up Mink Creek to destroy an American boatworks. But a Roche warned the British to turn back while still out of range. She went on to maintain that Roches were Confederate sympathizers during the Civil War and participated in a rebel raid on St. Albans, whereas two Marshes died at Vicksburg. She proposed that Roches Ridge be renamed Marsh Ridge for the bicentennial. The proposal was voted down.

"All right," said Waneeta, scowling, "if you want your town named after a bunch of crooks and creeps and cowards."

The committee finally found something to agree on when Clea suggested posting signs on each road into town, reading: "Welcome to Roches Ridge, chartered in 1787." Only Waneeta Marsh voted against them, sourly maintaining hunters would just use them for target practice.

After the meeting Clea went over to Ishtar and asked if they could have a word in private. Ishtar invited her back to the Karma Café, where she served chamomile tea at a table for two.

"I hardly know you, Ishtar," began Clea, elbows propped on the table, cup cradled in both hands, "but I feel as though I can trust you." She had no choice. Her concupiscence had reached a new low. She had come to the end of her rope and was tying it into a noose. But if she could establish once and for all that Dack was beyond reach, maybe she could get on with her busy life.

"I know what you mean." Ishtar nodded. "I feel as though we've known each other before. Do you know who you were in any of your previous lives?"

Clea cleared her throat uneasily, scarcely knowing who she was in *this* one, now that she was chasing teenagers around her backyard.

"Forgive me. I'm making assumptions regarding your belief system. And as you say, we hardly know each other. Supposedly." Ishtar sat back in her chair and sipped her tea.

Clea wondered if being here wasn't perhaps a mistake, but she was so desperate that she blundered ahead. "Uh, I of course know that you used to live down on Mink Creek."

Ishtar nodded warily.

"So I assume you know the young woman down there named Morning Glory."

Ishtar blushed violently to the roots of her overgrown crew cut and nodded again.

"What you may not know is that my neighbor Dack Marsh is in love with her."

Drawing a sharp breath, Ishtar went from fluorescent pink to deathly white in a moment. She dropped her head against the chair back and gazed up at the spider plants near the café ceiling.

"I seem to have distressed you," said Clea. "I didn't mean to stir up painful memories."

Ishtar sighed, then laughed weakly. "What *you* may not know, Clea, is that I also love Morning Glory."

"God, I'm sorry."

"It's okay. I need to know this. You see, Morning Glory wants a baby, and that's something I can't provide, however much I may adore her. I knew she'd been scouting around for sperm. I just didn't know it went farther than that."

"I don't know what her feelings are, Ishtar. All I know about are his. He's my neighbor. I wouldn't want him to get hurt." Clea studied her fingernails.

Ishtar's eyes narrowed. "So in other words, you're in love with Dack?"

Clea started. Then she laughed nervously. "But that's ridiculous. I'm old enough to be his mother."

"Maybe you *were* his mother," said Ishtar. "Look, don't be embarrassed, Clea. After all, you're talking to a woman who loves another woman. The body is just the heart's current packaging."


As Maureen unlocked her front door following the festival meeting, she could hear *The Sound of Music* sound track blasting through the door, stuck: ". . . doe, a deer . . . doe, a deer . . . doe, a deer . . ." She'd told her mother never to touch that record. Flinging her pocketbook on the sofa, she looked around wildly.

Where was the old bitch? No point in calling her. Her hearing aids lay in Maureen's pocketbook, and without them May couldn't hear any sound softer than the highest volume on the stereo. Maureen tiptoed across the shadowy living room, looking behind the sofa and chairs, in her mother's usual hiding places. She lifted the stereo arm, removed the record, and studied the deep scratch across it. Then she returned it to its jacket, trying to remain calm. It wasn't enough that her mother scared away Earl Atkins. She had to wreck Maureen's favorite record as well.

Entering the dining room, Maureen surveyed it carefully, seeing no sign of her mother. With horror she discovered that her *Sound of Music* plate was missing from its wall brackets. Her mother knew how much that plate meant to Maureen. It'd be just like her to take it with her in an escape. This was the last straw.

Entering the kitchen, Maureen screamed. Pieces of her plate lay scattered around the floral linoleum. In the midst of them lay her mother, in a crumpled heap. One of her hands clutched a shard of plate. The other hand was extended over her head, a puddle of blood dribbling from the wrist.

Maureen rushed to the fragments on the floor and began frantically fitting them together, trying to work out where she'd put the Super Glue. Her mother moaned. Maureen looked up from her china jigsaw puzzle to hiss, "This time you've really done it, Mother!" Walking on her knees to her mother's side, she studied the wound in her wrist. Sighing irritably, she got up and phoned the rescue squad. Then she went into the kitchen cabinets in search of the Super Glue. Finding it, she tried to mend the halves of Julie Andrews's torso, gluing two fingers together in the process.

"Poor Mother," Maureen explained to Earl Atkins, a volunteer Rescue Leaguer, in his Australian slouch hat with the emu feather. "She fell on a plate. You know how shaky old people get." Earl looked at her with what she thought was wistful sadness. She added softly, "My best plate too." When Earl remained silent, she realized he'd rush home and tell Astrid, who'd immediately pass this on to all her customers. Yet there had been a time when Earl Atkins' loyalties were to her.

Holding up her glued fingers, she asked with an uncharacteristic flutter to her eyelids, "Earl, do you know first aid for Super Glue?" He nodded no, holding the oxygen mask to the old woman's face while Sam Silvers, the holistic dentist, took her pulse.

As Maureen sat in the hospital waiting room, she searched *Parents' Magazine* for the *Sound of Music* plate advertisement. She'd order a new one and hang it so high her mother would never reach it. Father Flanagan appeared, short of breath, wearing his stiff collar and his expression of bemused horror.

"I just heard about your mother," he said. "I'm so sorry."

Maureen regarded him expectantly, awaiting words of solace. But he just shrugged helplessly, sat down beside her, and studied his hands.

Glancing up, Maureen saw Jared and Gordon McQueen rush through the door, Jared in suede jeans, with that ridiculous patch of turquoise at his crown, Gordon in his closely cropped beard and tight denim. Good-looking boys, those McQueens, thought Maureen. Jared got hair-styling magazines in the mail all the time, and Gordon got printed matter in plain brown wrappers. When Maureen steamed one open over the electric kettle at the back of the post office, she couldn't believe her eyes. The things that went on in this world!

Spotting her and Father Flanagan, the McQueen brothers waved, faces grim. Jared's eyes were red, as though he'd been crying. Daisy Wagner came dashing down the tiled corridor, blond hair floating around her head. She fell weeping into Jared's arms. Father Flanagan made a move to stand up, then sank back into his chair with a helpless grimace. Little Danny must have died. Maureen felt sad. He'd been such a cute little boy, bicycling into town in his khaki shorts to pick up his family's mail. She'd miss his love letters to Daisy Wagner. She always looked forward to those envelopes from Camel's Hump Community College. He was very tender and romantic describing the things he wanted to do to Daisy. Nothing like what went on in those disgusting pictures in his brother Gordon's plain brown wrappers.

Zeno Racine lumbered through the woods by Colonial Manor Estates, a fifty-pound bag of rock salt on his shoulder. Reaching the Wagners' side yard, he halted. The light in Daisy's bedroom was out. She was either asleep or not home. Her father's Audi wasn't in the driveway. Through the picture window Zeno could see Bethany Wagner, multi-colored hair sticking out like sharpened candy canes. She stood in an orange bikini, holding a barbell at chest level, the theme from *Rocky* blaring on the stereo.

Zeno scuttled over to the dwarf fruit trees. Dropping the rock salt, he tore it open, then spread salt around the trunk of an apple tree.

On his fifth tree, bag nearly empty, Zeno heard a low growl from the bushes behind the house. Grabbing the bag, Zeno ran for the woods just as Poo, fangs flashing, leapt from the shadows to fling himself at Zeno's throat. Flailing wildly, Zeno hurled Poo halfway across the yard and raced for the highway.

## 35 September

Sitting in Darius' truck cab beside the road from Colonial Manor Estates, Clea watched Darius hammer the last of the bicentennial signs with a post maul. Roches Ridge was finally getting into gear. At last some visible results from all the hours of meetings. The signs looked wonderful, a white shield with black script: WELCOME TO ROCHES RIDGE, CHARTERED IN 1787.

"How do you like them?" asked Clea as Darius drove back through town, along the green past Casa Loretta.

He sat in silence for a long time, sucking thoughtfully on his empty pipe. "Not too bad," he finally replied.

Clea smiled. This was Darius' highest possible praise.

"Just hope folks'll let 'em stand."

Loretta, beehive swiveling like a beacon, stood in the window of Casa Loretta, watching Clea Shawn ride past in Darius Drumm's battered black Ford pickup. John Denver was singing "Rocky Mountain High" on the Wurlitzer. It sounded different without Dylan Scarborough strumming "The Anne Frank Waltz" in the kitchen. He'd just quit and gone to Nashville, in pursuit of a recording contract.

From the corner of her eye Loretta spotted Daryl's yellow van lurking behind the bandstand across the green. Loretta hadn't been sure what to feel when Daryl's number failed to win the Megabucks lottery. She felt sorry for him, of course. It had really rocked his faith. Of course, that faith of his could use some rocking. She hadn't seen him to talk to since she closed her curtains and declined the number that night last month. But he'd been skulking around town ever since. She hoped he'd get over feeling sheepish soon and come on in for a taco pizza.

But Loretta felt guilty knowing how much she'd have hated it if Daryl's number had actually won. She'd stayed true to Ray and not let another man touch her beehive. And her loyalty had been vindicated. But at Daryl's expense. It was an impossible quandary.

But talk about impossible: That night of her trial, when she'd chosen to keep her beehive unsullied, Ray came back to her trailer from his acupuncturing at Ishtar's carrying a suitcase. He explained that Ishtar's needles in his Third Eye had put him in touch with a past life as a closeted lesbian teacher at a girls' boarding school in Victorian England. Ishtar had been one of his pupils, with whom he'd been unrequitedly in love.

From his suitcase Ray pulled two long white Edwardian gowns, camisoles, corsets, and knickers, borrowed from Angela McGrath. Ishtar told Ray his cure lay in acting out with Loretta his thwarted love for this pupil (since Ishtar in her current life as a lesbian wanted Ray embodied as a man no more than she had when he was a lesbian and she a heterosexual schoolgirl). So Loretta was supposed to pretend she was a reluctant student, while Ray put on Victorian drag and slowly worked up to a seduction. This had been going on for some time now, and Loretta had her doubts. But Ray's foreplay involved various chocolate treats in reward for homework, so Loretta was content to adopt a wait-and-see attitude, especially if it got Ray over Ishtar.

Sonny Coffin stood in his black polo shirt, slacks, and jacket, displaying his best graveside manner, hands folded before him, somber expression on his gray hollow-cheeked face. The box holding Dan McQueen's remains moved along the conveyor belt toward the kiln doors. The viewing had been last night. Afterward, Orlon Marsh had done his thing, then departed for his back shed with the payload in his van. This was the moment, equivalent to that at weddings when the minister asks for objections to the union, when Sonny wished he could put the belt in overdrive and hurl the box into the flames before anyone asked for one last look.

Angela McGrath, in her white high-necked gown, was playing the Grateful Dead's "If I Had the World to Give" on her harp. The McQueen family had agreed to let Dan's girlfriend, Daisy Wagner, select his favorite song. Daisy really looked the part of Miss Teenage Roches Ridge today, her cloud of blond hair floating around her head. Despite her eyes, which were red and puffy from days of weeping. Daisy's mother, Bethany, in an alarming new fluorescent punk hairdo, stood with her muscled arm around Daisy, whispering consolations and eyeing Jared McQueen across the room. The entire McQueen family was devastated. Gordon, in a suit and tie, was sobbing in the arms of a man who could have been his twin. So apparently the rumors about him were true. Old man McQueen was down from Burl-ington with a buxom young broad on his arm, and on his face the startled look of a reformed alcoholic just beginning to realize there was an entire world outside his own tormented ego. Father Flanagan stood off to one side looking hopeless and useless, like the eunuch he was.

It had been easy to talk the McQueens into cremation. Sonny merely mentioned worms and putrefaction. He didn't even have to pull out his decay photos. And once one member was cremated, often the entire family converted. These twelve assembled McQueens on the hoof represented several thousand dollars in Sonny's Swiss bank account.

Sonny watched Angela plucking furiously at her harp, blond waist-length hair swaying with the beat. She was working out very well in-deed. Live music was just the touch lacking here in the Gloom Room. Angela was flourishing as well. There was color in her cheeks and a sparkle to her eyes. She said Deathworks had given her something to live for. Sonny had additional responsibilities to add to Angela's job description for the future. He couldn't say exactly why he was deter-mined to destroy Ian both professionally and personally. It had some-thing to do with Ian's having been an all-American shortstop at Indiana University.

As Clea sat at her desk, sorting through photos for *The Town That Time Forgot,* she spotted a bandannaed young woman in faded jeans sneaking up the hill from Mink Creek and across Clea's backyard. The young woman slipped a piece of paper under a rock beside the shed in the Marshes' backyard.

Clutching her robe around her, Clea rushed downstairs, out the door, through the stand of wild asters, and over to the stockade fence. Peering around the fence into the Marshes' yard, she saw no one. From the shed she heard the hum of power equipment. Orlon's van stood outside. Watching the shed door, she slipped over to the rock, reached under it, and grabbed the note, which read: "Meet me at the fishing access at 3 p.m. M.G." Replacing it, Clea raced on bare feet through the purple wild asters back to her house.

Clea watched from her upstairs window until Dack came out of his door in his low-slung jeans. Looking all around, he sauntered over to the rock, turned it over, picked up the note, unfolded it, and read it.

As his gloomy face broke into a beatific smile, Clea felt her spirits descend like an express elevator to hell. That look was love, if Clea had ever seen it. And she had.

Knowing she already possessed all the information she required, Clea nevertheless phoned Ishtar at the Karma Café. Ishtar said she would be over as soon as she finished making Brussels sprout fritters.

At 3 p.m. Clea and Ishtar hid in the bushes by the fishing access at the lake. Morning Glory arrived and tensely surveyed the surrounding woods, which were splattered with vivid fall colors like a Jackson Pollock painting. Dack soon appeared, in his jeans and down vest. He and Morning Glory gazed at each other across the vacant parking lot for a long time, like two wild animals catching each other's scents. Warily they edged toward each other.

Ishtar gripped Clea's arm, a grimace on her face, as Dack and Morning Glory embraced, lower torsos pressing fiercely together, heads falling back, eyes closing, mouths gasping. Clea glanced at Ishtar, who'd shut her eyes so she wouldn't have to watch the mouths meet and the hands begin a tender exploration of unfamiliar flesh.

Eventually Dack pushed a rowboat into the water, erection straining through his jeans toward Morning Glory like a divining rod. Morning Glory climbed in, and he rowed them across the bay toward an evergreen-camouflaged duck blind, one among several rising out of the water on stilts.

"I can't believe she's letting him do all the rowing," moaned Ishtar.

Ishtar and Clea watched across the still water, which reflected splashes of color from the woods, as Dack reached down from the blind to pull Morning Glory up into it.

"Enough?" asked Clea weakly.

Ishtar rubbed her wet eyes with her forearm. "I need to see this through. Do you mind?"

"I can think of ways I'd rather spend the afternoon. But I suppose this'll cure me if anything will."

They pulled the Boudicca canoe out from under some evergreen boughs, climbed in, and began paddling across the marsh toward the stand of stilted duck blinds, which looked to Clea like the Philippines. She reached for her camera, then realized she'd left it behind for once.

They arrived at the blind beneath which Dack's rowboat bobbed. It was swaying and trembling on its two-by-eights, dried evergreen needles showering down onto the water as though from a dried-out Christmas tree. They could hear Morning Glory moan, "Yes, Dack, yes!"

She cooed endearments and gasped expletives in a rhythmic pattern that left little to Clea's and Ishtar's imaginations.

Ishtar buried her face in both hands. Then she sat up straight, cheeks shining, tears dripping off her chin, and grabbed her paddle.

As they stashed the canoe, Clea finally said, "Well, I guess that's that."

Back at her house, Clea invited Ishtar for tea. Ishtar had said nothing since the duck blind, and she continued her anguished silence in Clea's kitchen as the teapot began to sing. A shaft of light from the descending sun came through one window and bathed the hooked rug in gold. Flames danced in the walk-in fireplace.

"God, I love her so much, Clea," Ishtar finally whispered. "How do I let her go?"

Seeing someone else, especially a young person, in such pain was allaying Clea's own. Besides, she'd known Dack only a few months and had blessedly never translated the attraction into a physical connection. "I know you do," said Clea, sitting down beside Ishtar on the couch before the fire. "And I'm so sorry. I wish I could help."

"If only I were a man this time around, I could give her a baby and then she'd want to be with me."

Clea wasn't certain it was that simple. But maybe it was. She was trying to figure out how to convert her absurd passion for Dack into something more neighborly, when Ishtar ducked under her arm and said, "Hold me, please, Clea. Just hold me."

Clea obliged, gently rocking Ishtar and stroking her hair as she wept softly. It reminded her of times when she'd held Kate and Theo like this, comforting them over playground quarrels. Before Clea fully realized what was happening, Ishtar's hands were under her turtleneck, and Ishtar's face was buried between her breasts.

Amid her momentary consternation, Clea discovered she actually liked what she was feeling. It reminded her of her babies, soft and warm and sweet, very late at night at the top of the darkened town house, while the rest of the city slept and rain pounded at her windows. Relaxing into the cushions, Clea sighed with pleasure.

Eventually Ishtar sat up and smoothed her hair.

Pulling down her turtleneck, Clea said, "Ishtar, I don't know what to say."

"Don't say anything, Clea. We've been together like this before. I'm sure of it. You may have been my mother in some other life. Whoever you are, thank you. I needed that."

"You're welcome," said Clea.

After Ishtar left, Clea went upstairs and wrote in her journal: "Darius has replaced the missing slates on the roof and the broken panes in the fanlight. Tomorrow he's insulating the attic. Almost ready for winter!"

In a daze she went back downstairs, grabbed a hand scythe, and headed for the back field, Brandy nipping at her heels. Nature was winning the battle for her backyard. Wild asters, raspberry canes, wild grapevines, and Virginia creeper were so thick she couldn't even get at the remaining garbage.

Life in Roches Ridge certainly wasn't turning out as she'd planned. She'd bargained on solitude and peaceful coexistence with aloof Yankee neighbors. But since her arrival, she'd loved and lost a teenage hillbilly. And adding incest to injury, she'd made love, of a sort, with her daughter from another life. . . .

As Clea began to hack at the weeds, she discovered that the purple wild asters were covered with thousands of migrating monarch butterflies. They perched on the blossoms, slowly fanning orange and black wings, while the golden light of late afternoon warmed them, and the dark-blue sky awaited their departure. Brandy threw himself at some as they drifted from bloom to bloom.

Clea raced back to the house and returned with her camera. Hastily making some adjustments for light and exposure times, she focused on the astonishing scene and began snapping. Eventually she lay on the ground, with the butterfly-filled asters at eye level. Life would be so simple if she'd just stop meddling, reflected Clea, pausing in her orgy of picture-taking. Maybe Elke was correct to maintain that Clea stirred up chaos wherever she went. After all, she'd fallen in love with Dack and dragged him to New York. She'd helped him earn the money that had gotten him beaten up by Orlon and had given him the confidence to pursue Morning Glory. Clea had given Ishtar the news about Morning Glory, which had driven her into Clea's arms with grief. From now on she'd rein in her rampaging emotions. She'd use them to fuel her work, as Elke did. These butterflies among the asters were an omen: Life in Roches Ridge, close to nature, was meant to be peaceful and full of beauty. She'd been complicating it with her city-bred lusts and lunacies. . . .

Brandy was barking and whining, tail wagging frantically. Clea got to her feet and began to photograph his contortions. He was circling some object on the ground behind Orlon's shed, lunging at it, tugging it, then falling back to howl in distress. A dead chipmunk or rabbit or something. Moving closer and extending her zoom lens, Clea squatted and focused on Brandy, surrounded by wild asters. And then she saw, lying amid the purple flowers and the orange-and-black butterflies, a mangled human foot, bloody and bruised.

# III

## 36 The Simple Life

"You hear Calvin Roche auditioned to be the new Marlboro man?" asked Waneeta Marsh, handing Astrid Starr her food stamps. Waneeta wore an olive rayon Calvin Klein jumpsuit with tab epaulets. A carbine belt girthed her belly.

"He get it?" asked Astrid listlessly. The foot had left all gossip before or since in its dust. Trooper Tommy Trapp sauntered in to buy Camels the day Clea Shawn found it. His smug expression alerted Astrid to the fact that he knew something she didn't. She refused to sell him cigarettes until he told her what it was. He threatened to go to the Grand Union.

"Go," she said with a shrug, knowing he'd never make it to Route 7 without a nicotine fit, even if he turned on his flasher and pretended to be chasing a speeder. Finally he whispered the news in her ear. Astrid froze, mouth falling open, aware this was the stuff town records were made of. Tommy grabbed the pack of Camels she'd been waving beneath his nose, tore it open, extracted a cigarette, and lit up.

"Whose?" Astrid finally asked.

"Dunno. Too darn chewed up to tell. But all the feet in this state are present or accounted for." He exhaled with relief. "Must be from outa state. Mafia or something. We're checking with the FBI on missing persons."

Setting her Casio, Astrid handed off this information to an astonished Loretta Gebo as she sprinted past the register, arms full of supplies for hot fudge dessert tacos. Shortly, Ishtar raced into the IGA to pass the foot news along to a jubilant Astrid, who punched her Casio at twenty-one minutes.

But Astrid's jubilation faded quickly, and now all she felt was despair: The twenty-one-minute rumor constituted a barrier far more unbreakable than the four-minute mile. The sound barrier was surpassable, but the speed of light was not. Earl wouldn't cruise to Anchorage with her, the nuts were in with the flour, and the town's new record was inviolable. Astrid had nothing left to live for. At this week's WOW meeting at the Center for Sanity, she intended to work on giving herself permission to exit early.

"Nope. Calvin didn't make it," said Waneeta, picking up her brown bag.

"Too old." Astrid sighed.

"Too ugly." Waneeta chuckled. "Jeezum, Astrid." She gestured to the Halloween decorations in the front window—pumpkins, dried corn shocks, cardboard skeletons, bags of candy treats, all draped with fake cobwebs like tent caterpillars. "If I'da wanted cobwebs, I'da stayed to home."

"You heard any more about that foot next door, Waneeta?" Astrid couldn't see killing herself before finding out whose it was.

"They been poking around out there for days. But they ain't found nothing. Too bad Calvin's not around. Sounds like something he'da done. Chopped it off and thrown it in his cellar." Waneeta's face went blank, and Astrid suddenly suspected she knew more than she was saying. "Someone tried to kill Wagners' apple trees t'other week."

"Umm," said Astrid, to indicate her refusal to be bought off so cheaply.

"Rock salt around the trunks. They think maybe Conrad Bohring done it. Sometimes Wagners' dog does her duty on Bohrings' lawn. And t'other day the dog dug up them plastic mums Frieda grows alongside her house come fall. Bethany Wagner says Conrad's wired his lawn now, so's an alarm goes off if anything gets on it."

Astrid saw that Waneeta was desperate to fan any embers of inter-est Astrid might exhibit into a smoke screen. But to conceal what?

All in a rush, Astrid's taste for life revived, as though Waneeta were waving ammonia beneath her nose. By Jeezum, she'd beat Tommy Trapp at his own game and find the owner of that foot herself! After all, who knew more about what went on in this town than Astrid Starr? She'd been moping around feeling sorry for herself when there were crimes to be solved.

Orlon Marsh's bait and tackle van roared past the display window, Orlon hunched over the wheel like the bootlegger in *Thunder Road*. He was wearing his Scottish plaid golfing cap, and he ran the Stop sign.

Orlon balanced his golf ball on the tee with the three remaining fingers of his right hand and said to Sonny Coffin, "All I'm saying is that we'd better lie low."

"Well, it was a damn stupid mistake."

"Yup. Sorry, boss."

"I don't like it one bit," said Sonny, teeing up beside Orlon. "If we don't fill our quota, they may find another source. After all, the only reason they started dealing with *us* was that Mother Teresa dried up the supply from India."

"Look, boss," said Orlon, leaning on his driver, tongue darting out to lick his mustache. "It was pure luck I'd just sent Rayon to New Jersey. So's when Trapp looked in, the shed was empty."

"You can be replaced, you know," said Sonny, eyeing Orlon in the tweed plus fours he'd salvaged from some car wreck. "In fact, the whole damn trade *is* being replaced. By plastic."

"Ayup," said Orlon, taking a practice swing, knowing if he let Sonny fret, he'd soon be fine. Sonny took half a dozen ferocious practice swings, as though imagining Orlon's head on his tee.

"Well, all right," Sonny finally said. "But just until Trapp stops nosing around."

"I put him on the scent of them goddam lezzies down to Mink Creek. Told him I'd seen them roast a live rooster over a bonfire. What was to stop them doing the same to a human person? Everybody knows how they feel about men."

"Good man, Orlon. Now let's drive 'em home!" Sonny hit his ball two hundred yards down the fairway. "This may be our last match before the snow flies. If so, let's start meeting in your ice-fishing shanty. But not too often. We don't want to attract attention. Besides, I'm really busy with my stock offering. Deathworks is going public."

"Good job, boss," said Orlon, glancing knowingly at Sonny. There were other reasons Sonny was such a busy man right now. Orlon's mother, Waneeta, who cleaned Deathworks, said Angela McGrath was doing more over there than just plucking her harp. Waneeta had found a Victorian corset under Sonny's desk the other day.

Grip askew because of his missing little fingers, Orlon sliced his shot into the rough. Riding in the cart in search of his ball, Orlon recalled asking Tommy Trapp, as one father to another, to scare the shit out of Crystal Sue if she was down to Mink Creek when he got there. So she'd stay home and be normal. Threaten her with jail or something. Tommy winked and said, "You bet, buddy." It was exhausting trying to get Marshes to be respectable.


Trooper Trapp stood outside a plastic tent on the bank of Mink Creek, listening to a deep female voice within saying, ". . . so I won't always be with you. Each of you must hone her own survival skills. . . ."

"You girls know anything about a stray size twelve man's left foot with an ingrown big toenail?" asked Trooper Trapp, removing his flat-brimmed hat to stick his head inside the tent, where twelve dripping Boudiccas sat naked in the lotus position around smoldering coals.

Starshine looked up, startled. "Probably belongs to some jerkoff who stepped in his own leg-hold trap. Get the fuck outa here, Trapp."

"Unlike you girls, I got a job to do."

"Well, go do it in someone else's sweat lodge. We don't allow men on this land."

"Well, that's too bad, ain't it? You better watch your mouth, lady, 'cause I can get just as nasty as you." Trapp patted his holster. That Starshine woman was ugly as a dead woodchuck. So fat her friends would have to hide her during a famine.

"Stick it in your ear, boy," said Starshine. The Boudiccas were unfolding and crawling toward the door as water dripped down from the plastic ceiling. Outside, several Boudiccas assumed the karate fighting stance.

"Look, I don't want to arrest you girls, but I will if I have to."

"Arrest us?" sneered Starshine, flexing her fingers into claws and blowing out breaths with a rhythmic hiss. A soggy blue-and-yellow parrot hunched on her shoulder. "We're minding our own damn business.

Circling quietly in our sweat lodge. Sending energy to the stock market. And some goon for the patriarchy comes in and stares at us and lets in cold air. Pack it in, Trapp. You can't arrest us, asshole."

The parrot croaked, "Power to the People!"

"You're harboring an underage runaway and corrupting a minor." Trapp nodded to Crystal Sue, shivering off to one side, covered with nothing but goose bumps. "Your daddy wants you home, Crystal Sue. And you're gonna get your friends here in big trouble if you don't go back with me right now."

"Get outa my face, Trapp," snarled Starshine, nodding to her karate guard, who advanced one step.

"No," said Crystal Sue. "I'll go. I don't want no trouble." She struggled into tourniquet-tight jeans and T-shirt, slipped on a denim jacket, and followed Trapp through the trees up to the road into town.

"Hop in, honey," said Trapp when they reached his cruiser. Her lips were blue. He'd turn on his engine and warm her up.

"My house is just down the road," said Crystal Sue. "I better get on back there."

"Wait just a minute," said Trapp, irritated to have his caretaking dismissed. "It's not quite that simple. I'm gonna have to run you in, missy."

"Run me in? What for?"

"Hop in the car there and I'll explain."

Crystal Sue did so, sitting nervously, hands pinned between denim knees.

"Now look here, Crystal Sue," began Trooper Trapp. "I got daughters at home, and I know what you been putting your daddy through, running off down there with those weird women."

"They're not weird, they're wonderful," murmured Crystal Sue.

"But they're not normal, are they? And if you're not normal in this country, you get put in jail." He took off his flat-brimmed hat and laid it on the back seat.

"No, you don't neither. 'Cause this is a free democratic country."

"For normal people it is. But not for weirdos." He unbuckled his belt and laid it, with the attached holster and gun, across the back seat.

"They're not weirdos." Crystal Sue wrenched open the door and scrambled out. "Go chase a speeder, Trapp."


Zeno Racine lurched past four trick-or-treaters on the green, who were disguised as a ghost, a pirate, a skeleton, and a gypsy. He'd been down at the graveyard spying on Daisy Wagner, who was wearing her headphones and grieving over Danny McQueen's brass plaque. Every evening at sunset she'd accompany the tape in her Walkman in a wavering voice: " 'If I had the world to give / I'd give it to you / Long as you live. . . . ' " And at that point she'd start crying.

"Everybody in favor of skipping McGraths' this year say aye," said the pirate.

"Aye," said all four.

"Yeah, she's too strange," said the ghost. "Playing crummy songs on that harp all day long."

"Yeah, and hanging out in the cemetery in that ratty old dress with those soggy teddy bears. I bet she cut the foot offen that corpse. Dug one up and cut the foot right off!" suggested the gypsy.

The group shuddered.

"My mama says she probably puts glass in her treats," said the skeleton.

"Hey, neat-o!" The pirate pointed at Zeno. "Check out that monster costume!"

"That's not no costume, dummy," whispered the ghost. "That's Zeno Racine. He's mental."

"My dad says he probably cut off that foot," whispered the gypsy.

Zeno scowled, making his hands into claws and lunging at them. He wished he *had* cut off that foot. Some murderers got all the breaks.

The trick-or-treaters scurried off into the dark, clutching their IGA sacks of candy. Zeno's own sack contained Milk-Bones soaked in Tri-Die, which he was taking to Daisy Wagner's to poison her dog. They'd think their neighbors the Bohrings did it, just like that rock salt around their apple trees. Once that fucking dog was dead, he could climb right up the trellis and into Daisy's bed. (He couldn't attack her in the graveyard because Angela McGrath was always around.) Now that her boyfriend was dead, Daisy would be happy to wake up and find Zeno there. She'd let him touch her and love her. And if she put up a fuss, he'd tell her he cut off that foot, and if she didn't shut the fuck up and let him screw her, he'd cut off her goddam boob and feed it to her dog. Except the dog would be dead. . . . Zeno scratched his head.

Clea lay in her bedroom, a damp towel across her eyes. Brandy gnawed quietly on her Nikon case by the bed. A vision of the mangled foot among the violet asters, surrounded by orange-and-black butterflies, kept drifting through her brain. She'd knelt there studying the foot in her zoom lens for a long time, *earlobes dripping blood, pistol barrel caressing her temple* . . .

Eventually she wandered into the house and called the state police. A hearty, genial man named Trooper Trapp arrived. "Trapp's the name," he said. "Tommy Trapp, as in Maria von. We're probably related, but I couldn't carry a tune in a sap bucket!"

He then proceeded to grill Clea as though she were a prime suspect. She made every suggestion she could think of: The Sooner or Later garbage truck sometimes belched debris near that spot when it began revolving. The Boudiccas often marched through her backyard en route to Mink Creek, carrying the contents of the IGA dumpsters. But no identification of either the foot or the maimer had yet been made. FBI investigators in dark topcoats had been poking around among the wild asters for days.

Clea moaned and rolled on her side, clutching the cool cloth to her head. Darius had installed dead-bolt locks on her doors, and she'd been cowering behind them, venturing out only to the IGA for supplies. Roches Ridgers eyed her uneasily as she pushed her cart down the aisles. Rumors were circulating regarding her Mafia connections: Her purchase of Calvin's house was an attempt to launder drug money. Clea in turn eyed *them* uneasily, wondering who was capable of such horror.

At the checkout one afternoon, Astrid Starr reported that some were claiming Daryl Perkins, the Jesus freak in Granite Gap, had done it during an exorcism. Walking home, Clea considered returning to Turtle Bay until the crime was solved. But that might make it look as though she had something to hide. And without her presence, God knew what turn the rumors might take. She could picture her house being sacked and torched, as happened to Elke's family home on the Oder after Elke and her mother's escape to England.

Also, Clea had burned all her Big Apple bridges by now. Elke and she were finished. The children were away at school. (Kate's reaction to Clea's news about the foot had been, "*Gross!* Mother, get *out* of that weird place.") Turner in London sympathized smugly about the foot. Then he educated her on the struggle in Europe between tooth powder and paste. Even her career eggs were all in the Roches Ridge basket now. She had an advance and a deadline on *The Town That Time Forgot*. But how was she to finish a book that had been revealed as a farce? The anonymous, gratuitous violence that had helped drive her from New York now perched like a vulture in her own backyard.

Besides, she had responsibilities in Roches Ridge. Turner and the children had reluctantly agreed to come for Christmas. She wanted the house comfortable and attractive by then. And the bicentennial festival was only a few months away. Yet nothing had been agreed on except the welcome signs along the roads.

Out her window, in the spotlight over the auto graveyard, Dack Marsh was hanging half a dozen dead ducks from the clothesline by their webbed feet. Clea studied his lean muscular body, his shiny black hair, and his aquiline nose. Rolling on her stomach so she wouldn't have to look at the ducks, she pounded the mattress with her fist, in frustration at the complexity of country living. Brandy began racing around the room, growling and barking. Clea eyed him uneasily. Ever since he'd tasted human flesh, she'd been wary of him.

# 37  The Mountains of the Moon

Elke and Terence sat at their oak-pedestal kitchen table, eating cheese and fruit. Clearing his throat, Terence said, "Elke, I'm really proud of you for making this break with Clea."

Elke glanced up at him. He looked as though he'd won a footrace. "I can't imagine why. It doesn't seem to be doing me much good. I mope around my studio all day, boring that poor graduate student to death. I'm sure she's thinking if this is the life of a sculptor, she'd rather be a gravedigger."

Terence smiled. "Just give it some time."

Elke got up and washed her dishes in the sink. Perhaps in time it *would* be all right. But for the present, her life felt as barren as the mountains of the moon. Terence had always provided security; and Clea, excitement. But without Clea, Terence was suffocating her. Yet she felt guilty because she knew he loved her with his entire being— head, heart, soul, lungs, and liver. So why did she increasingly grit her teeth to stop from saying unkind things to him? Why had she begun working late in her studio so he'd be asleep when she came to bed? But so total was Terence's devotion that he hadn't yet noticed. He adored it when she worked, and never grudged her that time, as he did her time with Clea. She headed for the studio stairs.

"Be sure to come to bed early tonight," called Terence. "I'm worried about your cough."

Pausing on the steps, Elke turned to observe him, hunched over his plate cutting up a pear, gazing at her with loving concern through black-framed glasses perched halfway down his nose.

She heard herself reply with exasperation, "Terence, my love, please stop it."

Terence's face took on a bewildered and hurt expression, and Elke hated herself for a moment. She felt like a caged macaw, pampered in every way, but longing to fly free. Yet afraid to throw herself into the air.

In her studio she stepped over a deflated beach ball globe and some plastic tubing. Beth, her graduate student, had plans for them, but Elke couldn't recall what. The tubing was going to be a placenta or something. Stanley Stoddard had persuaded her to take Beth on as an apprentice for the fall term. Elke agreed, thinking perhaps an alteration in her work process would generate some new ideas, as it had when she joined Arts Alive after Clea's move to Paris. Historically, sculptors used assistants for their dirty work. Beth was eager and capable, but Elke had remained devoid of inspiration all fall. She'd tried every trick in the book to jar her psyche. She'd doodled endlessly in every medium. She'd listened to Bach's Brandenburg Concertos at top volume. Like an impotent octogenarian drooling over *Penthouse,* she'd studied plates of other artists' work and visited museums and galleries, hoping to strike sparks of emulation or competition. She found a set of gears in the street one day and experimented with sending fragile objects—a silk flower, a child's mitten—through the teeth. But when she saw the time and concentration required to continue, she tossed it all in the trash. Another day she began a collage, drawing a still life of some ordinary kitchen implements and surrounding them with varnished newspaper headlines about rape and wife beating. But she quickly became bored and stashed it behind a cabinet.

Beth watched all this like a proper apprentice, joining in when invited. She was young and still fancied herself the Brancusi of her generation. Dressed like a sixties hippie in gauze peasant garments, she began to initiate academic discussions of the sort Elke most detested, with the sibilance of "ism" in every other phrase. But Elke dutifully accompanied her on these rambles through the thickets of her unpruned intelligence, and on the more personal rambles that followed regarding her family life and love life. Elke soon found herself offering sympathy and advice, as though to Kate or Theo.

Elke could feel Beth becoming besotted with her. Beth longed for an older woman who'd successfully run the rapids Beth was eyeing fearfully from above. Elke realized she could teach Beth all she herself had learned about graphics, sculpture, and life in general. She could recommend her to gallery owners and patrons. Beth would lave her with an adoration that might salve the wounds left by Clea. For the first time, Elke understood the function of Clea's endless crushes: If you kept moving, you never had to mourn what you were leaving behind. You could avoid the void, so to speak. If it worked for Clea, maybe it would for her too.

For a while Elke managed to dredge up feelings of solicitude for Beth, and she relished being perceived as flawless. After a couple of months, however, she found herself unable to keep the magic going. Her attempts to define a new project remaining fruitless, Beth's adoration began to moderate into grudging respect for an aging dignitary whose future lay firmly in the past.

In addition, being a mentor just didn't do it for Elke. She'd had the real thing—a mutually fructifying friendship with Clea. There had been occasional strife, but they had been equally equipped for it. Over the last year she'd systematically terminated this friendship because it was too ghastly to have Clea always gone or in love. But some days Elke had felt like crying out with the pain of it all. It often seemed as though Clea had taken with her all the light and life in the immediate neighborhood. But this pitch of agony was impossible to sustain, and by now it had given way to ennui. Having experienced such an interchange, however, she was unable to settle for simple worship from Beth. Especially knowing that Beth would eventually need to move on in her pursuit of MOMA, kicking up dust clouds of recrimination to conceal the real reasons for her desertion.

The week before, Elke had suggested that Beth work on her own stuff during their hours together. This morning Beth, as she repeatedly blew up and deflated her beach ball in search of the perfect degree of flaccidity, announced, "When you think about it, Elke, abstract forms seem so much more expressive. Because there are no external referents to dilute the impact."

Elke, who was studying her face in a mirror for a possible self-portrait, glanced at Beth. Elke's main body of work had been at least marginally representational. Elke felt wary. Since she'd barely tasted the adoration, surely she didn't yet merit the diminishment.

"I mean, the impulse is closer to its primal origins," mused Beth. "No identifiable objects, with all their distracting associations, intervene between the artist and her audience."

"If those are your goals," replied Elke, "why not just hook yourself up to an EEG machine in the middle of MOMA and leave it at that?"

Beth, missing the sarcasm, fell silent as air hissed from her beach ball. She was evidently considering whether Elke's suggestion would constitute Art.

"I've found," said Elke, softening, "that whatever forms, styles, materials, or techniques I've used, I keep turning out metaphors of myself. Whether I want to or not."

Elke circled Beth's beach ball and plastic tubing, trying to figure out what they were saying about Beth. That she really *would* be happier digging graves, Elke concluded. Self-expression probably ought to be denied people until they'd reached an age at which they had something worth expressing.

Studying her own charcoal self-portrait from that morning, which lay on her drawing table beneath the skylight, Elke saw fatigue and stagnation in the eyes. Her current sterility was almost worse than a full-blown depression. Where there was passion, whatever its coloration, at least there was the possibility of transmutation. But the barren wasteland she was presently scouting offered only parched desolation. Stretching before her lay years and years of clipping her toenails, feeding the cat, and throwing out junk mail.

No one and nothing mattered to her anymore—not Terence, not Clea, not Beth, not Kate or Theo. Even her work—a source of such exhilaration and sense of purpose in the past—had failed her. She had no new ideas because she had nothing to say. And the best way to say nothing was to shut up about it. She was shrinking and shriveling, her circle of contacts contracting. She was, in short, dying, gradually but inexorably, like everyone else on earth. And though she longed to be dead, she was afraid of the dying. But the extinction past the pain of getting there—oh, yes, that was something worth wanting.

Opening the bottom drawer of her file cabinet, Elke pulled out her sketches, made while Clea was in Paris, of two women making love. Flipping through them, she wondered how this topic had ever inspired her. The women—Clea and herself, she supposed—looked like two pale fleshy slugs slithering all over each other. They were disgusting.

Sinking into her chair, drawings in one hand, she smiled. Nearly twenty years of mutual fascination reduced to this—slugs copulating. The workings of her mind horrified even herself. She supposed that deep down she was still furious with Clea, although she felt only indifference. The minute Kate and Theo left home, when Clea and she could have finally spent some uncomplicated and uninterrupted time together, Clea hit the road in search of a new circus. It wasn't fair, after all the effort Elke had put into helping raise those damn kids. She felt used. All used up, in fact. Oh well, never mind. It was finished now.

One by one she took the erotic drawings and ripped them in quarters. Rising, she tossed the scraps into the trash can, reflecting that being a practicing artist was like being adrift on a life raft: First you devoured your comrades and jettisoned the remains, then you began to gnaw your own flesh.

# 38  Born Again

Daryl Perkins sat brooding by the green in his Dodge Ram van. Ever since the Megabucks debacle, he'd been realizing his Lord was an elusive kind of guy. You might say, "Thy will be done," but you couldn't say for sure what that will was. For instance, Daryl was beginning to wonder if the world really *would* end on Deuteronomy's third birthday. And he also wondered if the Lord still meant for him to save Loretta Gebo. If his plan failed, he'd be humiliated in front of her yet again. He hadn't dropped by Casa Loretta since the Megabucks defeat. Loretta probably thought he was either a lunatic or a con man. This plan to save her for Christ was his last chance. But if it worked, Loretta would know Daryl was only the humble servant of a wily Master.

Closing his eyes for a quick bracing prayer, Daryl opened the door and swung out on his aluminum crutches. Unlatching the rear doors, he put some equipment in a bucket and hung the bucket by its handle from one crutch. Then he lurched along the green toward the Stop sign. From the corner of his eye he could see Loretta in her window, wicked beehive held proudly aloft, a monument to her godlessness. "Please, Lord, let this work," he prayed. "But Thy will be done," he added.

Loretta stood in her front window, sucking the mousse from a Godiva chocolate walnut. She'd earned it from Ray for her arithmetic the night before. She was embarrassed to admit that she was enjoying these schoolgirl games. Ray had finally moved into her trailer, so they could play them more often. Several nights a week they'd pull the shades and put on Angela McGrath's elaborate Edwardian rigs. Ray wore a chestnut fall Loretta had bought from Mane Magnifique, pinned up in a severe bun. He'd give her assignments, rewarding her with chocolates and punishing her with a ruler across her palms. Then they'd undress and let down their hair. Each would don a starched white Victorian nightgown. Ray would lie on the living room sofa, and Loretta on her own bed. After the lights were out and all was still, Ray would steal into her room and whisper girlish secrets. Sometimes she'd giggle and let him kiss her cheek. Other times she'd turn away petulantly. He'd beg and cry and bribe her with chocolates to let him hold her hand.

Ishtar said that when Loretta finally gave in, it would free Ray from his lifetimes of obsession with Ishtar herself. Loretta was fascinated with this past-life stuff. Ishtar maintained, for instance, that the foot in Clea Shawn's backyard might be a time-warp meteor from one of Daryl Perkins' past lives. But since Daryl felt lesbians were emissaries of the devil, he refused to let Ishtar acupuncture him to discover the scenario for which the foot had been a prop.

Poor Ishtar was suffering horribly over Morning Glory's romance with Ray's baby brother, Dack. Ishtar said Morning Glory's rejection of her had activated her early experience of abandonment by her birth parents. Feeling she needed a major change to take her mind off it all, she was thinking of selling the Karma Café. Loretta was uneasy about a new owner. Better the competition you already knew.

Loretta watched Maureen and May Murphy come out of their house and get into Sonny Coffin's black Mercedes. Sonny in his black turtleneck and sports jacket loaded their suitcases into his trunk. As he walked around to his door, he waved to Angela in her front doorway. She blew him a kiss. He glanced around uneasily. So, reflected Loretta, it was evidently true that Angela was working overtime at Deathworks. God knows, Loretta was in no position to judge other people, but she did feel sorry for poor Ian McGrath. He was so earnest and kind that he'd never find another wife.

Maureen Murphy was also kind, taking her mother to South America to recuperate from falling on that *Sound of Music* plate. May had been in the hospital a long time, and she still looked pale and tired. It was thoughtful of Sonny to drive them to the airport. Loretta had never regarded Sonny as thoughtful. When he was a boy, he'd been downright evil, soaking barn cats in kerosene and setting them on fire. She didn't know Sonny and Maureen were friends. She didn't know Sonny *had* friends. But people were always surprising her.

It looked as if May was trying to get back out of Sonny's Mercedes. Maureen reached across the old lady to hold the door shut. It was sad what Alzheimer's did to people. Sonny drove off with a screech, running the Stop sign. Why did Tommy Trapp bother keeping a Stop sign at that corner? Drivers always ignored it. The only thing it was good for was spray-painting by the various loonies around town.

Speaking of which, Daryl Perkins was swinging toward the sign now, a bucket hanging from one crutch handle. He halted before the sign and studied it. Balancing himself on one crutch, he took items from the pail and set it on the ground. Poor Daryl, he was still so sheepish about that Megabucks fiasco. Loretta wanted to tell him it actually gave her hope to know that even God lost lotteries.

After many agonizing minutes, Daryl managed to tape a stencil to the Stop sign. Then he propped himself on one crutch and aimed a paint gun at the stencil. As he tried to spray, he lost his balance and crumpled to the ground.

Loretta rushed out her door, calling, "Are you okay, Daryl?"

As she lifted him up, he said, "Thanks, Loretta. Can you help me finish this?"

"Sure. Here, give me that." Taking the sprayer, she misted the stencil on the Stop sign.

"Would you take the stencil off, please?"

Loretta did so. And then she stepped back and read aloud, " 'Stop SATAN.' " Pondering this, she glanced at Daryl, who was studying her expectantly.

"Well?"

"Well what, Daryl?"

"Don't you feel nothing?"

"Feel what, honey?"

Daryl reached out and poked her behind the knees with a crutch, so her legs buckled and she collapsed to the ground.

"Woman, fall to your *knees* in the presence of your Lord God!" Daryl thundered. "Raise your eyes to heaven, and praise your Savior for showing you the Way here this afternoon!"

"Daryl," said Loretta evenly as she got to her feet. "You know, sometimes I'm sorry you were born the first time, much less again."

.  .  .

Jared came to a halt halfway across the green from Mane Magnifique when he saw that Loretta was already helping Daryl. Jared was
disappointed, wanting to carry Daryl back to his van. It would be a
piece of cake with his new muscles. Bethany had agreed to keep her
spikes if Jared would be her body-building partner. It was the best deal
of his life. Several clients from Colonial Manor Estates, who now had
Julie Andrews specials, were flirting with spikes after seeing Bethany,
and he was certain a couple would convert.

Plus which, he was self-sculpting one terrific body. Alone at night
in his boyhood bedroom, he'd spend hours before the mirror in his
hot-orange posing trunks, flexing a muscle every now and then. He
knew Gordon in the next bedroom was allowing Randall to watch him
in the knothole in the woodwork through which he and Gordon had
passed notes as kids. Gordon had been so torn up over Dan's death
that Jared was happy to see his playfulness reviving. Gordon claimed
Jared's new fascination with muscles was sibling rivalry, since Gordon
had had muscles for years. Maybe so, but it was also a way to stay so
busy that Jared had no time to grieve over his brothers—Dan already
dead, and Gordon perhaps under fire.

The trickle of rumors about Gordon's homosexuality had turned
into a sluice ever since Maureen Murphy accidentally put his *Gay
Community News* into Astrid Starr's mailbox. Astrid, not noticing Gordon's name on the wrapper, had opened it—which was like throwing
a zebra carcass to a leopard. Within minutes it was all over town that
the severed foot resulted from a gay S&M orgy in Gordon's milking
parlor.

This rumor, however distressing to Gordon, was a relief to Jared
because it replaced the one attributing the foot to punk rites performed by Bethany and himself. A more likely foot possibility—that
Astrid's husband, Earl, was involved, since Earl was one of three men
in town who knew butchering and owned a cleaver—never made it
onto the airwaves, since Astrid was anchorwoman.

Mrs. McQueen had agreed to let Jared and Bethany set up their
weights in Danny's old bedroom, beneath his Wayne Gretzky posters.
Always accepting of her sons, Jared's mother had become downright
burdensome with her approval since Dan's death, intending to savor
each child while she had the chance.

Bethany's husband, Ken, just barely tolerated her dumbbells in their living room. Bethany claimed if Ken knew she had a partner and plans to compete again, he'd beat her senseless with her Ms. Empire State trophy. But with Ken at Xerox composing memos half the night, and with Bethany's daughter, Daisy, always down at the graveyard singing Grateful Dead songs to Danny, and maybe refusing to participate in the Miss Teenage America pageant in Dubuque, poor Bethany needed a diversion.

As Loretta trained a spray gun at the Stop sign, Jared turned back toward his shop, where Astrid Starr sat under the dryer, setting a body wave so her hair would look like Angela Lansbury's on "Murder, She Wrote."

"But, Astrid, Jessica Fletcher's hairdo is so suburban. How about a spike or two?" he'd asked earlier.

"The only spike I'll allow on this head," grunted Astrid in the styling chair, "is one through my brain if I ever let you punk this hair, Jared McQueen."

# 39   The Nativity

Clea handed paper bags to Kate and Theo as they headed out the door to Clea's BMW with their skiing gear.

"Really, Mom," insisted Theo, "we'd rather buy lunch at Alpine Glen."

"Let her do her trip, Theo," murmured Kate, nudging him.

Theo dutifully took his lunch. Clea stood waving in her apron in the doorway as they drove down the driveway. Turner came up from behind and kissed her ear. "Alone at last," he whispered.

He'd just arrived from the Burlington airport, and they hadn't seen each other in weeks. Clea felt remote from him. His proposed solution to the foot affair had been for her to sell the house and return to New York. This determination to resuscitate dead horses made him a successful businessman: He overcame obstacles by refusing to acknowledge their existence. But it made him a lousy husband. Turning to embrace him briskly, Clea said, "I've got a turkey to stuff."

"Later." He led her by the hand up the stairs and pulled her down beside him on her bed, where he stroked her hair out of her eyes. "I'm amazed at all you've accomplished, darling. The house is so handsome and comfortable. I had no idea."

"Thanks. It's been like this for about five minutes. Until the day before yesterday it was furnished with sawhorses."

Clea cooperated as Turner removed her apron. And when his hands and mouth began their familiar ministrations, she performed her role. But her heart wasn't in it, nor were her other body parts. Out the window she could see dried asters against the snow, over the spot where she'd found the foot. For the moment she wasn't associating human flesh with pleasure.

Turner paused, hand on her breast. "You're not really up for this, are you?"

"I guess not. I'm sorry, sweetheart," said Clea, proud of him for noticing. It always amazed her how he could get right into this. She required some wooing, particularly today. It was an old quandary for them. He needed sex in order to feel connected to her, and she needed to feel connected to him in order to enjoy sex.

"It's okay. Look, why don't we try this later?"

"Don't mind me," offered Clea. "Just carry on."

"But it's like doing CPR on a corpse."

Clea smiled wanly. "Maybe I'd better stuff my turkey, then."

"Maybe you had," he said, sitting up. "And I'll watch the Giants game."

As Clea chopped celery for the stuffing, she looked out her kitchen window past the new calico curtains to the auto graveyard, drifted over with fresh snow. On the clothesline in the foreground hung several webbed feet, Dack having cut down the ducks. Dack was incandescent these days, wandering the woods in his down vest and jeans, warmed by his love for Morning Glory. One afternoon last month he stopped by to break the happy news to Clea, unaware of her distress as she valiantly consented to his request to use her barn for trysts. Apparently she was now going to plumb the depths of masochism. She'd been so busy readying the house for Christmas that she hadn't yet had time to observe Dack and Morning Glory sneaking across her yard to the barn. But what would happen after New Year's, when her family departed and the snow piled soft and deep around her windowsills? She was frankly frightened.

At dusk Theo burst into the kitchen, calling, "Hey, Mom, that Dack Marsh is an okay dude."

"Yes?" Clea felt her heart wobble.

"We just gave him a ride home from Alpine Glen," explained Kate, unzipping her jumpsuit. "His car collapsed in the parking lot."

"I'm not surprised," said Clea fondly. "It's tied together with baling twine."

"He likes you," said Theo, tearing a crisp piece of skin off the roasted turkey on the stovetop. "He said we really lucked out with our old lady."

Clea winced.

"And we agreed," added Kate, putting her arm around Clea and hugging her.

Clea glanced at the arm with suspicion. From *persona non grata* at Easter to *mater familias* at Christmas? Kate was vibrant, eyes bright and cheeks rosy. To be in such a good mood, she probably had a new girlfriend, or boyfriend, or both.

"Did you know he's getting hitched?" asked Theo.

Clea looked at him quickly.

"He's knocked up his girlfriend," added Theo cheerfully.

Clea turned back to the stove and leaned on it, feeling the remnants of her obsession with Dack fall away like clay from a roasted pigeon. Babies needed their parents. As Theo would put it, she was history.

As they gathered around the pine harvest table in the wainscoted dining room, Clea asked Theo, "Would you like to say grace?"

"Naw," he replied. "I'm not into all that Christian shit anymore."

"Well, praise the Lord," said Turner, clasping his hands at the head of the table. "What happened?"

"Aw, I was dating this wench at school who was born again. But she was always on my case. So I dumped her."

Turner laughed, face ruddy from the Scotch he'd drunk during the Giants game. "So what sect are you into now?"

"Sect, Dad?" Theo grinned.

"Sect, not sex," said Kate.

"I'm seeing this fox who's on the Junior Olympic ski team. Maybe I'll bring her up here for a weekend, huh, Mom?"

"I'd be delighted," said Clea, baffled by her sudden popularity with the youth of the land.

As they began to eat, Kate asked, "So what happened to Elke and Terence this year?"

"I invited them," replied Clea, picking with her fork at her cranberry relish. "I left a message on Elke's machine. But she sent a note saying they couldn't handle such a long drive in holiday traffic." The note had contained no endearments, and Elke had simply signed her name in closing. To Clea it had felt like one more nail in the coffin, this one piercing her heart.

"Too bad for them," said Theo.

"So bring me up to date," requested Clea, eager to change the subject. "What are you all up to?"

Clea recognized her mistake in not being more specific. Just as in the old days, each vied with the others to monopolize her attention with news about course work and corporate mergers. Clea sat back, still weakened by Dack's matrimonial plans and the reminder of Elke's withdrawal. But as she observed the struggle to dominate the conversation, she found herself for once actually enjoying the tug-of-war, knowing that the participants would vanish in a few days and that her meals would again become silent and perfunctory.

When each had talked himself out and subsided into silence, Theo asked, "So, Mom, how's it going with menopause?"

They all looked at her, and Clea realized this was why they'd been humoring her so assiduously. Turner had probably warned them to treat her gently. They were worried about their eccentric wife and mother, alone in the woods with a psychopathic foot fetishist. She smiled faintly. "It's going fine, thank you, Theo. And I appreciate your asking."

"So what about this foot thing, Mother?" asked Kate, frowning.

"What about it?"

"Dack says it hasn't been solved."

"Not yet. But I'm sure it will be."

After dinner they turned out all the lights in the living room except those on the tree and the candles in the windows. As they sang carols, sprawled on cushions on the wine-and-teal Oriental carpet, Clea felt her sorrow catch up with her. Elke had always loved this phase of their Christmas ritual. She did descants to Turner's baritone and Clea's alto in a pure soprano, like the ring of tapped crystal. If Terence had been a tenor instead of tone deaf, they could have done barbershop. She wondered how Elke and Terence were celebrating, if at all. She pictured Elke at the Turtle Bay dinner table the past Easter, wearing the navy-blue silk dress that matched her eyes, silver hair piled atop her head and escaping in wisps all around. It was so painful to believe you had a best friend who'd stick with you through anything, only to discover it was all a mirage.

Clea began to listen closely as they sang: "O little town of Bethlehem, / How still we see thee lie. / Above thy deep and dreamless sleep /

The silent stars go by. . . ." This was how she'd seen Roches Ridge—silent and peaceful. But that was a mirage too. As in Flanders, mangled limbs lay scattered about the rolling fields. And her family members, harmonizing by the hearth, would soon go back to their real lives, in which they regarded her with the remote gratitude and affection a rocket probably felt for its launch pad. In the past the children had alternately clung and clobbered. They were able to be so solicitous today because they no longer needed her. But why couldn't they just leave? Why did they have to keep coming back, to pick the fragile scabs off her heart? She began to cry.

The children lapsed into silence and gazed at her with alarm, simultaneously irritated and pleased. They needed not to feel guilty for growing up and going away, yet they needed to know she missed them. How was one mother to fulfill all these requirements at once?

"Please don't stop singing," she said. "I'm just so moved to have you all here in my new house for the first time." Her life to date had been entirely sustained by illusions. Without them, what was left?

In bed that night Turner held her in his arms and said, "Clea, I'm afraid to leave you here alone like this. Please come back to New York with me."

She replied briskly, "Nonsense. I'll be fine. Don't worry."

"You keep saying that. But I *do* worry."

"You never have before. Why now?"

Each pulled back and inspected the rancor behind this remark.

Turner eventually replied, "I've done the best I can, Clea. Given the considerable limitations to my personality."

"I'm sorry, Turner. That was a low blow. I know you have. And so have I."

"But it's not good enough, right?"

"It's been better than good. It's been marvelous."

"But you're speaking in the past tense. What about the present?"

Clea sighed. "I don't know, Turner. So much has happened so fast. I'm confused." She felt she was watching Turner recede through a retracting zoom lens. He was a man of action. He wouldn't allow his domestic life to lie in shambles for long. Yet Clea felt unable to sort through the rubble for him. She had her own rubble to deal with.

"That makes two of us."

"Well, never mind. Things will be fine. They always have been."

"I hope so," he said, turning his back and clutching a pillow to his chest.

# 40  The Hunger Moon

Clea lay in her rumpled bed, gazing out the window across the sloping back field of snow, which was illuminated by moonlight. With the leaves down, her view extended over the cliff to the Boudicca tepees, and along Mink Creek to the frozen lake, where duck blinds had perched like shore birds in September. A hide of ice on the lake now hosted an infestation of multicolored ice-fishing shanties. According to town records, the early settlers had called this February full moon the Hunger Moon. At this time of year stored supplies started to rot and give out, and the weak and ill began to die.

Since her family's departure after Christmas, Clea had left the house only once. To stock up on groceries at the IGA, and to hand in her resignation as bicentennial chairperson to Conrad Bohring at the bank, pleading her book deadline, a lame excuse: She hadn't worked on her book since the foot, and doubted she ever would again.

Throughout January Clea had lain under her duvet, watching the sun rise out one window and set beyond the opposite one. Followed by the moon in its fluctuating configurations. Patterns of light and shadow had shifted in a stately time-lapse gavotte across the pine floorboards, occasionally interrupted by dark snow clouds like bruises on the sky. Roches Ridgers had passed by outside, insects on parade. Zeno Racine would hide in the bushes at twilight and jerk off to the sizzle of the Marshes' bug light. Crystal Sue Marsh would sneak down the cliff to the Boudicca tepees. Dack would plod across Clea's field on snowshoes, and down through the woods to check Orlon's traps. Orlon would nose around the Boudicca tepees in search of Crystal Sue. Sometimes he'd enter his green fishing shanty on the bay, to be joined by the saturnine owner of Deathworks, who'd drive across the ice in his black Mercedes. Astrid Starr once stepped into a leg-hold trap along Mink Creek while wearing a Sherlock Holmes cape. The Rescue League had to pull her out of the valley on a toboggan. Boudiccas hiked through Clea's field toting rotting produce from the IGA Dumpsters. Orlon was in and out of his shed at all hours, running power equipment. Ray Marsh dragged home wrecked cars behind his blue tow truck and deposited them on the heap out back. Waneeta Marsh emerged in designer dresses to go clean houses at Colonial

Manor Estates. At night, spotlights flashed in the valley, where Orlon was jacking deer.

All this passed before Clea's eyes like *Friday the 13th, Part II.* Her Roches Ridge, the Roches Ridge of *The Town That Time Forgot,* where harp music floated across the green on zephyrs off the lake, was a figment of her imagination, as wispy as wood smoke on winter winds. The real Roches Ridge was an abattoir, a snake pit, a creep show. The foot atrocity was insoluble because almost anyone in town could have done it.

As the Hunger Moon cast its silver light across the yard, Clea saw Dack Marsh emerge from the snowy trees carrying a limp fox that trailed black gore. Her Lawrentian man of the woods, her Native American folk artist, was an ignorant brutal youngster who murdered helpless animals in a swamp and performed voodoo with their remains. She felt nothing for him anymore except anger at his betrayal of her vision.

In the beginning of this bedbound vigil over her backyard, Clea had been assaulted by the familiar restless boredom that in the past had propelled her out onto the streets and into some mess. But this time her vitality failed her. Lacking the energy even to change her sheets, she lay there and endured the agitation, finally sitting quietly with no amusements, as Pascal counseled. And eventually the agitation passed. To be replaced by utter terror, which her relentless activity had evidently been keeping at bay all these years.

The reality was that she perched on a globe that spun and wobbled in a penumbral vacuum. This globe had witnessed with indifference as thousands of living species marched to extinction. Even now this globe was being struck by lightning bolts and meteorites, swept by tidal waves and tornadoes, rent by earthquakes, racked with famine and epidemic, convulsed with war. The landmass bristled with missiles. The seas were a stock pot of toxic waste, and the air was a blanket of noxious fumes. In time the sun would burn out and the oceans would freeze over. Every inhabitant of this globe, under a lifelong sniper attack, would eventually be picked off by Fate, after years of being beaten, robbed, raped, and mutilated by fellow creatures. The modern male killing machine had filled the hospitals with casualties and the countryside with corpses. This very stone house looming around her had no doubt witnessed murder, suicide, sexual assault, psychological torture of every sort. All Clea's loved ones would eventually desert her—by departing or dying—after suffering ghastly wasting diseases and gory accidents. Clea's own organs were even now in a process of gradual collapse, which would perhaps render her deaf, blind, lame, incontinent, senile. And after several decades of pain and sorrow without limit, she'd end up alone in a narrow grave, where she'd turn into green slime and be devoured by worms, while a hot wind whined through a hollow black void.

This was the world Elke inhabited all the time, the world she'd grown up in, the world memorialized by her bleak etchings and tangles of torn steel. This was the world Clea's parents tried to blot out with their alcohol. Most people understood that this world was an inferno. But Clea had managed to levitate above it for years. Now, however, she was sinking into it. She longed to abbreviate her torturous descent by wandering into the woods one subzero night and waiting for a fresh snowfall to settle over her like a shroud. Elke could perhaps have told her how to subvert this impulse, but Elke was gone.

Was it any wonder Elke called her pollyannoid, and her photos "decorative"? Clea thought with chagrin about her travel books, showing elaborate buildings and their privileged inhabitants, scenic vistas and national monuments. Elke had once chided her for discarding a photo of the ornate Victorian train station in Bombay because of a limbless leper in the foreground. "This is the best picture in the bunch," Elke had insisted. "It sums up life on this earth. When will you face it?"

Pulling on her bathrobe, Clea stumbled downstairs, weak from eating too little and lying in bed too much. After building a fire, she retrieved her photos for *The Town That Time Forgot* from her office. Sitting by the fire, she studied them—the mossy headstones beneath the drooping elms, the peeling colonial cornices, the children leaping off the War of 1812 cannon, Gordon McQueen and his draft horses, Angela McGrath playing her harp in her Edwardian gown. Lies, all of them. The latest in a lifetime of lies. Those children on the cannon were probably being sodomized by their fathers at night. One by one she laid the pictures on the altar of flaming logs and watched them turn brown, curl up, and dissolve into ashes.

The phone rang. Clea started, then turned her head and stared at it. It rang so rarely these days.

"Your husband says you're weepy and depressed. Is this true?" inquired Elke.

"Elke." Clea felt like bursting into tears.

"Is it true?"

"I was just thinking about you," she mumbled.

"Is it true?"

"I resent being discussed behind my back," said Clea carefully, feeling anger, elation, fear, and relief.

"What do you think is going on up there in Rooster Ranch, or whatever you call that place?" Elke sounded nervous.

"Point well taken. Weepy and depressed. Let me see," said Clea, beginning to thaw around the edges at the sound of Elke's familiar wry voice. "Yes, I guess so."

"Well, I'd like to come visit. Does my invitation still hold?"

Clea said nothing for a long time, struggling for clarity. Elke had rebuffed her so many times in the last year. Why now? Finally she replied, "Forgive my hesitation, Elke. But it annoys me that I have to be demoralized for you to come."

"I don't blame you. But would it help if I pleaded demoralization also?"

"What about?"

"You, for one thing. God, what an awful Christmas without that boring dinner at Turtle Bay."

Clea laughed weakly. She felt equally capable of picking up where they'd left off or hanging up and never speaking to this wretched woman again.

"My work, for another."

"Not going well?"

"Not going at all. I must have filled a dozen dust bins with sketches. But I can't find my way."

"That makes two of us. I just burned my entire book."

"I'm impressed," said Elke.

Neither said anything for a long moment, each no doubt tasting her ambivalence. Could they open up again after all the pain they'd put each other through?

"Won't Terence mind?" Clea finally asked.

"He won't be thrilled. But he's never thrilled, so what difference does it make?"

Clea tilted her head quizzically. This was a new note to Elke's connubial rondeau. "Well, I don't know, Elke. Maybe we can heal together. Yes. Do come. Soon." She added tentatively, as though sending a canary into a coal mine, "I've missed you."

"Me too. But you do realize it's your fault?" teased Elke.

"Of course," said Clea, lapsing readily into their standard tone of gentle mockery. "Everything always is. Just ask my kids."

After hanging up, Clea stood perfectly still for a long time, hand on the receiver. She hoped this wasn't a mistake. Her poor old heart couldn't take much more.

# 41   The Cosmic Fandango

Upon reaching the snow-blanketed green, Clea discovered a new sign over the Karma Café, reading: SCHUSS KEBAB. And another over a colonial house beside the bank, which read: NEW AGE TRAVEL. For a town that hadn't changed since the eighteenth century, this one certainly looked different from last month, she thought sourly. Once quaint to her, Roches Ridge now looked ramshackle, and its citizens, as they went into and out of the IGA, demented. Clea felt baffled by her sea change. It was like waking up after a night of passion to find a grinning death's head on the sheets beside you. Which version was real, or was neither?

Clea raised her camera and framed a shot of New Age Travel. But her index finger refused to press the shutter release. Turning to focus on the Victorian bandstand, Clea found her finger still frozen. She wiggled it, trying to limber it up, but it resolutely declined to perform. Great. Now she couldn't practice her profession even if she wanted to.

At the IGA, Astrid Starr seemed to have forgotten all about the foot. She buttonholed Clea by the pasta shelf with news of May Murphy's death at New York customs upon her and Maureen's return from Colombia. German shepherds trained to detect drugs had lunged at the old woman, triggering a heart attack. While doing CPR, officials found plastic bags of cocaine taped all over her body beneath her clothes.

"Maureen, of course, is in a terrible state," confided Astrid. "She blames herself, poor soul, for leaving her mother alone in the ladies' room in Bogotá before boarding their flight. Some smuggler must have taken advantage of her Alzheimer's."

Clea excused herself after Astrid's briefing and escaped to the produce aisle. She felt alarm, recalling May Murphy's note: HELP. With her revised outlook on Roches Ridge, it seemed distinctly possible that something awful had been going on. And Clea had failed to intervene. But she couldn't dwell on this just now. She had a lot to do before

Elke's arrival, and not much energy with which to do it. The Avon woman, Ida Campbell, sat behind a card table by the greeting card rack. Some paperback books, titled *Sir and Her,* were stacked before her. The cover featured a woman with lashing hair and a ripped see-through blouse.

"Hello," said Clea, unable to maneuver her cart past the table. "How are you, Ida?"

"Just dandy." Ida smiled. She was wearing Vuarnet sunglasses.

"I've finished my house. I could use some cleaning products, if you want to stop by sometime," said Clea, to be neighborly.

"Oh, I don't do Avon anymore," sniffed Ida. "I'm an author now."

"Really?" said Clea. "Congratulations. Is this your book?"

Ida nodded.

"May I buy one?"

"That's what I'm here for." Ida beamed.

Ida handed Clea an autographed photo of herself as well. "Keep smiling!" it said. The signature was punctuated with a happy face.

"Your family must be very proud of you," said Clea listlessly, wanting to be back in bed. She felt raw and vulnerable, as though a Marsh brother had stripped her of her hide.

"Less than you might imagine," sighed Ida. "In fact, my husband has taken the children and moved to his mother's."

"Oh, dear. I'm sorry."

"Well, the lot of the artist has always been a lonely one. We pay a high price for the privilege of telling the truth." She removed her Vuarnets to reveal a black eye.

"Your husband?"

Ida nodded.

"What happened?" So Roches Ridgers were brutalizing each other all over town, not just in Clea's backyard.

"He thinks I'm having an affair with Ken Wagner of Xerox. He can't understand the fantasies we authors need to stoke our creative imaginations."

At the checkout, Astrid nodded toward a woman in a maroon velour sweat suit. Psychedelic spikes, stiff with styling mousse, protruded from her head. "Remember Daisy Wagner?" Astrid asked Clea.

Drawing a blank, Clea shook her head no, wanting only to get out of this freak show and back home behind her dead-bolt locks. No one seemed to realize she was insane. She must be putting on a convincing act, a thought that made her even more uneasy. They were *all* probably putting on acts.

"Last year's Miss Teenage Roches Ridge?"

"Oh. Yes."

"That's her poor mother, Bethany Wagner."

"Poor?" asked Clea weakly, desperate not to hear about any more atrocities.

"Haven't you heard?"

"I haven't been out much lately."

"You haven't, have you?" said Astrid, looking at her with curiosity. "Well, Daisy went to Dubuque for the Miss Teenage America pageant. She hears the Grateful Dead have a concert in Kansas City. So she hops a bus and never turns up for the pageant. Someone saw her at the Dead concert in Saratoga last week, wearing torn jeans and a Jerry Garcia T-shirt. Selling rainbow decals from a psychedelic van."

Clea shook her head. This was too rich a mix. She was getting engine knock after her weeks of silence. She'd forgotten about small towns—how all one's fears and failures were soon swamped by the ceaseless flux of new events.

In the display window Clea spotted a new poster: "You've traveled *out* of your body, why not travel *in* it as well? Swim with the dolphins off Key Largo. Mine the moldavite crystal in Czechoslovakia. Climb the Andes with Shirley MacLaine's shamans. Tour faraway lands where you have lived in past lifetimes. Contact Barbara Carmichael at New Age Travel, located on the Roches Ridge green."

Through the window of New Age Travel, Clea spotted Ishtar, dressed in a robin's-egg-blue rayon skirt and top, her blond hair spiked. Clea's weary heart gave a faint nervous lurch as she recalled stroking that hair before her fire while Ishtar nuzzled her breasts. Curiosity overcame her, however, so she climbed the steps to the door. The ceiling was filled with spider plants and wind chimes, which tinkled in the breeze through the door.

"Welcome! What do you think?" asked Ishtar, gesturing around the office.

"Gosh, Ishtar," said Clea. "When did all this happen?"

"First off, I've gone back to my original name, Barbara Carmichael. For professional reasons."

"Okay. So how's it going, Barbara?"

"Mail order sales are great. But local business is slow."

"Did you sell the Karma Café?"

"Yup. The Schuss Kebab is for skiers down from Alpine Glen. Their specialty is shish kebabs skewered on miniature ski poles."

"But I thought you loved your restaurant."

"I did, but there's a limit to the number of ways you can cook tofu. And Morning Glory's marriage has finally set me free. I've lost her in this life, and have to wait for the next. So why suffer in the meantime? Where have you been, by the way? I haven't seen you around lately."

"Oh, I've been lying low," said Clea with forced ease. "Actually," she added, "I've been having a tough time. Over Dack, over my book, over this foot business." Over *you* a time or two, thought Clea, but she didn't say this, since Barbara apparently hadn't given their interlude by the fire a second thought.

"Let them go," suggested Barbara. "They're just missteps in the cosmic fandango."

"Easier said than done."

"True. Speaking of which, I've been meaning to stop by and thank you. But I got all caught up in selling the restaurant."

"Thank me?"

"When we got back from the duck blind that afternoon, I felt so demolished—deserted by Morning Glory and by my birth mother. But when you accepted me like that, with all my neediness, it set off echoes of other lives in which I *wasn't* abandoned by loved ones. That was a real gift you gave me, Clea."

"Any time," said Clea, embarrassed.

"Once is enough, if it works. And it did."

Astrid Starr walked in, wearing her dark-blue polyester jacket, setting the wind chimes to clanging. "Hello, ladies. Am I early for our meeting, Barbara?"

"I'm just leaving," Clea assured her.

As she walked home along the frozen dirt road, with the winter sun sinking behind a bank of snow clouds, Clea felt relieved to know there were apparently no unresolved issues between Ishtar and herself. So what if she'd been Ishtar's mother? That was in another life. In this one she was now free to obsess about Elke's arrival tomorrow. She was longing to see Elke, yet afraid to. A stiletto plunged into the heart was even more deadly than a cleaver lopping off a limb. Should they apologize and forgive? Pretend nothing had happened? Accuse and dispute? Clea had no idea.

Jared McQueen lifted the brass knocker on Bethany Wagner's oak door at Colonial Manor Estates. Glancing around nervously, he thought he saw Frieda Bohring peeking out an upstairs window next door. Poo was growling softly behind Bethany's door. He'd been one sick puppy, near death at the animal hospital for a long time. The Wagners suspected Conrad Bohring had poisoned Poo for peeing on his perfect lawn. The boy who delivered the *Gazette*, Waneeta Marsh who came to clean, Ida Campbell with her Avon products, the missionaries from the Church of the Holy Deliverance, and Jared himself had been in a state of jubilation. What a pity veterinary medicine had made such giant strides in recent years.

Bethany flung open the door, wearing only her hot-orange posing bikini. She pulled Jared inside. "Glad you could make it, partner. It'll be great to practice with the music blaring. And without Randall and your brother spying on you. You turn into such a show-off every time you hear them at that knothole."

"I do not." Jared smiled. "When's Ken getting home from Louisville anyhow?"

"Not till tomorrow. So we can practice all night long if we want."

"Great," said Jared, plucking at one of Bethany's teetering turquoise spikes. Poo growled softly.

"Here, I've hidden my equipment in the basement." She opened a door and flipped a light switch.

As they carried the bench, rack, and weights upstairs to the living room, Jared said, "You know, Bethany, sometimes I feel really guilty toward Ken, doing this behind his back."

"So do I. But now that Daisy's run off with the Dead, my life's pretty empty. So either I get my needs met elsewhere, or I leave Ken." She put the theme from *Chariots of Fire* on the stereo and turned it up loud.

Jared threw off his sweat suit, buckled on his four-inch-wide leather belt, and began stretching in his orange trunks, muscles rippling. "God, I can't believe we're really all alone," he murmured.

"Just you and me and the barbell," sighed Bethany, looking up from touching her toes.

"Let's take it slow, and make it last." Jared picked up a dumbbell and curled it to his biceps.


Zeno Racine snipped the wire to the alarm outside the Wagners' house. Then he scrambled up the rose trellis, lath breaking underfoot. When he reached Daisy's window, he broke a pane, reached in and undid the latch, raised the frame, and climbed through.

The theme from *Chariots of Fire* blared up the stairs. Looking around at Daisy's canopied bed and skirted dressing table, Zeno shook with a sob. Daisy had run away with the Grateful Dead, and he hadn't even gotten to rape her yet. He flung himself on her bed, buried his face in her pillow, and wept. No rape, no "Mink Valley Crimestoppers," no prison. It wasn't fair.

Eventually Zeno realized that the music downstairs had stopped. Voices were being raised in anger. Zeno leapt up, rushing around the room like a shark in a feeding frenzy. Daisy's Miss Teenage Roches Ridge tiara sat on her dressing table. Zeno grabbed it and stuck it on his head. Then he climbed out the window and down the trellis. Upon reaching the ground, he stumbled in a haze of misery through the snowdrifts on the Wagners' lawn, over to Conrad Bohring's yard, which Conrad had cleared with a snow blower.

An alarm went off, and searchlights lit up the yard. Zeno froze in place like a deer paralyzed by headlights, tiara perched like antlers atop his head. Conrad rushed out his door, sighting down a shotgun barrel. Realizing as he pulled the trigger that Zeno was not a small defecating poodle, he managed to jerk the barrel to one side. The blast dug a crater in his flawless lawn. Within moments Trooper Trapp pulled up in his cruiser, blue flasher whirling. Trapp in his flat-brimmed hat climbed out at a leisurely pace.

"Hold on there, Zeno," he said in a genial drawl, opening the back door to the cruiser. "I'm gonna have to run you in, son. This time you've gone too far."

Conrad was trembling with anguish over the blackened hole in his lawn.

"I have?" asked Zeno, wiping his tears with his parka sleeve.

"You can't go around trespassing on no bank president's lawn."

"No, I can't," Zeno confirmed gleefully, climbing into the cruiser. "You'd better send me down the river, sir."

"And to think I trusted you, Bethany." Ken Wagner, scowling, stood in the doorway in his tweed topcoat and cashmere scarf, suitcase in his hand. Bethany was lying on the bench, her face a study in horror, barbell extended overhead, elbows locked.

"Oh, God, Ken. I'm so sorry you had to find out this way."

Jared was scrambling into his sweat suit, face dark red from exertion.

"At least you could help her rack that damn thing," snarled Ken.

"And you call yourself a man." Jared scuttled over to Bethany and guided the barbell onto its pegs. "Now get the fuck out of my house, you musclebound scum. You hair wrecker."

"I'm sorry, sir," stammered Jared as he sidled toward the door, pulling on his leather bomber jacket.

With a sigh of relief to escape with his tanned flesh unbruised, Jared closed the door. Damn. If Ken made Bethany give up body building, she'd probably get rid of her spikes. Then her ambivalent neighbors would never convert from their Julie Andrews Specials. He jogged down the sidewalk to his car.

Conrad Bohring's house was lit up with spotlights, and a whooping sound was coming from a loudspeaker under the eaves. Conrad, in his steel-gray flattop, stood cradling a shotgun and ululating over a crater in his lawn. Trooper Trapp's cruiser pulled away from the curb, blue light flashing.

As Jared started his car, Bethany dashed down the sidewalk in her raincoat, a dumbbell in each hand. Ken carried her barbell out the door and threw it in a snowdrift. Reluctantly Jared rolled down his window.

"Can I sleep at your place tonight, Jared? He's kicked me out, and I have nowhere to go."

Jared was appalled. What had started out as a little harmless flexing was turning into the real thing. "Sure," he said. "Hop in. You can sleep in Danny's room, with the weights." The *Chariots of Fire* record came sailing through the air and shattered on Jared's windshield.


Ken Wagner was sitting in the den, dictating a power memo, when the doorbell rang. Probably Bethany, full of empty promises to give up her weights and try to save their marriage. Why couldn't she be like all the other Xerox wives, and keep her legs open and her mouth shut?

Ken ignored the doorbell and continued dictating. This memo was going to ensure his rise from level 3 to level 2. Poo began to growl. Ken looked up. Poo usually wagged his tail when he picked up Bethany's scent. Must be someone else. Setting down the Dictaphone, he got up and went to the door.

A skinny woman carrying an imitation-leather briefcase and wearing Vuarnet sunglasses stood on the porch. "Hi. I'm your Avon lady."

"I'm sorry, but Bethany's out," said Ken irritably. She certainly wasn't *his* Avon lady.

"Could I show *you* our new household products, then?"

"No, thank you. You see, I'm in the middle of a memo just now."

"I may as well stop playing games, Ken." She swept off her sunglasses, to reveal a black eye and a watery gaze.

Ken studied the woman, startled she knew his name. But probably Bethany had mentioned him.

"I'm Ida Campbell." She waited for him to indicate recognition. "The author?" Still nothing. "My new novel, *Sir and Her,* has been the number one best-seller at Starr's IGA for the past month."

"Well, congratulations. But I'm afraid you'll have to excuse me."

"And I've brought you an autographed first edition, Ken, because you've been such an inspiration for me. My muse, I might almost say." She extended a paperback with a cover featuring a woman having her clothes ripped off. Ken took it gingerly, as though it might transmit AIDS.

"But I don't even know you."

"Now you do," pointed out Ida with a plucky smile. "I used to see you in your Audi 5000, Ken, wearing your silk ties and cashmere scarves. I have to confess, I even peeked through your window here a time or two, and saw you dictating at night in your recliner while your wife worked out in the living room. And I've dreamed of what it would feel like to reorganize your file drawers. . . ."

"Well, it's sure been nice talking with you, Ida," said Ken with a hearty smile, taking her upper arm and ushering her out the door. "And hey, thanks for the book."

"Oh, and Ken," added Ida, playing her trump, "I type one hundred twenty words a minute."

"Oh, yes?" said Ken, looking at her with sudden interest. "And would you like to fix us a cup of coffee, Ms. Campbell?"

# 42   Sea Changes

Elke got out of her Honda Civic, which was crammed with art supplies. Clea stood in the doorway to her stone house in tweed trousers and a turtleneck. They looked at each other uncertainly for a moment, then moved together and kissed the air beside each other's cheeks.

Stepping back, Elke said, "Clea, you're too thin." Brandy came dashing around the corner of the house and wiggled up to Elke.

"Compared to what?" Clea folded her arms tightly across her abdomen.

"Compared to your robust urban self." Elke reached down to pat Brandy.

"It's been a hard winter."

"Obviously. But is a teenager really worth it?" Elke raised her eyebrows and smiled mockingly.

"Probably not. But Dack is twenty-three."

"Oh, well, then." Elke laughed.

"But Dack is the least of it."

"Yes. Turner told me about that foot."

"And you still wanted to come?"

"You forget my past. The odd mutilated foot means nothing to me." In fact, Elke had been unnerved on her drive to Roches Ridge by all the woods, fields, and rural byways, which reminded her so vividly of her wartime flight across the ravaged European countryside, when every copse contained a corpse.

As they carried things in from the car, Elke said, "This house is stunning, Clea. I can't imagine how you did it in such a short time. It must have seemed as daunting as constructing a pyramid." Elke refrained from mentioning Roches Ridge, which had looked like an ideal setting for witch trials. And Clea's immediate neighborhood, if located in New York, would have been slated for urban renewal.

Putting on water for tea, Clea replied, "As no one knows better than you, Elke, raising Theo and Kate was the toughest job I ever tackled. Everything else is a piece of cake."

Elke nodded agreement, inspecting the comfortable room with its wide pine floorboards, hooked rugs, and huge stone fireplace.

"But thanks. I'm glad you like the house. The yard, however, is a nightmare. Wait till the snow melts."

"After London in the blitz, nothing could faze me."

"My backyard might. It's a garbage dump, cleverly concealed by a mat of impenetrable vines and bushes."

"Sounds charming." Elke sank into a tapestried wingback chair before the fireplace. As Clea knelt to feed the fire, Elke studied her. Her face was haggard—and more handsome than ever, in a feverish sort of way. But it was the vitality of anxiety, not health. Her crisis appeared to rival Elke's own. But it was startling to find Clea, always doggedly upbeat, in such sorry shape. Whereas Elke's current gloom was just business as usual. Better than usual, in fact. Although she couldn't work, she had not slid from the listless desolation of the past autumn into a winter of despair. In fact, she'd even experienced some moments of what could only be that heretofore unknown quality—peace.

One afternoon the week before, she had been sitting in her studio, alone and inactive, instructing herself in the Zen of futility. The images of violence and destruction that had always fueled her art had departed with the scraps of steel from her bayoneted baby the previous spring. Since nothing had arrived to take their place, she'd been trying to learn to value her void, telling herself that it was freeing to be living in an era when all the isms had failed. There were no guidelines to help you through bad times, but there were no psychic straitjackets either. Anything was possible—even hope.

No sooner had she entertained this uncharacteristic thought than into her void seeped an unfamiliar intimation of well-being, like an underground spring in a freshly dug grave. She inspected this sensation with surprise and suspicion, a gold coin in a handful of lead slugs.

Disoriented, she forgot not to answer the phone when it rang. Turner's jovial voice greeted her. Following her cool staccato replies, Turner said, "All right, Elke, I know you and Clea are on the rocks. And that I shouldn't interfere. But I'm really worried about her. She's weepy and depressed and all alone up there in that strange little town. If you could find it in your heart to contact her, I know it would help."

Elke smiled as he explained about the foot in Clea's backyard. This delegation of responsibility was so Turner-like. The corporate executive taking care of business. As though Elke hadn't mopped up after his disjointed emotional style for years.

"I'll think about it, Turner," she finally replied. "You see, I've got troubles of my own just now."

"I'd be even more in your debt than ever, Elke. Because I've got to dash to Rio."

Elke managed to refrain from saying that if she did anything at all, it would be for Clea, and for herself, not for Turner. Hanging up, she considered Clea's situation. And in reaction to her own lingering sense of well-being, she dialed her.

But ever since their decision to get together, Elke had been on edge, wondering if they had anything left to say to each other. Considering how long it had taken to convert agony over Clea into ennui, perhaps it would have been best to let sleeping dogs lie. But now, as

Clea chatted about work on her house in the wingback chair opposite, Elke started to picture her at their first meeting, in the studio doorway in her long black Clara Barton cape, dark hair tumbling down her shoulders.

Clea stopped talking in midsentence and began to smile, setting her teacup in its saucer on the coffee table before the hearth. "What?" she asked Elke.

"What what?"

"Why are you looking at me like that?"

"Like what?" asked Elke.

"Like you like me again."

Elke laughed. "Just because I hated you for a few months doesn't mean I didn't like you."

Both laughed uneasily.

"That wasn't very nice of you not to answer my notes or return my calls," said Clea.

Elke studied her rough hands. "I know. I hope you'll eventually forgive me. It was a question of survival."

"I thought you were appalled by Dack. With whom I *never* slept, by the way."

"I was appalled by my own need for you, Clea. I was constructing my cocoon, as you once advised. But can we just drop this? I mean, I proved I can get along without you. So now I'm back."

Clea studied her intently before saying, "You could have told me what you were doing."

"No, I couldn't. Because I didn't understand it myself until recently."

"Well, I'm glad you're back, Elke. God knows I don't like a lot of hatchets lying unburied around the place."

Both laughed.

Clea helped Elke carry her suitcases upstairs to the guest room, which contained a spool bedstead covered with a patchwork quilt, and a pine chest. A bathroom opened off it, and a couple of the windows overlooked the backyard. While Clea cooked supper, Elke unpacked and washed up, feeling ambivalent. The awkwardness had faded quickly. They'd begun talking as though months of estrangement hadn't intervened. But Elke was on guard. Clea's charm, her sweetness and courtesy even when she was depressed, alarmed Elke. She didn't want to fall in love with this woman all over again.

They ate chicken flecked with lime peel and broccoli with cheese sauce at the coffee table by the walk-in fireplace, a wind whining at the kitchen windows. Brandy twitched in his sleep on the hearth.

"I'm glad you're here, Elke." Clea laid her fork and knife on her plate and leaned back in her chair, feet extended, hands hanging off the chair arms. "Thanks for coming. I know you hate the countryside."

"Thanks for wanting me." Elke lowered the bone she was gnawing to study Clea, sprawled in her wingback chair. If Elke hadn't renounced her profession for good, she'd have liked to sketch that posture, so typical of Clea's casual grace. Elke had almost forgotten during the months of animosity that there was something truly magnificent about Clea. Clea coped effortlessly with so many things—renovating houses, raising children, managing money, entertaining, traveling, running a career, conducting love affairs. Elke felt for a moment almost childlike by comparison. Just getting herself out of New York City and up here had seemed as complicated as D-day. "So you burned your book, huh?"

"Yup. And good riddance too."

Elke raised her eyebrows quizzically, continuing to pick at her chicken bone.

"But I haven't been able to snap a picture since. My finger won't press the button. A hysteric index finger. Freud would have a heyday."

"What's the problem?"

"I have no idea." She looked at Elke expectantly.

"What, you're asking me?"

Clea nodded.

Elke heaved a sigh. "Let me see, what do I think?" She laid her chicken bone on her plate and rested her forehead in her hand, elbow on the chair arm. Brandy, eyes still closed, began sniffing. "I guess what I think, Clea, is that there's something deep down inside you that doesn't resonate. Something armored and guarded. You never really lose yourself. I think you need to let your subjects speak *to* you and *through* you, not *for* you."

Clea continued to stare at Elke, silent and motionless.

Elke became uneasy. She'd gone too far for their first meeting in months. But Clea had asked. And their pact was always to tell the truth when it came to work. Unable to endure the silence, Elke said, "I'm sorry, Clea. I'm probably wrong."

Clea waved her apology away. "Don't worry. I'm not upset. I'm speechless. Because I know you're right. I *do* choreograph reality. I've been realizing this ever since that foot turned up in my backyard."

"Oh?"

"I lay in bed all last month looking out my window as townspeople passed below. And I wondered what ghastly atrocities each was enduring or imposing in those bland little houses and trailers that line the roads into town. And I realized that if we could hear the screams of every creature on earth who's being raped or tortured or murdered or starved right now, the cacophony would deafen us. I've been photographing châteaux while most people are huddling in shacks."

Elke drew a sharp breath and frowned. "Well, well," she said. "Welcome to the charnel house. I always wondered what would happen when the dervish stopped whirling."

They sat in silence, the wind snuffling at the windows. Brandy dragged himself on his belly to the coffee table and laid his head beside Elke's chicken bone, slowly pounding his tail on the stone hearth.

"You *have* had a hard winter, haven't you, darling?" Elke said softly.

Clea began to cry quietly, until tears dripped off her chin. "You have no idea, Elke."

"I think I might." Elke fought down a wish to take Clea in her arms. Too much too soon. But Clea didn't cry easily. Or hadn't. She must be in a bad way.

"So in other words," said Clea, impatiently wiping her eyes with the sleeve of her turtleneck, "I guess I can't push the button on my camera because I'm afraid I'll uncover another maimed limb beneath the flowers."

"That's a valid fear, given this world."

"Why do you think I've stuck with the flowers all these years?"

"I *knew* why. I just didn't realize *you* did."

"I didn't until this month. I didn't understand a lot of things until this month. You, for instance. How do you stand it, Elke, gazing into that inferno day and night? Just a few weeks of it makes me want to gouge out my eyes like Oedipus. Or thrust my head into a leg-hold trap."

"Do you really mean that? Or are you just making unfunny jokes?"

"Yes, I mean it. What keeps you here, Elke, seeing what you see?"

Elke began to massage her temples, unnerved by this role reversal. What if Clea's despair dragged her down? Her cocoon was still so fragile. Yet she'd experienced the urge toward self-destruction so many times that suicide no longer impressed her. "Clea, if you want to kill yourself, that's certainly your prerogative. However devastated I and everyone who loves you would be. But I think it's a mistake to take the death wish at face value. It's a metaphor. Read it. Your psyche is telling you it wants you to die to certain ways of thinking and feeling. Or at least, that's what I tell myself when my urge to visit the Empire State Building becomes strong."

Clea nodded numbly.

"Look, Clea, try something, will you? Go out and shoot what's really there, instead of what you *want* to be there. You can always kill yourself later."

Clea nodded again, watching Brandy lick tentatively at Elke's chicken bone, chin resting on the coffee table.

"Promise?"

Clea looked at her irritably. Finally she replied, "Yes, I promise. After all, I'm your hostess."

Elke whisked the bone away as Brandy lunged for it, tossing it into the fire. Brandy stared at her resentfully.


In her bedroom Elke put on her purple velour robe and padded in bare feet to the window. Moonlight on the snow lit up the night sky with an eerie luminescence. A dying elm cast a black net of shadows across the white. Elke felt a stab of terror. What horrors were lurking in those shadows? All this pastoral splendor was definitely going to take some getting used to. After her escape from Germany, the entire world had held only terror for her. But she had discovered, via her art, images to contain and subdue her urban terror. Rural terror, however, was still uncharted territory.

Elke steadied herself by inspecting the light and dark of elm shadows on snow for a woodcut. But the mere idea wore her out. Clea didn't know when she had it lucky—some fussing with shutter speeds and focus, the flick of a finger, some messing around in a darkroom, and it was done. Besides, a woodcut could never convey that sparkle of moonlight on ice crystals.

Terence had fluctuated among grief, indignation, and concern when she announced her journey up here. Did she know how to unlock the gas cap on the car? Could she read a map? She should phone him if she had a flat. Et cetera, et cetera. She departed in a flurry of guilt, anxiety, and resentment, not looking around at him as she drove to the end of their block.

But once on the Palisades Parkway, the city skyline at her back, she was swept with elation, wanting only to live her own life, free of

Terence's urgent need to take care of her, feeling no longer able to go on year after year in their familiar humdrum way. And now, with Clea in such sorry shape, she definitely wouldn't be going home anytime soon. Besides, she was sick of being Terence's raison d'être.

# 43   The Discipline of Parting

Clea laid a fire in the kitchen fireplace, then began to put away dishes, trying to keep the clatter down because Elke was still asleep. Clea awoke at dawn, full of anxious energy, whereas Elke slept until daylight and woke up groggy, blue eyes bleary. So Clea usually cooked breakfast and let Elke deal with dinner.

The kettle began to whistle. Grabbing it, Clea poured water over the coffee grounds in the filter. After adding milk, she carried the mugs upstairs to the guest room. She set one on the bedside table next to Elke, who lay sleeping, hair a silver swirl on the pillow, cheeks flushed, the quilt over her breasts steadily rising and falling. Placing her own mug on the windowsill, Clea threw open the homespun curtains. Grackles were fighting over sunflower seeds in the clear plastic bird feeder on the windowpane. The sky was bright and clear. The snow in the back field looked as heavy as wet cement. Ice floated in chunks on the bay.

Elke began to groan. Clea went into the bathroom and turned on the taps, pouring some rose-scented bath oil into the water. Then she returned to the window and sipped her coffee. Picking up Elke's brush, she swept back her own dark hair with some long, vigorous strokes.

"I don't know where you get all this energy at this hour of the night," grumbled Elke, scooting up against some pillows to sip her coffee.

"Yeah, but it's all I can do to stay awake for Dan Rather." Laying down the brush and picking up her mug, Clea left the room.

Back downstairs, Clea lit the fire and put some oatmeal on to cook. Sitting down by the fire, she sipped her coffee and listened to Elke stumbling across her bedroom floor to the bathroom. It was odd living so closely with her. Apart from their trip to Saint John, they'd kept the physical routines of their daily lives separate. But in the weeks since Elke's arrival, they'd developed a soothing interplay of solitude and companionship. In contrast to the violent spasms of visceral agitation Clea had been accustomed to label "love," she and Elke had been experiencing a slow, steady elaboration of their eighteen-year interdependency.

Terence, meanwhile, was wailing his loneliness at the mouth of the Hudson in frequent phone calls. This was throwing a pall over their easy intimacy. Both knew without having to spell it out that they'd better not start counting on each other's presence because, as usual, it was about to be interrupted by the requirements of others. And perhaps by their own inner requirements as well. Although Elke's departure felt to Clea at that particular moment almost as desirable as major surgery. Still, they'd been through years and years of this discipline of parting. It never got any easier, but each knew by now that she'd survive it.

Elke descended the steps in her burnt-orange coverall and work boots as though sleepwalking. She plopped down beside Clea and stared glumly at the fire.

"Here," said Clea, handing Elke a bowl of oatmeal topped with cream, raisins, melting butter, and brown sugar. "Give your blood sugar a boost."

"To say nothing of my cholesterol level," grumbled Elke. "Thanks."

They ate in silence, preferring to talk as little as possible in early morning, when dreams, like fish, were closest to the surface. Clea valued this discretion in Elke. Turner and the children usually babbled mercilessly at the breakfast table, uninterested in whether she was listening.

Elke washed her dishes in the sink and departed for the ell, calling, "See you later, Clea. Good luck." Elke had hired Darius Drumm to install a wood stove in an empty storage room with a concrete floor and several north-facing windows. She said it was the nicest studio she'd ever not worked in.

Despite Elke's advice to photograph what she saw instead of what she wanted to see, Clea's index finger still wouldn't function. But today Clea intended to shoot a series in the very spot where she'd found the foot, to convince her stubborn finger that it was gone.

Standing by the kitchen window reviewing this plan, Clea watched Morning Glory, dressed in a green corduroy smock, emerge from the Marshes' house with a basket of wet laundry. As she hung graying sheets on the line alongside the webbed duck feet, Clea could see the bulge of her belly, like the mound of a fresh grave. It was a relief to have recovered so quickly from Dack, after hearing at Christmas of his impending fatherhood.

An image drifted into her head of Elke in her funky black Betty Grable bathing suit, asleep on the wicker lounge chair on the Saint John terrace. Clea inspected it with curiosity. Where had this come from? She knew Elke too well now for her to be a candidate for Clea's passion. Passion required ignorance and self-deception, and Clea was beginning to learn to live with the truth. Ushering Elke out of her head, Clea pulled on her mahogany leather jacket and headed out the door, grabbing her camera from the counter.

Strolling across her backyard, leaving treaded pits in the wet snow with her Sorel boots, Clea fondled her camera, savoring its familiar heft and contours. Arriving at the spot where she'd found the foot, she inspected the crust of snow that sparkled in the sun. Crisp dried asters and their shadows made dark lines against the glittering white. Raising her camera to her eye, she saw that a photo of this would look like an abstract etching, chilly and intellectual. Yet a shot here last August would have featured dazzling purple flowers. And in September, a mangled human foot. Soon the snow would melt into muck. And that summer she might plant a hydrangea in this spot.

Lowering her camera and glancing around, Clea reflected that these desiccated asters were a minute segment of a landscape that stretched miles in every direction. To her left were the Marshes' junked cars, gray sheets, and duck feet. To her right, the melting lake with the snowy mountains beyond. Both there, both "real." Elke had suggested photographing what was really there, but it was impossible to encompass this entire expanse. Yet if you extracted a fragment from its context in time and space, you were falsifying reality, representing a part as the whole, the fleeting as permanent. All Clea's profession had to offer was lies. Just like the lies Clea had fabricated throughout her entire career, with soft-focus lenses, backlighting, retouched negatives, staged shots for travel brochures, and oil brushed on peas. Removing the woven strap from around her neck, she hurled her camera into a snowdrift.

Elke, work boots propped on a nail keg, sat in a captain's chair by the black wood stove, gazing out the window at the wings nailed to the peeling gray clapboards next door. Huge wings they were, from eagles, hawks, blue herons. And beside them, antlers from deer, elk, and moose. A Peeping Tom would have assumed Elke was in a state of stagnation. But he'd have been mistaken. She hardly knew how to discuss it, even with herself, but something important was happening. The whole point seemed to be *not* to discuss it, not to put it into words. To lull that analytic capacity of her overtaxed brain to sleep. To become a passive receptacle for sensory input. To drift on the stream of well-being that had first begun to trickle in her New York studio before she'd come to Roches Ridge.

Day after day Elke had sat in this chair, unable to work, unwilling to think, merely observing the Marsh family through this window. Dozens of people came and went, laughed and cried, hugged or screamed. It was like an Italian opera with no sound track. Waneeta, the head diva, rolled through the collapsing house and junk-strewn yard like an avalanche down a mountainside, bossing everyone around in her designer outfits. Her sons dragged home dead animals and wrecked cars. Her daughters appeared with babies on their hips and in their bellies. Her grandchildren bathed in mud puddles in the driveway. At that moment several children were playing "Miami Vice" on the heap of junked cars, pretending to shoot at each other with what looked like real pistols and rifles. A pregnant woman in a green smock was hanging underpants the size of flour sacks on the clothesline. A small girl was dressing a dead fish in doll clothes and placing it in a doll carriage.

If Terence had been here, he'd have launched into a condemnation of American capitalism for allowing such rural deprivation in the wealthiest nation in world history. Yet the Marshes seemed to be enjoying life more than she and Terence, with their overdeveloped cerebral cortexes, had ever enjoyed it. Waneeta Marsh appeared to be the Falstaff of Roches Ridge.

As several children next door leapt behind steering wheels throughout the junk pile for a mock car chase, Elke recalled lying in bed at their age in her family's house on the Oder and watching the corner of her room elongate until her doll, sitting in a child's chair, looked as tiny as an ant. And then the process reversed and the room collapsed around her, until the doll loomed large as a house. She had laughed and laughed. It had confirmed her child's sense that nothing was as it appeared, and anything was possible. It had been like a drug trip without drugs. This occurred several times, but ceased once she entered school.

Eyes fixed vacantly on the eagle wings next door, Elke began to picture sunlight across a red-checked tablecloth on green grass. A china platter of spicy sausages. Her father lying in his shirtsleeves in the shade of a linden tree. Showing her how to draw a cow on a prescription pad. His delighted smile as she gravely covered each page with trees, flowers, and animals. Her mother pausing, as she spread pale butter on dark seeded bread, to admire these drawings. Her blond brother in shorts and knee socks, teasing her as she chased him through a field of poppies. Riding atop her father's shoulders to a river, where he rowed her out to inspect a pair of snow-white swans.

While Dack Marsh came out of the woods carrying several dead muskrats by their feet, Elke sat stunned in her captain's chair. So indelible had the images become of Elke's father hanging by his neck, her mother dead on the parlor carpet, her brother in a grave beneath a white swastika, that Elke had forgotten there was a time before the war when her family—whole, healthy, and happy—had gone on picnics in sunlit meadows.

Elke watched Clea stalk past the windows, blocking the view of the eagle wings next door. She looked irritated and perplexed. But this was at least progress away from despair. During their weeks together they had taken walks nearly every day. At first Elke literally trembled with fear whenever they entered woods, expecting to encounter shell craters and escaped POWs. Once snow slid off an evergreen bough to plop on the forest floor, and Elke started as though at an incoming artillery round. Clea was pretty timorous herself, braced to encounter another severed body part protruding from a melting snowbank.

Elke asked Clea, by a way of distraction for them both, to point out what she found so appealing about the natural world. Clea tried to comply, even while confessing that her muscles for appreciating it had atrophied from her weeks of brooding in bed. In time, however, she did manage to point out the glitter of sun on snow, the flash of a cardinal's wing in a spruce tree, the sound of ice shattering on the lake, the fresh scent of pine needles, the trampled area in a stand of pines where deer bedded down, the sawdust thrown down by woodpeckers beneath a dead elm.

Watching Clea skulk past the windows in her worn mahogany leather jacket and faded jeans, Elke remembered her in that same jacket standing in Elke's studio doorway fifteen years earlier, home from Paris, slouching like a rebellious teenage boy, inviting Elke to the Waldorf for a night of passion. Elke smiled. She'd turned Clea down. But why?

. . .

As Elke and Clea strolled into town in the afternoon sun, Clea announced, "I've decided to give up photography for good."

"Oh, yes? How come?"

"I've been trying to photograph what's there, instead of what I want to be there, as you suggested. But I've concluded it's not possible. Everyone edits all the time. I mean, whenever you focus on one thing, you're automatically excluding thousands of others."

Elke shrugged. "Sorry. You should never listen to me. If I had any answers, do you think I'd spend my days sitting in that drafty ell staring at those wings on your neighbors' house?"

"And if you photograph something, aren't you automatically giving it an emphasis it would lack in its original context?"

Elke sighed. "Clea, another word of advice, for what it's worth: You're thinking too much. As your favorite son, Theo, would say, 'Lighten up, Mom.' "

Clea gave a startled laugh. "What's going on here? The doyenne of disaster is telling *me* to lighten up?"

Elke smiled. "You've been going all earnest on me lately. I liked you better as the Wife of Bath."

As they went through the IGA checkout with some haddock for dinner, Astrid Starr gave them an update on the bicentennial festival in July. Genevieve Paxton from the Center of Sanity had been brought in to facilitate at meetings, and consensus had actually been reached. There would be a Decoration Day at the cemetery, with a barbecue contest in the evening. A body-building competition in the town hall. A parade. Clea's original vision of sack races on the soccer field behind the school had been replaced by something called Bossy Bingo.

"It sounds fun," said Elke as they crossed the green toward home. "I wish I could be here for it."

Clea looked at her quickly. "Yes, I know you have to leave soon. It's been wonderful of you to stay so long."

They walked on in silence, the snow wet and dense beneath their boots.

Finally Clea added, "But one of these days maybe we'll stop running away from each other."

Both inspected this remark. Elke drew a sharp breath and looked away to the melting snowbank across the road. Then she smiled and said in a tone of teasing flippancy, "I don't see why. We've been doing it for nearly twenty years now. We've got it down to a science."

"Don't we," said Clea dryly.

Back at the house, Clea and Elke sipped tea by the fire and watched Oprah Winfrey. A bearded psychologist was instructing the women on stage, who wore casts and bandages, how to negotiate with battering husbands. Oprah was weeping into her microphone.

Clea's phone rang. Picking it up, Clea said, "Hello there. I'm fine. And you? . . . So how are things in New York today? . . . Yes? . . . Yes, she's right here. Nice talking with you, Terence." She stoically handed the phone to Elke.

Elke walked around the corner of the chimney. Clea could hear an irritated edge to her voice. She spoke about the thaw. After several minutes of scarcely audible murmurings, she hung up. Clea glanced at her as she resumed her seat. Her face was tense and anxious, and she began to rub her temples with her fingertips.

"He wants me to come home," she said.

Clea felt a flash of anger and panic. Yet she'd known this was coming. "Well," she replied in an ironic voice bordering on sarcasm, "I guess you'd better go be with your husband, then."

Elke grimaced, recognizing the valediction with which she'd consigned Clea to Paris all those years ago.

"I told him I wouldn't."

Clea looked up quickly.

"Clea, you've left me, and I've left you. I think we're just about even now. But this time I won't go until we both agree I should."

Clea stared at Elke with a flicker of alarm. Then she broke into a grin. "Forgive me for smiling, Elke. It's just a nice feeling after all those nights when Terence kicked me out of your studio."

"He was just trying to protect me," murmured Elke, defensive and guilty.

"I know. But it's enough already."

"I agree. And now would you like to hear how I regard your marriage?"

"Not especially."

"Let's just say I've never seen a marriage I admire," said Elke, nodding at the television.

# 44 A Surge of Sap

Clea stood on her skis, hands resting on her poles, watching Elke careen down the beginners' slope in a wavering snowplow. She slid to a halt not far from Clea, short of breath, cheeks flushed, eyes triumphant.

"That was spectacular," said Clea. "I think you're ready for the chair lift."

"Come on, Clea. I'm being a good sport. Don't push it."

"Trust me, Elke. You're ready for bigger things."

As they moved forward in the lift line, Clea spotted Dack helping skiers into the chairs. He wore plaid wool pants with red suspenders. Clea nudged Elke and nodded.

"Ah, our noble savage," replied Elke, pushing herself along with her poles.

"I never knew you were an athlete."

Elke laughed. "I never was."

"But you're very coordinated," insisted Clea. "You've picked this right up."

"Terence always said I couldn't walk and chew gum at the same time."

Clea raised her eyebrows, but said nothing.

Reaching the front of the line, Clea said, "Dack! Hello. We've got a beginner here. First time up. Can you slow things down a bit?"

"Sure thing, Mrs. Shawn. How's it going?"

"The snow's pretty soft, but all this sun makes it worth it. You remember Elke from New York?"

Dack nodded to her shyly.

"How's Morning Glory these days?"

Dack grinned as he helped Elke into the chair. "The baby's moving in there. It's really something."

"I remember." Clea smiled, watching her own grown babies, visiting for the weekend with their girlfriends, come zigzagging down the hill beneath the lift line like a pack of startled jackrabbits. She reached absently for her missing camera. The lift started again, carrying Clea and Elke up the hill.

"You mean I have to do that?" gasped Elke as Theo jumped off a large mogul and did a midair split with his skis.

Clea laughed. "What, are you crazy? That stuff's for teenage boys who're showing off for their girlfriends. Not for old ladies with bursitis."

"Well, thank God for that. It's fun having them here, isn't it?"

Clea nodded.

"I want to congratulate you, by the way. You've done a wonderful job as the mother of my children."

Clea looked at Elke, in her reindeer headband and racing goggles, touched to have her acknowledge her role in Clea's household, however jokingly. "Despite everything," she murmured in a choked voice.

"*Because* of everything," said Elke, patting Clea's Gore-Tex-padded knee.

Both were so moved that their skis tangled as they got off the lift, bringing them crashing to the ice in each other's arms. The operator shut down the lift and eyed them impatiently from his hut as they disentangled and sorted out equipment.

After supper that night, the four young people and two women played Pictionary on the Oriental carpet by the living room fire. At first Clea and Elke won constantly, translating the words into pictures quickly and easily.

"No fair," Kate finally insisted. "You're both artists. You need a handicap. I think you should draw with your left hands."

"I'm no artist," protested Clea. "I'm your mother."

But Elke and Clea complied, and the game became more even. The two young couples, however, were having trouble keeping their hands off each other long enough to draw. They were continually tangling fingers, stroking thighs and shoulders, locking eyes. Each couple moved as a unit, like a pas de deux. Kate's girlfriend, Sally, was blond, petite, and shy. Theo's Lyn, an Olympics-bound ski racer, was tall, dark, lean, and androgynous, not unlike Clea herself.

Clea watched her children with a mix of delight, amusement, and envy. She remembered loving like that, unable not to be in constant physical contact. But this was a state available only to the young, with their uncertain psychic boundaries. By middle age, such a blending and flowing into another person became impossible, if your lifelong search for identity had been successful. Yet wasn't this what Elke maintained was lacking in Clea's photos? She claimed Clea never really lost herself, but hadn't Clea been struggling her entire life to outgrow this kind of adolescent self-obliteration? Since recovering from Dack Marsh, she'd been delighted to be free of that sensation of crazed absorption with another person. Why would she want to court it for her work?

Clea watched Elke sketch what looked like a cross. "Cross?" guessed Clea. "Annoyed? Irritated?"

Elke put a stick figure on the cross, with a jagged crown on the head. "Crucifixion?" Elke kept pointing to the stick figure. "Christ?"

Elke cheered. Clea watched with amusement as she scribbled down the score. She was really into this dumb game. Clea smiled, remembering Elke's calling her "the mother of my children" on the ski lift. Was tonight's easy give-and-take what family life could have been like with Elke? Turner had rarely been around, and when he was, he vied with the children for her attention. Elke, in contrast, allied herself with Clea. As the adults, their job was to draw out and interact with these children. But of course Elke had just had Clea's undivided attention for several weeks, whereas Turner was always flying in from Eastern Europe. Also, with their own partners present, Kate and Theo had less need of their mother's attention than usual. Nevertheless, Clea glanced at Elke with gratitude.

"Hey, Mom," said Theo, "let's call Dad."

"Good idea," said Kate, disentwining from Sally and hopping to her feet.

As they raced to the kitchen phone, Clea looked at Elke with an apologetic shrug. Over the years, Elke had supplied much of the grit in this family, yet garnered none of the glory. But you couldn't fight biology. Besides, it was a choice they'd both made.

Elke shrugged, gauging Clea's reflections exactly. "Don't worry. It's okay. Go talk to him."

Kate handed Clea the phone as she sauntered in from the living room.

"Hello there, stranger," said Turner.

"Hello yourself. So you're home?"

"Yes, I got in last night. The water pipes froze while I was away, and the kitchen flooded."

Clea was assailed by guilt. "Is there a lot of damage?"

"The ceiling fell in." His voice was grim and bitter. She was struggling not to apologize. It was his house as much as hers.

"Have you found someone to fix it?"

"I've put my secretary onto it."

"Good. And how are you?" asked Clea, resolutely changing the subject, trying to remember that the proper running of the entire world did not hinge on her.

"If you really want to know—which I doubt—I'm lonely as hell."

"So now you know why I left." Clea laughed.

"Look, I know I've been away a lot over the years. But it's my career. It's how I put meat on my family's table."

Clea cleared her throat. "I know it's your career, Turner. But this isn't Davy Crockett, and I've been buying my own pork chops for years. So I'm sure you'll excuse me if I don't feel a lot of loyalty to Fresh-It, Inc."

"I thought you said when this Roches Ridge nonsense began that you'd come to New York when I was home."

"I did. But I've got company."

"How long is Elke staying?"

"I don't know. Until we get sick of each other, I guess."

"Terence called me tonight."

"Oh?"

"He's pretty upset."

"Well, that's between him and Elke."

"Not entirely."

"Elke's an adult. Though Terence may not realize it. She does as she pleases. I'm not making her stay here. And I understand it was you who sent her here in the first place." Clea was thoroughly annoyed. She walked around the corner of the chimney so the children wouldn't hear. "Look, Turner, I don't know what to say. I'm sorry you're lonely. I'm sorry the kitchen's flooded. I'm sorry Terence is unhappy. I love you, and I like him. I really do."

"I'd come up there and shake some sense into you if I didn't have to go to Brussels in a few days."

Clea gave a startled laugh. "Shake some sense into me?" she said incredulously. Turner was the mildest and most tolerant of men. "Look, darling, get some sleep. I think jet lag must be getting to you."

"Perhaps you're right."

"And I do love you, you know."

"I love you too," he said in a defeated voice.

The kids were dumping Kahlúa into cups of hot chocolate in the kitchen and making noises about hitting the hay. Their real goal was to get Clea and Elke to turn in so the long night of lust could begin. Clea had put Sally and Kate in adjoining bedrooms upstairs. Lyn was in Clea's office downstairs, and Theo was on the living room couch. All last night Clea had heard creaking floorboards, whispers, and giggles, like a haunted house. Clea noticed Kate eyeing Lyn with admiration. The potential complications boggled Clea's mind. She was amused to find herself thinking that she'd kill her daughter if she stole her baby brother's girlfriend.

Clea strolled into the living room, troubled by Turner's distress. She found Elke lying on the Oriental carpet, gazing into the fire, eyes filled with tears. Kneeling before her, Clea said, "Damn it, Elke. I'm sorry. I know that must have hurt."

"What?" Elke looked up, tears glistening.

"The kids running off like that to call their father when we were having our own domestic idyll right here."

"Why shouldn't they? That's the reality of the situation. Whatever it might have been had you and I not been such cowards, or . . ."

"Or so smart?" Clea concluded for her with a smile.

Elke smiled back. "Smart. Stupid. Who's to say? We did what we did. You may be disappointed to hear that I'm crying about something that has very little to do with you. I've been thinking about my parents a lot since I've been here. And feeling grateful to them for all they gave me. And I was wishing I could have known them as an adult. Because what you have with Kate and Theo now looks lovely to an outsider."

"When they left for school last fall, I thought I'd lost them for good. But I now realize I'll never get rid of them!"

Elke sat up and put an arm around her. "No, you won't, Clea. You'll never get rid of any of us."

Clea studied Elke in the firelight, which was making dancing shadows beneath her cheekbones. "I love you too," she finally replied, responding to the look in Elke's eyes rather than to the words on her lips. "But you already know that."

Elke nodded. "Clea, you've given me so much happiness during all these years. Thank you."

In reply Clea put her arms around Elke's neck and kissed her gently on the mouth. The kiss hovered in some no-man's-land between affection and passion. Confused, both quickly disentangled and got to their feet, making a great show of yawning and stretching. Calling good night to the children, they went upstairs, and into their separate bedrooms.

Clea lay awake, watching the quarter moon move across her window. From Kate's bedroom next door she could hear the squeak of bedsprings and an occasional murmur. Into her head drifted an image of Elke bending over to shake her breasts into her brassiere in the shadowy bedroom on Saint John, while the wooden fan turned slowly overhead.

Inspecting this scene with dismay, Clea felt her palms turn clammy for the first time since she'd found that foot. Evidently the only way to eliminate the life force was to smother it with the death wish. But spring was nearly here, and her sap was apparently stirring. If Elke were someone else, Clea would have sneaked down the creaky hallway and into her bed right now. But she and Elke had their pact, so Clea wrapped her arms across her chest and tried to pretend she was dead— free of her body and no longer plagued by the unexpected delight of burgeoning desire. Heaving a sigh, she felt her heart hopping beneath her palm, as a muffled giggle came through the wall.

# 45 Basso Continuo

Clea stood on the tableland above the lake, breathing deeply of warm spring air. A breeze was tossing some wispy clouds as though they were scraps of paper. Melting snow was running in rivulets down toward Mink Creek, which was swollen and turbulent, threatening the Boudicca tepees. New shoots on the willows lent a mustard hue to the valley. Way below, the dirt road past Clea's house was a swamp through which a car was struggling like a prehistoric sloth in a tar pit.

On the path up here Clea had passed several good photo ops, as the photojournalists in New York called them. One involved round hay bales stacked three stories high in a pasture. Using a telephoto lens, you could fill the frame with spirals. Printed, they would look like cells under a microscope, or a honeycomb. And from the top of this cliff Clea had discovered beneath her a sea of black-and-white Holstein cows, their mottled hides resembling an aerial snowscape. And right in the middle, a single plaintive staring bovine eye. Her hands had grabbed for her camera, but she'd left it at home. Over the years this camera had become an appendage. The rub of its woven strap on the back of her neck was as familiar as the swing of her hair against her ears. Through its viewfinder she'd inspected the world. But that was why it had to go. Like blinders on a draft horse, it had distorted her peripheral vision. So trained were her eyes, however, that she automatically framed shots without its assistance. And as she surveyed the panorama, she kept chopping it up into discrete photogenic chunks.

Studying the mountain range beyond the lake, Clea reflected that a photo of it would suggest a female torso, all smooth mounds and curves, knees parted, chest heaving, as if surrendering to the sky. The lake, still and glassy, reflected this image. But there'd be no way to photograph it. The sweep was too vast. It wrapped around Clea on three sides, enclosing and including her. She felt naked and exposed without her camera to shield her from this enveloping immensity.

Clea began to speculate that if you could compare hay bales to a honeycomb, cow hides to a snowscape, a mountain range to a woman's body, perhaps there was some underlying unity that pervaded these forms. Diverse appearances might be irrelevant. The reality might be that unifying pulse that throbbed beneath all the surface beauty and horror.

As Clea struggled to develop the ramifications of this concept, her brain abruptly shut down, as sometimes happened in the moments just before sleep, when a train of thought would derail into incoherence. Yet Clea was wide awake. The lake vista seemed to tremble under her gaze. A sound like rushing wind filled her ears. She was shaken, almost as though she'd grabbed an electric fence. Catching her breath, she sank to the ground in the melting snow. And a visceral knowledge, as indisputable and as unprovable as anything she'd ever known, swept over her—the knowledge that she was not alone. That her existence was not pointless. That the ghastly suffering of all living creatures, however hard to bear, was not without its function. That a steady reliable basso continuo hurtled along just beneath the range at which the human ear could hear. That for all her extensive exposure to this world, there were other ways and other worlds she had not yet glimpsed.

Clea sat very still, like a cat watching a mouse hole, eyes shut, breaths shallow, hoping to prolong this experience. She was tasting the sense of connection and purpose she had searched for her entire life— and had occasionally found with family, friends, and lovers, in sporadic fits and starts, like an engine struggling to turn over on a subzero morning. And for the moment she knew with certainty that no pain was permanent, and no loss was real. That even though people treated each other abominably, even though they left, even though you let them go, even though you never laid eyes on them again, this fugue that linked you continued, whether you liked it or not.

Clea sat there under a twisted pine tree, trying to fan this fading vision like dying embers. But it guttered and went out. And when she opened her eyes again, the lake scene below her appeared just as it had moments before. Except that she viewed it through a haze of tears that also bathed her face. And the tears continued as she sat in the soggy snow, feeling once again her own irrelevance and isolation, as though a procession of surpassing dignity and significance had just passed by, leaving her behind to grovel in the mud.

Clea stood up and brushed damp snow off her jeans. Then she wandered down the path off the hillside in a daze that fused elation and grief. Her previously short-circuited brain, indignant, kept trying to kick in and explain what had just happened. It had something to do with generative energy. Perhaps the bright spring sun had stimulated the pleasure center of her brain. Was this mania, the flip side to her winter of depression?

She recalled Elke's maintaining that Clea never really lost herself. It was true that over the years she'd been working at cross-purposes, trying simultaneously both to connect with other people and to protect herself from them. Her profession had reinforced this stance by interposing a camera lens. In the process she had dug herself a foxhole so deep that even a direct hit with a mortar shell wouldn't have moved her. Today, however, for some unknown reason, a bombardment had rocked her.

It all seemed alarmingly mystical now as she reached the foot of the plateau and headed home through a fir forest. This kind of thing happened to medieval Spanish nuns, not to twentieth-century Cornell graduates. It was embarrassing. Yet she still felt as though for a brief amazing instant she had seen life through a corrective lens after decades of myopia. And although the blur was now back, she carried within herself a faint imprint of that caressing clarity. But how could she describe this to Elke without sounding like a Hallmark card?

Squishing through the mud up her driveway, Clea discovered Elke talking with Dack by the stockade fence. He wore his dirty jeans. His muscled copper chest was bare and sweaty against the backdrop of rusted autos. Clea thought Elke disliked Dack. So why was she smiling at him so coyly?

The next morning Clea plunked Elke's coffee on the bedside table and stationed herself by the window, where she began to brush her hair furiously. She'd just spent an agitated night, buffeted by incompatible emotions. The seizure of pantheism in the hills had put her into a state of self-contained exaltation similar to what she'd felt after first learning she was pregnant with Kate. A secret new life was sprouting within her, unbeknown to those around her. But seeing Elke smiling at Dack had aroused jealousy as fierce as any she'd ever felt. She'd been examining it with distaste all night because she didn't approve of jealousy, believing real love should make no demands on its object. At first she was uncertain whom she was jealous *of*. But she realized Dack meant nothing to her now except as a neighbor. It was Elke toward whom she felt possessive. Which was ridiculous after all these years. And inexplicable if she truly accepted yesterday's message about eternal connectedness. But there it was, a green-eyed Gila monster in the Garden of Eden.

"So what's wrong with you this morning?" asked Elke, as she sat up to sip her coffee.

Clea stopped brushing and regarded her friend coolly. "Nothing's wrong with me." She laid down the brush and opened the window.

Elke sighed. "For God's sake, Clea, after all this time I know when something's wrong. But I don't know what it is. So please tell me."

"I thought you hated Dack Marsh."

Elke looked at her with surprise. "I guess I was jealous of him when you were so besotted with him. But I didn't exactly hate him."

"You thought he was a child," snapped Clea.

"Maybe."

"So why are you hanging out with him now?" Clea was appalled with herself.

"I wasn't hanging out with him, Clea. I just chatted with him for a few minutes yesterday." Her voice was perplexed and faintly annoyed.

"I saw you smiling at him like some goddam ingenue."

"Well, that pagan vitality of his *is* quite attractive, isn't it?" Her dark-blue eyes flashed amused malice. "This is ridiculous, Clea. I've talked to no one but you and your children and Astrid Starr for weeks. Surely you can't begrudge me some human contact. After all, I—" Elke started laughing.

Clea glared at her.

"Forgive me, darling," gasped Elke, overcome with amusement. "It just strikes me as so funny—two sophisticated middle-aged women squabbling over some backwoods juvenile delinquent. Look, I was talking to Dack about his wrecked cars. My new sculpture is finally taking shape, and I need some materials."

Clea smiled reluctantly. "I'm glad for you. Can you talk about it?"

"I'd rather wait until I can show you something. By the way, I think you've recovered. You've been moping around here like a beaten cur. It's great to see you angry again."

"Thanks a lot," said Clea, relaxing into amiable sarcasm. "Hey, look," she suddenly whispered, pointing at the window. An orange-and-black Baltimore oriole on the window ledge was reaching in with its beak to pull some hairs from the brush that lay by the open window.

# 46   The Bonfire

"So are you two in love with each other, or what?" asked Terence glumly, removing his beef cubes from the miniature ski pole in the Schuss Kebab. The room looked bare without Ishtar's spider plants hanging from the ceiling.

"Of course they're in love with each other," snapped Turner. "They've been in love with each other for years. That's not the question. The question is, 'When are you coming back home to New York, where you belong?' "

Elke shrugged, poking at her salad. "My work is going well here. I want to stay until I finish this piece."

Turner and Terence had driven up from New York for the weekend to extract an explanation from their wayward wives. If there was anything Clea hated, it was a showdown. "And I have a deadline on a book about this town," said Clea, "so there's no way I can leave." She glanced out the window to the green, struggling to subdue her annoyance. Turner had almost as much right to this new role of Outraged Spouse as she did. Terence, however, was another matter. The bicentennial festival band was practicing in the Victorian bandstand under the direction of Sam Silvers, the holistic dentist. Clea could see Earl Atkins puffing into a tuba and Genevieve Paxton beating the snare drums. Their current tune bore a faint resemblance to "Blame It on the Bossa Nova."

Terence was twitching with irritation. Turner flashed Clea a hostile smile. "So what are *we* supposed to do?" asked Terence.

"Deal with it," said Clea. She was doing her best to remain unengaged with their pain, because to relieve it would mean returning to New York. Her eyes met Elke's for a brief moment of mutual support.

"There's no lack of attractive women to help a lonely man cope," said Turner, refilling their wineglasses as though with battery acid.

"Oh, do shut up, Turner," requested Elke.

Someone's knee was pressing against Clea's beneath the small table. Clea felt confused, unable to formulate a response since she didn't know whose it was. She solved the dilemma by shifting hers to one side.

"I just don't see the appeal of this ghastly little town," muttered Terence.

"But nothing has ever appealed to you," said Elke sweetly.

"Except you."

There was a sudden commotion in the restaurant. Diners rose from their tables, and waiters surged toward the outside doors. Through the window Clea could see a newly lit bonfire in the center of the green, flanked by the bandstand, in which the bicentennial band sat in disarray. Flames began to lick the night sky.

Brandy, waiting by a tree, dashed over to Clea as she came out. She bent over to pat the whimpering dog, her eyes on the bonfire. Around it stood the women of the Holy Deliverance, in their blue veils and ankle-length dresses, eyes lowered, hands in pockets. Daryl Perkins, propped on his crutches, eyes as red as his hair in the firelight, was preaching to the gathering townspeople in his thick Southern accent about the end of the world, which was apparently scheduled for July.

Sam Silvers tapped the music stand with his wand to restore order among his musicians. He raised his arms, and the band launched into "I Left My Heart in San Francisco."


Doomsday was just around the corner, and Daryl felt desperate to get the word out. Deuteronomy's third birthday was nearly here, and these atheists before their tables of plenty needed to repent of their greed and prepare for Armageddon. He hurled John Denver's "Rocky Mountain High" from the Casa Loretta jukebox into the fire. Loretta had had her chance for salvation. His only regret was that witch burning had gone out with buckle shoes. He'd have adored watching these flames lick at that beehive hairdo, reducing it to ashes that would swirl away in a hot whirlwind from hell.

A man from Daryl's congregation hurled bingo cards seized during the raid on the Rescue League into the conflagration. Other men followed these with the contents of the IGA book rack—Joan Collins' autobiography and a huge stack of *Sir and Her*.

Astrid Starr, still limping from her ordeal in Orlon Marsh's leg-hold trap while investigating the origins of the foot, stood outside New Age Travel with Barbara Carmichael. Astrid had turned the IGA over to Earl. WOW had persuaded her to take some space so she could decide whether she really wanted the nuts in with the flour. She was now organizing cruises for New Age Travel, which she had been bankrolling in any case. She'd already developed a trip to explore the possible sites of Atlantis. A second involved cruising the Caribbean with prominent channelers from all across the planet. Astrid felt invigorated finally to be owning her own power. At the last WOW meeting she'd given herself permission to be fat and rich.

"Jeezum," said Astrid. "What's Daryl up to *now?*"

"God knows," sighed Barbara. "If only he realized he'll get born again and again and again, he wouldn't have to be so frantic about it this time around."

Father Flanagan and Theresa came out of the rectory, Father Flanagan still holding his dinner fork. As he gazed at Daryl Perkins, silhouetted against the blaze, shouting and gesticulating in competition with the discordant music from the bandstand, Father Flanagan felt envious. Imagine feeling such conviction about your faith. Across the green he spotted Ishtar in the doorway to New Age Travel. When he'd stopped by the other day, she informed him she'd reverted to her real name, Barbara Carmichael.

Forgetting himself, he'd said, "My daughter is named Barbara."

Ishtar looked at him oddly.

"I mean, my brother's daughter. My niece."

She studied him in silence.

"She lives in Iowa City," he'd babbled on. "But I haven't seen her in years."

Father Flanagan glanced at Theresa, his unacknowledged mate, as she walked back into the parsonage. Following her, he stood by the sink, watching her adroitly halve and peel an onion for tomorrow's stew. In a rush he realized he didn't even know how to peel an onion. He was no closer to the divine than in seminary, yet he had forfeited his humanity.

He fell to his knees by Theresa's feet. "Forgive me, Theresa, for I have sinned. Against you and against our child." He grabbed her hand and pressed it to his cheek.

"Father! What are you doing? Get up."

"However it may have appeared, Theresa, I've been wed to you in my heart for all these years."

"Don't be ridiculous." She tugged at his armpits to get him to his feet.

"Please marry me, Theresa."

"It's too late, Father."

"As long as there's breath in our bodies, it's not too late to correct a horrible mistake."

Theresa hacked furiously at the onion, scattering pieces all around the counter and the floor. "Nonsense. You're a priest."

Father Flanagan embraced her knees. "I'll wash pots at Casa Loretta."

"You don't know how to wash anything."

"I can learn. Let me try to make it up to you, Theresa."

"Nothing you could ever do would make it up to me." She grabbed her straw pillbox and marched out the door, the bonfire casting dancing shadows on the kitchen wall.


This was all she needed, thought Clea. Turner and Terence would send men in white coats to drag her and Elke in nets back to New York City for lobotomies. The two couples stood among the napkin-clutching tourists, the lederhosened waiters, and the aproned kitchen help, being harangued by Daryl about their soul-corroding hedonism. Elke's face was strained from the dinner-table confrontation. Clea slipped an arm around her waist and gave her a quick hug. Elke shifted her troubled eyes to Clea's and gave her a faint, anxious, rueful smile.


Starshine and Conrad Bohring stood on the steps of Mink Valley Savings and Loan, watching the wailing children of the Holy Deliverance deposit Barbie dolls, G.I. Joes, Care Bears, and Smurfs in the conflagration.

"I don't get it," said Starshine, Che on her shoulder. "What's wrong with Smurfs?"

Conrad shrugged. "Daryl says they're idols. Like the Golden Calf."

Starshine had finally completed her word processing correspondence course and felt deeply relieved to have a marketable skill. There was an oversupply of gurus in the marketplace at the present time. She spotted Anita Perkins by the fire, eyes lowered. Anita had one hand in the pocket of her long skirt, clutching a fistful of dirt to remind herself of her unworthiness. With her other hand she patted Deuteronomy, who wore flannel Dr. Dentons and Mickey Mouse slippers. He kept rubbing his eyes with his fists, heartbroken at the loss of his G.I. Joe.

The previous week Starshine spotted Orlon Marsh planting dozens of marijuana seedlings in the Boudiccas' women-only graveyard. After he departed, she pulled them up. She had no quarrels with herself as a guru. She'd protected and nurtured her devotees to the best of her considerable ability. But it was time to move on. There had to be more to life than deification.


As Maureen Murphy set down her suitcases to open her front door, she was greeted by the sight of Daryl Perkins' disciples heaving the Megabucks lottery machine into a bonfire on the green. Maureen smiled pleasantly, off for the weekend to her time-sharing unit at the Trapp Family Lodge, which she'd bought with her inheritance. After her mother's accident with the German shepherds at customs, Sonny Coffin had offered to cremate May for free, on the condition that Maureen tell no one about their foiled arrangement for the cocaine. Maureen had asked Angela McGrath to play the theme from *The Exorcist* on her harp while May's wooden box slid into the oven. Now Maureen no longer felt a need to destroy postal patrons' love letters or to rob the change drawer. She didn't even mind that the bicentennial committee had voted to replace the dying elms on the green with birches instead of maples. It was amazing that one little death could give you such a boost.


Gordon McQueen limped down the road, leading his workhorses, followed by fifteen other men. The wagon for the annual Gayride had broken down eight miles outside of town. Approaching the WELCOME TO ROCHES RIDGE sign, which was pocked with bullet holes, they saw a rosy glow above the green, and heard a cacophony of shouting voices and snatches of music that sounded like "The Naughty Lady of Shady Lane."

"Looks like poor old Daryl has finally lost it completely," said Loretta, standing outside Casa Loretta with Tommy Trapp, Ray, and several customers. Ray hooked his thumbs through his belt loops and assumed a cowpoke slouch. The flames leapt, causing shadows to play across Daryl Perkins' bearded face as he picked up the condom machine from Al's Getty station with one hand and prepared to hurl it into the fire.

Loretta was pissed. Daryl had not only stolen her John Denver records, he'd wrecked her Wurlitzer while doing so. No doubt this was his revenge for her failure to convert during the miracle of Our Lady of the Stop Sign. She'd have liked to oblige him, but Satan just didn't impress her.

But hey. What was a minor annoyance like Daryl Perkins in the face of such happiness as she was now sharing with Ray? They'd finally consummated their schoolgirl crush. One night after lights out, Ray had sneaked into her room and removed his starched nightgown. To reveal his penis, poking through the ring in a black leather harness. Pretending it was a dildo, they enjoyed the best sex ever.

"I guess this is illegal," mused Tommy Trapp. "Perkins has got no permit." He scratched his forehead beneath the brim of his trooper's hat. He was at a loss, being preoccupied with tomorrow's raid on the Boudiccas. An anonymous male voice over the phone, which Tommy immediately recognized as Orlon Marsh's, told him the Boudiccas had planted a marijuana crop in their women-only graveyard. Trapp, Sheriff Spokes, and the half-dozen other troopers who constituted DESTROY (Drug Elimination and Seizure Team to Rescue Our Youth) were going to check it out. Of course, Orlon had had it in for the Boudiccas ever since Crystal Sue changed her name to Beaver Dam.

Starshine marched up to Trooper Trapp, Che flapping his wings to keep his balance on her shoulder.

"Listen, Trapp," she said, "I'm outa here tonight. But if you search Orlon Marsh's shed tomorrow, you'll find two doe carcasses. And if you don't, I'll hear about it, and I'll contact your superiors."

"Jeezum," said Trapp to Loretta. "When it rains, it pours, don't it?"

Starshine sauntered up to Anita. In a low voice she said, "You know me, don't you, Anita?"

Anita said nothing and continued looking at the ground.

"We bought frozen peas together at the IGA last week."

Still Anita remained motionless.

"Make love, not war!" shrieked Che.

Deuteronomy pointed a chubby finger at him.

Taking another tack, Starshine said in a forceful voice, "Anita, I've got a BMW and one hundred thousand dollars in unregistered municipal bonds."

Anita continued to study the ground. Deuteronomy looked up and said, "Mommy, who dat fat lady?"

"Anita,' said Starshine, as though to a Boudicca, "I want you to throw down that damn dirt. And pick up your obnoxious little boy. And come with me right now."

Anita stood still and silent. Then she abruptly raised her eyes and studied Daryl, who held the condom machine aloft in one hand, eyes fixed on Loretta Gebo's beehive. Anita withdrew her hand from her skirt pocket and flung her handful of dirt into the fire. Then she picked up the little boy and perched him on her hip.

Slowly she turned her head, until her eyes met Starshine's. They smoldered and flared in the firelight as Anita said in a husky Southern drawl, "Well, praise the Lord."

While Starshine, Che, Anita, and Deuteronomy walked away from the fire, Daryl came out of his trance to call, "Anita, where are you going? Get back over here, woman!"

"Can't, Daryl," she replied cheerily. "Your world's just come to an end, honey."

Che spotted Brandy outside the Schuss Kebab, dashing around Clea in circles, barking frantically.

"Sit!" screamed Che.

Halting in his tracks, Brandy looked in every direction.

"Sit!"

Brandy sat, wrinkling his forehead. Then he began tentatively to raise his haunches.

"Stay!" shrieked Che.

Brandy sat back down, whimpering and looking at Clea, who was uneasily eyeing her husband.

Daryl Perkins held a condom machine over his head. Behind him stood Gordon McQueen, his Clydesdales, and a dozen other men. A gang of children arrived at the fire with marshmallows on sticks.

Clea glanced at Elke with a grimace of resignation, while Turner and Terence went inside the Schuss Kebab to settle their bill. "He'll never let you stay," she said in a low voice.

"I'm afraid it's no longer a question of 'let,'" said Elke.

As the two couples strolled along the dirt road back to Clea's house, Turner said, "This place is a lunatic asylum, you do realize that?"

"No more so than any other place I've ever lived," replied Clea. "Perhaps less so, because no one pretends otherwise."

# 47  Flesh and Blood

Clea was stripping sod off the rock ledge in her backyard. Having watched for weeks from his tower of wrecked cars as Clea grappled like Laocoön with wild grapevines, Dack Marsh had come over with his chain saw one morning the week before. Together they turned her field into a desert, hacking down and burning the brush and bagging the remaining debris for the Sooner or Later truck. As Clea began to dig up areas for planting, she discovered the soil was mere froth atop fathoms of granite bedrock. Her vision of perennials and ornamental shrubs faded. But then she recalled the concept of rock gardening, and now she was determined to make the barren stone bloom.

Hearing a commotion in the valley, Clea laid down her spade and strolled over to the cliff, Brandy at her heels. Half a dozen men in combat gear wove through the birches down the hill toward the Boudicca tepees. Trooper Trapp was yelling through a bullhorn, though Clea couldn't catch his words. Brandy began to bark. Starshine, the Boudiccas' shaman, had eloped with Daryl Perkins' wife the night of the bonfire. Daryl had also left town, to scour the back roads in search of his wife and son, leaving the Church of the Holy Deliverance leaderless. So there were many disgruntled devotees roaming the roads of Roches Ridge at present.

Boudiccas began appearing from jobs in the woods, to gather in the clearing before the house trailer. Several assumed karate fighting stances. A heated discussion ensued between Trapp and Crystal Sue Marsh. The camouflaged men fanned out and scurried through the woods like a pack of blue ticks following a coon.

Should she somehow intervene? Clea wondered. It was outrageous to think private property could be simply invaded like that without warning. Over the past several months, as she slaved over her rocks, she'd chatted often with various Boudiccas as they crossed her yard to their encampment, bearing armloads of rotting produce from the IGA. She'd come to admire their naive idealism and felt almost as protective of them as of her own children. But her support would probably constitute a liability for the Boudiccas, she being the owner of the land on which the foot was found. So she returned to her rocks.

Gardening was so satisfying compared to her wretched book, she reflected as she collected broken glass on the granite beneath the sod. You planted a bulb; you weeded, fertilized, and watered; and you eventually beheld a tulip. Yet, although her finger was finally pressing the shutter release on her camera, her book was as far from completion as ever.

During the weeks after that cosmic Muzak on the plateau overlooking the lake, she'd thought she was on the trail of a productive new method. She hiked over to Gordon McQueen's milking parlor one afternoon. As he rinsed udders and attached suction cups, Clea explained *The Town That Time Forgot* and her difficulties. When she asked for his help, Gordon readily agreed. For a couple of days she hung around, discussing his daily life with him—how he saw himself, how he wanted others to see him, what he liked and disliked, hoped and feared. Eventually he became so used to her sympathetic listening presence that he went about his chores unself-consciously. She followed him around, waiting patiently, for what she wasn't sure.

Late on the third afternoon, as Clea was about to pack it in and go home to the solace of a bottle of gin, Gordon's brother Jared drove into the barnyard and climbed out of his car. Gordon, who was leading a workhorse in a leather collar, went over to him and began chatting.

All at once Gordon threw one arm across Jared's shoulders and the other around the horse's neck. Behind them loomed the blue silo with LONG LIVE THE GANG OF FOUR on it. In the foreground was a sea of muck. Clea raised her camera, quickly adjusting for light and focus. Something about Gordon's expression as he glanced over at her, lips parted in the beginnings of a delighted smile, eyes frank and gentle and unguarded, stirred in Clea a faint tantalizing echo of that baroque fugue in the hills. Gordon was revealing himself to her. And she was allowing him to, rather than trying to coerce him into some preexisting scenario. She, the two brothers, and the horse all seemed to partake of a moment of mutual recognition—acknowledging in concert the wonder and weirdness of living on this earth, of being inexplicably linked up with one another in a seemingly insoluble mystery. And Clea's stubborn finger finally consented to press the shutter release, freezing this fleeting instant of connection on film.

Excited, Clea had employed this new method with other townspeople. Her sole goal became to present her subjects in their intriguing uniqueness and eccentricity, not to choreograph or interpret them. And she savored those critical moments when her subjects, after hours or days, finally lowered their elaborate defenses—and she hers. But today it seemed to Clea as though this technique had yielded only a pile of pointless photos of strange and unattractive people and places.

Soon Turner, Terence, and the kids would be arriving for the bicentennial festival, with their various needs and demands. Who knew when she'd be free to get back to her nonbook? These months alone with Elke had been her big chance, and she'd blown it. She used to get more work done when little children were beating down her door.

Elke, on the other hand, was in her ell studio at that very moment, finishing her new sculpture. Clea had been listening to the clanging of hammers and the rasping of saws for weeks. Often Elke skipped their routine of walks, tea, supper, and TV in order to work into the night, the blue flame of her blowtorch casting eerie shadows on the windowpanes when Clea took Brandy out for a lonely midnight stroll.

Clea was pleased for Elke. But she was also envious and resentful. Elke had moved right in, commandeering all creative energy in the immediate neighborhood. She'd held tête-à-têtes with Dack right up until his departure the day before for basic training at Fort Dix. (About to be a father, he was now devoting himself to some serious breadwinning.) Elke's appropriation of Clea's life in Roches Ridge was especially galling since she'd originally disputed Clea's move so mercilessly.

Clea listened to the workings of her own mind with astonishment. Elke might have taken over Clea's energetic optimistic mode, but Clea had taken over Elke's: Querulousness had always been Elke's preserve. Clea had been relentlessly cheerful. Clea reminded herself that it was she herself who'd urged Elke to visit, to stay on, to appreciate Dack's vitality, to turn the ell into a studio. Gradually her annoyance with

Elke faded. She was irritated with *herself* for her inability to assemble this wretched book. It wouldn't do to shift the irritation onto Elke. Besides, this irritation was Clea's high-octane fuel. Without it she'd never find her way.

An hour later several forest-green state trooper cruisers pulled into the Marshes' driveway, flashers revolving. On their doors was painted the Vermont state seal, featuring antlered deer, cows, haystacks, and evergreen trees. Trooper Trapp and his camouflaged colleagues leapt out and ran in crouches down the driveway. Orlon rushed from his shed and leaned against the door, beady black eyes darting around the yard.

Clea heard Trapp say pleasantly, "Poaching much these days, are you, Orlon?"

Orlon snarled, "All right, how much do you want this time, Trapp?"

"Why, I oughta run you in for that alone, Marsh. Never mind that you gave me a bum steer about some damn marijuana crop down to Mink Creek."

Orlon said nothing, tongue prodding his mustache.

"Got something in that shed, have you, Marsh? Something you don't want us to see? Stand to one side there."

Waneeta, Penny, Polly, Esther, and Morning Glory rushed from the huge rambling house, still clutching bones, skulls, and bits of fur. Orlon had them assembling Abenaki totem sculptures for Dack's gallery in SoHo. They clustered uncertainly in the driveway.

"Get offen my land, Trapp," called Waneeta, handing her rodent skull to Polly and rolling forward like a boulder down a mountainside in her slate-gray Benetton knit pants suit. "I know my rights. I watch 'L.A. Law.' "

"Got a search warrant, m'am," mumbled Trapp, respectfully removing his flat-brimmed hat. "Sorry not to give you no warning, but that's the whole point."

"So he had a body in there," Clea told Elke in a stunned voice as they sat by the kitchen fire with mugs of tea later that day. "In an acid bath. As well as a couple of poached does."

"In the bath as well?"

"No. Hanging from a beam."

"Whose body?"

"Somebody from Rutland who'd supposedly been cremated yesterday at Deathworks. Once they broke into his shed, Orlon confessed everything."

"Confessed what?"

"Do you really want to hear this?"

"How do I know, since I don't know what it is?" mused Elke, sipping her tea.

"All right. Here goes. After the viewing of a body at Deathworks, Sonny Coffin would have Orlon trim off the flesh and remove any gold fillings from the teeth. The flesh was then cremated, along with some dead woodchucks to make up the extra weight. Sonny would give the ashes to the family. Orlon would chop up the skeleton and take it back to his shed, where he'd soak it clean in acid. Then he'd hide the bones in pelts and have Rayon drive them to a medical supply house in New Jersey. Medical schools use them for teaching purposes."

Elke sat with her mouth wide open, a deep crease of disbelief between her eyes.

"So the famous foot fell out of his van during transit from Deathworks. And my puppy found it and dragged it over to my yard."

Elke was massaging her temples with thumb and forefinger. "To whom did it belong?"

"Danny McQueen. A local boy who died from a hockey injury."

"How could anybody do such a thing?"

"I can't believe you're asking me that, Elke. You, who, as you continually point out, spent your childhood watching the Oder run red with your neighbors' blood."

"Okay." Elke nodded, eyes closed, head against her chair back.

"Orlon said Sonny told him it was no different from someone's donating his organs for transplant. It was in the interests of science."

They sat sipping tea in silence as the sun sank behind the trees and tepees down on Mink Creek.

"So that's why I can't do this book about Roches Ridge," Clea concluded.

Elke looked at her questioningly.

"When I first moved here, I thought nothing had changed since the French and Indian War. But now I realize that change is all there is. One damn thing after another, each more horrifying than the last. On and on."

"There's your theme," said Elke. "The flux. Stop trying to pin it down or make sense of it. Just observe and record it."

"That's what I've been trying to do, but it hasn't worked." Clea sighed and stood up. "I'm going to make us some supper."

"Not yet," said Elke, rising. "The moment has arrived."

"For what?"

"I want you to see my new piece."

"Good God," said Clea.

They walked down the hallway to Elke's studio. Clea was terrified. What if she didn't like it? As Elke's best friend and most valued critic, she was honor bound to say so. Besides, Elke could always tell what she really thought.

"Wait here." Elke went into the studio, switching on the light and bustling around. "Okay," she called faintly.

On a nail keg in the center of the room stood a bust of a woman with wings, rising up out of an inferno of torn, twisted steel and shards of bleached bone. The breasts, large and smooth, were of rusted steel from a wrecked car. The clavicles and rib cage were the bones of wild animals, some carved into lacy filigree. The fringed wings were from an eagle. The face was also of rusted auto metal, pinched, creased, gouged, and hacked to form hollow eye sockets, a howling mouth, high sharp cheekbones, and leathery skin. Small antlers rose from hanks of fur atop the head. It was surreal, representational, and abstract all at once. Maternal tenderness mixed with a fierce primal exuberance, strength with pity. The woman seemed at once firmly grounded— earthbound even, buried to her waist in ruins, seemingly assembled from the debris itself—yet poised for flight.

Elke was studying Clea anxiously, but Clea was too overwhelmed to respond. The space around the piece seemed almost to pulse with an electric current, that same current Clea had tapped into atop the plateau. For a moment she felt as though someone had punched her in the solar plexus.

"It's magnificent," Clea finally said in a weak voice, aware that she was witness to a minor miracle. "The best thing you've ever done."

Elke gazed intently into Clea's eyes. "You're not just saying that?"

Clea turned and embraced her. "It's absolutely stunning."

Elke started laughing. "God, I'm so relieved you like it."

"Like it? I'm speechless." Clea stepped back and held Elke at arms' length, studying her as though she didn't know her at all. In fact, she *didn't* know the genius who must have inhabited her while she was making this. "I can just imagine what that *Voice* critic will write: The triumph of the life force over destruction and chaos. The fusion of the natural with the technological. A comic *Rite of Spring.* . . ."

"Blah, blah, blah." Elke laughed.

"Let's go open some champagne," suggested Clea.

As they stumbled upstairs to bed after no supper and much champagne, Clea shyly handed Elke some file folders of photos. "Look at them in the morning when you're sober. Tell me if they're hopeless."

Clea swept into Elke's room the next morning and threw open the curtains and windows to warm May sunlight, oblivious to the fact that Elke was already sitting up in bed, studying the photos. Turning around and seeing her, Clea said, "Oh, God, I forgot I gave you those. I must have been really drunk. Here, give them back."

"No way," said Elke. "I've just started looking. Go away, will you?"

Clea went into the bathroom and turned on the taps for Elke's bath, pouring in some sandalwood oil. Her stomach churning, she returned to her spot before Elke's window and rolled up the sleeves of her coral-and-white-striped silk shirt. Then she grabbed Elke's brush and started stroking her hair furiously in the morning sun. There was a mist over the lake, which would burn off by noon.

Clea leaned forward out the window and took several deep breaths to calm herself. She resumed brushing, singing in a soft alto, "Sheep shall safely graze and pasture in a watchful shepherd's sight. . . ."

"Quiet, please," requested Elke with an irritable stab of her hand.

Clea pulled the hairs from the brush and set them on the window ledge for the scavenging Baltimore oriole. Then she went downstairs to make coffee. From the kitchen window she could see Orlon's shed. She was almost relieved finally to know about his grisly cottage industry. She'd slept better last night than in months, and it wasn't just the champagne. Horrible as the foot story was, it was less horrible than some of her imaginings. Better the psychopaths you knew . . .

Clea kept feeling stabs of panic at the thought of Elke sitting up in bed studying those photos. They were awful. She didn't need Elke to tell her. In fact, she'd put Elke in an awkward position. It was from some element of competitiveness, she supposed. The winged woman was dazzling. Clea had hoped her own work might have thriven in the atmosphere that produced Elke's triumph. But this was wishful thinking.

Clea trudged up the steps, carrying two coffee mugs. With resignation she entered Elke's room and set one mug on the bedstand. Then she returned to her station by the window and glanced at Elke. Who was smiling. Clea's fears were well founded: Her photos were laughable. Pathetic.

Elke looked up at Clea, shaking her head. "My God, Clea, you've finally done it."

Done what? wondered Clea, studying Elke's face.

"You've caught the mix—the fear and humor and pathos and courage of real people." Her voice wavered with emotion.

Clea did a double take. "Look, I know I've put you in an awkward position, Elke. You don't have to perjure yourself just because I raved about your woman last night."

"I'm not perjuring myself, Clea. I wouldn't, however devoted I may be to you. Don't impugn my integrity."

Clea smiled, amazed.

"So what's your problem with this book, Clea? It's all right here. Life as a state of permanent transition. Each person peering out for a moment of connection through a bubble of self-absorption. The mix and the flux. It's fantastic."

Clea sidled over to the bed and glanced at Ishtar before the New Age Travel sign, which hung from the eaves of a handsome old colonial. She wore a large crystal on a chain at her throat and was trying to convey an esoteric expression. Gordon, his brother Jared, and his horse before the spray-painted silo, which rose like a graffiti-covered lighthouse from an ocean of swelling mud. The Boudiccas in karate postures before their tepees, the distant mountains lying like a naked woman in the background. Dack with his stern Abenaki features posing proudly with his crowbar atop the mountain of junked cars.

"Well, I don't know." Clea returned to the window and leaned on the sill with her elbow. They weren't too bad technically. "Maybe there's a book there somewhere." A faint feeling of excitement began to stir in her.

Elke looked at her with exasperation. "There's no maybe about it. Organize them and send them off to Karen."

Clea detected movement on the window ledge from the corner of her eye. The Baltimore oriole was picking at the hairs Clea had put there earlier. Boldly seizing the entire clump in its beak, it flew off. Clea leaned out the window and watched it land on a maple branch alongside the house. Its mate plucked out a few hairs and began to weave them into the rim of a pouch-shaped nest.

"My God," whispered Clea.

"What?" asked Elke with alarm.

"Come over here quietly."

Elke tiptoed over in her robe and looked out at the birds' nest. It was almost entirely composed of interwoven hairs—Elke's silver ones, and Clea's black and gray.

"I think it's an omen," said Clea softly. "We'd better call Ishtar."

Elke was studying the mountains across the lake. "God, it all passes so quickly, doesn't it?" she murmured.

"What does?"

"It seems like only last month that I was sitting in my studio after you photographed me for *American Artist*, rejoicing to have a new friend. And now we're both going gray and menopausal." She turned to face Clea, eyeing her tentatively. "Look, I know I'm not supposed to say this. But it *is* a unique occasion in our lives. So how about just once, before we die?"

Clea started, then turned to meet Elke's dark-blue gaze. She ran her eyes down Elke's velour bathrobe. After all these years of enforced etherealization, it was strange suddenly to have permission to regard Elke as flesh and blood, possessed of a physical body that sometimes craved stoking and stroking.

"I thought you'd never ask," Clea finally replied, reaching out to untie the belt on Elke's robe.

"But you're the hostess," said Elke, putting her hands around Clea's neck and guiding their mouths together.


Clea lay in the spool bedstead and watched the vermilion sun setting behind the mountains across the lake. Elke's robe and Clea's silk shirt lay in a heap on the floor, and a tray with the remains of a meal sat on the night table. Clea was propped against some pillows, the duvet pulled up over her breasts.

Elke, who was having a hot flash, lay on her stomach across the foot of the bed, silver hair damp with sweat. "You know, I really like menopause," she observed. "It's like having a tropical vacation several times a week."

With languid eyes, Clea traced the curve of Elke's back as it descended to her waist, then rose to her white buttocks. "We're fools not to have done this years ago."

"Probably. But I bet we'd have made a mess of it."

"No doubt. Well, we must do it again sometime. Before we die, as you so convincingly put it." Clea stubbed out her cigarette in a dish on the tray.

"Judging from the last several hours, I'd say you've got a lot of life left in you, old girl," said Elke. "But you do realize it would never be quite like this again? After all, we've had almost twenty years of fore-play."

"Not unless we wait another twenty years."

"It might be worth the wait," said Elke, sitting up and leaning against the footboard.

Clea studied Elke's breasts in the apricot light through the window—firm ivory orbs that had never seen the sun or been suckled by the greedy gums of an infant. She held out her arms. "Come here, you gorgeous creature."

Elke crawled up the bed, under the duvet, and into Clea's embrace.

"I'm so glad finally to know what you look like when you're making love." Clea stroked the hollow under Elke's cheekbone with her finger. "There's been a gap in my contact sheets all these years."

"And how *do* I look?"

"Absolutely breathtaking. Savage and tender, just like your winged woman," said Clea, as the crimson sun sank behind the hyacinth hills.

## 48   Bossy Bingo

The citizens of Roches Ridge sat in bleachers along two sides of the soccer field behind the elementary school. A snow fence had been erected to form a huge square in the middle of the field. This square had been crisscrossed with lime to form a giant bingo card. One of Gordon McQueen's Holsteins wandered around the squares, cropping grass and placidly chewing her cud. Townspeople had bought chances on the squares. The prize was an all-expenses-paid weekend for two at Ausable Chasm.

Gordon and Randall sat in the bleachers in their tank tops, muscles bronzed from haying in the sun, Gordon silent so the cow wouldn't try to find him and ruin the contest. Everyone was watching the black-and-white cow and chatting desultorily, sunstruck. Most had just come from Jared McQueen and Bethany Wagner's victory in the First Annual Mink Creek Body-Building Classic at the town hall, which had drawn contestants from all over New England.

Yesterday had been Decoration Day at the cemetery, capped off by a barbecue contest for the men in town, who used their wives' favorite sauce recipes. Families weeded and decorated forebears' graves, then sampled ribs at each man's grill and voted. Tommy Trapp, wearing a high white chef's hat in place of his usual flat-brimmed trooper's hat, had won. Not necessarily because he was the best barbecuer, but because everyone considered it wise to stay on his good side.

Earl Atkins, in his Australian slouch hat with the emu feather, had been deeply dismayed, knowing full well that Astrid's sauce was second to none. Unfortunately, Astrid wasn't there to browbeat the judges with threats of exposure on the gossip circuit. She'd hired a fishing trawler to take her into the Bermuda Triangle, to check it out as a possible cruise destination during the Window of Light weekend.

Earl was disgruntled. He resented being left to mind the store while Astrid hung out day and night with that occult travel agent. So when Maureen Murphy stopped by his grill for a rib, Earl raised his eyebrows and said in a gruff voice, "Like your new hairdo, Maureen." Her bangs, freed from their usual Scotch tape, were curly and girlish.

Blushing, she said, "Thanks, Earl. I decided I could use a change."

"So could I," Earl replied, gazing at her with meaning.

"Like your ribs," stammered Maureen, short of breath.

Earl raised his eyebrows again. "Thought I might come by your place some evening and catch *The Sound of Music?*"

"You and Astrid?"

"Astrid's in the Bermuda Triangle."

Maureen swallowed her mouthful of pork and stared at Earl in his HOG WILD T-shirt. "What would people say?" she finally managed to ask.

"No one would hear about it because Astrid's away."

Maureen smiled, Astrid's sauce on her lips. "Maybe you'd like to see my time-sharing unit at the Trapp Family Lodge sometime."

"Maybe I would," said Earl, jaw set but eyes twinkling, just like Christopher Plummer in *The Sound of Music.*


Ian McGrath III sat in the bleachers beside Angela, whose belly was bulging beneath her long white Edwardian gown. Angela, pushing her harp across town on a skateboard, had turned up at Ian's door shortly after Orlon Marsh's and Sonny Coffin's arrests. Ian answered the door, unshaven, eyes bloodshot. The object of his grief was standing before him, her golden harp on a skateboard.

"We've come home," Angela whispered, nodding at the harp. "If you still want us."

Never one to bear a grudge, Ian opened his arms to both. Angela explained that her months in Sonny Coffin's Gloom Room, like a homeopathic remedy, had finally gotten death out of her system. She now felt able to face life again. Ian carried Angela in his arms up the stairs to their mahogany sleigh bed, where they made love throughout the evening, while the shadows of the dying elms stretched across the green and faded into the night. A few weeks later, a pregnancy test kit confirmed Angela's suspicions that Ian V was in the works.

Meanwhile, Deathworks had been closed down as a health hazard. And yesterday, during Decoration Day, the traitors who had been seduced by Sonny's brass plaques found they had no headstones to hang wreaths from, and no weeds to pull or trim. Several spoke contritely to Ian about purchasing headstones. Ian McGrath III was a happy man. Plaques were out, and stones were in. And all his family members were back where they belonged—Ian IV in the tomb, Ian V in the womb, and Angela out of the Gloom Room.

Around Clea sat Elke, Turner, Terence, and the children. Brandy had had to stay home so he wouldn't chase the Bossy Bingo cow. Theo, in tight torn jeans and a white T-shirt, appeared to be doing a James Dean imitation. His new girlfriend, lean as Twiggy, wore a leather miniskirt. Kate had a cotton knit sweater hanging down her back like a cape, tied around her neck by the sleeves. Her new Yalie boyfriend wore chinos and penny loafers. Turner, who catalogued men according to which fraternity they'd have pledged at Cornell in the fifties, said he was classic Sigma Chi.

Clea watched Elke clasp and unclasp those sturdy hands that had recently been doing such interesting things to Clea's body. Elke was nervous. She was about to take her winged woman to Anya in SoHo. Anya had done well off Elke's previous work and might not care for this departure from despair, since she tended to regard art as a product that, like Ivory soap, ought to remain consistent from one bar to the next. Elke, Clea, and Waneeta Marsh had organized an arts and crafts show in the town hall for the festival. It included Elke's winged woman, Clea's framed photos of Roches Ridgers, and the Marsh family's Abenaki totem sculptures. All weekend long, gangs of giggling children had surrounded Elke's woman. And the Little League team had stolen Clea's photo of themselves from the exhibit.

None of Clea's loved ones could believe that such an unpromising heap of garbage as her backyard could have been transformed into sheets of handsome gray stone, carved with glacial fissures and dotted with pockets of tiny alpine flowers and mats of greenery. Clea could hardly believe it herself. Nor could she believe that Karen liked her new version of *The Town That Time Forgot* much better than the old one. Anya had been in touch as well, finally proposing a one-woman show. Although Clea accepted, she was struck by the irony of being offered a show now, when she no longer cared.

On the afternoon before Turner's and Terence's arrival, as Clea and Elke lay in deck chairs overlooking the sloping rock garden, Elke had asked hesitantly, "Clea, what would you think about having me for a neighbor part of the year?"

Clea looked over at her with amazed disbelief. "I'd think: How incredibly wonderful."

"Well, I don't want to get your hopes up, but it's on my mind. I keep picturing myself in a cottage in the woods. Odd, since I hated trees until about last week. But I've grown to love this bizarre little town. To say nothing of you."

"You've always loved me," said Clea smugly.

"True."

"With Terence or without him?" asked Clea.

Elke shrugged. "I love Terence, but I'm tired of playing Cassandra on the ramparts with him. The world will probably limp along just fine without my lamentations."

Following their first day in bed together, Clea and Elke had been as awkward and shy as schoolgirls, blushing violently when their eyes met over breakfast. And each had traversed the creaking hallway between their bedrooms several more times in the middle of the night. Clea's emotions had been tugging at her like a team of wild horses eager to run amok. Part of her wanted nothing more than to spend the rest of her days in Elke's arms, making up for all the lost years. But both had other things to do. Also, in the past Clea had had repeated proof of how easy it was to devour in a few greedy sittings all the nourishment a sexual connection had to offer. They had to treat theirs with reserve and respect if they wanted it to endure. No doubt the delicious delirium would eventually fade. It always did, thank God. But all their old love would remain.

Clea's uncharacteristic restraint was made easier by the memory of her experience on the hilltop, which she carried within her now like a radioactive tracer. Once you'd heard the full orchestra, the strains of any individual instrument, however haunting, became slightly less overwhelming. As though you were a raindrop that had finally encountered the sea.

After Turner's and Terence's arrival and a lengthy dinner, Terence and Elke adjourned to Elke's bedroom for an interminable domestic debate. Clea and Turner sat in the deck chairs in the deepening dusk, listening to frogs croaking along Mink Creek.

"You know," said Turner, "I've realized I might as well fly out of the Burlington airport as out of Kennedy."

Clea studied him in the lamplight through the living room window. He looked very handsome and distinguished with his salt-and-pepper beard, fringe of graying hair, and white dress shirt with rolled-up sleeves. She remembered him as a fair-haired lad, ladling milk punch with a basketball sneaker.

"That would be delightful, Turner," she finally replied. "And I'd be happy to put you up until you find a place of your own."

"What're you saying?" he asked in a panicked voice.

"Turner darling," she said, groping for his hand, "there is no one in this world who could ever take your place, in my heart or in my mind."

"If not in your bed," muttered Turner.

"We've grown up together, and we're growing old together," continued Clea, unwilling to be diverted from her prepared speech. "We've produced two wonderful children. You've seen me drunk on whiskey sours and screaming with agony during childbirth. You introduced me to passion on your raincoat among the rhododendrons. Although we've been about as unfaithful as two people could ever be to each other, it seems to me there's something indestructible between us. But I don't want to be married to anyone anymore. I'm not the type. Besides, Ishtar has told me if I don't fulfill my karma as a lonely old lady, I may have to come back in another life as a forest ranger."

"This isn't amusing," said Turner.

"Maybe not. But it's not tragic either. Let's find out what's really between us, Turner. Without all the claptrap of marriage and parenthood. It'll be fun. Trust me."

Turner smiled ruefully. "As the captain of the *Titanic* said to his passengers as they steamed out of port."

"There's my party chairman," said Clea, leaning over to kiss his bearded cheek. Terence and Elke descended from her bedroom for a nightcap, Terence looking ashen and mute.

Turner, sitting beside Clea on the bleachers today, was tense and unhappy. Clea began to brace herself for the pain it was going to give her to cause *him* pain. After everybody left the next day, it was up in the air who, if anyone, would return and for how long. Yet Clea was unconcerned. She at last knew how to sit quietly in her own room. As though her inner eye had gotten used to the dark, she was beginning to detect unfamiliar shadowy forms within herself, which the flares of excitement from past passions had previously concealed. In addition, she now knew that solitude was an illusion. She was traveling in the same convoy with every person in these bleachers.

Calvin Roche had come home from Abilene for the bicentennial celebration at the committee's expense, on the condition that he be allowed to ride in the parade on a white stallion with silver-studded tack. Since he was the oldest extant Roches Ridge Roche, the committee acquiesced. At yesterday's opening parade, he rode ahead of the color guard, making the horse rear in profile like the Lone Ranger and Silver, waving his Stetson by its brim to the cheering crowds, while the bicentennial band played "Happy Trails to You" in march cadence.

Clea was saying to Calvin, who sat behind her, "That was some house you sold me."

Calvin chuckled and slapped his leather chaps. "That old bathtub finally fell into the cellar, did it, Mrs. S.?"

Clea smiled. "Yes, it did, you fox. But it's been worth it. I love that place."

"Well, honey, you can have it. Give me a sleeping bag on the open range any day of the week."

"Is that how you live?" asked Clea with concern.

"Well, not exactly," he said, picturing his studio apartment in the Last Roundup Rest Home.

Father Flanagan and Theresa in her straw pillbox sat on either side of Barbara Carmichael. All three had scarcely stopped smiling since the day last week when Maureen Murphy went to confession under the guise of repenting for her years of giving incorrect change. She reached through the screen and handed Father Flanagan a letter with an Iowa City postmark. The letter looked as though some dog had chewed it for breakfast.

"Congratulations, Father," said Maureen, as he read the reply to his letter to the Iowa courts and learned that his and Theresa's infant daughter, Barbara, had been adopted by a California couple named Carmichael. Several years previously, Barbara had placed her name on file from California, updating her address to Roches Ridge, Vermont.

Father Flanagan wore a sports shirt today instead of his stiff collar and dickey. He and Theresa were being married next week. Theresa said spending her twilight years servicing an elderly defrocked priest was a concept she could resist, but not the chance to make amends to the abandoned daughter she thought she'd lost forever. Father Flanagan was going to be Earl Atkins' number two man at the IGA. His face had relaxed, and his myopic eyes shone in the sun with happiness.

"You know," Barbara was saying in a dazed voice, distracted by recent developments from the fact that no one had heard from her New Age Travel partner, Astrid Starr, since her excursion into the Bermuda Triangle, "I still can't get over the fact that it's *this* life we used to know each other in, Dad and Mom. And that I came back to Roches Ridge. Probably I was once a salmon. . . ."

A hush came over the crowd as the Holstein paused in her chewing and stood still, tail swishing. Tension mounted around the perimeter of the field. But the cow merely strolled across the square to a fresh patch of grass and resumed grazing.

The Boudiccas in their crew cuts and headbands sat along one row of bleachers. They'd spent the weeks since Starshine's desertion circling and processing. They'd hired Genevieve Paxton from the Center for Sanity to come down to the sweat lodge and facilitate. Genevieve's hair, which looked like a gray fiberglass insulation batt, became sodden with moisture as she helped them explore their potential for subsumption by unreliable authority figures. Eventually they reached a consensus to reach all future decisions by consensus.

Jared McQueen and Bethany Wagner sat beside each other in orange satin robes, blue first-place sashes across their muscled chests, gold-plated Mr. and Ms. Mink Creek trophy on the bench between them. Their vivid spikes of hair were color coordinated with their robes and their sashes—and the maroon curtains on the town hall stage.

Ken and Bethany had negotiated a reconciliation under the arbitration of Genevieve Paxton at the Center for Sanity. It would be an open marriage. They would put an addition on their house at Colonial Manor Estates. Bethany would allow Ken to dictate memos to Ida Campbell in his new home office whenever he liked, in return for his allowing her and Jared to toss iron in the new weight room whenever *they* liked. The metaphor Genevieve gave them was of a three-legged race—Ken and Bethany hobbling along in concert, but with one leg free.

When Astrid Starr first heard about this, rather than setting her Casio, she had shrugged and gestured around New Age Travel. "Well, I admit it's kinky. But hey, who am I to talk kinky? Whatever floats your boat, right?" The new town record of nineteen minutes was held by Astrid herself. The topic was Astrid's abdication as the queen mother of hearsay. Townspeople felt like Israelites delivered from the pharaoh.

Sitting on the other side of Bethany was Daisy, in her torn jeans and Jerry Garcia T-shirt, her potential Miss Teenage America title having gone up in marijuana smoke. Daisy was off the Grateful Dead trail only long enough to watch her mother and Jared make town history. But Jared's and Bethany's aspirations now stretched far beyond this tiny town. They would become the first punk Mr. and Ms. World!


Again the crowd fell silent as the cow raised her head, ceased chewing, and stood in the middle of the field, swishing at dive-bombing deerflies with her tail. Loretta Gebo felt her heart in her throat. Her life was already perfect since Ray had asked her to marry him and had agreed to let her be the bride. But if only she could win something just once in this life, Ishtar said it would free her from coming back in the next as a casino croupier. Besides, the weekend at Ausable Chasm would be a perfect honeymoon for her and Ray. She grabbed Ray's hand and crunched it.

The cow's tail lifted, and the crowd buzzed. Someone yelled from the bleachers, "Go for it, Bossy!"

"Ray, she's doing it!" screamed Loretta, pounding his thigh with her fist. The cow's sphincter muscle relaxed. "Right on my square, Ray!"

Manure emerged, plopping to the ground in the middle of a grassy lime-lined rectangle, while the crowd in the bleachers went wild. Loretta was on her feet jumping up and down, beehive tottering, bleachers swaying.

"Jeezum crow, Loretta. Calm down," suggested Ray.

Sighting through her Nikon, Clea snapped some shots of Loretta in her victory dance across the soccer field. She hopped, jumped, and howled like a Comanche on the warpath.

Lowering the camera and looking around, Clea thought about the people who were absent today—Sonny Coffin, Orlon Marsh, Zeno Racine, Daryl Perkins, Starshine, Dack, Astrid Starr. All off pursuing their impossible dreams. But there were some new faces to take their place, and who knew what bizarre activities these newcomers would soon be generating?

Waneeta Marsh, who was sitting in front of Clea in a batik halter top and harem pants, turned around and smiled, to reveal several missing teeth.

"So how's Orlon managing in prison?" asked Clea.

"Not too bad," Waneeta said. "Sonny Coffin and Zeno Racine are up there to keep him company. They play Go Fish together." Waneeta surveyed the crowd, who were cheering Loretta Gebo as she embraced and kissed the Holstein cow in the center of the grassy bingo card.

"Jeezum," said Waneeta. "Ever stop to think this whole dang town might be a few logs short of a cord?"

Clea smiled. "Well, it's not what I expected when I first arrived here. But it'll do just fine."

And they all lived happily ever after, a few logs short of a cord.

A NOTE ON THE TYPE

The text of this book was set in a digitized version of Electra, a typeface designed by W. A. Dwiggins (1880–1956). This face cannot be classified as either modern or old style. It is not based on any historical model; nor does it echo any particular period or style. It avoids the extreme contrasts between thick and thin elements that mark most modern faces, and attempts to give a feeling of fluidity, power, and speed.

Composed by Creative Graphics, Inc.,
Allentown, Pennsylvania

Printed and bound by The Haddon Craftsmen,
Scranton, Pennsylvania

Typography and binding design by
Dorothy Schmiderer Baker